CALL OF THE PENGUINS

Hazel Prior

BLACK SWAN

TRANSWORLD PUBLISHERS
Penguin Random House, One Embassy Gardens,
8 Viaduct Gardens, London SW11 7BW
www.penguin.co.uk

Transworld is part of the Penguin Random House group of companies
whose addresses can be found at global.penguinrandomhouse.com

First published in Great Britain in 2021 by Black Swan
an imprint of Transworld Publishers

A CIP catalogue record for this book
is available from the British Library.

ISBN 9781784166243

Typeset in 11/14.5pt Sabon by Jouve (UK), Milton Keynes.
Printed and bound in Great Britain by Clays Ltd, Elcograf S.p.A.

The authorized representative in the EEA is Penguin Random House Ireland,
Morrison Chambers, 32 Nassau Street, Dublin D02 YH68.

For Ursula,
who has also heard
the call of the penguins
and followed it

Vancouver

ONTARIO

Edinburgh

Ayrshire

Madrid

Buenos
Aires

Falkland
Islands

South Georgia

Ushuaia

'Bolder Island'

'Locket Island'

Veronica's Travels

Christmas
Island •

'Ginty
Island' •

Melbourne •

Snares
Islands •

ANTARCTICA

1

Veronica

The Ballahays, Ayrshire, Scotland

'I HAVE ASKED Eileen to find us some penguins in Scotland.'

Daisy gives a small shriek of delight and springs up from the sofa. I do worry that all her bouncing is not good for it, and I always ensure it is me who is seated in the more valuable Queen Anne chair whenever we are in the snug, the smaller of the two sitting rooms at The Ballahays. Daisy's fervour borders on vandalism at times.

'You don't need to ask Eileen,' she proclaims, her voice imbued with cheekiness, which, as she is not a healthy child, I decide to let go. 'I can find the Scottish penguins on my phone.' She rummages inside her dizzyingly multi-coloured bag, pulls out her phone and waves it around. The phone is no more than a small, flat rectangle, but I know she can she operate it with ferocious efficiency.

'Put that thing away,' I tell her. 'It is an abomination to see a nine-year-old frittering her life away on such pointless gizmos.'

'A bomination? That sounds fun!'

'It isn't, believe me.'

She tosses the phone back into her bag. We seem to have wandered away from the subject already, which is a little dangerous as far as I'm concerned. This is not because my memory is at fault (it is, as ever, in tip-top condition), but one often loses track when one is in conversation with Daisy, whose young mind darts about all over the place. I return to the topic with haste, before we lose the thread altogether.

'Penguins,' I remind her, 'are not only a source of endless entertainment; they are an example to us all. They are well worth seeking out.'

'I know,' she says. '*Remember the penguins!*'

This was the little mantra I often cited to cheer her along when she was undergoing chemotherapy before Christmas. Penguins, as well as being quite charming, have for me come to represent bravery, determination and resilience. With their daily challenges of long treks across snowy wasteland, swimming in icy waters and trying to avoid becoming meals for seals, they are paragons of good cheer in the face of hardship. I'm pleased that Daisy has fully grasped this concept.

She scrambles back on to the sofa and kneels up, looking over the arm and out of the bay window, as if she might see one of her favourite birds waddling about on the lawn. The Ballahays garden boasts several sweeping herbaceous borders, a fountain and a fine collection of

2

rhododendron bushes, all lovingly tended by Mr Perkins, but alas, there is a complete dearth of penguins.

'Perhaps I will commission a penguin statue to be made,' I muse. 'It might look rather splendid in the shrubbery.'

Daisy is overexcited at the very idea of it. Her eyes have lit up. They are unusually big and blue. She has a scattering of freckles across the bridge of her nose, which, although she is growing at an alarming rate, is still the small, button-ish nose of childhood. Her mouth, when not busy, settles into the shape that is commonly described as 'rosebud'. She is a pretty girl in spite of her hair loss. The orange scarf wrapped around her head does her no favours, however. I have offered to buy her a wig, but she won't have it. A very determined young lady is Daisy.

It was, I am proud to relate, her first wish to come and visit as soon as she was out of hospital and well enough to do so. Her parents and brother accompanied her here for the first few days, but they have now returned to Bolton. Although she must still rest every day and take various medications, Daisy asserts that she feels less tired when she is here. I, on the other hand, feel more tired. It is absolutely worth it though.

It is gratifying that the McCreedy charm is still intact, but the ramshackle Jacobean elegance of The Ballahays may also have played its part in seducing Daisy here. As well as the three acres of formal gardens, it has much that appeals to her vivid imagination: oak panelling, ingle-nook fireplaces, several staircases, and twelve bedrooms filled with assorted antiques and objets d'art. She is particularly smitten with my padded footstool that is shaped like a donkey, my carriage clock, my pianola and my globe on legs. Not to mention the special photograph which hangs in my hall.

'I'm going to go to Antarctica one day, just like you did, Veronica,' Daisy proclaims. 'And I'm going to see Pip.'

She rushes to fetch the photograph now. I do wish she wouldn't do that, as it resides in a large, heavy frame and I worry that she will drop it. It is a particular favourite of mine, having been gifted to me by the magnificent television presenter Robert Saddlebow, whose wildlife documentaries inspired me to go on my epic voyage. I must proudly now refer to him as *Sir* Robert, since the New Year Honours list was announced last week, when 2013 quietly slipped into 2014.

In the photo, Pip's outline is crisp against the snow. When I knew him, he was a teacup-sized grey fluff-ball with big feet. He is quite grown up now, with the typical Adélie penguin snow-white frontage and sleek black every-where else. He has clearly been caught mid-waddle because one foot is lifted slightly higher than the other. His flippers are outstretched. His head is cocked forward, his beak is open, and there is a bright, inquisitive look on his face.

'He's saying, "Hello, Daisy and Veronica," isn't he?' Daisy decides.

'Yes, Daisy, I'm sure he is,' I reply. Lies tend to be so much simpler and kinder than reality.

I wonder what is really going on in Pip's head. In the background you can see a blurry mosaic composed of other penguins going about their daily lives. The picture always has the power to take me back. I would give any-thing to see again those sparkling landscapes and wander amongst that vast, rowdy congregation of black-and-white birds. Daily life here is humdrum in comparison: eating, sleeping, reading, litter-picking; decisions as to whether to take tea in the Wedgwood, Royal Crown Derby or Coalport china; Eileen bustling in and out with a vacuum cleaner or tin of beeswax polish . . .

I am grateful that I am able to live in comfort. There remains, however, a kind of grief in my heart. Never again will I have such an adventure. Travelling across the globe is bad for the planet and, in any case, my eighty-seven-year-old body would find it hard to tolerate. The longings are there, nonetheless.

'There aren't any penguins in Scotland.'

Daisy's brother, Noah, although he is only seven, is what is commonly called 'a geek'. 'You only get penguins in the southern hemisphere,' he asserts. We are communicating with Noah by means of a device called Skype. Skype (even the name lacks musicality) is another of those tiresome technological doo-dahs considered essential by the younger generations. It was set up at The Ballahays by Daisy's parents, who thought they should have daily visual contact with her whilst she is here. Eileen and I are equally panic-stricken by the intrusion of Skype into this calm household, but we have come to accept it.

Daisy is now arguing with Noah in a voice that sets my hearing aid aquiver.

'THERE ARE PENGUINS IN SCOTLAND!' she screeches. 'AND I WILL PROVE IT TO YOU!'

'HOW?' demands her brother, in equally ear-splitting tones. I am surprised that Skype hasn't exploded into a thousand smithereens.

'Please, Daisy,' I beg. 'Consider the chandeliers!'

She glances up at the Waterford crystal suspended above her, which is indeed jangling slightly.

She lowers her voice and delivers the next line in an urgent hiss. I can hear the hiss but cannot make out the words at all.

After her call has ended, she skips off into the dining room to pester Eileen, who is flicking dust around and humming something tuneless. Eileen has become adept at doing housework and entertaining Daisy simultaneously, so I leave them to it and head upstairs for a little quiet time.

It is certainly a challenge having a child in the house, but nobody can say Veronica McCreedy fails to rise to any challenge. I believe my Antarctic adventures have underlined that point.

In my bedroom I leaf though the *Telegraph*, which renders the usual uninspiring catalogue of human quirks and misdemeanours. It is some relief when I alight on the crossword page. It is imperative to keep one's little grey cells exercised when one reaches an advanced age, and I delight in fathoming out cryptic clues. Unfortunately, I am quite unable to find my pen. I know I left it here somewhere, but the infuriating implement is determined to thwart me and hide away. Having searched every nook and cranny of the bureau, I discover it at last beside a stack of postcards.

Now, why did I need it? It must have been so as to write a letter to my grandson, Patrick. Eileen can then transcribe it into her computer and relay it to him via email. I must tell him all about Daisy's visit. I sink back into my chair to ponder the wording, but my head is feeling exceptionally heavy . . .

When I come to, my eye falls on the clock and I am alarmed to see that it is already half past two.

I rise stiffly and make my way downstairs.

'Come along, Daisy, dear. It is time for our walk.'

I usher her to the porch, and she scrambles into a puffy jacket that resembles a sleeping bag and pulls on a woolly hat with a pompom on top. Meanwhile I don my scarlet coat and stout walking boots. As always, I take my stick to steady me, and a handbag; one never knows when one might find oneself in need of a handkerchief or painkillers. It is useful to have Daisy accompanying me because she is keen to carry the refuse sack and litter-picking tongs.

Daisy's parents were insistent that she gets out in the fresh air every day. In this matter I am entirely at one with them. I owe my extreme toughness to my lifetime habit of daily walking along Ayrshire's coastal path. I persist with it no matter what the Scottish weather decides to hurl at me, be it snow, hail or sleet. Eileen often begs me not to ('Oh, Mrs McCreedy, it's too chilly today'), which only makes me all the more determined to go. As Daisy and I set out today, however, there is no precipitation, only greyness and murk, with a few pale smudges of snow on the ground. We step out of the Ballahays front gates and along the short lane that leads to the coast. The hedgerows on either side soon give way to fuzzy gorse bushes, scoured rocks and a sense of openness.

With her eagle eyes, Daisy is quick to spot the first item

of litter, a crisp packet caught in the bracken. She pounces on it with the tongs and stuffs it into the sack with cries of triumph.

The sea and the sky are melded in a silvery wash. The cries of the gulls seem muted and nature is infused with that January feeling of suspense, as if it's waiting for things to start growing again. I maintain a steady pace as Daisy runs about reaping further spoils: a disintegrated old wellington boot, a broken glass bottle, a curved piece of plastic that I believe is part of a container for animal feed, a squashed Coke can and a piece of thick orange twine.

Daisy loves using the tongs, and I think I will purchase her a pair for when she goes back home. It will be of benefit both to her and to the environs of Bolton, which are doubtless in far more need of a thorough cleanse than the Ayrshire cliff path. It is good to see her enjoying herself today. By the time we arrive back at The Ballahays, her eyes look brighter and her cheeks rosier.

Eileen is at the door to meet us. Her plethora of tight curls is unkempt, her chins are wobbling, and there is an air of excitement about her as she helps us off with our coats. She will later don her Marigolds and sort out the rubbish into what can be recycled and what will have to be consigned to the dustbin. I have increased her wages to amply cover the nastiness of this task in addition to all the other things she does for me.

Thankfully she has a freshly brewed cup of Darjeeling and a steaming mug of hot chocolate waiting for us on the kitchen table. As I claim my tea and Daisy her chocolate, Eileen proudly crosses her arms.

I look at her quizzically. 'I perceive you have something to tell us, Eileen. I beg you not to stand on ceremony. Please unburden yourself.'

A wide grin spreads across her face. 'I've found them,' she declares.

2

Veronica

EILEEN DRIVES US. I am quite capable of driving myself, but I gave it up three years ago. My reactions, as I told the doctor in no uncertain terms, are as lightning-quick as ever, and my long-distance vision is more than adequate. However, after that small scrape with the Jaguar and a very tiresome young man in his Vauxhall, I came to the conclusion I could live without the aggravation.

Last week's snow has been washed away and the day is replete with bright, lemony sunshine. As the daubed sky and green hills of Scotland fly past the window, Daisy is quiet in the back of the car (I suspect she is surreptitiously up to 'social medium' shenanigans on her phone) and Eileen hums to herself as she drives, occasionally making comments such as 'Lovely day for it,' and 'Pretty clouds, aren't they?'

Eventually we traverse a crossroads and swing left

under a low-hanging sign that says 'Lochnamorghy Sea Life Centre'.

'Veronica, we must do a selfie with the penguins!' Daisy chants behind me as we drive into a space at the far end of the car park. 'You *will* do a selfie with us, won't you?'

'That may be possible,' I assure her, not wishing to let on that I am vague about what exactly 'doing a selfie' involves. If it is anything like 'doing a handstand' or 'doing the splits' I have no wish to oblige, and indeed my limbs will permit no such thing.

Eileen, Daisy and I go in through a huge entrance with a rotating glass door. The woman at reception is brisk and efficient: 'Aquarium straight ahead. Go to the end of the corridor and follow the signs for seals, otters, seabirds and penguins.'

We follow signs through a maze of passageways lined with informative posters about sea life which we entirely ignore. We also ignore the baleful squids, octopuses, jelly-fish and other tentacled and scaled creatures in the grey waters of the tanks that line the walls. The three of us are equally focused on where we are heading. Daisy runs ahead and loops back to us like an excited puppy.

There will not be Adélie penguins here. With their Antarctic background, it would be unkind to keep them in these warmer climes. But there will be other breeds, those that are used to a more clement climate.

When we reach the enclosure, at first I can see nothing but human couples and families with young children jostling round. We shuffle forward. We are in a broad space with a netting roof and an artificially blue, kidney-shaped pool. Areas are partitioned off with red tape and behind them I perceive a collection of birds standing amongst rocks, sand and a few low brick caves.

Eileen elbows her way through, parting the crowds and calling, 'Excuse me, excuse me!' so that we can find a good spot to stand and watch. Daisy is bubbling with excitement. I, too, am straining forward to look. At last I see them.

The African penguins (otherwise known as Jackass penguins) have black-and-white markings around their heads, a strip of black circling their fronts, and pink patches of skin showing above their eyes. They are mostly skulking around, but a few slide off into the pool for a dip as we approach. They are extremely attractive. But the Macaroni penguins charm us even more, with their mighty headdresses of long yellow feathers that stick out where their ears should be. It is a bizarre and jaunty look. They are quite splendid.

'Are they named after macaroni cheese?' asks Daisy.

'I was wondering that, too,' admits Eileen.

'Because they have cheese-coloured tufts,' nods Daisy.

It seems unlikely but none of us know. We watch as two penguins stand on a stone and preen each other, long beaks rifling through shining plumage. Task completed, one of them hops off the stone. Noticing his audience, he waddles towards us and looks at us with one eye and then the other, his crest waving a little in the breeze. Then he points his beak to the sky and swings his head from side to side in a series of movements that look almost like a dance.

'Oh, look at him!' cries Daisy. Seldom have I seen a child so enthralled.

The penguin ruffles his feathers, opens his beak and lets out a loud, crooning sort of honk.

My eyes start prickling. For seventy-odd years I did not permit myself to cry at all because somebody once said it was a sign of weakness. I no longer believe that, but I am still uncomfortable with any demonstrative show of emotion in public. Nevertheless, my tears gush forth with embarrassing frequency these days, and there is little I can do about it.

'Here you are, Mrs McCreedy. Take this,' Eileen offers. I have a freshly laundered handkerchief in my handbag, but I graciously accept her tissue.

'Are you OK, Veronica?' asks Daisy, glancing up to examine my expression.

'It is a sinus condition. It troubles me sometimes,' I tell her sharply.

These penguins are not quite like my Adélie friends, but they manifest the same qualities of bumptiousness and enthusiasm. Our friendly Macaroni trumpets again.

'We call him Mac,' one of the so-called penguin patrollers tells us, stepping up. She's a young woman with a confident air and a swinging ponytail. 'He was hand-reared. From a chick,' she adds.

I look from her to the penguin and back again. 'So you will have used a syringe to feed him a carefully balanced formula of liquidized krill and tuna?'

Her eyes widen a little. She looks as if she is trying to calculate what the answer should be. 'Ummm . . . well, it wasn't me who—'

'This is Veronica McCreedy,' Daisy interrupts. 'She's been to Antarctica and saved a baby penguin called Pip and after that she was ill and Pip saved *her*! And' – Daisy takes a breath – 'she's friends with Robert Saddlebow.'

'*The* Robert Saddlebow,' Eileen adds.

'*Sir* Robert Saddlebow,' I point out.

I must admit, I am rather enjoying my protégée's admiration.

'Well, your nan is an amazing woman,' says the patroller, clearly not believing a word of what Daisy has told her. I wonder whether to correct her on the 'nan' front but cannot be bothered. In any case, most of my attention is focused on the penguin, who is utterly delightful.

'Can I feed it?' asks Daisy, all eagerness.

'Not now. It's feeding time in twenty minutes.' The patroller looks relieved to be back on familiar territory. She crouches down to Daisy's level and speaks to her in a big-sisterly way. 'You can watch them all enjoying their dinner then. In fact, I might let you have a fish or two and you can help.'

My legs are weary now. Daisy and Eileen trot off to find the enclosures with the seals and otters whilst I head for the tea shop. I purchase a slice of cherry Bakewell tart and cup of Darjeeling tea. At least, they call it Darjeeling (presumably to justify the extra pound on the price) but it is of a very disappointing quality. I am not one to complain, however.

I park myself at a small table by the window and look out at the chink of sea that is visible beyond the edge of the building. Having visited the Macaronis and Africans, it is perhaps inevitable that my mind insists on winging its way back to Antarctica, to the colony of Adélie penguins, to my friend Terry and my grandson, Patrick. I am

14

invested in the Locket Island research project both metaphorically and literally, as I have committed a monthly sum towards it, mainly because Patrick is now part of the team.

Terry and he have been together for a year now. Terry is really Teresa, you will understand, and 100 per cent female – although, with her lack of make-up or any particular hairstyle, she does little to flaunt the fact. Unlike Sir Robert, she is never likely to become a television celebrity but, like him, she is one of the few people on this planet who has won my respect.

Some would say that Patrick doesn't deserve Terry and there was a time I would have agreed with them. Patrick is like caviar. This is not because he is an upper-class delicacy (quite the reverse!) but because he is an acquired taste. The first time I met him, which was a mere eighteen months ago, I took an immediate dislike to him. With his scruffy appearance, unsophisticated mannerisms and seeming immaturity for his twenty-eight years of age, Patrick remains an unlikely candidate for my affection. I am not somebody who finds it easy to love and the blood tie alone would not be enough. But I have seen the sweeter side of Patrick. I have seen how he cares for others. I have seen how he adores Terry. And I have seen how he loves the penguins.

My hand automatically goes up to my neck and I run my fingers along the fine chain of the locket that I still wear every day under my clothing. Daisy spotted the chain the other day and asked me what it was, so I pulled it out to show her. She is very taken with the idea of having a piece of jewellery that contains tiny items of personal value. I did not open it for her, however. Unlike Terry, I am not skilled in the art of empathy, but I do recognize various aspects of human nature. I have found it useful to reserve some means of bribing Daisy if she becomes a little uncontrollable, along the lines of: 'If you do not come and sit at the table at once, Daisy, I will never show you what's inside my locket,' or 'If you do not give me back my lipstick, Daisy, the locket will always be a closed book to you.' My little ploy works well, for Daisy is possessed with an insatiable curiosity.

I drain my tea and flick the Bakewell crumbs from my lap with the paper napkin. I glance towards the door of the cafe and see that Eileen is already here to fetch me, Daisy dragging her in by the hand. We march back to the enclosure together. The penguin patroller with the ponytail is wielding a blue plastic bucket, from which she is throwing limp fish at the crowd of penguins. The fish have shocked, glazed expressions on their dead faces, but the penguins' enthusiasm is captivating. They hop about, grabbing the fish, gulping them down their greedy beaks and clamouring for more.

Daisy is offered the bucket. She extracts a fish with a mixture of revulsion and rapture, stares at it for a moment, then flings it at a penguin so hard that I fear she will knock it down like a skittle. She is relieved when Eileen, ever practical, hands her a wet wipe afterwards.

Most of the human spectators are taking photos.

'It's time for our selfie, Veronica. Our selfie with the penguins!' Daisy cries. 'So I can prove to Noah that there *are* penguins in Scotland.'

She holds the phone out at arm's length to take a picture

16

of us together but (as her arms are not very long) fails to capture all that she wishes. Eileen is then presented with the phone and forced to take hundreds of photos of Daisy and me with the friendly penguin called Mac. I am glad I reapplied my lipstick on my way from the tea shop and pleased I have brought a presentable handbag in complementary tartan reds. I ensure that I keep it well out of reach of Mac's beak. I have already, in my time, lost one handbag to the forces of penguin curiosity.

On the drive back, Daisy tells us she is googling Macaroni penguins. I am astonished when, contrary to my expectations, she comes up with some interesting information. Apparently, the birds were named after eighteenth-century dandies called 'macaronis' who often wore flamboyant tassels in their hats.

'Like the song about Yankee Doodle!' Eileen cries in a tone of wonder and revelation. 'Do you know it, Daisy?'

Daisy doesn't and Eileen insists on teaching it to her.

'Yankee Doodle went to town
Riding on a pony
Stuck a feather in his cap
And called it macaroni.'

My ears are assailed with one high-pitched voice and one deeper, ill-tuned voice singing these profound lyrics all the way home. Under normal circumstances I would find this unbearable but today, for reasons I cannot quite fathom, I don't mind it in the least.

3

Patrick

Locket Island, South Shetlands, Antarctica

THE SUN'S RAYS are glancing off wet rock, every crevice of the land is wedged with fleecy rags of snow, and I'm gazing across acres and acres of penguins. My nostrils are zinging with the smell of fish and guano. My ears are full of gabbling, squawking, honking and twittering. All around me cute, stumpy birds are waddling about in the pebbles and ice. Above is a great white drift of clouds. In the distance, a range of blue peaks and glaciers. It's one of those moments when it hits me.

I live here, I fricking *live* here; this small island off the Antarctic peninsula, shared with a collection of seals, albatrosses, skuas and gulls . . . plus three other human beings. And five thousand Adélie penguins. I never thought I'd end up counting penguins as a profession. But then I never thought I'd discover a rich, eccentric grand-mother who was obsessed with them, either.

Over the last year, I've fully adjusted to the Locket Island lifestyle. I don't miss Bolton one bit. Well, maybe I miss Gav and the bicycle shop and telly and fresh vege-tables, but not a lot else. It's amazing how quickly this wilderness has become my world. At this precise moment there's just one thing missing: Terry. It's such a bummer we have to work in different areas of the colony. It was much better when we were working together, even if it did mean we got distracted sometimes . . .

Terry always says I should relax more. 'We don't have to live in each other's pockets to prove we're in love, do we?' she said recently when I was coming on all posses-sive. But I can't help being passionate, can I? I'd spend every moment of the day with her if I could. Not that I'm complaining. It's pretty incredible she wants to spend any time at all with a loser like me.

I glance at my watch. I've been counting and weighing penguins for three hours.

'I think I've earned a kiss at least,' I mutter.

A cheeky little penguin looks up at me, his eyes beady, his stomach swollen with self-importance.

'No, I don't mean from you, mate,' I tell him.

We're not due back at the field base for another hour. I think I'll go and find Terry and escort her back for lunch. I pull out my radio but then change my mind and tuck it back into my belt. I know her whereabouts roughly and it would be much more fun to surprise her.

I pick my way through the rocks and scree and head as fast as I can up the slope. The temperature today is only

3.5 degrees Celsius but I'm wearing plenty of layers and the climb makes me hot. I take off my parka and bundle it under my arm. I pause, panting a little, when I reach the top. From here I have a good view of the mountains and the distant lake, which is mottled blue and white to match the sky. This island got its name because it's oval-shaped and on a map it looks like a locket, the semi-circular lake on the north edge making the hole that a chain would go through. I can see the ocean beyond, shining bright and decked with white blobs of icebergs.

The part of the penguin colony allocated to Terry is down on the other side. I can make out her orange jacket from here, a colourful dot amongst the thousands of black-and-white dots that are penguins. I head towards her, weaving my way around the pebble nests. There are so many tiny chicks. They're old enough to be active now so I have to be careful where I'm treading. The adults have super-smart plumage like glossy dinner jackets with white starched shirts, but the babies are dark grey and rather amorphous. You could easily hold one in the palm of your hand and you'd find it soft and squashy. I don't pick them up though. Rules is rules. Sample weights of the chicks will be collected just before they start fledging, but otherwise it's a 'don't touch' policy. Even the adults only get handled if we're tagging or weighing them, and then there's a special technique for that. I'm proud to say I now classify as a fully trained penguin wrangler.

The mums and dads are working unbelievably hard to get those chicks fed, taking it in turns to babysit and trek to and from the sea. When they return, they're stuffed full of krill, which they empty down the chick's gullet, beak to beak. Penguin language is a complete mystery to me, but those adults and chicks all recognize each other's calls. It's mind-blowing that they can find their own in amongst the clamour.

I get a real pang seeing all this parental love ... such mega commitment and devotion. It would've been nice to have some of that when I was growing up. Those chicks have no idea how lucky they are.

But enough with the self-pity.

There's Terry, straight ahead of me, looking like only Terry can look: 100 per cent absorbed in a massive sea of penguins. My heart lifts as she turns and waves. The sun is shining in her pale blonde hair and she starts pacing towards me, neatly skirting round all the nests.

'Patrick!' she calls over the penguin racket. 'Is something wrong?'

I shake my head emphatically. 'No, nothing wrong. Can't a man see his girl once in a while?'

She walks into my open arms, which I greedily wrap around her. We share a long, delicious kiss and I almost knock her glasses off.

'Why didn't you radio?' she asks, coming up for air. We're all supposed to let each other know where we are on the island, just in case.

'Do I really have to announce to the whole world that I'm in the mood for love?'

'Not the whole world,' she points out. 'Just me and Dietrich and Mike.'

'Dietrich and Mike don't understand.'

She frowns a little. I run my fingers over her brow,

21

smoothing out the wrinkles she's made. 'Relax. I didn't slip over and break my back, OK?'

'Yes, but—'

'I risked all sorts of terrible dangers to come and see you: ice, snow, rocks, seals . . . penguins. I thought you might come with me on a hot date now?'

She can't help smiling her incredibly gorgeous smile. 'Where did you have in mind?'

'Well, I believe there's a very comfortable if rather run-down research station not far from here, with sausage rolls that just need to be whipped out of the fridge and put in the oven.'

'I'll give *you* sausage rolls,' she answers in her mock-scolding voice, pushing me sideways.

'I wish you would.'

She won't let us leave until she's done another fifteen minutes of penguin monitoring, though, so I give her a hand.

It's a small operation we run here, not like some of the massive Antarctic stations which cover marine biology, oceanography and meteorology. Our speciality is penguins (and five thousand isn't that big for a penguin colony, would you believe it. Some are over thirty thousand). Still, four of us isn't really enough, which is why Terry is always pushing herself to get more work done. As well as running the project, she tries to engage the public across the world by writing blogs about our work. She featured Granny V in the blogs a lot last year which went down very well with the fans. Dietrich is the oldest and most qualified of the four of us. He's been studying the birds his whole life and calls himself a 'penguinologist'. Mike's special skill is bio-chemistry; he analyses blood, bones and faeces so he can work out details about the diet and health of the birds. We all muck in with the donkey work – the endless monitoring of penguins, counting them, weighing them and tagging them. These facts and figures are at the core of what we do. They tell us a huge amount about the health of our whole ecosystem; and penguin numbers are going up and down at an alarming rate at the moment.

'Do you mind having a girlfriend who's your boss?' Terry asks as we finally head back up the slope together.

'If you don't, I don't,' I tell her. She never gives herself airs or graces. In fact she's the unbossiest boss I've ever known.

'It would be nice to see more of you, though,' I add, looking at her sideways. I hope I'm not sounding too clingy again.

'Let me think. Which bit of me haven't you seen, Patrick?'

We snigger.

As we reach the top, she goes back to the subject though, which is clearly bugging her. 'Go on, admit it. You'd pre-fer me ordering you around if I was in a crisp suit or a sassily seductive police uniform.'

'Nope. Parka jackets, woolly jumpers and thermal vests absolutely do it for me.'

Dietrich and Mike are already at the field base when we arrive. They look at us knowingly as we come in, Dietrich with a benign smile and Mike with one that's a lot less benign. Mike doesn't really do benign. They both assume we've been spending time canoodling rather than penguin-counting. They already have the sausage rolls on the table along with a mountain of peas and oven chips.

'Tuck in,' says Dietrich, whose English is flawless.

We do.

'There's something wrong with the water,' Mike remarks, looking at me accusingly, as he does if any bit of machinery or plumbing is faulty.

'OK, mate, it'll be the reverse osmosis machine again. I'll take a look at it later.'

The reverse osmosis machine is used to purify sea-water, removing the salt and any chemical or biological nasties to make it drinkable. It's a great alternative to bottled water . . . when it works. The field centre is pretty dilapidated and things keep breaking. It was built for five scientists years ago, but dwindled due to lack of funding and would have died altogether if it hadn't been for Granny. Terry, Dietrich and Mike are trained environmental scientists and I'm just a humble techie-nerd, so I'm the one who ends up with all the fixing jobs.

'Did you see Pip today?' asks Dietrich, nibbling on a chip.

Terry shakes her head sadly. 'Not today, no.'

Pip is everyone's favourite rescue penguin. We all try to be impartial but when you've experienced the joys of a live-in miniature waddler, you're bound to go a bit soft.

After lunch I notice Dietrich is rubbing his hand back and forth across his bristly beard, a habit he has when he's anxious.

'Can I have a quick word, Terry?' he asks her in a low voice.

'Of course.'

They go into the lab together. Cue curiosity from Mike and me, as we head for the kitchen to make coffee.

'Stronger than that,' Mike tells me, putting in an extra spoonful. 'I need to stay awake.'

He suffers from insomnia and spends half the night prowling around the field centre, which is maybe one of the reasons he's always so tetchy.

'What do you reckon's up with Dietrich?' I ask.

He shrugs and taps impatiently on the side of the coffee pot. 'I hope he's not hassling Terry needlessly. She could do without it.'

When they come back in Dietrich looks relieved, but Terry is frowning and chewing her bottom lip.

'Right, I'm off!' she announces, already putting on her boots to go out again.

I wave a mug at her. 'Aren't you staying for coffee?'

'Nope. Lots to do,' she answers, darting out of the door so fast I can hardly catch the words.

I turn to the guys. 'Has she gone off me or something?'

'Of course she hasn't,' Mike replies promptly. 'You've got a rich grandmother who's keeping our research going.'

'I – er, yes, that's true.'

I glug down my coffee as fast as I can, wondering if I can catch up with Terry. But Mike's words clang and clatter and repeat themselves over and over in every corner of my skull. Does Terry only tolerate me because of Granny's funding? Yes, Mike loves a snide comment, but I can't help asking myself if there's an element of truth in what he says.

4

Terry

Locket Island

I HOPE I wasn't too short with Patrick. I need some head-space. I scoot out of the field centre and speed up the snow-laden slope, swinging my arms, sucking in the fresh air, trying to relax. I'm stressed after my discussion with Dietrich. I couldn't say no to his request, but I'm not sure how we're going to cope. I have a lot of rescheduling to do.

Poor Dietrich. I know he wouldn't have asked if it wasn't important. His eyes were full of concern as he ushered me into the lab, out of earshot of the others, then sat down heavily on the chair beside the microscope.

'Terry,' he began earnestly. 'A situation has come up.'

He gave his moustache a nervous tug. I knew already by his expression that it wasn't good news.

'Just tell me, Deet.'

'My wife has to have surgery next month. It's nothing too serious but she'll be in hospital for a few days and it will take her a while to recover afterwards. Would it be all right if I went back to Austria to look after her and the children? I would have to leave in a couple of weeks' time.'

We are already stretched here with four of us.

'Of course you must go,' I assured him. 'Family comes first.'

'I'd come back as soon as possible, but I know you'll be pressed. Are you sure you can manage?'

I nodded vigorously and gave him an encouraging smile. 'Absolutely.'

'Thank you. She will be so grateful. As am I.'

It was good of him to ask me rather than just telling me, in fact. He was the boss up until last year when he passed the job over to me, and his precise reason was that he wanted to spend more time away with his family. It's the timing that's so bad. It's the height of the Adélie breeding season and we're struggling to keep up with the workload as it is.

'It is a good thing we have Patrick with us now,' Dietrich said, picking up a test tube, looking at the grey contents (a sample of semi-digested krill from a penguin's stomach) and putting it down again. 'He's learned fast, hasn't he?'

I had to agree.

Dietrich beamed. 'But then, he's had a good teacher.'

I coughed modestly.

'Do you think he's happy here?' I asked.

'Why wouldn't he be, with mountains, icebergs, incredible wildlife and a lovely girlfriend?'

It was kind of him to say that, but I do worry about

Patrick sometimes. He's had to adapt so quickly and things here couldn't be more different from his life in Bolton.

I feel bad that I've run off, leaving him choking on his coffee. But if I can get ahead with gathering penguin data now, there won't be so much pressure when Dietrich has gone. I've left him to break the news to the other two. I'm sure Mike and Patrick will understand that we'll all have to work extra hard in the weeks to come.

I've been so preoccupied I've hardly been aware of my surroundings. I've already reached the crest of the hill. I gaze across at the wrinkled markings of snow on the distant mountain ridges. If I half close my eyes I can see faces in those markings, an eerie artwork formed by the natural contours of the land. Above me a trio of gulls circles high in the sky, dark Vs against a wraith of white clouds.

There's a nasty little niggle in my mind that I can't quite identify. I try to focus in on it. It's to do with Patrick. He's always so jokey and enthusiastic but sometimes, when he thinks I'm not looking, I catch him with a faraway look on his face. And I sense an underlying sadness in him.

I know Patrick has unresolved issues with his family. I remember having a conversation with him just the other day, when I was complaining about my parents. 'They think I'm completely bonkers to be living out here,' I grumbled. 'They'd far rather I was settled in Hertfordshire with a sensible job, a mortgage and a healthy bank balance. But I'm only twenty-six and nowhere near that dreaded "settling" stage. They just don't understand me at all.'

'At least you *have* parents,' he'd answered glumly.

I realized how tactless I'd been. I tried to cheer him up by finding a positive.

'You have a fabulous grandmother, though,' I told him. 'There aren't many Veronicas out there.' Then, stupidly, as if I wanted to illustrate that I was just as unfortunate as him, I went and added, '*My* nan got old at fifty-five, stopped going out altogether at sixty, and died two years later.'

'I suppose Granny V *is* cool,' he acknowledged. 'But parents are pretty important.'

The conversation moved on, but I still had the impression he was holding something down – a dark force, simmering below the surface; desperate to get out.

5

Veronica

The Ballahays

WHEN WE ARRIVE back at The Ballahays after this morning's litter-picking walk, I am ready for a rest in a horizontal position. I therefore decide to leave Daisy with Eileen for a short while. I have reached no further than the hall, however, when I am surprised by Eileen bursting out of the kitchen. She closes the door behind her.

'Mrs McCreedy, can we go into the snug for a moment?' she buzzes in my ear.

'What about Daisy?'

'She's quite happy looking at Pokémon for a while.'

'Very well. But I shall need a cup of tea.'

'Of course. Of course you shall,' she mumbles. She disappears back into the kitchen whilst I wander into the snug, wondering what all this is about.

She joins me soon after, teacup in hand.

'What is the problem, Eileen?'

'There's an email for you. From' – she lowers her voice in reverence – 'Robert Saddlebow.'

'Ah, my good friend, Sir Robert,' I answer loudly. I am possibly showing off a little.

'And another one from Locket Island. From your grandson, Patrick . . .'

'I am well aware of his name, thank you, Eileen.'

'I've printed them both out. Here they are.' She waves the pieces of paper at me and I snatch them from her. I look on the mantelpiece, the dresser and the coffee table, but my search is in vain. My glasses are nowhere to be seen. This happens often and is extremely trying. I do wish people would stop moving my things around.

'Mrs McCreedy, I'm sorry, I couldn't help glancing over them,' Eileen admits, referring to the messages. This is entirely normal; I am well aware that she reads every correspondence sent to me by email. She simply cannot resist.

'Shall I read them out to you?' she asks, obviously quite desperate to do so.

'Very well.'

'You may want to sit down, Mrs McCreedy.'

I lower myself into the Queen Anne chair, concerned now. I observe that she is in a state of extreme agitation, for as she takes back the two sheets of paper her hands are trembling.

'I'll read the one from Sir Robert first then, shall I?'

'As you wish, Eileen.'

'*My dear Veronica*,' she begins. At those words my heart lifts a little. It is many years since anyone has started

31

a letter to me in that way. To think that I only met Sir Robert for the first time a matter of weeks ago!

'*I hope you don't mind my putting down this strange request in the form of an email. I wanted to get the main facts down in writing, and in a form that will reach you without delay. I will come straight to the point. As I mentioned when we met at Christmas, I will be shortly heading for Australia and the Falkland Islands for a new documentary on marine birdlife.*'

Eileen looks up at me, a broad smile across her face.

'I pray you, be so good as to continue reading, Eileen.'

She obliges. '*I have been busily engaged in many discussions with the producers about how to give the programme more popular appeal. We decided that one solution would be to put an emphasis on penguins because they are such enchanting birds. However, as you know, I have already in recent years produced a documentary entitled* The Plight of Penguins *and we are very much looking for a new angle.*'

'I thought he said he was coming straight to the point,' I mutter, then wave Eileen on.

'*Most people feel helpless when it comes to climate change because we as individuals can do little about it. So the programme producers have decided to underline other ways in which we can help our wildlife to thrive. Bearing in mind your avid litter-picking, I thought of you. You have become well known through Terry's penguin blogs as a brave and colourful character and, you may not realize this, but you had quite a following of your own on social media when she posted photos of you and Pip. Your name is associated with penguins, with*

*saving penguins, and you have become . . . how may I put
it? . . . almost a penguin ambassador.'* Eileen pauses
again. 'A penguin ambassador! Hark at him!' she declares.
I give her a stern look and she resumes reading.

'*I also noted when we met that you have a delightfully
archaic way of speaking*' – I produce an involuntary snort
here – '*and a very good, clear voice which might well be
suited to presenting. Please don't hesitate to say if this is
out of the question but I have to ask: Would you consider
an all-expenses-paid trip to either Australia or the
Falklands – or possibly both – to join in with some filming on location as my co-presenter?*'

Eileen's voice has been rising steadily in pitch throughout this last paragraph and now she cannot help herself.

'Oh, Mrs McCreedy! Mrs McCreedy! More travels!
And with Robert Saddlebow! *The* Robert Saddlebow. Sir
Robert himself! And more penguins!'

I steadfastly maintain the semblance of composure. But
within I am assaulted by all sorts of emotions. 'Does he
say when?'

'Yes, there are lots more details. It's soon. Next month,
he says. What will you do?'

'The very idea of such a venture is both peculiar and
preposterous, Eileen.'

'But I thought . . .' She tails off and visibly wilts.

I take a sip of tea and lay the cup back in its saucer
with care. 'Indeed, the idea is peculiar and preposterous
in the extreme,' I reiterate with a degree of severity. 'I will
therefore seriously consider it.'

Eileen claps her chubby hands in glee.

I remain motionless but I feel a brimming sensation

that could most accurately be described as 'thrill'. Yes, I am thrilled. Thrilled, from the very tips of my white hairs all the way down to my ancient, knobby toes.

Then I remember. 'And what about the other email?' I ask.

Eileen's face darkens. She moves the other sheet of paper to the top and I see that there is a single line of print upon it.

6

Veronica

'LOOK, VERONICA!'

It is an offence having a computer on the dining-room table but I oblige by peering across at the screen. Daisy has selected a photograph. She, Mac the penguin and myself make an odd trio. The pink of Daisy's headband jars with the reds of my coat, handbag and lipstick and, together with the yellow feathers atop Mac's head, the overall impression is one of gaudiness. However, the composition of the scene is good, with me in the centre and the two shorter figures in front. Mac is surveying Daisy, his beak pointing up to her face. When one looks at the photo one's eye is immediately drawn to her smile, which is victorious.

'Is that the one you're going to send to Noel?' I ask her as I lay down my pen, having just completed the *Telegraph* crossword.

She huffs. 'Not *Noel*, Veronica! Noah!'

Not only does her brother have a name that is virtually impossible to remember; he persists in his belief that there are no penguins in Scotland. She is determined to prove him wrong.

Whilst Eileen is helping her to send the photograph into the ether (also sending copies to Terry and, at Daisy's insistence, Sir Robert), I sit silently, letting my mind wander. I am due to meet Sir Robert later, which is a source of great excitement, but I still have this nagging worry about the second email. A long sigh escapes from the depths of my lungs.

'What's up, Veronica?' Daisy asks me.

'Just something about my grandson.'

'Patrick, you mean?'

'Yes.'

She knows Patrick a little because her father Gavin (or 'Gav' as they all insist on calling him) used to employ him at his bicycle shop in Bolton.

'My dad misses Patrick,' she states simply. 'I expect you do, too.'

This had not occurred to me, but there may be something in it.

'Isn't it strange, Veronica, that you have a locket and Patrick works on an island called Locket Island,' Daisy comments.

'Ah, but it was due to my own locket that I was drawn to the island in the first place,' I explain. 'And Patrick ended up there because of me.'

'Is your locket magic, then?' she enquires.

'It may very well be.'

I consider the poignant memories that lie within.

'Now is probably a good time to tell me what's inside,' she hints.

'One day, Daisy. Not yet.'

Eileen starts clattering around with a dustpan and brush, but Daisy is remarkably still and pensive for at least half a minute. Then she rushes off and I hear her feet galloping upstairs. She returns a moment later and presses a scrappy little thing into my hand. I stare down at it. It is a thin strip woven out of brightly coloured strings, with daisy-shaped and heart-shaped beads threaded into it.

'It's for you, Veronica. Because I know you like jewellery,' she tells me. 'I made it myself.'

Eileen stops clattering and draws close to look, the nosy expression I know so well establishing itself on her face.

'It's beautiful, Daisy!' she exclaims, beaming.

Beautiful is not the word I would have used but I make a suitably appreciative noise.

It transpires that the object is a 'friendship bracelet', made from a kit one of Daisy's school friends gave her when she first became ill.

'My friendship bracelets are magic, like your locket,' she tells me.

If truth be told I'm not enraptured by the idea of wearing the fiddly thing, but I allow her to tie it around my wrist. It is a very sweet gesture, after all.

When he isn't busy filming, a job which takes him to all sorts of extreme areas of the planet, Sir Robert lives in Edinburgh. It is only a few hours away from The Ballahays and, if Eileen isn't available to drive me, it is quite doable by public transport or by taxi. I favour the latter these days. Comfort is becoming slightly more of a priority; not to my spirit – never that – but to my ageing body, itself a vehicle over which I hold little sway but within which I must operate as best I can.

I therefore leave Daisy in Eileen's capable hands for a few hours whilst I am borne by taxi to Edinburgh. I settle in the back and smooth down my skirt. Now that I have a brief respite from childcare my thoughts turn again to Patrick, and I experience a raw, scraping anxiety. Try as I might, I simply cannot understand my grandson. I ponder the words of his email. It merely said: *Sorry, Granny. You won't be too chuffed about this but me and Terry have split up. Patrick. x*

The very thought of it fills me with dismay. How could this have happened? The question flaps around the insides of my head. He does love her, I'm sure of it. I have always been convinced that those two go together like a teacup and saucer. They are both very practical in their different ways, both willing to make sacrifices and to compromise. They are people who care deeply about what's important, and they also care deeply about each other. They are tough nuts with soft centres. He needs her sunniness to ward off his dark moods and she needs his devotion to heal her loneliness. I wonder what on earth could have instigated so sudden a rift between them?

If I could be with them I'm sure I could find a way of gluing them back together again ... but how can I do anything from here? I will have to trust that they'll sort out the problem between themselves. I must hope that the next email will be along the lines of: *Forget I wrote that, Granny. All good again with Terry and me. x*

The taxi driver's voice interrupts my reverie and snaps me back to the present.

'Nearly there, ma'am.'

We are turning into Princes Street and the familiar outline of the castle rises sharply against a dove-grey sky. The prospect of my imminent meeting with Sir Robert lifts my spirits. No decisions have been made yet, but his proposal is undeniably marvellous. I am all aquiver with anticipation.

Sir Robert meets me punctually as the taxi pulls up. He is looking distinguished in his classic greatcoat, his thick white hair blowing about his pleasantly gnarled features. His face is solemn, but his eyes display that mischievous twinkle for which he is so well known. We walk arm in arm to Thurlstone House, our favoured restaurant. It is a handsome building with stone pillars at the front and views of the Tron Kirk and the Royal Mile. Sir Robert holds the door open for me, ever the perfect gentleman. I step inside to the warmth of a roaring fire and the tantalizing scents of herbs, garlic, roasts and freshly baked bread. Each table is well dressed with a white tablecloth, linen napkins, a candle and a small vase of heather. Real flowers are a mark of quality, I always think.

We settle near the fire and order poached wild turbot followed by a nice sweet cranachan.

Sir Robert observes me earnestly across the table and I have the feeling he is looking right inside me. This would be unsettling if it were anybody else, but I sense that Sir

Robert is someone who seeks out the good rather than the bad.

'When I first heard about you through Terry's blog, I thought how very brave you were to travel to Antarctica in your . . . eighties? I hope I have that right?'

'Yes, my mid-eighties.' I do not wish to be too specific.

'Very brave and intrepid,' he remarks.

I would not normally trust anything akin to buttering up, but in Sir Robert's case I am prepared to make allowances. 'Oh, it was nothing,' I reply with a modest air. 'As you know, Sir Robert, the South Shetlands are situated only on the perimeter of Antarctica, north of the peninsula. And I went in the Antarctic summer. On Locket Island that is on average thirty-five degrees Fahrenheit, much the same as these Scottish winters to which I am fully inured.'

He tips his head a little to one side. 'Ah yes, I remember Fahrenheit,' he replies, which is reassuring (Eileen only comprehends Celsius). 'But I know that field centre isn't well equipped. I recall there's very little in the way of creature comforts.'

'It was indeed a far cry from the lap of luxury I have been enjoying at The Ballahays for the majority of my life. However, I have lived through a war and such physical disadvantages bear no terrors for me. It was more the attitude of the naysayers that was the problem.' I think back to how Dietrich and the team had done their utmost to dissuade me from staying with them.

Sir Robert nods sagely. 'Ah yes. I've had some problems with naysayers myself.' He is about a decade my junior and in robust health, but I know that the general public have been expecting him to retire for many years now.

In his presence I feel able to voice my opinions without worrying too much about niceties. 'Because we are past our peak the younger generations assume we've had our time,' I grumble. 'They think we shouldn't be impertinent enough to have any more of it. The fact is, though, that I didn't. I didn't have much of a time at all.' I am aware of how irascible I am sounding, but there you are.

Sir Robert is sympathetic. 'Well, I hope you feel that's changing. You've had one big adventure and I'm offering you another. On a plate,' he adds, as our lunch arrives and is laid in front of us. He takes a sip of wine and graces me with a rakish smile. 'And it's up to you and me to prove the naysayers wrong.'

'Absolutely, Sir Robert. So, tell me about this filming project.'

The contours of his face settle into an expression of intense seriousness.

He informs me that seabirds are in terrible danger. Taken as a whole, they are one of the most threatened groups of vertebrates in the world, which is why he is so anxious to make this programme. Some of the documentary has already been filmed, apparently. Last year he went to Skomer and the Faroe Islands to film puffins, and he has already done some work on albatrosses.

'And I will be looking at boobies.'

'I beg your pardon?' I adjust my hearing aid slightly.

He repeats the phrase.

I am quite sure I heard him right, but cannot believe that Sir Robert could be indulging in schoolboy-style humour. He goes on to explain, however, and I am relieved to find out that the booby is a type of bird that is closely related to the gannet. 'The Abbott's booby is an extraordinary bird with a long bill and bright blue feet. It is a seriously endangered species. I will be flying to Christmas Island in the Indian Ocean to do a presentation on it, and from there onwards to Australia.'

He will do something on albatrosses, petrels and skuas in the next leg of the venture, but he'd like me, Veronica McCreedy, to cover the penguins. If I am willing, this would involve just over a week's worth of on-site reporting about Little penguins.

After that he will be flying straight on for five weeks of work in the Falklands, to which I am also invited should I have the stamina for further reportage. The archipelago is, he says, made up of over seven hundred islands, many of them uninhabited. Quite a few others have a population of fewer than ten people, but these, he assures me, are welcoming and friendly. The projected filming will be in various locations, island-hopping on a little eight-seater plane, so there will be plenty of scenic flights.

For me the idea of the Falklands primarily conjures images of Margaret Thatcher's war, but Sir Robert paints a picture of a natural paradise: mile upon mile of open spaces punctuated by tiny settlements, sheep and bird colonies, all surrounded by seas of brilliant turquoise-greens and silvery blues. The islands are on the same latitude south as the UK is north and so next month there it will be late summer. Our Scottish January has dragged on in a very dank and dull fashion this year and I must say the idea of long sunny evenings, blue skies and the smell of summer meadows is severely tempting.

'It would be too much for the scope of the programme

to report on every species of penguin,' Sir Robert tells me. 'But we hope to cover several.'

I ask him to name the different species and he lists each of the eighteen, counting on his fingers. His memory is quite extraordinary – almost as good as mine. There are apparently five different species of penguin living in the Falklands, and I am pleased to discover that Macaronis are one of the five. I am therefore able to slip into the conversation my recently acquired titbit of knowledge: 'Ah yes, Sir Robert, the species is named after the eighteenth-century fashion called Macaronism, as in the song "Yankee Poodle".'

'"Yankee Poodle"?' Sir Robert raises his delightfully bushy eyebrows, impressed with my know-how.

I consume a mouthful of turbot with great satisfaction.

'My producer is very keen for us to tailor this programme to popular tastes,' he goes on to explain. 'And I feel that people are tired of hearing my voice—'

'Never, Sir Robert!' I protest.

'And you would bring something highly original to the programme, Veronica.'

I can feel a smile breaking out across my face. My role as far as the presenting goes will not be arduous, he assures me, as the lion's share of the work will be his. Slightly disappointed that *I* am not to have the lion's share, I nevertheless feel electrified at the prospect of seeing penguins in the wild again, and soon. I therefore give Sir Robert my acquiescence to his proposals and commit myself to a new role as his co-presenter in both the Antipodes and the Falklands.

*

Hitherto I have assumed that my trip to Locket Island was my last great adventure upon this planet. Yet now I stand on the cusp of another adventure and I can scarcely believe my good fortune. This time it will not be 'basic conditions' and the coldest continent on the planet; it will be relative luxury with good facilities and as many cups of tea as I like, in the company of a BBC filming crew and the most charming gentleman I know. Moreover there will be penguins – penguins in their thousands.

7

Patrick

A ship in the Antarctic Ocean

GRANNY SAYS THAT impulsiveness runs in the McCreedy blood. I think I may have just proved her right.

I lean over the side. The cold pinches out here on the open sea. Icy gusts of wind sting my face. The cries of gulls and skuas ricochet around the hard white sky. All around me jags of icebergs are throwing light around, so bright it hurts my eyes. In the distance I can see some spouting whales but I'm furious with them for looking so damned joyful. It's not on, not when I'm leaving Locket Island.

I couldn't hack it any more. I'm not going to play happy families and pretend. Fact: I can't work with Terry now. I had to get out.

I'm sore, raw and kind of spiky, too. Like a porcupine, I think I might just send a load of sharp spines into anyone who comes near me. What's the point in talking to the other passengers anyway? These are people who pass through, wrapped up in their own lives just like I am in mine, and I've got enough to be thinking about without any overlap, thank you very much. I avoid them all and stay out on deck as much as I can. My bones are frozen. Good. I can't seem to eat much. Good. I feel sick to the core. Good. I'm a sad lonely git, yet again. Good.

It's good, good, good that I've managed to step out of that crazy phase of my life, but scenes from it keep flashing up in my brain. The crunch of snow and glint of ice. Flopping seals, soaring gulls, shining snowmelt streams. Slopes covered in penguins. Walking amongst them, watching, weighing, counting, tagging. The steam of our breath rising, the gloves frozen solid, the hardship, the laughter. The four walls of the field base. Dietrich stroking his beard, Mike stomping the snow off his boots, Terry with her hands wrapped round a mug of tea, me stirring hot tomato soup. Dietrich picking a pen from the pot and starting on one of his penguin cartoons, Mike examining a specimen of bone in the lab, Terry sat in front of the computer, pushing her glasses up her nose, focused on choosing the right words for her blog. The four of us gathered round the table stuffing porridge into our mouths. Dietrich putting on a jazz CD, me rewiring a plug, Terry wrapping her scarf round her neck five times, Mike tapping the barometer, Dietrich crying 'Mein Gott!'

Terry with a penguin under one arm and a pencil between her teeth. Terry laughing because she has somehow got penguin crap in her hair. Terry leaning towards me to show me the latest pictures in her camera. Terry putting her lips on mine. Terry peeling off her layers of clothes and slipping under the duvet, her soft, warm shape sliding against me, sending fire through my veins.

But now the dark episodes of the past week muscle in on those memories. After Mike's hint I kept seeing little signs that Terry didn't really care for me, that she was only with me because of Granny's funding. Once I'd noticed them, those signs were bloody everywhere: the way she looked at me, the way she talked to me – I could even see it in the way she fricking *walked*. And she was forever staying out late to do extra work. She made excuses when I made advances . . . and then tried to make up for it by being extra lovey-dovey. What a class idiot I've been. It never even occurred to me before that I wasn't wanted for my pathetic, over-inflated self; I was only wanted for my granny's money.

The crunch point was the blasted reverse osmosis machine. I'd already had several attempts at mending it with no luck, and we'd spent three vile days with stinking water and stomach cramps. I wasn't in the best of moods about it and I spent most of last night trying to fix the wretched thing. It wouldn't work and wouldn't work, and then, in the small hours, it went and died on me al-together. I let out a roar of frustration and anger.

They all tumbled out of their bedrooms, rubbing their eyes to see what was wrong. Dietrich's face was scrunched up with disappointment, Mike's was covered in an enormous smirk. Terry was all over me with concern. I shook her off and yelled at her, at them all. The more she flinched, the more I fumed. My outburst was met by a tight, judgemental silence.

Terry's voice cut through, quiet but icy.

'I sometimes wonder if the pressures of Locket Island are too much for you, Patrick?'

Then I really flipped. Another hurricane of words came whooshing out of my mouth. Words I probably should have bitten back, but it's too bloody late now, isn't it?

That was when she said it. 'If that's how you feel, then maybe our relationship's a mistake.'

It was as if she held my heart right there in her hands and ripped it into little pieces.

I'll never forget that rejection and pain. That need to get out.

So get out I did.

8

Terry

Locket Island

'I SUPPOSE THAT'S it then.'

Mike is quick to condemn, quick to see the worst possible scenario. I pretend not to know what he's talking about and turn my face towards him with a questioning look.

'That's it for the Locket Island project, isn't it?' He spits out the words. 'Patrick will go whining to Veronica and Veronica will stop the funding and we're completely stymied.'

I want to spring to Patrick's defence. Instead I spring to Veronica's. 'She'll make her own decision. She's supported us ever since she's known us, and I can't believe she'd drop us just like that.' I click my fingers in a vague suggestion of speed. But even as I do it, I'm aware that Veronica *does* react to things quickly and might swing either way.

Dietrich lifts his head from his papers at the table. His eyes are anxious but he's keen to counteract Mike's pessimism. 'Remember, Veronica saved Pip,' he points out. 'There's an emotional attachment there.'

'She also has an emotional attachment with that wa— with Patrick,' Mike argues. He knows how to underline to me just how selfish Patrick has been without actually spelling it out. As if I need reminding.

I'm not going to agree or disagree out loud. If I even mention Patrick's name I might burst into tears and I don't want to do that now, for their sakes and mine. I've cried in front of Dietrich a few times over the years since we've been working here as a team, but in front of Mike only once before – and that was when we all thought Veronica was dying. Now it is positive, practical action that's required, not uncontrollable sobbing.

I've made some quick calculations to see how long our research here can continue if Veronica stops supporting us, and it's not long: three or four months at most.

'I'll write to Veronica,' I decide. 'I'll be honest and tell her how much we still need her monthly payments.'

Dietrich scratches his beard. 'Thank you, Terry,' he says finally. 'I think it's the only way.'

Mike curls his lip. 'Be sure to mention Pip.'

I nod. 'I mention Pip every time I send Veronica an email anyway. She'd be furious if I didn't.'

The field centre has lost its normal homely atmosphere. It's still early but I need to get out. I pull on my gear as fast as I can and leave for the morning's rounds. The day is cloudy, with a speckling of snow in the air. I trudge up the slope, pausing as always at the top to look at the view: the

50

soft white line of the land, the mirrored rocks, the distant range of mountains and the half-moon lake. And there, spread out across the valley, the pulsating community of birdlife that means so much to me.

The penguins, it must always be the penguins who come first.

I pick up pace and launch myself down the hill into the midst of the colony. What a therapy it is to be knee-deep in these noisy, smelly, glorious birds. Some are shaking the dots of snow off their plump bodies, others hunkering down in their nests. Many are just a few weeks old, comical and cute in their grey baby down. On the outskirts of the colony, penguins are coming and going, waddling with flippers stuck out or slithering along on their bellies, pushing themselves forward with their strong, rubbery feet. They leave dark trails in the snow, like messy creases in a white sheet.

I throw myself into my work. The human population of this island might be back down to three but I have five thousand Adélies for company.

Patrick must be hundreds of miles away by now, but he keeps pushing into my thoughts. Does he regret getting on that ship? Whatever possessed him! I hate being angry – it feels as if an invading army is stamping about inside my head – but I can't help it. Bigger things are at stake than his bruised ego and I can't believe he did that to us.

I wander under the milky sky and tag a few more penguins before self-doubt and accusations start to reel in. Was I unreasonable? Was it all my fault?

Maybe Patrick and I were doomed from the start. We

fell for each other so quickly, and under such strange circumstances here on Locket Island. I'm out of practice with relationships and I've never been great at them anyway. Past boyfriends include smug Stevie who didn't mention he was a vegan until the moment my mother had put a pork chop in front of him, handsome Sam who never forgave me for not owning a single dress, and arrogant Damian whose definition of a date was me watching him play in his band. I worked hard at each of these relationships but always had this uncomfortable feeling they should be so much better. When I came out to Locket Island it was such a relief. I could forget about men and focus on penguins instead.

Then came Patrick and I experienced a completely different kind of love. It was like the love you get in books and songs. It was a love that actually made me happy, the way love is supposed to.

I could have sworn I made him happy too.

My eyes are starting to go fuzzy. I have cordoned off an area and I'm trying to do a count to find out the ratio of adults to chicks. I have a clicker but I still keep losing track. I set it at 00 and start all over again.

It's useless. I veer off for a while and head for the shore, breathing deeply and trying to get a grip. The clouds have rolled back now and rays of sunshine stride out, leaving golden footprints on the surface of the sea. The icebergs make up a great, gleaming flotilla. Small flat pieces jostle beside the huge craggy sculptures, all composed of blue shadows and white light. Yet even on this bright day, with the sea throwing glitter and diamonds into the air with each wave, the wind at my back and the noise of five thousand penguins in my ears, I can't shake off the shock of what has happened.

I wonder how we're going to manage, with Dietrich taking time off soon, too. I'll have to work out what we can still do and what we simply can't. And how will Veronica react to all this? She's fair-minded, but she's headstrong. I hope Patrick won't poison her against us. I know he's hurting, but surely he wouldn't do a thing like that?

Loneliness engulfs me. I shed a few tears, then head back to the hub of the colony. There are tiny grains of colour in amongst the mingling patterns of black and white: the yellow tags we have attached to the birds' flippers so that we can track individuals. My eyes scan the penguins for an orange tag amongst the hundreds of yellow ones. If I can find him, Pip might bring me solace.

It isn't long before I spy him. I pick my way through the other birds, over the pebble nests, shingle and slippery pink guano. He is engaged in a lively exchange with a tight gaggle of other penguins. Simultaneously they turn their heads and look at me, with typical Adélie curiosity. Pip arches his head and shakes his tail feathers.

For the first time since Patrick left, I smile. Pip is an adolescent now and not the sweet pompom he used to be, but I still adore him. When it comes to all other penguins I'm ruthlessly detached. I can witness Adélie corpses littering the ground around my feet after a blizzard, or a chick being pecked to death by skuas, or a bloodied penguin being bashed on the rocks by a seal and then gulped down its throat inch by inch. Like a surgeon before operating, I've learned to put a line between myself and the suffering creature, otherwise I'd be no use. But when it comes to Pip there is something else. It's all down to Veronica. She's somehow transmitted to me her feelings for this little Adélie penguin, feelings that I know are all mixed up with her past.

Mike and Dietrich know about my unscientific soft spot. Mike says it's 'soppy and unprofessional'. Dietrich says: '*Ja*, but it doesn't stop her doing the work.' I justify it by reminding them Pip is a one-off, and anyway, he's won us a lot of public support. Besides, I do think love has got to be a good thing, on any level.

Pip bobs his head and pulls at the material of my trouser knees. He's still too young to be mating and having babies, so his pals are important to him. One of them is already tagged. I make a note of his number, or maybe *her* number – it's hard to tell with Adélies. Then I take advantage of the situation and swiftly tag the other three. They protest when I scoop them up, but I'm very careful as I tuck them under my arm and fasten the bands securely at the base of their flippers. I only get pecked once. Pip watches the process with interest.

'So, we'll see now if you always hang out with the same friends,' I tell him.

Soon I'll post my next blog about him and the other penguins of Locket Island. Nothing is more important than the future of our world, so I bang on a lot about our research, the rate of ice-melt and the danger this poses to our beloved penguins, as well as our planet generally. I draw people in by including news and photos of Pip, who is incredibly popular. I also share something about our own lifestyle. I'm not going to mention the fact that Patrick has left us, though. The public gets told about our personal troubles on a need-to-know basis and it's better to keep bad news from them if I can.

I will write that email to Veronica as soon as possible. I mustn't and won't play the blame game, but she needs to hear our side of the story.

9

Veronica

The Ballahays

AFTER A YEAR of relative inertia I had well-nigh resigned myself to stagnancy. Yet now two occurrences have simultaneously appeared to stir up my life again: firstly the sudden prospect of a gallivant across the globe with Sir Robert Saddlebow, and secondly the imminent arrival of my grandson.

The latest from Patrick, which came in an email from some South American airport, is extremely disappointing, to say the least. I had thought the boy had gumption and sticking power, but it appears he has no more backbone than a jellyfish. In my own mind I am sure that he and Terry would have sorted out their differences if he had only stayed on Locket Island. There is slim chance of any sorting out now. He hopped on to the ship that was docking at the island the very morning he split with Terry, thus throwing the troubled team into even more turmoil.

Terry will no doubt battle on, putting her feelings to one side, immersing herself in her work. But as for Patrick . . . Oh, the silly boy. Silly, selfish oaf! I am furious with him and I will tell him so in no uncertain terms. I am not accustomed to dishing out grandmotherly advice but I shall do my utmost. He must endeavour to find something worthwhile to do with himself. On no account will I have him frittering away his life.

It is unfortunate, however, that I will be departing myself for six weeks so soon after he returns. I would have hoped for more time to discuss the future with him.

The Locket Island team will surely have to find a replacement. Keen as I am to support their worthy endeavours, I am disinclined to fund somebody who isn't Patrick to assist them.

Terry's email comes shortly after Patrick's second missive and is more eloquent and thoughtful. She is clearly having problems skirting between the professional and personal, and I imagine she is far more upset than she implies.

Dear Veronica,

I do hope you and Eileen are well, and your corns are not playing up. We often think of you and remember the wonderful adventures we had together.

I'm afraid I have to tell you some sad news, which you may have already heard from Patrick. He and I have decided to go our separate ways and he has left

Locket Island. It's been tough for him here with just Mike and me and sometimes Dietrich for company ... and me acting as both his boss and his girlfriend. I've had some difficult decisions to make and found it hard too, always splitting myself in two to try and do the right thing.

Dietrich, Mike and I will miss him. He's been a wonderful all-round help and a real asset, and we honestly wish him well. We are, of course, worried about the future of our mission to study the Adélies and protect them. Please be assured that the three of us are determined to keep going if we can.

Pip is well and happy. He seems to have made three particular friends and I'm monitoring the little group so I can keep an eye on his social life. He's as handsome and strapping as any of them. Who would have thought he was once so feeble? He always reminds us of everything you have done for him, our project and the bird colony here on Locket Island.

With love,
Terry xx

Terry looks on all her fellow creatures with a charitable eye and is more forgiving of Patrick than I am myself. I still have no clear idea about what happened, though. I wonder if my grandson has done something inexcusable and Terry is reluctant to tell me what it is. I wonder also if Terry, who is an annoyingly conscientious girl, might have prioritized some matter of penguin welfare instead of prioritizing Patrick. He would not like that.

I wander into the drawing room, deep in thought. Daisy is currently at the table, pounding her fists into a piece of pink, sparkly plasticine-like material. As soon as she sees me she is bursting with questions. 'Is that bad, then, that Patrick's coming home? Will the penguins manage without him? Will he be mending bicycles for my dad again?'

'I'm not sure about the answer to any of these, Daisy.' Were I to analyse the peculiar shades of emotion I am experiencing, I would detect that, amidst my rage at my grandson's imprudent behaviour and stress about what this sudden change portends, I feel some elation at the prospect of seeing him again.

'Is Terry coming back too?' enquires Daisy.

I shake my head glumly.

'Are they going to get married?' She is determined to marry Patrick off. In her own way, Daisy is an incurable romantic. She is unshakeable in her belief that marriage equates with living happily ever after. (I am made of much more cynical stuff, my own affairs of the heart having been more deadly nightshade than honeysuckle.)

When Patrick and Terry came home for a whirlwind visit last summer, Daisy witnessed them being 'couply'. Daisy hero-worships Terry and avidly follows her penguin blogs; thus she knows all about the rhythms of the penguin colony, the moulting season, winter on the pack ice, and the return to land in October for breeding. She keeps up with news about Sooty, the all-black penguin, and above all she adores Pip. She's interested in the humans of Locket Island too. She gulps down any references to my grandson, and whenever I mention Terry and Patrick together she will start singing pop songs about love – or 'lurve', which, as far as I can see, is a sentimental variety of the same thing. She has even hatched great plans to be a bridesmaid at their wedding.

I field Daisy's questions by pretending not to hear her. But when she abandons her glittery pink dough and shouts into my hearing aid, 'ARE TERRY AND PATRICK GETTING MARRIED?' I cannot avoid supplying some sort of answer.

'I fear not,' I reply.

'Not now or not ever?' she asks.

All I can say is: 'Daisy, I am not God. I do not know.'

'If I am bridesmaid, I will have to grow more hair quickly though, because bridesmaids can't be bald,' she tells me, as if she could attain this goal by willpower alone.

'I don't think you need to worry about that at the moment, dear,' I tell her.

She is still for a full thirty seconds and then goes back to her pounding.

10

Patrick

Bolton

FROM THE ANTARCTIC Ocean to Ushuaia, from Ushuaia
to Buenos Aires, from Buenos Aires to Madrid, to Heathrow and then, finally, after days of whizzing round the
edges of the planet, here I am: Bolton.

Home? Maybe not. It used to be, but that was fourteen
months and several thousand penguins ago. The cruddy
flat where I once lived is rented out to someone else now,
and my few possessions are in storage. I'm stopping off at
Gav's. I texted him as soon as there was a signal and he
said, yes, OK, I could stay with him for the time being. Top
man, Gav. He used to be my boss at the bike shop but was
always more of a mate. He and his family are sagging with
relief at the mo. Their Daisy is much better after a terrible
time with chemo last year. The doctors won't quite say

the word 'remission' yet but they are full of hope. She's staying with Granny V right now. She and Granny seem to have taken a liking to each other.

Gav and his wife, Beth, and even their younger kid, Noah, are very good to me, but I'm in a weird state of mind. I need to think, but thinking isn't my forte. The few brain cells I used to have seem to have gone AWOL.

I walk the streets of Bolton and gawp at everything. This is the town where I've spent most of my life, but even the familiar sights look alien and grotesque. I guess I can't really blame Bolton; I'd feel the same in any city. It's as if Antarctica's got into my bloodstream and messed with my senses. I can't breathe here without choking on the stink of diesel and chips and piss and perfume. The poor land has been completely smothered with buildings, square upon square, oblong upon oblong, block upon block. And the tarmac! Whoever thought it was a good idea, this flat, grey network, sprawling over the earth, crawling with traffic? Cars roar past, an endless stream of hard metal capsules driven by highly complex mechanisms that churn out noise and fumes. The racket never stops. Even underground is this vast grid of tunnels, cables, pipes and sewers carrying water, waste, electricity, gas – all these things that humans have to organize and funnel about endlessly. It's bloody frantic. Penguins just crap in the snow and that's fine, get food from the water and that's fine, get light from the sky and that's fine, get entertainment from each other. Why do humans have to over-bloody-complicate every little thing? I've lived most of my life amongst this clutter. How the hell did I put up with it all?

Wherever I go, a tide of people sweeps me up and carries me along. All done up in fancy gear, yelling into phones, gabbling about the latest gizmos and what's on telly. Humans, humans everywhere. And none of them is Terry.

Not that I care. I'm over all that now. I don't give a bat's bumhole. And it will serve her right if her precious penguin project gets shut down.

Gav sets a pint in front of me. We're wedged into a corner of the Dragon's Flagon. We've drunk many, many beers here in the past, but now the place has gone weird. It's cramped and fetid and the din feels like drills in my eardrums.

I try to block it out and look at Gav helplessly. 'Man, I'm a mess,' I tell him.

'What's new?' he asks, grinning.

I don't manage to smile back. 'I can't snap back into the old life just like that.'

'I can see that, mate,' he says. 'It sounds like you're suffering from culture shock. I expect you need to be somewhere quieter for a while.'

'Yup. Too right, mate. It's just as well I'm heading for Granny's next.'

He nods and takes a swig of beer. 'Check up on Daisy for me while you're there, would you? I bet she's running circles round them.'

I promise I will. But there's no doubt in my mind that Granny will be reigning supreme. I'm also pretty sure she's going to be mad at me. She'll probably make me do penance for the rest of my life.

Gav hasn't commented on the fact I've left Locket Island, which is pretty amazing when you think about it.

'So you're not going to tick me off?' I ask.

'What good would that do?' He knows me too well.

I wonder for a moment if he might offer me my old job back – Mondays spent with inner tubes and axel hubs and customer service. He doesn't.

'I'm not proud of myself,' I confess.

Irresponsible. That's the word that best describes me. Gav thinks it and Granny V will be thinking it and the whole bloody team at Locket Island will be thinking it, for sure. It's the word that should go at the top of my CV in big block capitals because, hell, I'm going to have to start thinking about CVs again very soon.

I pour half a pint down my throat. 'Irresponsible is in the fricking genes,' I tell Gav. 'Look at my dad. Buggered off when I was a week old.'

Where there should be memories of Dad there's just this black hole. I remember some stuff about my mum, though. I remember her kneeling to blow on the embers of a fire in a dim light. I remember her shouting at me when I climbed on top of a stone wall she thought was unsafe. I remember her leaving tights in a knotted tangle on the floor of the caravan. When I think of her, I can smell rose soap and cheap shampoo with an underlying bitterness like sour beer. I can hear her recordings of Joni Mitchell on loop. I can see the dirt under her nails. I remember the ache in her voice, too. And her words – 'You have no father' – every time I asked her about it. Even though I was only six years old when she left me, I do remember all these things.

But Dad? There's a total blank where his face should be. There haven't exactly been many role models in my life, and now it strikes me that he should have been one, like a map telling me how I ought to behave, what you're supposed to do when your world falls apart.

'What's up, mate?' asks Gav, leaning forward and viewing me anxiously. 'You look like you've seen a ghost.'

'Just thinking about my dad. He kicked the bucket ages ago, but I hate his guts all the same.'

'How can you hate someone you don't remember?'

I try to explain. 'I feel mad at him, as if all the mistakes I've made throughout my entire life are his fault.'

Gav looks unconvinced. 'And?'

'OK, in spite of it, I want to find excuses for him. I want to believe he had a good reason for abandoning Mum and me. I want to know he was sorry and lived the rest of his life regretting it.'

Gav pauses with his beer halfway to his mouth. Then he says exactly what I'm thinking. 'Maybe now's the time to find out.'

11

Veronica

The Ballahays

WE GATHER IN the driveway. A large, dishevelled figure climbs out of the taxi and throws a rucksack on to the ground.

'Great to see you, Granny!'

I allow myself to be engulfed in Patrick's impressively muscular arms.

Daisy runs at him and he whisks her into the air and round in circles a few times.

'You did a Dietrich!' she cries, once he has set her down again. She has seen photos of all the members of the Locket Island team and thinks that Dietrich's facial hair is hilarious. Patrick is now almost his equal, follically speaking. He is in possession of a dark, straggling beard.

'I hardly recognized you,' I admit.

'Well, *you* try shaving every morning in the Antarctic,' he protests.

'I have no intention of ever doing that,' I assure him.

I do occasionally discover a whisker ungraciously sprouting from my chin these days, which is the source of unimaginable chagrin. Why hairs become so thin on top during the ageing process and yet persist in appearing on one's upper lip, chin and other inappropriate places is beyond me. It is one of the many flaws in nature's methodology. But I digress.

Patrick looks up at the house and gives a low whistle.

'Great to be back at Ballahays! I'd forgotten the size of the place!'

Eileen steps forward and squeezes his hand. 'It's lovely to see you again, Patrick. Tea? Hobnobs? Fairy cakes?'

'I made the fairy cakes earlier,' Daisy is keen to inform him. 'Eileen helped but I did the icing all by myself.'

'Well, a fairy cake it is, then!'

Patrick is being excessively jolly, but I perceive the bags under his eyes and detect that, behind the beard and stubble, his face is tight with strain. He has plenty to think about.

Over tea our conversation is largely about Pip. ('Oh, he's a big guy now. Goofs around a lot. Typical teenage behaviour. You'd laugh.') Then, after we have settled Patrick in, we all take a tour of the garden together. This morning's frost has melted and trickled into the porous ground, waterlogging the lawn.

'It's like treading on a sticky chocolate sponge cake,' announces Daisy, squelching through it in her red wellington boots. The rest of us follow the paved paths past the borders and shrubberies. The year has not yet found its feet so I cannot show off my finer specimen plants, but there are a few signs that life will spring anew in the fullness of time. Stubby green catkins have started to form on the hazels and the first snowdrops are sprouting in clusters in the back area I call the wilderness, some of them even cautiously showing a thin band of white.

When he was here with Terry last year Patrick was buoyant, but now there is a marked difference. Terry, although never trivial, always manages to keep things light. Without her my grandson seems more solemn and earnest about everything.

Daisy is plaguing him. 'When is Terry coming?'

Patrick grits his teeth. 'She's not.'

Daisy looks startled at his hard tone of voice. But Eileen soon distracts her by escorting her around the garden looking for feathers. I am granted a few moments for a confidential chat with my grandson.

When I ask about Terry, he winces and looks uncomfortable. It turns out that there were various issues with her being a workaholic, granting him too little of her time. And Mike, as moody as ever, kept putting in barbed comments at every opportunity. 'One comment really got under my skin,' Patrick tells me, but doesn't mention what it was.

Then there was apparently an argument over some machine, which escalated to a fit of shouting and swearing. It was Terry who suggested the split.

'I realized right there that she'd never really loved me . . . she'd just been nice to me because . . . because . . .' He glances across at me and gulps. His fists are bunching and unbunching and there's a vein standing out on his forehead. 'Anyway, it cut me so much I just snapped back at her, "OK then, that's it. We're finished."'

For the rest of the night he hadn't slept. His hurt and fury had burned, seethed and fed on itself until, by morning, it had reached such epic proportions that he'd flung his belongings into a rucksack, shouted that he was leaving and pounded out towards the ship. He hadn't stayed to see his colleagues' reactions but had been vaguely aware of three figures struggling to understand what was happening. None of them had run after him.

He drags his feet and looks at me with pain in his eyes. 'I just don't know what to do with myself. Is this a kind of mid-life crisis?'

'At twenty-six? I sincerely hope not.'

'I'm twenty-eight, Granny.'

'A mere baby, then.'

I had intended to vent my rage at him but he seems such a very lost sheep that it is now impossible. I am aware that Patrick was brought up by a string of foster families. It is perhaps not surprising that the boy finds it hard to make attachments or put down roots. I suspect that he has abandonment issues and would rather reject others than risk being rejected again himself. It is indeed a sad legacy his parents have left him.

I walk by his side in silence.

After a long while he starts up again. 'But anyway, I thought that maybe now I'm back in your hemisphere' (*your* hemisphere indeed! As if he hasn't spent most of his life in Bolton!) 'you and I could start looking up that stuff to do with my dad.'

I stop in my tracks.

He stops too. Gesticulating wildly, he goes on, 'He's the middle link between us, but what do we know about him? Hardly anything. Just that he died in a mountaineering accident. We don't know if he knew he was adopted or if he ever wondered about you, his birth mother. We don't know why he came to England or why he left again just after my birth. We said we might track him down and I really think now's the time to do that. What do you think? I'm keen to find out more.'

What I think is *yes, yes, yes*, but I don't say anything. My heart silently convulses.

12

Veronica

My own tragic story was a tiny drop in the worldwide crisis of those wartime years. Despite my best efforts, I could find no trace of my son for decades. Then it was only to receive news of his death due to a tragic accident. I unexpectedly discovered the existence of *his* son, Patrick, years after that. But Patrick is as ignorant as I am about Enzo's life. There is still much to be discovered and I am quite desperate to discover it.

The old wound still smarts, but I have always hoped my boy had a fine life with his adoptive parents in Canada, better than if he had stayed with me. When Enzo was mine, he only had one toy, a cat puppet I'd made for him out of an old, over-darned sock. He adored it, especially when I made it purr and rub against his cheek. As he started to crawl about, I improvised more entertainments for him, putting conkers into an old saucepan for him to rattle and roll around. The nuns didn't like that because it was noisy. So I read aloud to him from books I found in the convent library, even though he didn't understand the words. Once he tore a book's pages. The nuns didn't like that either. I had plans for us to run away from the convent when he was old enough. In those days I also still hoped that my Giovanni would come and rescue us.

Over the years I have conjured many an image of Enzo growing up. I know that his adoptive parents were wealthy and that he was renamed Joe Fuller. I picture him as a small boy, the age of Daisy's brother, in short trousers, grasping a toy tractor, fascinated by dinosaurs or spaceships. Then at Daisy's age he'd be growing taller, reading books, learning about the world, having dreams and already beginning to follow them. Then I see him slipping into adulthood, Patrick's age – possibly resembling Patrick in behaviour and appearance, but alas, already hurtling towards his death. Not for the first time I am overcome with intense anger that he had to die so young whilst I, his mother, linger on and on . . .

Patrick and I originally said we'd research his life together as soon as he came back to the UK, but his summer stay was too brief and he had Terry with him, and her family to visit, too. Now he seems as eager to learn about his father as I am to learn about my son.

'I am aggrieved about you and Terry, and deeply dismayed that you have taken it upon yourself to leave Locket Island,' I tell him finally. 'But this issue of your father has always been hanging over you. Perhaps if we can uncover his life, you'll be able to settle more into yours.'

He nods emphatically. 'I didn't want to leave it too

long. On Locket Island I did a bit of googling whenever I could get at the computer. I searched for the name Joe Fuller, and there were a few around who dated back to that time in Canada, but I couldn't find anything that quite fitted. We could work on this one together, Granny, if you're up for it?'

I most certainly am.

He squares his shoulders. 'Do you still have the letter from Chicago, from the cousin who wrote to you about my dad's accident all those years ago?'

'I do.'

'Let's start there.'

We head back inside immediately, leaving Daisy threading feathers through Eileen's hair in the orchard.

The aforementioned letter is locked up in the Georgian oak bureau in the dining room. Frustratingly, we cannot find the key for some time and I have to resort to calling Eileen in.

'What is it, Mrs McCreedy?' she asks in the porch, looking somewhat like a long-eared owl with her wide eyes, round face and two feathers sticking upright out of her curls.

I enquire after the whereabouts of the key.

'I expect it's in the blue Chinese pot on the mantelpiece, the one where you keep all your spare keys, Mrs McCreedy,' she answers.

I know I most definitely would have kept it somewhere less obvious than that, but Patrick takes a look and produces a small key which does, in fact, bear a resemblance to the bureau key.

'Let's try it, just in case,' he insists.

I am astonished when he inserts it into the lock, declares 'Bingo,' and the drawer slides open.

'Well, I don't know who put that key in that jar,' I exclaim. 'It most certainly wasn't me.'

He smiles in a way I do not like.

Fortunately, my memory is faultless, so I am able to find the letter in amongst the other papers with very little trouble. It is distressing to read again those lines that tell of my son's life and death: so few words, such sparse, bald facts. Susan Warlock, cousin of the woman who adopted my son, is mildly apologetic. She states that she only met my Enzo a couple of times because of the distance to Vancouver. She doesn't leave a full address. However, 'West Ridge, Chicago' is written at the top of the page.

'I might be able to find her on Facebook or something,' Patrick declares. 'Assuming she's still alive.'

He pulls out his phone and spends some time searching on it. But Facebook renders nothing, and neither do any of the other social thingamajigs.

In the evening we gather in the snug and watch television. I feel no enthusiasm for any of the programmes available, but Patrick says it's five months since he's watched anything and he is desperate for his fix. Daisy is also keen. We end up watching a cosy crime drama, then a programme all about wishes being granted to children (Daisy particularly likes that one), then some dreadful celebrity quiz show. My eyelids are drooping, and before I know it the programme has ended and Daisy is putting her arms around me. 'Eileen says I have to go up now. Goodnight, Veronica.'

'Goodnight, Daisy. Sleep tight, and remember the penguins.'

'I will.'

After she's taken herself upstairs, the news comes on, bringing the usual frightful tales of murder, destruction and depravity. The more I see of humans the more I like penguins. I am glad I will be spending another episode of my life devoted to these joyful birds. I have found that one's happiness very much depends on where one chooses to put one's focus. I would do well to follow my own advice and at all times remember the penguins.

As I am performing my night-time ablutions I reflect on Patrick's state of mind. When I told him I would shortly be voyaging southwards on a wildlife adventure, he seemed sulky. Jealous, perhaps? I wonder whether there is any possibility he might tag along, but I baulk at the idea. Much as I love my grandson, I feel that Sir Robert and I have our own elegant dynamic, and Patrick's somewhat childish manner and demands would not make for an easy atmosphere. Especially bearing in mind he is such an unquiet soul at present.

Nevertheless, the thought of leaving Patrick alone at The Ballahays fills me with dismay. It isn't that I don't trust him with the house. It's because in the past he has turned to drugs at times of stress and I am apprehensive that this might happen again. His knee-jerk decisions about Terry and Locket Island have thrown doubt on his whole future. I can only hope that the mission to find his father will bear fruit.

It would be truly wondrous to discover more about my darling Enzo. I fall asleep to soft memories of being sweet sixteen again, rejected by society but nevertheless lit up with hope because I have my beautiful baby in my arms.

13

Veronica

It is the second time that Sir Robert has called in at The Ballahays without prior warning. Last time was on Christmas Day, when he presented me with a bottle of champagne and the framed photograph of Pip. This time he presents me with a bottle of sherry and a request. His perfectly white hair is combed back, exposing his artistically craggy brow. He is wearing his woollen greatcoat and a mischievous smile.

'My dear Veronica, I hope you don't mind my surprising you like this. Could I trouble you for half an hour or so?'

'My dear Sir Robert, it is always a joy to be troubled by you,' I reply. I am almost audibly purring.

'I would like a quick word with you, if you're sure. And after that I'd like to meet a young lady who goes by the name of Daisy, who I believe is staying with you?'

'She will be delighted to make your acquaintance.'

I usher him into the snug and locate my best crystal sherry glasses. He pours us both a tipple that is neither skimpishly small nor vulgarly large, but just the perfect gentlemanly in-between.

'Were you aware that Daisy has written a letter in Irish?'

'In Irish?' I am baffled. 'Pardon me, Sir Robert. My hearing aid is being a nuisance. I don't believe I heard you correctly.' I adjust it and it gives a small, high-pitched squeal.

'Daisy has written a letter to *I Wish*.'

Well, that is quite different, but I am none the wiser. He explains, '*I Wish* is a TV programme. Children write in to it with their wishes and the programme-makers attempt to grant them those wishes.'

'Oh, I see.' I have a vague recollection of Daisy viewing some such programme only recently. I had thought it very gimmicky, although I suppose some would label it 'heart-warming'. 'And what did Daisy wish?'

'She wished she could come with you and me to see the penguins.'

I am so stunned that I fear I will spill sherry over my dress, so I hastily set down my glass. 'You are not seriously suggesting . . . ?'

He nods.

'But she is still recovering from chemotherapy! Her parents only let her stay here with me because she absolutely wouldn't accept no for an answer, and even so they are in touch with her almost hourly. They would never allow such a thing.'

Daisy must have written to *I Wish* the moment she knew I was going away. Sir Robert informs me that he

78

was contacted by the producer of that programme as soon as Daisy's letter arrived. The letter had been accompanied by the photo of herself looking like a very sweet child with cancer, myself looking rather striking (though I say so myself) and Mac the Scottish penguin looking suitably magnificent, and the combination of these things had proved quite irresistible to the programme's host. He, a minor celebrity, had virtually begged Sir Robert, who is a far more major one. Sir Robert had at once consulted with the directors and producers of both programmes. It was decided that Daisy would not only benefit herself from such a trip but, with her innocent charm and the added pathos of her illness, would bring something special to the viewers as well.

Her parents, Gavin and Beth, were contacted the same day. Had this been a trip to Antarctica they would have been less than enthusiastic, but since conditions will be relatively luxurious they were willing to consider it. When it was pointed out to them that the Falklands is renowned for the freshness of its air, they started to warm to the idea. When assurances were given that Daisy would also be allowed ample time to rest, they warmed a little more. Her doctor had given the go-ahead. And didn't she deserve a holiday after all she had been through? After two days discussing it, Gavin and Beth gave their answer: it was a yes. She could come on the Falklands part of the trip, on the condition that one of them could come too.

Sir Robert relates all of this with admirable speed and clarity. 'It remains only for me to confirm with Daisy herself that she really does want to go.'

When I last saw her, Daisy was hooting with laughter

and videoing Patrick on her phone as he made faces at her. Now all is quiet, and I believe she is upstairs, writing a postcard to her parents with Eileen's guidance. I call her down. She goggles at Sir Robert when she sees him.

'Do you know who this is, Daisy?' I ask.

'Yes, it's Robert Saddlebow from TV.'

'*Sir* Robert Saddlebow.' I will not tolerate her being impertinent to him, especially bearing in mind the huge favour he is about to bestow.

He shakes her hand and addresses her seriously, as though she were an adult. At first, he engages her in what seems a random conversation about her home in Bolton and her hobbies, and delicately enquires after her health. Daisy becomes more and more talkative. She confides that she feels so, so much better than she did at Christmas and even a tiny bit of hair is beginning to grow back, and how I told her to remember the penguins and how the penguins always help her. Just thinking about the penguins helps her. But it would help her even more if she could get to see some. She looks at him very pointedly here. She is endowed with much perspicuity for her age.

'Well, Daisy, I think you have proved your commitment. I'm here to officially invite you on the expedition to the Falklands,' Sir Robert concludes. 'Will you come with us?'

She stretches her arms outwards as far as they will go, and her voice is so loud I nearly drop my sherry glass again.

'YES!'

14

Patrick

The Ballahays

I'D LIKE TO loll about here and watch wall-to-wall daytime TV, but of course, Her Royal Bossiness isn't going to let that happen. In between my entertaining Daisy and looking things up on the web, Granny has roped me into helping Eileen with the cooking. Eileen is very giggly about this and can't seem to grasp that this is one of the few things I'm actually good at.

'You wouldn't catch my Doug anywhere *near* a saucepan,' she comments as I tie one of her frilly aprons around me. She took me on a shopping trip to Kilmarnock yesterday and I came back with a good haul of fresh ingredients. I start laying them out on the worktop now.

She eyes the arborio rice, ciabatta and parmesan suspiciously. 'Foreign food?'

Surely Eileen isn't feeling competitive? Her own cooking tends to be old-style. Meat and two veg with lots of salt, lots of stodge and all the vegetables boiled to death.

She lingers at my shoulder. 'Did I mention that I cooked Christmas dinner for Sir Robert himself along with Mrs McCreedy and my own clan?'

'You did, Eileen.'

'And do you know what Sir Robert said?'

I do, because she's mentioned it at least twice already.

'He said I have a way with sprouts!' Said with total rapture.

'I'm sure you do, Eileen.'

She has been allocated the pudding today, however, and now goes to the other side of the palatial kitchen and starts slapping out flour and suet for a jam roly-poly.

Granny sails in. She has an atlas under her arm and a firm look in her eye. I worry when she has that look.

'A word, Eileen, if you wouldn't mind.'

She beckons to Eileen, who scuttles after her. I hear them murmuring together in the next room. I dread to think what they're up to.

I don't like being left on my own because that's when all the negatives come flocking in. I still keep obsessing about my dad, Joe Fuller, or 'my Enzo' as Granny insists on calling him. She named him that because it was the only Italian name she knew at the time, apart from the name of her lover. Oh yes – she may seem prim and proper, but Granny's past is full of naughtiness. She had a fling with an Italian prisoner-of-war when she was only fifteen, and my dad was the result. Her own parents had already been killed in the Blitz and her mean old aunt bunged her off to a nunnery, where she stayed with baby Enzo, scrubbing floors and doing laundry as if she was their slave. Then what did those nuns do? They only went and gave her baby away to a childless couple from Canada. The first she knew of it was that Enzo was gone and never coming back. Unbelievable they'd do that to her. No wonder she became a bit odd.

This morning I had my first bit of luck trying to track down my dad's adoptive family. The name in Granny's letter was Susan Warlock. Twitter and Facebook led nowhere, but on a heritage website I finally found a record of a Susan Warlock (deceased) who lived in the West Ridge district of Chicago and who'd be about the right age. It had details of her children. I managed to find one of them on LinkedIn – Denise Perry (née Warlock) – and messaged her. She messaged back later. She now lives in Vancouver, which is where the family came from originally, and vaguely remembers meeting my father when they were children. Somebody remembers him!

Granny and I both said nothing for a long time after I read out the message. We were feeling too much.

Granny comes back in now, as I'm chopping the shallots.

'Patrick,' she says, fixing me with steely eyes. 'Tell me, is there any chance at all you might go back to Locket Island?'

My reactions are fast when it comes to this one. 'Nope.'

I'll never see Terry again. Or Dietrich or Mike. No way would they have me back after I left them in the lurch like that, and I couldn't face them anyway. No more penguins for me. My bridges could hardly be more burnt.

Granny pouts. 'And what, may I enquire, are your plans for the future?'

'Look, I'm not exactly in a state to decide anything at the moment, what with all this stuff about Dad, and you going away and Daisy and everything.'

She frowns. 'I feel a certain responsibility towards the penguin project, as my own experience in Antarctica was a significant one. Since I am about to benefit from a free nature holiday and a generous payment from the BBC, I will continue funding the Locket Island project until the future has made itself clear. I will do this for the sake of Pip, for Terry, for Dietrich, and even for the less-than-amicable Mike.'

I shrug. 'Whatever.'

'In the meantime, I have asked Eileen to book your flight to Canada.'

I nearly slice my fingers off in shock. Bits of shallot go skittering across the worktop. 'You *what*?'

'Whilst I am gallivanting in the Antipodes with Sir Robert, you are to go to Canada to find out what you can. It seems to me there is a limit to what your endless googling can achieve. Somebody needs to go in person to delve into the past, and the sooner the better. Yet again you and I will be in different hemispheres. But after that you will fly to the Falklands. You can join us there and be my assistant. I'm sure Sir Robert won't mind.'

I'm sure he will. I don't say it, though, I just stare at her, open-mouthed.

She is relishing my shock. 'Would you kindly put your jaw back where it belongs and resume cooking lunch? Daisy is used to having her meals ready promptly.'

She turns and leaves the room before I can say anything else.

I'm in a daze as I carry on chopping. I think of how my father's shadow has been looming over me. I want to find out what happened more than ever. But now the search is beginning to feel sinister, as if I'm a character in a horror film being lured through swirling mists to the edge of a cliff. And I think for the first time, *Hang on a mo, maybe this isn't such a good idea.* Granny clearly believes her darling boy grew up into a wonderful human being, but don't I already know the opposite? At best he was a scumbag. Do I really need to know any more?

Everything's simmering in the pan when Eileen reappears. She gives me a thumbs up. 'Flight's booked.'

Jeez, that was quick. Granny and Eileen can be lethal when they get together. I don't know what to say. I can't believe I'm being sent off round the fricking world again. I hate that I haven't even been given any choice in the matter. Granny is a total control freak.

Somehow, I manage to get lunch on the table. The risotto goes down well and Daisy especially likes the ciabatta. She's intrigued by the name and keeps chanting 'shabbatta, shabbatta, shabbatta'. I'm getting a bit pee'd off with it, to be honest.

Suddenly she stops.

'Patrick, are you sad?' she asks, pointing her spoon at me.

I don't want to say 'yes', but 'no' would be an outright lie, so I stuff a forkful of risotto into my mouth and make a grunty noise that could be either. Daisy doesn't know why I'm here. She's been told I'm just having a little break from my Locket Island work. She's got no idea I messed up big-time.

'Sometimes I get sad, too,' she says. 'Are you hurting anywhere?'

Of course, Daisy's reasons for getting sad are because she has been through terrible, unthinkable physical pain, far more than a child should have to bear.

'No, Daisy,' I tell her. 'I'm not hurting.' Then add: 'At least, not in that way.'

15

Terry

Locket Island

DIETRICH HOLDS THE drawing up for me to see. Four jolly Adélies dance across the page, flipper in flipper, each of them wearing a different kind of hat: a top hat, a bonnet, a beret and a bobble hat.

'Fabulous!' I tell him. He's so talented. If he wasn't a penguinologist he could easily illustrate children's books. Any spare time he has here at the field centre he spends drawing for his family. I'll ask him to email it to Daisy as well.

'Is one of them Pip?' I have to ask.

'Maybe, but I couldn't decide whether he was top hat or beanie.'

'The children will know.' I haven't met Dietrich's three, but when I was introduced to Daisy last summer she struck me as a girl who is very sure of her opinions.

But I can't think about last summer without thinking about Patrick. We were together for the whole of our UK trip, visiting Veronica in Ayrshire, his friends in Bolton and my family in Hertfordshire. We were breathlessly in love and the weeks passed in a giddy haze. My parents didn't quite know what to make of Patrick when they met him, but I overheard Mum's scathing comment to Dad: 'He's probably just a phase.' How cross I am that she was right.

Veronica has promised to keep our penguin project going for the time being, but of course our future depends on whether she'll be pouring her finances into setting Patrick up somewhere else. It's a huge weight hanging over us. Even Veronica can't have an endless supply of money, and I can see why her only living relative would be her priority. If only Patrick had stayed with us . . .

Dietrich is still fretting over his artwork. He scrutinizes it at arm's length and then brings it closer. 'Do you think I should have done more background?'

'No, no, it's perfect,' I assure him.

He smiles gratefully. 'I'll go and scan it, then.'

I feel my shoulders sag as he marches off to the computer room. He has cheered up at the prospect of seeing his family soon, but for me life feels like one huge Patrick-shaped hole at the moment. I have to force myself to get out of bed, force breakfast down, force conversation with Mike and Dietrich. I force smiles too, so that they don't worry about me, so that they know I'm not falling to pieces, that I can hold what's left of the Locket Island project together.

*

Everything's changed since last year. The ship comes once a week now, bearing its cargo of provisions for us and the other few intrepid humans who stay on these outlying islands. The ship also brings a handful of tourists; these are on their way to more hospitable places, where they can view the wildlife in relative comfort. They come via Ushuaia on the tip of South America, the southernmost city in the world, their aim to explore our South Shetlands and the arm that sticks up from mainland Antarctica. They stay on Locket Island just a matter of hours before travelling onwards. Some don't even get off.

Dietrich will use this ship as a means to come and go. He will be gone next week and the dynamic here will change once again.

'Don't fret, guys,' he told us over the washing up last night. 'I'm going to change the return journey, so you two don't have to hold the fort for too long. I'll be away for three weeks, at most.'

But three weeks with only two of us is going to be hard. It's risky too. There should be at least three of us around at any time in case of emergencies. Yet it would be crazy to try and employ anyone else at this stage, when we're quite possibly closing down anyway. The worry keeps clawing away at me. I'm just praying that nothing else goes wrong.

Today is a grey wash, with light, powdery snow that creaks rather than crunches underfoot. The clouds hang low, and all I can hear is the tinkling of running water trapped under pockets of ice. A large seal is slouching in front of me as I make my way to the colony, her huge body spread flaccid, right across my path. Her skin shines and her round, bland face is turned towards me. She eyes me but remains motionless. We both know that we're not enemies. Neither of us is interested in eating the other and we're not competing for food, mates or territory. There is just mild interest on both sides. I can't feel for seals the passion that I feel for penguins, but they have every right to be here too, and they sometimes have to eat my flippered favourites in order to survive. I don't bear this one any ill will. Her lugubrious eyes remain fixed on mine. Then, without warning, she raises her head and lets out a giant's roar. It shatters the silence, makes the air quiver. The noise jolts me – yet for a moment I wonder if it was me who made it rather than her.

I take a detour to skirt round her and continue on my way, a little unnerved.

At the colony I find Pip almost immediately. He's not far from where he was last time, involved in a skirmish with another penguin. They are pecking at each other and doing a bit of flipper-slapping but it seems flirty-friendly. I check the tag of this other penguin and find that it's one of his friends from the other day. Pip leaves off when he sees me and points a curious beak in my direction. Several penguins come close and form a little troop around me, as they often do. They waddle after me and I lead them round in circles a few times before they lose interest. Pip waddles away too and I feel a pang of loneliness.

I radio Mike and Dietrich and tell them I am heading north to the far edge of the colony to check on Sooty. It's important that each of us always knows where the others are.

The wind has picked up and is whistling in my ears as

I clamber over the rocks. The sculpted ice gleams eerily in pale hues of iridescent blue and green.

Sooty (who's a bit of a wonder, with his all-black feathers) and Mrs Sooty (who has the usual snow-white chest and belly) laid two eggs, but, as is usually the case, the smaller one didn't hatch. The surviving chick keeps the parents busy though.

Patrick and I witnessed Sooty earlier in the season when he was building his nest. He kept us entertained for hours with his mischief. His neighbour, a sturdy male, was going to great lengths to select his pebbles, taking them one by one in his beak and laying them carefully into his little dip in the ground. Sooty casually had his back turned, feigning innocence. But every time the other male went off to find the next stone, Sooty waddled over, nabbed one of his pebbles and placed it in his own nest. The other guy didn't cotton on at all that, no matter how hard he worked, his nest didn't seem to be growing . . . while Sooty's was getting bigger and bigger.

Patrick couldn't stop laughing. 'Jeez, this is way better than watching *Doctor Who*.'

I shook my head. 'He's terrible! And to think we used to feel sorry for him!' Last year Sooty sat on his nest all by himself for ages and ages. We thought he'd never get a mate. But this season he has such self-confidence you'd almost think he was a different penguin.

It was the day I took Patrick to meet Sooty that we shared our first kiss.

I shouldn't let myself dwell on the memories but as soon as I've wrestled them out they're creeping back in again. I'm still furious with Patrick but I miss so much about him:

his cheekiness, his corny jokes, his dynamism, his bright way of looking at things. His little acts of kindness, like putting a hot water bottle in my bed when I complained about cold feet, or sneaking cookies into all our pockets when we had to go out in fierce weather. He was fabulously passionate, too. We'd rush back to the field shelter while the other two were still penguin-counting so that we could get some privacy. It felt as if we were a couple of naughty teenagers snatching moments when our parents were out.

But perhaps even more than the hot, addictive dance of sex, I miss the precious moments afterwards, lying with our arms around each other, skin against skin, mouths touching and breaths mingling, our two hearts beating together. The love poured out of us and enveloped us. I'd thought we were unbreakable.

'Need some company?'

I turn. My glasses have steamed up a little but it can only be one of two people and I recognize the thin outline tramping across the snow towards me. I feel grateful.

'Hi, Mike.'

Penguin heads turn to watch his progress. They are pleased to have not one but two of these tall, gangly beings to amuse them.

'Are you OK?' he asks. 'You look awful.'

'Thank you, Mike. Kind of you to say so.'

'Seriously, though. You do look pale.'

I'm tired of saying 'I'm fine,' but I say it anyway.

'It's hard,' he acknowledges. His brow is a fretwork of worry. There's me being all sorry for myself because I've lost Patrick but of course it's catastrophic for Mike too. He and Patrick weren't exactly close, but they got along all right and Mike must be feeling horribly betrayed by his desertion. Mike is as fanatical about the project as I am.

Soon we'll be the only humans left on Locket Island. Thank goodness we get on so well. Mike isn't the easiest of people: he is sharp in every sense of the word. To go with his super-sharp brain and the sharp angles of his face he has the sharpest tongue of anyone I know. Some people find him rude, but I've known him for years and have a different perspective. We've been through a lot together and I've seen his hidden qualities. Yes, he can be grouchy, but he's strong and steadfast and I'd trust him with my life.

It's nice that he doesn't mention Patrick and we can talk about Sooty and his family for a while. Sooty has been left in charge of the chick today but is looking a little bored. His front is grubby but, with his black plumage, he can get away with it more than his white-chested companions. He shovels at the snow with his beak and swallows a mouthful to quench his thirst. Then he inspects his feet. He can't go back to sea until his lady returns, and she's clearly taking her time. The chick is playing nearby with a group of others.

Mike and I watch for some time. We share a thermos of coffee and he tells me that today he has sighted a couple of vagrant Emperor penguins on his patch. We don't have a colony of Emperors on Locket Island, but we've occasionally seen the odd one or two. They have a very different lifestyle from our Adélies. Gluttons for punishment that they are, these giant birds breed in the Antarctic winter and can walk up to seventy miles to their chosen site.

'I don't know what these ones were up to,' Mike comments, 'but it would be interesting to study them too.'

I nod. 'If only we had the resources.' I think of Veronica again.

'I'd like to understand how it's possible to operate with such fearsome efficiency.'

'What? Oh, the Emperors. Yes, they're clever.'

Emperors have various strategies for counteracting heat loss. As well as a double layer of feathers and plenty of fat, they pack themselves together in huge huddles. While the temperature around them can drop to a bone-chilling −50 degrees Celsius, at the core of the huddle it can be as much as 37 degrees. The penguins are constantly shifting positions within the huddle so as not to roast or freeze. No other creature on the planet can rival their survival skills.

'I suppose if they can adapt that well, then so can we,' I tell Mike, trying to be cheerful but, as ever, wondering if we'll even be here in a few months' time.

Mike looks sullen, then lightens up a little. 'We could always adopt their tactic and huddle together for warmth.'

'I don't think Charlotte would appreciate that,' I point out. Charlotte is Mike's girlfriend. He doesn't talk about her much but they must be experts in long-distance relationships. She used to live in London but is now based in Cheltenham and they've been together for years. I'm curious about Charlotte but only know she works in PR, has elaborately flicked hair, and (judging by the photograph Mike has beside his bed) is quite beautiful.

We head back our separate ways across the icy scree and snow to get on with the work we're supposed to be doing.

As I scramble down the bank, I look back and see Mrs Sooty returning to her nest, waddling fast on pink feet. Sooty hops forward eagerly to greet her. Yet again, I'm reminded of Patrick.

I feel stupidly jealous of the penguins. They have a tough time battling for survival, for sure, but their relationships are so straightforward compared with ours. They're not forever tussling with issues and self-doubt. They never waste time engaging in behaviour which suggests one thing and means another. Their 'I love you' is gentle eye contact, a nuzzling of beaks and feathers, a sharing of fish . . . and their 'I love you' doesn't lie.

16

Veronica

Southeast Australia

'How were the boobies?' I ask Sir Robert.

'The boobies were fabulous, thank you, Veronica.'

He is here to meet us at the arrivals area. He is in a tasteful avocado-coloured cotton shirt, dark trousers that are almost but not quite jeans, and thick brown walking boots. With his slim physique, his sparkling smile and air of buoyant confidence, he cuts a dashing figure. Having reapplied my lipstick and combed my hair in the airport conveniences, I hope I do not present too crumpled and crabby a version of myself.

I had thought that when we landed in Melbourne we were near our journey's end, only to discover that we had another regional flight ahead of us. The whole voyage was tediously long. I was, however, accompanied all the way by a very polite young man whose name escapes me but who helped me with my hand luggage and smoothed the way at customs. We did not engage in much conversation apart from pleasantries, but he seemed a little nervous. For the first part of the flight he kept his head down in a book; for the latter part, as it was night-time, I was able to sleep in a semi-recumbent position. I also spent some time reading up on penguins over a small glass of sherry. My exact wording for the documentary will be determined by the filming opportunities that present themselves as we progress, but I still have homework to do and need to learn various penguin facts and figures.

'Did Liam look after you well?' Sir Robert enquires.

I correct him firmly. 'I looked after him well.' The shy young man smiles sheepishly.

Outside the airport we are met by a small cluster of people, Sir Robert's entourage connected with the TV production. The temperature of the air is a welcome reminder that we have landed in midsummer. I realize I am wrapped up a little too warmly. I am also feeling the metaphorical warmth of being part of a group. This is nothing like my arrival in Antarctica. Instead of being perceived as an interfering old bat, I now represent a respected and valued part of a team.

There is little to see so far but a large expanse of car park. We pile into a minibus. As we are driven through brightly lit conurbations, Sir Robert and his companions tell me about the challenges of making a wildlife documentary: the team have worked together now in many remote, unforgiving environments, contending with weather that doesn't often cooperate, trying to coax shy and elusive creatures in front of the cameras. Each part of the programme is storyboarded in detail but then half of it always ends up getting scrapped again.

'You try to choose the moment but usually the moment ends up choosing you,' the quiet Liam informs me, suddenly emboldened to share information now that he is amongst his colleagues. I try to absorb what they are telling me and to take in my surroundings, but I feel tired, cramped and rather disappointed in the urban sprawl around us. But finally, the minibus breaks out into open countryside and green fields run past the windows. Then there is a flash of blue sea and we are driving alongside a sandy, rock-strewn coastline.

Sir Robert, at my elbow, points to a swathe of slate-grey lapping across the tawny sand to my right. I strain my eyes and then realize the grey shape is made up of myriad smaller shapes. At first, I think they are pebbles. But then I see that they are too upright. What I am looking at is a throng of penguins.

'Little penguins,' Sir Robert informs me. 'You'll be seeing a lot more of them very soon.'

I reach inside my handbag and pull out a handkerchief.

'Are you all right, Veronica?' Sir Robert enquires as I blot my eyes.

'Indeed I am, Sir Robert,' I reply.

Indeed I am.

We are not due to spend any time on mainland Australia but are driven across a long spit of land to a flat, green island named Ginty Island. The whole island is a marine sanctuary, run mostly by volunteers although there are some permanent staff. Access to the island has been improved by development of the coastline, and this has made it easy for predators to cross the bay and attack the penguins nesting there. For this reason, a breed of sheepdogs called Maremmas have been introduced to protect the flippered residents.

In fact, as soon as we alight from the minibus we are greeted by two volunteers with dogs on short leads. I scarcely notice the humans but register they are both young, one is male and the other female. My attention is taken up by the two dogs. I hold back, rather alarmed at their size and vigour. I would have thought they were Golden Retrievers if I hadn't been told otherwise. They are good-looking beasts with flowing pale golden fur, large, paddy paws, lolling tongues and faces expressing extreme enthusiasm. Their tales wag wildly. Sir Robert, clearly at home with anyone belonging to the animal kingdom, ruffles their coats with glee.

'I'm Sandra,' declares the woman, a blonde with a tanned face and toothy smile. 'I'm the dog trainer here. And these two are Sugar and Spice.'

I put out a hand and timorously stroke Sugar's muzzle. Her tail wags a little faster and she looks up at me with eyes that are soft, brown . . . Or possibly Muscovado . . . or Demerara? I turn and stroke Spice, who presses a wet nose into my hand.

The humans and dogs escort us to a single-storey building which, although they call it 'The Cabin', is large and mostly constructed from concrete and glass. The dogs are tied to a post outside and the rest of us go in to inspect our quarters. As we are shown our bedrooms (warm and airy) and the facilities (clinically clean and decked with thick, fluffy towels), I reflect how very luxurious this is compared with the Locket Island field base. Thankfully there is an internet connection here so we will be able to stay in touch with Eileen, Patrick and the Locket Island team. I am more anxious than ever to keep reading Terry's penguin blogs, to know that the team there is struggling on in spite of Patrick's absence, and to reassure myself that Pip is safe. I do not have Eileen here to transcribe my letters and send them into the ether, but Sir Robert has most generously promised he will help.

Naturally we are offered tea straight away, and naturally we accept the offer with alacrity. The rest of the day we have to ourselves to settle in and recover from the journey. I have little idea what time it is, but a siesta will be most welcome.

I wake with excessively stiff limbs and a desire to explore. Sir Robert and I stretch our legs on a brief walk around, taking in the coastal views, and spend some time chatting. He tells me all about his stay on Christmas Island and the sightings of the Abbott's booby, with its wondrous blue feet. His enthusiasm is infectious. Tomorrow my own first foray into filming begins. I will be briefed about which information to include for each session, but I can choose how to phrase and present it. Sir Robert says I mustn't worry about making mistakes.

'I am not in the least bit worried, Sir Robert,' I tell him.

We return to the cabin and take our places at the long dining table along with the rest of the film crew. Our evening meal, prepared by the volunteers, comprises meat pies with side vegetables followed by a coconut sponge cake. The food is toothsome and the atmosphere is one of geniality and anticipation.

'There is an email for you, Veronica,' Sir Robert informs me as I am sitting with a cup of tea afterwards. He hands me a sheet of paper. I extract my reading glasses from my handbag.

Dear Mrs McCreedy,

I hope you travelled well and did not get any tummy wobbles. Doug says I mustn't worry too much because Sir Robert is with you. All is well at The Ballahays, but we've had more snow this week. It must be lovely to be in summer.

Something exciting happened yesterday, when I called in to water the plants. I had just got as far as the African violet when there was a knock at the door, and you'll never guess who it was. It was a smart young man asking questions, so many questions – and it turned out he was a journalist come to find out all about you! He was from the Scots Times, *no less! I told him about how you went to Antarctica and saved Pip and now you're in Australia with penguins again. He was very keen to know about Robert Saddlebow – Sir Robert, I mean – and how you got to know each other, so I told him about that too. I also mentioned Daisy being on* I Wish *and going to the Falklands with you soon. Maybe I shouldn't of said that. I do get carried away sometimes.*

It looks like you'll be in the paper, Mrs McCreedy. It's just a shame the man didn't catch you before you

*went away – then he could of put in a lovely photo
of you as well.*

*Mr Perkins says do you want him to empty out the
compost?*

*Please stay well, Mrs McCreedy, and thank you
for the marshmallows.*

*Yours,
Eileen*

I recall now that I left her some Sicilian lemon-flavoured
marshmallows as a small token of my thanks for all her
hard work. I am slightly concerned about the journalist
though.

'All well with Eileen?' Sir Robert asks, pouring himself
another coffee.

I incline my head. How refreshing it is that he hasn't
read the email himself before giving it to me. He is a man
of honour and integrity.

17

Veronica

LITTLE PENGUINS, UNLIKE every other species of penguin, are nocturnal. It is therefore necessary for us to be out filming at the edges of the day. Jet lag has left me disorientated and I devoted much of the first twenty-four hours to sleeping. But now we are on day two, the sun is only just contemplating rising and we are already in the minibus en route to the first location.

I have brought the walking stick I used on Locket Island in case of rough terrain. I flung my stout boots in the back of the minibus because a little physical exercise may be required but I am currently wearing my smart court shoes, which are a better match for this outfit. I am decked out in my mulberry-red dress and a black mohair cardigan with a knitted pattern of large roses for the first session. My make-up has been applied with the utmost care and I am clasping my shiny new mulberry-coloured handbag, for maximum colour coordination. This is to be my first television appearance after all.

The location is a grassy stretch of land pockmarked with burrows. Many of them have a scattering of grey and white feathers around the entrances. A few penguins are toddling about in the dim light and I am surprised at how very tiny they are. They are not sharply delineated black and white like my beloved Adélies but have bluish plumage and a slimmer, more elfin physique. They lean forward slightly as they waddle. It is odd to see penguins in so verdant a landscape as opposed to ice and snow.

Sir Robert is keen to give me whatever guidance he can, at least whilst we are starting out. He has already filmed a charming little speech standing on the shore in which he introduced me, outlining my credentials – my passion for litter-collecting, my saving of Pip the Adélie penguin, and my support of the Locket Island project.

The crew consists of several sound and camera men and one camera lady called Miriam, but it is Liam who is specifically allocated to me. I am arranged beside a burrow, with the twinkling sea as my backdrop. A family of young penguins peers out at me, not quite convinced about my presence but tolerating it nonetheless. It is decided I need to be a little lower down so as to get the right framing for the shot, so somebody rushes to get a chair. Then I am artificially lit, which takes yet more time.

I have a microphone clipped to my lapel and I am asked to speak several sentences as a sound check. It now remains for me to deliver my first lines.

'Just your introductory spiel here, please, Veronica.'

I glance across at Sir Robert who gives me a thumbs

up. I clear my throat and begin my narration. No sooner have I started speaking than I am told to stop again whilst they adjust a level. This happens twice. Finally, I am able to deliver my piece.

'Dear viewers,' I begin, and I see that Sir Robert is already smiling. 'Unaccustomed as I am to public speaking, it is my duty and my joy to bring to your screens this marvellous, ebullient and fascinating bird: the penguin. And to start you off in fine style I am here, on the coast of Ginty Island, to introduce you to the smallest of the species, appropriately named the Little penguin. Little penguins are a mere thirty-three centimetres in height.' (I was originally going to say thirteen inches, but Sir Robert told me that centimetres are more familiar to most of the human population.) 'They frequent the coastlines of southern Australia and New Zealand. Due to their miniature size and enchanting ways they are often called "Fairy penguins" here, whilst in New Zealand they are known as Little Blue penguins or *korora*.' I have been carefully practising the pronunciation of their Māori name. 'Little penguins spend most of their lives in the ocean, coming to land only to moult and breed. As you can see behind me, during the breeding season they reside in burrows dotting the hillsides along the shore. They follow the same path to their burrow each night. You will observe how the continual tramping of webbed feet has worn trails in the soft sandstone.'

'Stop! Can you stop at "shore", please, Mrs McCreedy,' calls Liam. 'Small soundbites are what we need. And would you mind repeating all that first section again, please? The penguins are in a better position now.'

I glance round and perceive that now a larger cluster of

penguins have assembled and are waddling around the chair upon which I am seated. There are some impossibly sweet young chicks too.

'As soon as you can, please, Mrs McCreedy, before they lose interest.'

I clutch my handbag and dutifully repeat the same words.

Again. And again.

When the crew are finally satisfied, I ask about my narration of the next part. I am determined to explain to the public that the penguins' colouring is for camouflage whilst they are swimming; their blue backs are almost invisible from above, whilst their white bellies blend into the bright sea surface, disguising them from predators below.

'Remember, less is more, Veronica,' Sir Robert tells me. 'We can always add your extra information as a voice-over later and put it with some footage of penguins swimming in the sea.'

A break is in order, and Sir Robert pours a coffee for me from an enormous flask. I am more of a tea person, but caffeine is appreciated under the circumstances. It seems that most of the morning has been used up by a mere couple of sentences, and I am anxious to know if my performance was acceptable.

'Was I very bad?' I ask Sir Robert.

'Not at all,' he exclaims. 'My dear Veronica, you are a natural.'

His compliment sets me aglow with pleasure, but I feign a charming modesty. 'But it took so long,' I protest.

'That is quite normal. In fact, it was speedier than

usual. It takes an unbelievable amount of effort to make something look effortless.'

We are returned to our temporary place of abode for lunch and a rest. Then it is time for Sir Robert to engage in some work introducing short-tailed shearwater and black cormorants, some of the other birdlife on the island. I am given a break as it is assumed I must still be suffering from jet lag. I am indeed feeling a little weary.

Dear Mrs McCreedy,

I've found you. You're right there, on the second page of the Scots Times! *I've been telling everyone I know. I feel so proud. And they've even used a quote of mine! I managed to scan it in this morning with the help of a very kind library assistant in Kilmarnock, so here it is attached for you to see.*

> *Yours ever,*
> *Eileen*

I am astonished even at the headline: *Millionairess McCreedy in on Penguin Action with Sir Robert.*

My eyes greedily take in the article.

Veronica McCreedy, 87, of Ayrshire, who travelled last year to Antarctica, has been enlisted by television presenter Sir Robert Saddlebow for his latest wildlife documentary. McCreedy became known as a penguin ambassador when she appeared in blogs written by the Locket Island scientists. Originally intending a short holiday to see the penguins, she ended up staying months and rescuing a penguin chick. She has been contributing generously towards the research project ever since her grandson became part of the team.

McCreedy was approached by Sir Robert about his filming venture soon after his knighthood was announced this January. The trip, which has already begun, will take them to Southern Australia and the Falkland Islands. Eileen Thompson (53), Mrs McCreedy's carer, said: 'We mustn't worry because she's ever so good for her age. She took off with Sir Robert just a few days ago. So romantic, isn't it? She always watched Sir Robert's TV programmes before but now she's going to be in one! It's wonderful that she's away with the penguins again.'

There are two pictures. One is of Sir Robert, a very good headshot in which he is looking straight at the camera with a magnificently inscrutable expression in his fine blue eyes. The other one is of me. I recollect it vaguely. It is lifted from one of Terry's blogs, a photograph she took of me when I had just arrived on Locket Island and was setting eyes on the Adélie penguins for the very first time. There I am, in my bright red Dynotherm jacket, with handbag and lipstick to match, transfixed by the thousands of penguins all around me. I do indeed look like a penguin ambassador.

With mixed feelings I show the article to Sir Robert. 'Ah,' he says, after reading it. 'That's unfortunate.'

I ask him why. Although there are several factual errors in the news story (and I am rather affronted that Eileen has been called my 'carer', as if I were in need of any such thing!), I thought it was fairly innocuous. In fact, I am feeling a small tingle of pride.

'This won't be the only one,' Sir Robert explains. 'Now the news is out there will be more, and the journalists will probably dig for dirt. Be warned, Veronica.'

I shrug my shoulders. There is little dirt to be found unless they go right back to my teenage years (and there is no record of that particular dirt except in my diaries, which have never been seen by Eileen and are safely locked away). I cannot get too worked up about it. I am slightly annoyed with Eileen for blabbering so openly, but crass enthusiasm is in her nature and I know she meant well.

At the moment, amidst the penguin-populated pleasures of Ginty Island, any tittle-tattle produced by the British press seems both distant and irrelevant.

18

Veronica

THE NEXT STAGE of the filming is to explain the Maremma dogs' role in guarding the penguins.

'Can we see Veronica being introduced to the dogs as if for the first time?' Liam asks. I note with some disgust that he has stopped calling me Mrs McCreedy, but do not comment on this.

I am rather appalled that everything is so very staged and orchestrated, but Sir Robert tells me that is the way of filming. The toothy volunteer Sandra walks briskly up the path, the dogs padding at her side to meet me. I try to react as if I've only just met them, shrinking back with an expression of horror on my face.

'Can we take that again, please,' calls Liam. 'Veronica, could you step forward and make a comment to one of the dogs such as *Aren't you beautiful?* or something? With a nice friendly smile.'

I glare at him. I am not accustomed to being told what to say or how to say it.

When the camera is rolling again, I pet Sugar and Spice but tell my viewers: 'I had the pleasure of meeting these two dogs yesterday. As you see, they are good-tempered, docile beasts, if rather slobbery. However, they are large and forbidding enough if you happen to be a fox, I'm told.'

I catch Liam looking helplessly across at Sir Robert. He mutters some words under his breath which I can't catch and then calls out to me again: 'OK, can you give us some dog and penguin facts, please, Veronica?'

For Sir Robert's sake, I do.

'My dear viewers, several hundred Ginty Island penguins have, alas, been gobbled up by foxes. At one stage the population here dropped to a mere four penguins. Thanks to these dogs it has risen again to nearly a hundred.'

I explain that dogs such as Sugar and Spice, traditionally protectors of chickens, are now trained to guard the native wildlife. As puppies they're made to sniff the penguins and therefore recognize them as a species that belongs to the territory; the foxes, on the other hand, they perceive as alien so they will bark and chase them away.

Having done a few takes of varying length whilst sitting with a dog on either side in front of the research building, I am to have a brief interview with Sandra.

'Which of these two is the better penguin guard, in your opinion?' I ask her.

'Oh, I'd say definitely Spice. Sugar is still in training, and anyhow she's naturally too nice. Given half a chance she'd just invite those foxes in for a friendly cup of tea . . . but Spice will see them off.'

The sweet nature of Sugar does have some advantages. Liam is able to capture a very lovely sequence of her cuddling up with a penguin chick, her pink tongue delicately licking the soft down of the chick's head.

I come away from the morning's session with tender feelings in my heart but dog slobber on my silk scarf, which will have to be hand-washed at the earliest opportunity.

I am very much enjoying these days of being amongst penguins once more. However, it does bring back a certain nostalgia for my time with the Adélies of Locket Island. With Sir Robert's assistance I have looked up Terry's blog on the computer. There are many photos and I am glad to see Pip featured again and again in these. Terry doesn't mention the gaping absence of my grandson or write about her own concerns. I do wonder if there is any way I can persuade Patrick to return there. Would she have him back? Not as her boyfriend, for that would be too much to expect after his disgraceful desertion, but there's a minute possibility she might accept him as a worker, if it meant I continued to fund the project. By bringing him to the Falklands, I cherish a faint but persistent hope of seducing him back to the world of penguins. But I fear that even I, Veronica McCreedy, am not possessed of powers enough to change Patrick's mind.

Still, the trip to Canada will surely do him good. He may discover the reason his father abandoned him. For his sake and mine, I hope it will be an explanation that proves my Enzo to have led an honourable life. I am inescapably emotional when I think of dear Enzo, which I

112

have been doing more and more of late, and it is just as well I have so much here to distract me.

Sir Robert was right. The day after Eileen's startling email, he takes a little time in our lunch break to put a search into the computer and finds that several more newspapers have taken up the story.

'You don't know whether to laugh or cry,' he grunts, showing me the headlines:

PENSIONERS UNITE IN PENGUIN MISSION
HAS SIR ROBERT MET HIS MATCH?
THE MILLIONAIRESS AND THE KNIGHT – A LATE-LIFE
    ROMANCE
PENSIONERS SADDLEBOW AND MCCREEDY – A MATCH
    MADE IN PENGUIN LAND?

If I were the blushing type, I would blush. Instead I throw up my hands, enraged at the bald cheek of it. Whatever might be my feelings towards Sir Robert or his towards me, it is outrageous to circulate these assumptions and insinuations.

It is not just this salacious gossip-mongering that galls me though. There are other headlines of an even more offensive ilk.

HYPOCRITE MCCREEDY ON CARBON-SPEWING ROUND-
    THE-WORLD TRIP
GERIATRIC ENVIRONMENTALIST TAKES GAS-GUZZLING
    FLIGHTS
MILLIONAIRESS MCCREEDY, FIRST CLASS HYPOCRITE

'Don't look,' Sir Robert warns, but my eye has already taken in a few phrases before he can stop me:

Veronica McCreedy, self-styled penguin ambassador, has not only chosen to fly thousands of miles herself, she had also forked out for her grandson to zip across to the other side of the world. McCreedy, who is currently joining Sir Robert Saddlebow on a wildlife-filming venture, drank champagne on the flight that endangers the penguins she claims to love.

'I did not!' I bawl at the screen, clenching my fists. 'Not a drop of champagne was imbibed on the flight. It was sherry!'

'They never bother to get their facts right,' Sir Robert sighs. 'Once the press is involved, things always become distorted and complicated. They're keen to drag your name through the mud because it makes a good story. But, as they say, "all publicity is good publicity". Ironically the penguins and other marine wildlife will benefit much more now they've reported this, so it's a worthwhile sacrifice, my dear hypocrite.'

This is a little unfair, I feel. My travelling to Australia to report on wildlife is not hypocrisy. Hypocrisy is when people who claim to be Christian lock up a young girl and steal her baby away . . .

I peruse the article again and feel the muscles in my neck tighten. It is an extremely unpleasant sensation to see my good name so besmirched.

'I note that all the criticism is aimed at *me*,' I complain.

'*I* am the one who is singled out as a hypocrite for flying across the world, even though you, with your booby escapades, have flown considerably further.'

Sir Robert nods sadly. 'You're absolutely right, Veronica. It isn't fair, and I'm sorry.'

'It is bullying of the worst order,' I snap. 'And like all bullies, they are cowards. Because you are a popular TV presenter and the public's darling, they don't dare accuse you, only me. No doubt they also pick on me because I am a woman.'

'That may be so,' he admits. 'I shall have to issue a statement via my agent and explain, as succinctly as possible, how we are careful to offset every flight with contributions to green charities. Also about the overwhelming advantages given to wildlife from making these documentaries and increasing awareness of the issues, which far outweighs the harm of flying.'

I am almost mollified by his good sense and beginning to regain my equanimity when I glance towards the bottom of his screen and see, to my horror, another headline that sends my blood pressure rocketing: CANCER CHILD VICTIM EXPLOITED BY GREEDY MCCREEDY.

Now I am incandescent. 'How dare they drag Daisy into this?'

Sir Robert lays a hand on mine. 'Breathe, Veronica. And try not to worry. This will blow over.'

'I sincerely hope so.'

'Let's see if there is an email from Eileen which might cheer you up.'

His hands ripple impressively over the keyboard and a message leaps on to the screen.

Oh Mrs McCreedy, I am so sorry. So very, very sorry. I can't tell you how sorry I am.

I had no idea this would happen. Doug says I was silly to talk to a journalist ever at all, but I only said good things, I only sang your praises, I promise, because I was so proud of you, Mrs McCreedy. I don't know why they had to go and twist everything and make it sound bad. I know you must be angry. I am angry myself – and angry AT myself. If you feel I shouldn't work for you any more and want to let me go, I will totally understand, but I hope very much you will let me stay on working for you at The Ballahays. I just want you to know I only ever tried my best.

Sorry again and yours very truly,
Eileen

How ridiculous she is. Of course I shall keep her on. How would I ever manage at The Ballahays without her?

As we head out for the afternoon's work, we pass the two dogs stretched out by the door of the centre. They both lift their heads and wag their tails. They look so similar that I can hardly tell them apart, but I remember what Sandra told me about their different attitude to the foxes.

I seem to have acquired some of my own predators – the journalists. If we were to draw parallels, my own bodyguarding dogs would be Eileen and Sir Robert. Eileen is rather like Sugar, naturally kind but much too trusting, inviting the foxes in. Sir Robert, I hope, is more akin to Spice; he will bark and drive them away.

My thoughts turn to dear Daisy. If she has been hounded by the press, I will personally seek out the perpetrators and give them a piece of my mind. I may even resort to physical violence.

I shall see Daisy very soon, but a further flight is obligatory. I curse under my breath. Due to those wretched headlines I am now feeling guilty about stepping on a plane again. Guilt is a peculiar presence. I am not accustomed to questioning my own actions or to doubting them, and the discomfort is similar to that of wearing somebody else's clothes that neither fit nor suit me.

The newspaper articles have also presented my imagination with the concept of a new connection with Sir Robert. *Late life romance?*

It is ridiculous, of course, and impossible.

But it is an undeniably interesting idea.

19

Terry

Locket Island

DIETRICH HAS GONE. We waved him off this morning, standing on the shore. The view of the sea from here is always different because of the ever-changing icebergs. The smaller chunks flock together, bob and tinkle in the wind. The larger ones resemble cathedrals with vast craggy facades, ornately carved pinnacles and shadowy blue archways, chiselled by the wind and waves. They melt, break up, clump together and combine once again in new formations. Some are blown away and others drift in, an endless slow dance of towering crystal.

I watched for ages as the ship ploughed through the glassy waves, passed between the crags and became a black dot on the distant shimmer, carrying Dietrich away from us.

Dietrich has always been more than a colleague, filling in sometimes as father and sometimes as close friend, and I felt bereft seeing him go. Even though he had a small rucksack this time and is booked to return in three weeks, I can't drive away this creepy feeling that he won't ever come back.

I still have no idea what will happen. Patrick is researching his father in Canada apparently, his own future equally vague.

'And then there were two,' I comment, as I take my place at the table with Mike at the field base in the evening.

'Where's the problem?' he says. 'All we need to do is twice the work we did before.'

'Yup,' I reply with forced heartiness. 'Simple!'

I delve into the cauldron and ladle dinner on to our plates.

'What the hell is that, Terry?'

'Comfort food,' I answer defensively. 'Sweetcorn, baked beans and mushy peas, shaken but not stirred, nestling on a bed of Frankfurter sausages. Otherwise known as tinned dinner.'

'Are you trying to kill me off so you can have the island to yourself?'

'Maybe.'

Standards have slipped since Patrick left. He was the best chef we could have asked for and always found ways of getting round the lack of fresh fruit and veg. Now we're tending to throw any old thing together. We're just too tired to make anything fancy. We strictly take it in turns to cook and I'm a little dismayed that I'm now going to have to do it every other day. I seem to have reached an all-time low this evening, just opening and chucking together whatever I could find in the cupboard. It does look pretty unappetizing, I admit. I shovel some into my mouth and make 'yum' noises.

'It's lovely,' I tell Mike. 'Try it.'

He gingerly loads his fork, brings it to his mouth, chews, swallows and grimaces.

Unlike him, I really am finding my creation surprisingly tasty, even if the texture is a bit odd.

Mike clears his throat. 'This has reminded me: can we discuss penguin poo?'

'Of course. Be my guest.' Anything to avoid dwelling on the emptiness of the place without Dietrich and Patrick.

Mike surveys me seriously. 'You probably don't want to hear this but I have to tell you: in one of the faeces specimens I was looking at yesterday I found micro-beads.'

'As in microscopic granules of plastic?'

'Yes, quite a lot of them.'

I pull a face, now even gloomier than I was before. 'Antarctic penguins have been eating *plastic*? Is nowhere sacred?'

'It was going to happen sooner or later.' He stabs one of his sausages viciously. 'Plastics flow into the sea via rivers from every corner of the world.'

'I've read stuff about that,' I reply, thinking. 'It's because rich countries dump their non-recyclable rubbish on poorer countries, and the poorer countries don't have any proper means of eliminating it.'

'That's part of the problem.' He washes down his mouthful with a swig of water. 'Plastics float, too, so they're easily driven thousands of miles by the currents. Did you know, when plastic has been drifting in the ocean for months it releases a volatile compound that smells like food, so the birds are confused and gobble it down?'

'That's awful. Poor birds.'

'Nobody should be producing plastics at all,' he growls. 'There are alternatives now. Corn starch and so on.'

I can't argue with him on this. Humans will always do what's easy and what's profitable rather than what's right. The conversation has depressed me more than ever. I don't know what to say.

Mike holds out his plate. Unbelievably he's eaten every last pea and bean. 'Give us some more pig slop then.'

Snow spits in my face. A low, grey mist has obliterated the view of the mountains and lake. The stones glint darkly and stiff grass blades prickle up from their thin, fleecy covering. Every crack and dip of the land is crusted with ice. The cold penetrates my jacket and gnaws at my bones. My muscles are strangely stiff and heavy, as if they're made of concrete. The walk feels longer than usual and I propel myself into the midst of the colony, needing the hustle and bustle of penguins. The fishy, guano-y smell is very pungent today.

I am determined to get as much work done as I possibly can and not let this sense of doom get in my way.

My heart lifts as I see Pip. He's in a patch by himself, standing erect with his beak pointing into the wind and a thoughtful expression in his white-rimmed eyes. Perhaps I'll just take a picture or two of him for Veronica, and for me. I crouch down with my camera to get a better view of his face and he immediately starts trundling towards me. Maybe he's feeling lonely too.

The camera is a new one, and was a Christmas present from Patrick, although it's top of the range so I suspect Veronica may have helped him pay. Veronica also forked out for some satellite transmitters that can be fitted to the penguins so we can track them during the winter months when they're away. I have already fitted one on to Pip.

He waddles straight into the camera and I take a video of his bill clacking against the lens, revealing the pink inside of his mouth and his barbed tongue.

'Steady on, Pip. I'm sure this camera can't taste that good.'

He shakes his feathers and pauses to look at me as if waiting for *me* to do *my* next trick. Then he lunges forward and tugs at my sleeve. He won't let go and his head wobbles back and forth as I push and pull. His antics make me laugh. I topple over sideways. He clambers right on top of me and I giggle uncontrollably as he prods me gently and then slaps my cheeks with his flippers, knocking my glasses askew. 'Oh, Pip. I needed this.' He honks loudly, sharing the hilarity.

Other penguins are interested now and several chicks venture towards us, heads bobbing, to see what's going on.

Delighted as I am, this isn't getting the work done. I sit up quickly. A wave of nausea spreads through me and suddenly I have to push Pip to one side so that I don't throw up all over him. He utters an injured cry and seems alarmed at my retching and heaving. Then he potters back to inspect the pool of sick I've just produced on the rocky, snow-speckled ground.

It looks as if tinned dinner wasn't such a bright idea after all. I hope Mike isn't suffering the consequences too. It's not like me to be so delicate. It must be the extra workload and all the stress of holding things together. I take deep breaths. Beaky faces and blurry little black-and-white bodies are all around me. I feel light-headed. And tired, unbelievably tired. Oh God, I hope I'm not coming down with something.

Then it hits me. It might not just be my bad cooking that made me sick. It might not just be the stress that's making me so exhausted.

Patrick and I were careful, but maybe we weren't careful enough. My cycle is never that regular but I need to stop a minute and calculate how long it's been. Over five weeks now. More than six when I think about it.

There's no way I can get hold of a testing kit, but I can't deny all the signs seem to be there.

20

Veronica

Ginty Island

'YOU COULD SPEND months in New Zealand and still scarcely tap into the abundance of wild beauties that make up the country,' Sir Robert tells me. 'But I shall be there for less than a week!'

It is our last evening on Ginty Island and we are setting out for an after-dinner leg-stretch. Whilst Sir Robert travels south tomorrow, I am to fly to the Falkland Islands in the distinctly less interesting company of Liam. Sir Robert will join us there later.

New Zealand, I'm told, is a country replete with mountain ranges, geysers, lakes and crystalline terraces formed from layers of mineral deposits, and I am somewhat envious of Sir Robert. The country also boasts three species of penguin, but we simply cannot fit them in along with all the other seabirds Sir Robert wishes to cover: shear-waters, petrels, mollymawks and whatnot. Be that as it may, I am greatly looking forward to seeing Daisy again, not to mention the Falkland penguins. Sir Robert is evidently quite used to zipping about from one country to another and has a remarkable metabolism that seems to thrive upon it. I am not quite so inured to this frenetic lifestyle.

'I will miss you, Sir Robert,' I admit.

'I will miss you too, Veronica. You and I will have to make the most of this beautiful evening.'

'We will indeed.'

The light is beginning to fade. We are wandering along a rugged path, accompanied by the sounds of a recklessly crashing sea. Sir Robert takes my arm when we reach a slight incline. Although I do not need any help, being quite accustomed to the roughness of the Ayrshire coast, I fully appreciate his solicitousness and courtesy. The bay, which lies a little below us and to our right, is washed flat by the continual visits of the tides. The shingle becomes rockier round the edges, turning into sharp spines and cragginess. On our left is scrubby vegetation. Birds wheel overhead and their cries float on the wind, but my eyesight isn't good enough to identify them. Not far away I can make out a mottled patch of blue-black and white.

This time of day is Little penguin rush-hour.

The film crew, set up on the beach, are all busy trying to capture the penguin assemblage on camera. The penguins have a safety-in-numbers policy and tend to come ashore in groups. Sir Robert and I, for once, can enjoy the luxury of merely looking.

Sunset is painting the sky in layers of amber folding into salmon-pink, cream and dark bilberry-grey. We stand in awe and gaze as the tiny figures are battered about by powerful waves and knocked back just as they are reaching the shore. They persist, always persist in their efforts, aiming themselves again and again until they are hurled aground. It is incredible that they find their feet so quickly amidst the white froth. Then, flippers pointing outward, they join the procession, crooning and gabbling together. They seem to be comparing notes about their time out at sea.

I gaze in wonder. It is hard to grasp that this is real, for it looks like a scene from a fairy tale. The dim light brushes the streams of tiny figures in shades of gleaming silver, so that they resemble a gathering of elves.

'Are you glad to be here?' Sir Robert asks gently.

'Yes, indeed,' I sniff. 'But drat this cold air! It is making my eyes water.'

The last stragglers of the penguin community dissolve slowly into the dusk. A shy moon peeps out from behind the clouds. The sky is deepening into a sheer, dense black, pierced by myriad pinprick stars. Sir Robert produces a small torch from his pocket. We leave the film crew to pack up their vast array of equipment and pick our way back along the path. The cabin is empty of people when we arrive. The volunteers are out on their rounds with the dogs and it will be some time before Liam, Miriam and the others return.

We make cocoa and sit in the front room, nursing the hot mugs, listening to the whisper of the wind and the odd calls of nocturnal birds. This is the first time Sir Robert and I have been completely alone together. I relish having him to myself and yet feel I should make more of it somehow.

At this moment I am keenly aware that the man before me has never had a wife or children. I know this not because I have been prying into his affairs, but because Eileen, who is always happy to poke her nose in, decided to investigate his personal life by means of her googly whatsit and took it upon herself to share the information with me. The background of any renowned personage is appallingly accessible on the internet, so it seems. However, the details about Sir Robert were, according to Eileen, rather scant.

Still immersed in the romantic quality of the evening's penguin-watching, I am emboldened to broach the topic. I clear my throat delicately first. 'Have you ever been married, Sir Robert?' I ask, feigning ignorance.

'No, Veronica. No, I haven't.'

Before I can ask anything more he throws the question back at me. 'And you, Veronica? You've been married, haven't you?'

My face gives an involuntary twitch of disdain. 'My husband was a lying, cheating slime-ball whose caddishness exceeded even my exceptionally low expectations.'

Sir Robert's eyebrows lift a little. 'No love lost there, then.'

'None. The only lovely thing about Hugh was his wallet.' Lest I have now cast myself in the role of gold-digger, I hasten to explain. 'The divorce left me well provided for, but I did not marry him for his money. I married him because I thought it might be fun, which was something I was very much lacking at the time. It wasn't.'

'Your grandson Patrick is not his grandson also?'

A diplomatic way of asking, as befits a real gentleman.

'No, indeed, Sir Robert. My child Enzo was born many years earlier and from a very different genre of man. I adored Giovanni with every fibre of my being, although I was so young.'

'Giovanni? An Italian?'

'Yes, and a true romantic. It was the 1940s and he was an Italian prisoner-of-war. In those days having a baby out of wedlock was viewed as wickedness, having a baby with the enemy a further travesty, and added to this was the fact I was merely sixteen. Giovanni was my first – and arguably my only – love.'

Giovanni, the father of my Enzo. The nostalgia hits me like a tidal wave. It is a longing not so much for Giovanni specifically, but for the passions of youth, so vivid and thrilling; so brimming with possibility. I remember how my teenage heart somersaulted when I spotted Giovanni striding through the fields towards me. His arms were wide, his dark eyes full of ardour. I remember how he pulled off his cap so that his hair sprang up, and how I dizzied with delight as he whisked me off my feet. How my pulse quickened as I heard his voice call me 'My own darling Very' in his exotic foreign tones. I, a teenager, conscious of my own allures, fragile in my fresh grief for my parents, glorying in the challenge of this new, forbidden love . . .

Sir Robert's voice breaks through my reverie. 'What happened to him, if you don't mind my asking?'

I shake my head. 'Swept away by the war, like so many thousands of other brave young men.'

I have always assumed my Giovanni did not make it to the other side of the war. If he did survive, he never came back for me. He never knew I had given him a son.

Love is a slippery fish. Many of us catch it but few manage to keep hold of it.

Sir Robert, I notice, is lost in his own thoughts. He has deflected the conversation away from himself but he will not get away with it so easily.

'You never fell in love?' I am compelled to ask him.

His eyes widen. 'I wouldn't say that, no,' he replies softly.

This is a somewhat tantalizing answer and I wait for him to reveal more. The silence expands and fills the room, along with the freesia and light citrus scent of my Estée Lauder eau de parfum, with which I earlier daubed my neck and inside wrists. Sir Robert looks as if he is working out a difficult maths equation. But his lips remain firmly closed. I sip my cocoa and wonder whether it would be socially acceptable to ask him another question. I have just decided it would and mentally formulated it into words when he finally speaks.

'You'll be thinking that I'm married to my job.'

My imagination had actually wandered far further than this, but I nod my head. 'I suppose it is inevitable.'

'You are right,' he returns with considerable abruptness. 'I *am* married to my job.'

His job, I conclude with some regret, is very lucky.

21

Patrick

Vancouver, Canada

I'M GETTING USED to civilization again, but Vancouver is something else. It's all made up of shiny skyscrapers, with mountains on one side and a bright expanse of sea on the other. The city has more than its fair share of well-kept parks, swanky bars and cafes, and if I was into shopping this would be heaven. The window displays are works of art, some displaying chicly dressed mannequins, others with a full range of sports and outdoor equipment, others decked with fancy household objects that only the privileged would ever think of buying. I wander about, wondering what the hell I'm doing here.

I know I ought to be impressed but I'm not really taking much in. Two persistent thoughts keep plaguing me. They alternate in my brain like a switch that has two settings: Terry and my dad. Sometimes the Terry setting includes Locket Island landscapes and acres of Adélie penguins in the background; Mike and Dietrich's faces, even Pip and his escapades . . . but mostly it just homes in on Terry. I still feel bloody mad at her. I once thought she was everything lovely and I was the luckiest man on the planet. Now I'm wondering if I only fell for her because she was the only female around for a million miles.

Then there's the Dad setting. And that's a clutchy kind of need-to-know sensation. The dread hasn't gone but it's mixed with flashes of hope. Tomorrow I have an appointment to see Denise Perry, my father's adoptive cousin, who remembers him from her childhood. Surely she can tell me something? I'm straining towards answers, hoping for pinging revelations. I need it all to make sense.

It's hard to believe I'm here, the city where my dad grew up and spent most of his life. I look down at my shoes as they tread the streets and it occurs to me that they might be walking exactly where his feet have walked before. I stop on a bridge and gaze out. Did he stop on the same bridge and gaze out when he lived here? I eat waffles in a cafe. Did he eat waffles in this cafe too? It would be good to feel a connection with him but so far, it hasn't happened. I wish there was a grave I could visit, but my father's body was never recovered from the chasm he fell down all those years ago.

Weird fact: I had more friends in Antarctica than I did in Bolton. And I don't know a single person in Vancouver. This city is packed full of people dressed in smart, colourful woollens, marching along arm in arm, chattering and laughing, occasionally noticing me and wondering why I'm such a miserable sod.

131

Even my shadow looks lonely as it paces the broad pavements. I wish Granny was here and we could investigate Dad together, but Sir Robert and the penguins seem to have become her priority. I suppose I can't blame her. It was a timing thing . . . and anyway, she'd slow me down if she'd come with me. She probably thought I needed a mission, too. She was probably right. I question my own sanity sometimes. My mind's a rubbish dump, piled high with all the crap that's happened in my life. Mum's suicide, the foster families, discovering my granny for the first time only eighteen months ago and, soon after, convinced she was dying, ending up in Antarctica but then splitting with Terry, leaping on that boat to go back home . . .

'*Home?* What home? I have no home,' I grumble to myself.

A tantalizing image pops into my head: the two pot plants I used to have, Weedledum and Weedledee. I'd give anything for a spliff right now. I wonder where you can get hold of drugs in Vancouver.

I find a greasy spoon cafe, wolf down some junk food and then wish I hadn't. Tomorrow I'll eat properly. I wander back to where I'm staying. It's a hotel chosen and paid for by Granny. I would have gone for something cheaper but I can't exactly complain, can I? The building has a crazy number of floors and, as well as its own posh restaurant, there are several fully fitted kitchens you can use if you prefer to cook for yourself (I do. At least, I will do when I'm more sorted). The hotel even has its own grocery service so you can order in whatever food you want and have it delivered to your door. My bedroom has the hugest windows you've ever seen with views over a big green park, the Yacht Club, Coal Harbour and beyond. Look at me, with my mirror TV and my minibar and my ensuite bathroom with complementary white bathrobe!

I sprawl out on the king-size bed and flick through telly channels. Every so often I pick up my phone. My fingers keep itching to go to the bookmarked page that says *Terry's Penguin Blog*, but I don't let them. I try to clear my head of anything penguin-related, which is strangely hard to do. Those little guys have waddled right into the murky depths of my psyche.

Sleep doesn't come for ages. When I finally doze off, I dream of two people who are called 'Vancouver' and 'Bolton'. Vancouver is a sophisticated woman with flawless make-up and intricately styled hair, while Bolton is a street urchin, a grubby kid with mud on his knees and patches of grazed skin. He can't seem to stop picking his nose. Vancouver tries to clean him up. She scrubs his face with a pale pink flannel, but the dirt won't come away. She dresses him in a smart little suit, but he tears it off again. She tells him to say please and thank you but he just grunts like a piglet. Eventually Bolton climbs out of a window and runs away.

I wake up with a great lump of sadness in my throat. It's surreal to find I'm in a big plush bed all by myself. I scramble up, wrap myself in the white bathrobe and look out of the floor-to-ceiling windows at the city and harbour. The place is decked out with snow and the reflections of the skyscrapers glimmer silver and blue on the water. It's a perfect scene, the kind of thing you should be sharing with your girl.

22

Terry

Locket Island

IF IT WASN'T so terrifying it would be funny. I know far more about the breeding cycle of penguins than humans.

The next time I can get the internet to work, I check out what the NHS website has to say about pregnancy. Ah yes, of course, folic acid is one of the things you're supposed to take. There's a supply of vitamins in the store cupboard so I'll have a hunt. I'm determined to be responsible about this. I don't smoke and I'm physically fit, thank goodness. Alcohol isn't a big deal for me, so I'm sure I can say no to the glass of red wine I sometimes like with dinner.

All of this is the easy part. The hard part is actually grasping hold of the future and looking it straight in the eye.

There is a baby right here inside me. Patrick's baby. My baby.

No, it isn't a baby yet, it's a clump of cells, but it will already have the beginnings of a nervous system and heart, and it's becoming more and more human every day. I keep telling myself it's true, and not believing myself, and telling myself all over again.

And then I ask: do I want this new experience, this strange and life-transforming gift that fate has given me?

The answer comes back at me, sharp as a scythe: no. I can't help it. I don't want it.

Whenever Dietrich talks about his kids, his face lights up. But they are a proper family, two parents and three children. I picture them all sitting round a table together, such a cosy image. I've always thought that's something the future might hold for me; I'd have a baby in my thirties, maybe even forties. Not now, though. I'm only twenty-six and there's so much penguin work to be done first. The timing could hardly be worse. I'm newly single and my family is on the other side of the world. I don't normally mind being alone, but alone feels different and scary when you're pregnant. I'm angry, too, that I've been robbed of any choice in the matter. But it's my own stupid fault. I should have been more careful.

I try to think of what might happen next and it's a vast unknown country filled with impossible choices and complications. Abortion? No. I will argue to the death for a woman's right to choose but I couldn't take that path myself. There's no way I can have a baby and continue to live here on Locket Island, though. God, oh God. Why did this have to happen?

When it comes to decisions, I usually think hard but I don't avoid them. Now the question of what to do next keeps slipping away from me. I should tell Patrick before I tell anyone else, but I'm not ready to do it and I don't know how. Not by email, not for something this big. But I can't do it in person with him in Canada and me here.

Maybe I should just make my own plans without regard to Patrick. It's my body, my responsibility . . .

No. I have to try and tell him. It's his baby too.

I wander into the lab, just because I need to see a friendly face. Mike is labelling a sample that may or may not be something taken from a dead penguin's stomach. He carefully lays the container in a tray of similar samples before looking up.

'Yes, can I help you?' he asks, as if I'm a customer who has just walked into his shop.

'I doubt it,' I reply a little grimly.

'Something wrong?'

'Er, no.' *Yes.*

Everything is meticulously clean and ordered here. Mike takes great pride in his lab work. He lifts the tray of samples and slides it into the freezer. It will be defrosted and examined in detail later in the year, when we're less busy . . . if we're here at all, that is. *I* won't be, anyway. I won't witness the changes that the seasons bring, the hushed magic of winter, the fresh sunshine gradually inching over the glaciers and then the joyous return of the penguins. The sadness of this washes through me like a cold wave.

'Well, if you have nothing better to do, you could stop standing there like a muppet and go and get me a coffee,' Mike suggests.

I come to. 'OK. On my way.'

The kitchen is a homelier space and it's good to give my hands something to do that I don't have to think about. Kettle on, mug from the hook, jar of instant from the shelf, one heaped spoonful and wait for the water to boil.

Once Dietrich is back, I'll have to break the news to him and Mike. We were in doubt before, but this really does spell out the end of the Locket Island penguin project. I'm gutted for them both. Dietrich will find something else part-time, I'm sure; maybe he'll tour the Austrian universities giving lectures on penguins. But Mike? Bird conservation work somewhere else? Or Cheltenham with Charlotte.

Telling people is going to be difficult all round. My parents won't know whether to be delighted or devastated. They'll be pleased that the black sheep is returning to the fold . . . but maybe not so pleased at the prospect of a black lamb. They'd be so happy for me to 'settle down', but their idea of settling down would be an office job and a mortgage, plus a spouse who has signed on the dotted line. All of this, in their world, should happen before any baby is impolite enough to make its presence known.

I close my eyes and try to imagine a life for myself back in Britain as a single mother. Jobs in ecology are hard to come by and I'm never going to find one that fits round mum-life, so I'll be unemployed for years, relying on benefits. I'll be in a council flat with paper-thin walls and a second-hand sofa I don't like much. There'll be a cot next to my bed and every night will be punctuated by my baby's crying. Life will be measured in rounds of breast-feeding, nappy-changing, pulling Babygros and knitted jumpers round a little warm bundle that poos and burps and dribbles. If I'm lucky, my parents will come round and babysit from time to time, slightly judgemental although they don't mean to be.

Patrick may or may not want to be involved when he finds out. I just don't know. I still miss him horribly, and I'm sorry for him because I know he has issues ... but when I think of the way he left us, I never ever want to see him again. It's all very confusing.

The kettle reaches the peak of its crescendo and switches itself off. I pour the water into Mike's mug and add just a smidgen of milk, so that it's almost but not quite black, the way he likes it. Lost in thought, I take it back to the lab for him and place it on a surface.

'Not there!' he yells.

I've put it too close to some printouts of data, which will be ruined if it spills.

'A simple thank you wouldn't go amiss,' I tell him.

'Thank you,' he says, promptly but grumpily.

'It was my pleasure.' I'm good at being nice, but I don't feel nice inside.

23

Veronica

Bolder Island, The Falklands

'DEAR VIEWERS, I am delighted to inform you that I have arrived safely on Bolder Island, one of the many nature-rich islands of the vast archipelago that makes up the Falklands.'

I am feeling quite relaxed and on top of everything. A few tufted clouds dawdle across the blue expanse above us, which stretches out in every direction, spreading even further than the Scottish sky. Before me is an undulating green hillside with a tussocky coat of grass, a scattering of sheep and a few fine bright threads of streams. But my viewers will not be able to see any of this yet because the camera is focusing on my face.

I have paid the utmost attention to my make-up, but the thorough combing I gave to my hair this morning was all in vain due to a spiteful gust of wind. I can only hope I still look presentable.

'I am currently striving to ignore my jet lag in order to bring to your screens another bird, one that is plentiful here and as appealingly gregarious as any of their race: the Gentoo penguin.'

I pause whilst the camera pans out and reveals that I am standing in the midst of the colony. These penguins are some twenty inches tall and very handsome. They have bright orange beaks and white triangular-shaped patches over each eye that make a sort of bonnet over the bird's head. Their webbed feet are whitish-pink and their tails are long – the most prominent tails of all penguin species, I'm told. Hundreds of the birds are gathered here. Some are sitting on their nests, which are roughly circular piles of stones, whilst others are shepherding little fluffy chicks. Many of the adults have their heads thrown back and are indulging in loud trumpeting calls. I have to speak with considerable force and volume, but no matter; the raucous noise of penguins is sweet to my ears.

'The Falklands are home to the largest population of Gentoos in the world,' I continue. 'As you will see from this copious multitude, it is nesting season, and they have selected a convenient coastal site where fish are quickly accessible, and tufts of grass give them some shelter from the wind.'

A tubby specimen waddles towards me, her tail sticking out behind, sweeping from side to side. I automatically lift my handbag out of beak's reach. 'No you don't,' I tell her. She seems to regard this as a challenge and cranes her head towards it, uttering a braying cry, so I pass it to my other hand. She follows it round. I pass it back again and she pursues it again with a determined look in her eye. Our little dance continues for several minutes before she loses interest and waddles away.

'Cool! We'll keep that in,' declares Liam, emerging from behind the camera.

Daisy has been smiling and waving throughout my presentation. It seems an age since we were at The Balla-hays together and it's good to see her again, especially looking so happy. When the camera is rolling, she has to be continually shushed by her mother. She wants to see me reporting but also wants to summon our attention every time she sees one of the Gentoos lift its foot to scratch its head or waddle in a queue or tuck food into the open beak of a chick . . . and these things are happening all the time.

I inform my audience that, like Adélies, male Gentoos will often woo females by gifting them a choice pebble. 'Gentoos breed monogamously. Infidelity is, in fact, often punished with banishment from the colony. They also have a keen sense of ownership and jealously guard their nests from penguin trespassers. In these aspects their natural instincts are remarkably similar to our own.'

Liam smiles and gives me a thumbs up. We are finished, for now.

'You were fab, Veronica,' Daisy asserts.

I bow graciously. 'It is kind of you to say so, Daisy.'

I am glad the filming is minimal this morning, although it is due to my own insistence that I am filming at all today. According to the schedule, I am supposed to be resting and recovering from yesterday's flight. But the multiple discomforts and frustrations of long-haul travel were a mere trifle to me, a McCreedy, and Liam's presence, as before, provided very little hindrance to my comfort. Indeed, he proved himself particularly useful in the luggage-carrying department. I have many suitcases with me to accommodate my outfits and have also brought a few luxury items such as bath salts and fragrant loose-leaf tea.

The journey was over in a fraction of the time I would have expected, and I was pleasantly surprised when I found myself alighting on Falklands ground. We were then transferred to Bolder Island in a tiny eight-seater plane. This leg of the journey rendered exquisite views. First of all, we looked down on the town of Stanley, which, with its coloured roofs, appeared a little like one of Daisy's Lego villages. Then we flew over a chain of islands set in a limpid turquoise sea.

This flight was followed by a somewhat squashed ride in a Land Rover up a rough track through sweeping pastures of green and gold. Our temporary home is now a broad, wood-clad building with gently sloping roofs, wide windows and its own veranda. It is surrounded by a collection of small outhouses. Daisy and her mother were already here to greet us when we alighted, having arrived the day before.

After much deliberation Daisy's family had decided that Beth, her mother, was the chosen parent to accompany her on this new venture whilst her father, Gavin, stayed at home to look after Noah. I can only imagine what an excitable state Daisy must have been in for the journey, and I am glad that Beth is here to answer her questions and take care of her demands.

Beth is a woman whom Patrick always describes as 'waif-like' and I see what he means. She is so thin as to be almost hollow and the contours of her face are riddled with worry lines. Her short brown hair is soft like the fur of an otter and her taste in clothes is muted. I have so far mainly managed to avoid her company. This is not through any ill-will on my part, but merely because she is so softly spoken that I can hardly hear a word she utters, which is rather an annoyance, and it seems rude to keep asking her to repeat what she has said.

My filming done for the day, the Land Rover returns us to the lodge, although it is a mere ten-minute walk from the Gentoo colony. My joints are feeling rusty and I have need of a little quiet sit-down. There are comfortable chairs in the common room and I lower myself into one of these and rest my eyelids.

'Wake up, Veronica!'

I start and it takes me a moment to realize where I am.

'I wasn't asleep, Daisy. I was merely meditating.'

'You were snoring!' she giggles.

Beth, who is here too, scolds her with a 'Daisy, that's rude.'

It is apparently time for dinner.

The dining room has five small tables so we eat in groups, our meals tending towards fish dishes with ample side vegetables. The default portion size is large, which is just as well; the film crew swoop upon everything like vultures. All the meals are cooked by a local man named Keith who runs the accommodation side of things. Keith is a bouncy and beaming man in his forties with big hands, tanned skin and floppy dark hair. He is Falklands born and bred, he tells us, although his forebears were Welsh sheep farmers who immigrated here in the 1830s. He chats to everyone in between dashing about. He has a clipped way of talking and a tiresome habit of referring to himself in the third person: 'Keith is boss here,' 'Keith is your mate,' 'Yes, Mrs McCreedy, Keith can bring you extra condiments.' For the first two days I assumed that Keith was some other person entirely.

Keith, I will add here, has taken a great liking to Daisy: 'If Miss Daisy wants something, she just has to ask. Keith will sort it!' Daisy has taken a reciprocal liking to Keith.

The frustratingly quiet Beth has promised that she will take over the task of printing out Terry's blogs and any emails that come my way. I have therefore entrusted her with the details of the email account that Eileen set up for me. I sense that, like Sir Robert and *unlike* Eileen, Beth possesses enough self-control to pass on any messages addressed to me without reading them first.

We have been in touch with the Locket Island team already and exchanged penguin news. Dietrich is currently away, but has sent some drawings, which we print out for Daisy. Terry's communications are very brief, but I know she is extremely busy.

There has been nothing at all from Patrick since his arrival in Vancouver, and I must say I am disappointed. Still, there is much here to divert me.

A few more papers have taken up the McCreedy-Saddlebow story. They seem to fall into two camps, dwelling on either my gas-guzzling hypocrisy or my budding romance with Sir Robert. I am enraged at the former and incredulous at the latter. Romance has not been on my radar for so many decades now that I find the concept risible, especially when I look at myself in the mirror. That particular brand of love was wholly achievable when I was possessed of full lips, silky chestnut curls and a peaches-and-cream complexion, but now it is surely impossible. Romance, like sex, is the domain of the young and nubile. This I know. And yet . . .

I have long tendered admiration for Sir Robert, and although I have been acquainted with him personally for such a short time, I have often felt a . . . how shall we say . . . a certain 'flutter' in his presence. I am drawn to him as a butterfly to a rose. Tempted as I am to wax lyrical, I must stamp on any expectations in that department. He is a decade younger than I and, as he told me himself, he is married to his job in any case.

When Sir Robert joins us, he will report briefly on elephant seals, dolphins and sea lions in addition to the incredible array of birdlife here. But the penguins are my remit. I am to do a short narration about each of the five species of penguin that are Falklands residents (Gentoo, Rockhopper, Magellanic, King and Macaroni), although Sir Robert has already warned me they might not all be included in the final programme. As I have learned from Ginty Island, hours and hours of filming might be trimmed down to a mere ten minutes or nothing at all. Much depends on visuals with a wildlife documentary, and we will fit the narrative around the most spectacular and interesting footage caught by the cameramen.

Daisy will, of course, be filmed in her own right for the programme *I Wish*. The makers of *I Wish* have been in

cahoots with the makers of *Who Cares About Seabirds?*
And, to save money, the I-Wishers have given the Sea-
birders the job of filming Daisy as well, whilst she is here.
Young Liam is the allotted cameraman for her, the penguins, and my enthusiastic and indefatigable self.

This evening, as I sip my Darjeeling in the dining area,
Daisy is weaving threads to make one of her friendship
bracelets incorporating her daisy-shaped beads. Her
small fingers are very nimble.

'I'm going to make one for everyone here,' she confides
earnestly. 'This is for Sir Robert. Do you think he prefers
red or yellow?'

'Red,' I answer, certain that Sir Robert will agree with
my own preference. I am not so certain that Sir Robert
will ever wear such a thing.

'Did you bring yours with you?' Daisy asks me suspiciously, having noticed my wrist is unadorned.

'It's keeping safe in my jewellery box,' I assure her.

'But you are wearing your locket,' she retorts. 'Can I
see what's inside it now? *Please.* Now would be a good
time.'

'Not yet, Daisy. I will know when it is the right time.' I
change the subject, eager to move on swiftly. 'Liam has
said he'll be filming *you* tomorrow. Are you nervous
about being on television?'

'Nope,' she says. She tugs one of the threads in the
intricate pattern she is weaving until it is tight. 'I just have
to be me, don't I? It's not difficult.'

I think of my own concerns about looking presentable
for the camera and remembering my words, and I wish I
could agree. I never used to care what people thought of

me, but now it seems I do. Perhaps it's something to do with Sir Robert. Daisy, however, is blessed with abundant self-confidence.

'I only get nervous about one thing,' she tells me.

'Oh, what's that, Daisy?'

'When I'm really ill and have to go to hospital,' she explains in a matter-of-fact manner, still absorbed in her work. 'And I have to wait a long time because it's miles and miles away and I am hurting in the car. Then I am hurting when we go and talk to the doctors and nurses. And when they stick needles into me. Then I feel sick in my tummy and head and right through all my bones. I'm nervous when that happens, because of all the pain and maybe dying. But I don't get nervous about any of the other things. Not now.'

I put my cup down. The tea has suddenly become hard to swallow due to the enormous lump in my throat.

24

Veronica

SIR ROBERT IS back with us. I need hardly express how delighted I am to see him again. He seems to have had many adventures since I saw him last. He is pleased with the New Zealand filming, and tells us the evening of his arrival all about the extra footage they managed to get on the Snares Islands. I am to do a voice-over later which will feature the Snares penguin, an extraordinary bird that nests in forests.

'Are you sure?' Daisy asks him. She has heard so many of my stories of the Adélies of Locket Island that (although she's now seen the Gentoos on the coast here) she still associates penguins with ice and snow.

'Yes, Daisy,' Sir Robert assures her, as one scientific researcher comparing notes with another. 'I watched a gang of penguins marching into the forest myself. I didn't follow them in though,' he adds with a wink. 'That was the job of the film crew, and a very muddy one it was too. All those penguin feet waddling in and out cause a complete quagmire. Miriam and David had to slither on their bellies round thick roots and ferns, down a labyrinth of muddy, wet penguin paths, until they reached the clearing which is the penguin breeding site. They were plastered in mud head to toe when they came out again.'

Daisy laughs stridently.

On the topic of mud, I also have something to contribute. 'I recall a time during the war when, as a teenager, I squelched through a quagmire to save a piglet,' I comment. 'My dress was caked with filth and stank for weeks afterwards, even though I'd scrubbed it for hours.'

'I like mud,' Daisy asserts.

Beth makes a comment that sounds like 'Yes, that's true,' but I can't be sure.

Sir Robert smiles at Daisy. 'Too much mud is bad for penguins, though,' he explains. 'Their plumage is densely packed for insulation, but it won't work properly if it is clogged with dirt, so washing is incredibly important for them. They spend a lot of time rinsing off, then they waterproof their feathers from a wax gland at the base of their tails.'

Penguins cleanse themselves with remarkable efficiency, but I am reminded that in our human world, alas, mud sticks. The latest from the British press, citing me once more as Greedy McCreedy, has listed various machinations and flirtations of which I am apparently guilty. One article mentions Daisy and virtually accuses me of using child labour to serve my own ends.

Everyone tells me to ignore this outrage, but I do find

it extremely vexing. It seems I have lost my good name for ever.

This, my filming endeavours, the demanding presence of Daisy and the flutter of being around Sir Robert, would normally be quite sufficient to overtake all my thoughts. Yet no matter what I am doing, in the background there is always my son Enzo. And whenever I have any time to myself, I am assailed by the memories of the short time I had with him and intense longings to know more of his life.

I only hope Patrick discovers something soon and conveys it to me quickly. This level of anticipation cannot be good for one's health.

I watch.

Morning has breathed silvery puffs of cloud into the sky. Daisy is walking along the shoreline with her mother. She is sailing a kite and it rides aloft beautifully, swooping and dipping, bowing to the whims of the wind. The two figures become silhouettes against the honey-coloured sand. I observe as they shed their shoes and socks, leave them behind on a rock, and run hand in hand towards the sea. The kite tracks them from above. Bright white wings of water sprout sideways as they jump in.

I am lingering here with Sir Robert whilst the crew make preparations. It is a joy to see the mother and daughter skipping amongst the waves in a primal burst of exhilaration, especially when you bear in mind the stresses both have borne over the past months. The film crew have already taken advantage of the pale, buttery light and the touching sight of mother and daughter together, although

I'm not sure Beth will want to be included when it comes to the final cut.

Now they wander back up the beach, and their silhouettes become larger as they approach again. They are not far away when a strong gust seizes the kite and dashes it down with some force on to an outcrop of jagged rocks. I fear it must be damaged. Daisy and Beth rush to retrieve it.

A small, stocky figure with a wavy hairdo scoots out of the water and heads towards the site of the crash too. Ah, the insatiable curiosity of penguins! I see Daisy crouching down, reaching a hand towards it. I see it dipping its head towards the hand, which is quickly withdrawn. An anxious mother evidently telling her girl to beware of snapping beaks. A little more human-penguin exchange. Then Daisy and Beth walk again, bringing the kite with them, although I suspect it can no longer fly. The penguin waddles with them, trying to keep up, perpetually gregarious. It is a charming sight.

'Look who we found!' Daisy calls to me. 'It's a Mac!'

Beth is clearly benefiting from the fresh air almost as much as her daughter. She looks excited too and speaks in a voice I can actually hear.

'He's a cheeky chappy, isn't he?' Then she looks at Sir Robert quizzically. 'Is it a he or a she?'

He takes a careful look at the penguin. 'The size of it suggests it's more likely to be a she. It's not a Macaroni though, Daisy. There are other penguins on these islands which have yellow crests too: the Rockhoppers. Your little friend is a Rockhopper, or a Southern Rockhopper, to be precise. See the styling of her crest feathers? She has those yellow eyebrows that branch off the sides of her

151

head. Macaroni penguins have crests that start just above their beaks and flare out past their eyes. And it's a different kind of yellow.'

'This one's headdress is a primrose shade,' I observe.

'And Mac's was more sunflower, wasn't it, Veronica?' agrees Daisy, remembering.

The penguin is now jumping up the rocks with startling energy.

'Doink, doink, doink!' cries Daisy, thrilled. She cares nothing for the broken kite now. Her new friend has both flippers stuck out to the sides and is in the midst of the film crew, examining a camera tripod, pulling at the straps of a rucksack that is lying on the ground. She is a rambunctious little character and completely unfazed by finding herself surrounded by these great knobbly giants. As she hops around, she knocks over a cardboard cup of coffee.

'Oi, that was mine!' cries Sir Robert, sounding like a schoolboy. Then he turns to Liam: 'Quick! This is a gift. You need to be behind that camera again, filming this. I can do a voice-over later. Or Veronica can. And this would be perfect for *I Wish* too. See if you can get some footage of the penguin interacting with Daisy.'

Daisy is equally keen for this to happen. It is not difficult for her to attract the penguin's attention again. She stiffens her arms as if they were flippers too, flaps them up and down and starts moving round in circles, taking tiny steps like waddles and making squawking noises. The penguin is fascinated and follows her around, as if asking herself, 'Is this a penguin or a human – or a cross between the two?'

'This is TV gold,' Sir Robert murmurs.

We are enthralled. Daisy's face is lit up and her eyes are shining, as if all her dreams have come true at once. I feel a surge of fondness towards this lone penguin for the transformation she has wrought in the dear child.

'I love you!' Daisy cries to her new friend. 'I LOVE YOU!'

The penguin honks back at her.

25

Veronica

DAISY AND I, who are early risers, have fallen into the habit of strolling along the beach every morning before breakfast. I take my stick and handbag, but there is no need for the litter-picking tongs. The coast here, due to the lack of human beings, is particularly pristine. It is quite wonderful to see a colony of Gentoos first thing in the morning and does set one up for the day. Daisy's main purpose in the walk is not for my delightful company and conversation but to see them. Also, because she is hoping to find her particular new penguin friend.

The little Rockhopper seems to waddle about this area on her own rather than with the rest of her colony up on the rocks further along the coast. Like people, most penguins want to fit in with the crowd whilst just a few quirky individuals prefer to strike out and do their own thing. Daisy and I are both more interested in the quirky individuals; hence her obsession with the Rockhopper. There is mutual fascination and I am sure this penguin recognizes us, just as we are beginning to recognize her. She does look the same as the other Rockhoppers, but, as Daisy says, 'She's a little 'un,' and her audacious behaviour sets her apart so that even when she's with the others we can usually identify her.

'I think I'm going to call her Petulia,' Daisy announces over our kipper breakfast on the fourth day.

There is a chuckle amongst the assembled group: Sir Robert, Beth, two of the camera crew and me. She must be remembering my talk of the petunias at The Ballahays.

'Is Petulia too long for a name?' she asks defensively, looking round our faces.

'No, it's a lovely name, darling,' I manage to catch Beth reply. I turn up the volume of my hearing aid so that I can hear her better. Daisy appears to be thinking hard and now has her knife suspended in mid-air. She screwed her nose up at the kippers earlier because they were 'stinky' and is therefore going for the toast and jam alternative.

'We could shorten it to Petal?' she says, not quite convinced.

'Or maybe Petra?' her mother suggests. 'That means "rock" in Greek, so it would be a perfect name for a Rockhopper penguin.'

I had not credited Beth with much in the way of intellect, but now I am impressed.

Daisy is satisfied. 'Petra then, definitely her name is Petra.' Her knife springs to action and lavishes a quivering mound of jam on to her toast. 'Petra, rock, Petra, rock, Petra,' she says between mouthfuls. She is like a little sponge when it comes to absorbing new information and I can see that she will text her school friends along the lines of: 'My penguin is a Rockhopper penguin and we have called her Petra, which is the Greek for rock.'

'Remember you're in polite company now, Daisy,' says Beth, pointing to her daughter's jam-smeared lips and handing her a paper napkin. Daisy grudgingly takes it and wipes her mouth.

Then she eyes me. 'You need one too, Veronica.'

I am slightly shocked to find I do indeed have a spot of grease on my chin. I scrub it quickly away with my napkin, hoping Sir Robert hasn't noticed.

'If ever I get a wig, I want one like Petra's, all long and yellow and sticking up,' comments Daisy.

Beth smiles tenderly at her. 'If that's what you want, you shall have one, darling.'

I am on my second cup of tea and engaging with Sir Robert in a conversation about walruses when Daisy breaks in again. 'Can I make a friendship bracelet for Petra?' she asks him. She is still obsessed with making her friendship bracelets and has now presented one to several of the film crew.

'It's a nice idea, Daisy, but I don't see how she would keep it on,' Sir Robert answers. He always takes Daisy's suggestions seriously, no matter how whimsical they may be. 'Flippers are slippery,' he adds.

She furrows her brow. 'But you said you put bands on the flippers of the Locket Island penguins.'

'Yes, it's true,' Sir Robert acknowledges. 'Scientists place a numbered stainless-steel band around each bird's flipper. They do that to identify and keep track of individual

penguins. It helps us understand changes in their popula-
tions. But those ones are specially designed.'

'Couldn't we specially design one for Petra? With a
daisy on it. To show that me and her are friends for ever.'

Sir Robert wavers. 'I've noticed that some of the penguins are banded here . . .' he begins.

Keith (who is bustling around with a big shiny coffee
pot, seeing to refills) joins in the conversation. 'If Miss
Daisy wants something, she must come to Keith!' He
points at his broad chest with his spare hand. 'Keith
is the man to sort it! I'll bring you a penguin band
for your Petra penguin tomorrow. You can paint your
daisy flower on it, then we'll put it on her like so.' He
mimes slipping a band over the imaginary flipper of the
coffee pot.

Daisy claps her hands. 'Oh yes, Keith. *Please!*'

Daisy moves her counter along the board four places and
then nudges it slyly on a fifth.

'I saw that, young lady,' I tell her. 'No cheating!'

She scowls at me. She is due to be swallowed down by
a particularly long snake just as I am mounting my final
ladder.

'I'll just try again,' she says, grabbing the dice and shaking it furiously in a gripped fist. 'There was a little wrinkle
in the tablecloth so it might have been a five really.'

'No, you threw a four so that's how far you need to
move,' I insist.

She makes a pained noise a little like a yelp and zizzes
her counter down the snake back to square three.

Her mouth turns down even further when I throw the

exact number required for me to win. I move swiftly to the end.

She slaps the board closed in a gesture of extreme rage. I suspect her parents normally allow her to win just to keep the peace.

Indeed, she is so cross with me that I decide to give her the upper hand again by asking for her help. It is an issue that I have been pondering for some time. I should like to learn the art of googling. Googling seems to be one of the favourite pastimes of the young and I have become rather curious about it. Daisy can discover all manner of information about anything by a few rapid movements of her fingers across her miniature machine. I am in possession of no such machine but have full access to the computer in the office here, should I need it.

No sooner have I broached the question than Daisy's good humour is restored. She pulls me to the office and starts banging away at the keyboard and pointing to symbols on the screen. I have to tell her to slow down. Slowing down is not in her nature but she is willing to go over things ad infinitum, so after some twenty minutes of asking her to repeat what she just said I am beginning to grasp the basics.

'So listen, Veronica. If you want to google, say, *brontosaurus rex*, you go here and type in the words – oh, how do you spell brontosaurus?'

I start spelling it out for her but have only got halfway before she has found two million, eight hundred and sixty thousand items of information on said dinosaur.

She demonstrates again with *frisbees* and *Little Mix*. I assumed that Little Mix was a type of liquorice allsorts and am surprised to learn that it is a pop band of girl singers who are scarcely older than Daisy herself.

It is past Daisy's bedtime and she is called away by Beth. I decide to stay and use my newfound googling skills before I lose the knack. I key in the words *Sir Robert Saddlebow*. Curiosity has got the better of me. I peruse a few of the articles. There is an abundance of information about his filming expeditions and numerous awards and accolades. I also find a little about his personal life: he went to a private school, studied at St Andrews University before working his way up to the BBC, and currently lives by himself in Edinburgh. There is nothing at all about past relationships, which surprises me. Either Sir Robert is expert in keeping these things private or he is not romantically inclined at all. There seems to be some speculation that he bats, as they say, for the other side . . . but I do not believe a word of it.

26

Veronica

IT IS A truth universally acknowledged that a single penguin in possession of a good fortune must be in want of a friendship bracelet. Petra has now acquired one, thanks to Daisy's insistence and Keith's willingness to oblige. It is very pink and has daisies all over it, and I'm sure there is no other penguin flipper band in the universe like it.

Daisy has become extremely involved in Petra. She wants to feed her and is quite desperate to make a pet out of her. We cannot justify this though.

'But you adopted a penguin in Antarctica and fed him yourself, and he sat on your lap and everything!' Daisy whines.

'Yes, that's true. But, Daisy, Pip was only a tiny orphan penguin chick who would certainly have died had it not been for our intervention. Even then I had to beg and bribe the scientists to let me save him. They believe in letting nature take its course, but there was something about that chick . . .' I falter, scenes flashing back to my mind. I remember the little bedraggled creature as he floundered in the snow, his head drooping, his feet hardly able to lift . . . how the sight had reminded me of the pain of being an orphan, of being rejected . . . how the sharp pang in my heart had almost knocked the breath out of me. Then how, when I held Pip in my arms for the first time, all my motherly instincts had been rekindled. The fire of love, the rage at the cruelty of nature for letting this happen, the longing to protect, whatever the cost.

Daisy is looking at me curiously. I gather myself together and force my mind back to the present.

My voice comes out hard and cold. 'That was different. Pip would have died, without question. Petra, however, is a strong young adult penguin. She's more than able to look after herself.'

'But she needs me,' Daisy argues. 'She's lonely! That's why she wants to play.'

I don't want to disillusion her and tell her that all penguins are extrovert and unafraid of humans and she is merely anthropomorphizing, as children are wont to do. Penguins do resemble little waddly people dressed in tuxedos and it can be hard not to endow them with human characteristics. I myself do it at times. I am not prone to softness when it comes to other aspects of life, but I am positively gooey when it comes to penguins.

Sir Robert, I note, never falls into this kind of sentimentality. He shows the greatest respect for all wildlife but doesn't become maudlin or emotional at the bloodier side of nature. He has had a word with Daisy and told her that yes, she can go down to the beach every day and talk to Petra, but she must on no account feed or touch her.

Sir Robert makes his strictness palatable by relating more stories of his travels, dwelling particularly on anything penguin-specific. He tells us one evening about the Chinstrap penguins who live in circumpolar regions, who have a thin line of black under their white faces, so they look as if they are wearing helmets.

'They look sweet,' he muses. 'In fact, they look as if they're smiling but, as penguins go, they are cantankerous and aggressive. Sometimes they beat up smaller Chinstraps for no apparent reason.'

'One may smile and smile and be a villain,' I comment, recalling (as I often do) a portion of *Hamlet* from my schooldays.

Sir Robert nods sagely. 'You need to be careful of their back ends, too.'

'How do you mean?' Daisy asks.

'They have a penchant for projectile pooping.'

Her ears prick up. She is incomprehensibly fascinated by lavatorial matters.

'*Pooping* I get, but what is *pro-jec-tile*?' She draws the word out, trying each syllable on her tongue.

'Their bathroom etiquette leaves much to be desired,' I explain. I have seen similar traits amongst the Adélies, who sometimes squirt long-distance in order to keep the mess away from their nests.

'It's like being shot at, but with poo,' Sir Robert adds. 'Arcing jets of it. It can hit you from four feet away.'

'You mean, they fire it out of their bums at you?'

'Exactly that.'

'And you got splattered once?'

He fixes her with a steely eye but there is a definite twinkle in it. 'Many times, Daisy. Many times.' Even whilst making such a confession, Sir Robert surrenders none of his dignity.

Daisy collapses in a heap of giggles. It seems that Sir Robert has ascended several rungs in her estimation.

We see Petra often, waddling about on her own or with a group of friends (despite Daisy's insistence that she is lonely). I have heard Liam saying of Robert Saddlebow 'he is his own man' and it is evident to both Daisy and me that Petra 'is her own penguin'. She is full of bravado when with the others, playfully pecking and communicating in honks and caws, waddling around with them in a gang. And when she is alone, she manifests similar confidence. She seems to find Daisy entertaining, which is not really surprising as the girl will do anything to attract her attention, from holding out pebbles to singing pop songs at her.

'I want to do cartwheels along the beach,' Daisy tells me. 'And I think Petra would enjoy that. But my muscles won't let me yet.'

Still, she is able to walk further and further, and sometimes Petra waddles a short way with us. Daisy joyously sends messages to her school friends with multiple photographs, saying, 'Just taking my penguin for a walk.'

I expect this gains her many popularity points amongst her peers, although I fear many will be jealous of her. Knowing that children can be cruel, this worries me somewhat. Still, I sincerely hope there would be few who would bully a girl with cancer.

Daisy is looking so much better, in fact. Her hair has started to grow again, a soft brown gauze making her outline, which used to resemble a cartoon in pen and ink, now seem drawn in a gentle broad pencil. Her cheeks are rosy, the freckles on her nose have darkened with so much time outside in the sunshine, and her eyes, always noticeably large, have a liquidity and shine that I hadn't previously observed. I am glad she is here, and feel a fierce pride that she has only herself to thank for it. She has already conquered so much in her short life and I feel she will go far. I wish I was younger so that I could watch her grow and see how her life unfolds.

Perhaps it is because of Daisy that I have taken up my pen and started to write a journal again. I have not done this since my teenage years, and I stopped on the very day that my baby was stolen from me. My life had seemed pointless from that time on, but now I feel driven to write again. It may be because I am filled with a new hope.

Patrick has emailed to say that he has an appointment tomorrow with the woman who knew Joe Fuller, otherwise known as my darling Enzo. I am fizzing with excitement like a bottle of vintage champagne. At last, at long last, I am on the cusp of getting to know my own son.

27

Patrick

Vancouver

Denise Perry's street is a broad, tree-lined avenue. A few snowflakes are fluttering in the air and I wish I'd brought gloves. I walk along a row of biscuit-coloured houses with steep gables and big porches until I reach number thirty-four. By the door there's a tub containing a bush with bright red berries, bowed a little under the snow.

I can hear the blood pounding through my veins. My visit was postponed until today because Denise had double-booked herself, but this is it. This is finally it.

I press the doorbell. I hear shoes clomping on the other side.

'Hey, you must be Patrick,' cries the woman, opening the door. Her smile is promising and her voice enthusiastic. She has tightly curled hair that should be grey but is dyed brown with gold highlights. She's wearing huge, shiny earrings, a pink and grey buttoned dress, woolly tights and flat shoes. She's carrying a small, snub-nosed dog under one arm.

'You made it, then. Well done for coming all this way!'

She surprises me by reaching up to kiss my cheek, and I feel the snuffle of dog nose on my neck.

'It's a pleasure to meet you, Mrs Perry.'

'Oh, please call me Denise,' she says emphatically, and I realize I've overdone the formality. Note to self: relax. Try to relax, anyway.

She holds the dog out to be petted. 'This is Lulu.'

'Hi, Lulu.'

Before we can talk business, she seems to think it's necessary to give me a tour of her house (large and chintzy) and tell me her life story. She's a widow with three children (a doctor, a lawyer and a teacher) and several grandchildren. She waves a photo at me. I catch myself seeking out a resemblance but then remember they're not related to me by blood at all.

When we're finally settled in her lounge with mugs of tea and cookies, I can ask what she knows about my father.

'There's a few bits and pieces I remember, but not much, I'm afraid. Joe and I met quite a few times as children, you see, but then we moved to Chicago and I only saw him once as an adult. I was younger than him and used to think he was real handsome, with those dark flashing eyes. He did look a little like you.' She scans my features with interest then carries on. 'His parents, my mother's cousins, completely adored him. I did think he was rather spoiled and arrogant, but maybe that was just because I wanted him to pay more attention to me. Didn't I, sweetie?' This last comment was addressed (thank heaven) to the dog.

She goes on to tell me about my dad's adoptive family. His parents were apparently pillars of their local community who were into fundraising for the local church. Of course, I remember now that they'd first set eyes on baby Enzo when they were in the UK, visiting the convent where young Veronica was working for the nuns.

I ask Denise if my father knew he was adopted but she shakes her head. 'I don't remember. I didn't know it myself until after he died.'

So Joe Fuller probably never knew he was born Enzo McCreedy.

'He was quite a tearaway, quite a rebel,' Denise goes on. 'My mom told me he was always playing truant as a kid, then dropped out of school altogether. When he grew up, he became involved in extreme sports. Parachuting, rock climbing and snowboarding and so forth.'

I haven't learned a lot more than I knew already, but I make a mental note of 'arrogant', 'rebel' and 'sporty'.

'I gather he turned a bit odd later.'

'How do you mean, odd?' I demand, suddenly struggling to get out the words because my mouth has gone dry. Was this to do with Mum and me?

She wrinkles her brow. 'Well, I seem to remember his parents were quite down about it. He kept moving around and hardly ever came to see them, and if he did, he'd turn up unannounced, usually at an inconvenient time when they were involved in an important charity function or something.'

I bet – and I *hope* – he was racked with guilt about leaving us. I'm going to tell myself that was the reason for his going 'odd', anyway. But I'm disappointed it's all I've got. Denise's flow has stopped and she's looking down at Lulu, stroking her ears. I stir myself, glance at my watch, and start to make I've-really-got-to-be-going noises.

Then Denise surprises me.

'There's a box that belonged to the Fuller branch of the family, if you're interested. It's got some valuables and a few personal items that my parents didn't think they should get rid of. It's here, in the attic.'

I have to stop myself punching the air with my hand. At last we're getting somewhere.

'Could I go up and find it?'

'Sure! It's terribly dusty, I'm afraid. Nobody's been up there for years. Have they, Lulukins?' Seems like she needs the dog's confirmation every so often. Lulu sticks out a little pink tongue and licks the tip of her nose.

I assure Denise I don't mind dust and tell her as politely as possible that I'm keen to see anything connected with Dad ASAP. She clicks her tongue, tickled that I want to do it straight away and not wait until three weeks on Thursday.

'Well, I suppose you can go up there now, if that's what you really want, honey.'

'It is.'

She wasn't kidding. The place is furred with dust and a shower of it falls into my hair as soon as I've got the ladder in place. I climb up and find myself breathing in the stink of rot. There are lots of trunks and bits of furniture

168

and an old bike I'd normally be quite interested in, but I'm making a beeline for the heap of cardboard boxes I've seen in one corner. Luckily they are all marked with felt-tip on the sides or lid. 'Lorna's toys', 'Old crockery/picnic stuff', 'Sewing fabrics and oddments', 'Pans and tupper-ware' – and then my heart skitters as I see the one: 'Fuller stuff'.

I come back down, coughing, with it tucked under my arm.

Denise is in the kitchen, feeding a bit of cookie to the dog.

'Oh, you found it.' She's amazed at my ultra-efficiency.

I don't want to open it here, though. It could get emotional.

'Would it be OK if I took it back with me to the hotel?' I ask. 'I promise I'll bring it back soon.'

She waves a careless hand in the air. 'Whenever you like, honey.'

We make an appointment for me to call and return the box in three days' time. She might be pleased to get rid of it, but I don't want to be lumbered with the stuff if it's all old napkin rings or something.

It's awkward hefting the box through the crowded streets to the bus stop. I'm tempted to rip it open in the bus on my way back, but don't out of respect for the other passengers in case it spreads mould spores around. The hotel receptionist, a girl with a cute ripple of brown curls across her forehead, gives me a smile as I pass with my strange cargo and my own hair all cobwebby. Once I get back to my room there's no stopping me though. I dive in like a pirate with a treasure chest.

To start with I feel frustrated. It's mostly junk inside and I have no way of knowing what belonged to who. Then I start to put it together in my head from what Denise told me. A family Bible – well, that would belong to Mr and Mrs Fuller, wouldn't it? A few bits of jewellery sitting in dowdy velvet-lined boxes. Some china. Then I discover a couple of items that interest me more: a school trophy for high jump, some old records (mostly of Little Richard and Ray Charles) and a kind of spiral crayoned in red and black with a big letter J in the middle of it. The paper has drawing pin holes in the corners as if it's been up on a wall. I'm guessing these are things kept by my dad when he was a boy.

I think I'm having a eureka moment as I put my hand on a bundle of letters. It turns out they are insanely boring, though. They're all addressed to Mrs F from her sister, nothing written by my father at all. There are a few references to him, like 'I presume your boy is settling in better at school now,' and 'Sorry to hear about your boy's accident, and I hope the stitches will be out soon. I suggest you forbid him from climbing trees in the future.' I'm sensing a load of disapproval. Seems like the sister frowned on the adoption.

Having ploughed through the letters I wilt with disappointment. I haven't learned much. But I pull out my notebook and jot down my findings to make sure I don't forget anything:

– *liked to climb trees*
– *was accident-prone*
– *liked Little Richard and Ray Charles*

– didn't settle well at school
– could jump high
– liked spirals and the letter J

It's better than nothing.

Then there really is a eureka moment. Right at the bottom of the box, wrapped in brown paper, I discover a photo album.

My stomach clenching with excitement, I pull it out and lay it on the bed. I get this eerie feeling as I turn the pages. There, under my nose, is my dad, in full human form. There are quite a lot of landscapes and cityscapes in between and some pictures of the parents, who are always linked arm in arm and looking serene. But there he is: Granny's baby Enzo – probably not long after he left her and became Joe – wrapped in a blanket with a blue teddy bear tucked by his side. Being christened in a miniature sailor suit, adoring adults gathered round. Playing with plastic skittles in a garden. A cheeky toddler on a tricycle, a boy splashing about a swimming pool with his mates. A trip to the zoo with his parents, a school photo of him in a blazer with a fake, gap-toothed grin. It's all there.

But there's something odd. Underneath the pictures are handwritten notes in a small, neat hand that I guess must be Mrs Fuller's. And instead of the name Joe, the boy is consistently referred to as Joshua. I'm confused. Why the name change?

I can't stop staring at the little guy. He has dark hair and eyes, like me, and there's an air of mischief about him. He reminds me of myself at that age, but with one major difference: he was spoiled and cosseted, whereas I was busy being unloved and passed round social care.

Feeling very weird, I take photos of the photos with my phone and send them one by one to Granny's email address. I imagine her receiving them on her island in the Falklands, imagine her face as she sees her boy in his childhood for the very first time.

28

Terry

Locket Island

Oestrogen and progesterone are produced in early pregnancy to support your baby until the placenta takes over. The high levels of these hormones may make ligaments softer, putting pressure on the lower back and pelvis. They may also create symptoms such as heartburn, vomiting, reflux, gas and constipation.

Tell me about it!

Oestrogen and progesterone can affect your mood and make you feel more emotional than usual. Mood swings are common during pregnancy and may cause feelings of anxiety, depression, irritability and euphoria.

I seem to be working my way through the list. And yet I still haven't made any arrangements for the future. I can't leave Mike on his own so I can't go to England until Dietrich is back here anyway. Maybe by then I'll have a plan.

Lots of women give up their jobs for their children: Daisy's mother, for one. I've been wildly catastrophizing but now I'm beginning to see things in a different light. It might even be a relief to have my own little human to care for instead of a dwindling penguin conservation team. I know being a mum is no easy ride, but it will be an interesting challenge, and surely a worthwhile one.

If only I didn't have to abandon this seriously sinking ship. I've worked so damn hard to be where I am, and the project has been my baby up until now. How can I leave all this? It's not like I'd be able to come back – probably *ever*.

God, I'm going to miss this place. I cling to the memories . . . Like that day we all went out in the Ski-Doos to visit the Chinstrap penguins on the south side of the island. The Ski-Doos (aka snowmobiles) are old two-seaters. We don't use them much because the Adélie colony is within walking distance, but when we do it's so much fun. Mike and Dietrich were wedged into one that morning while Patrick and I shared the other. It was a dazzling day and we were all whooping as we whooshed across the snow, and inevitably the outing became a race. The terrain here is far from smooth, so we were flung around a lot and all suffered with sore bums afterwards. Dietrich and Mike won the race in the end, but only by a whisker.

Then there was the day at the beginning of the season when we hauled out the bundles of stakes that are used for marking nests. One thousand stakes, and each of them needed to be repaired and repainted because they'd been battered by the elements and decimated by the powerful beaks of albatrosses. We'd laid them out in front of the field centre and set about the work as a team.

'How would you like your stake?' Patrick asked with a wink. 'Medium, rare or well done?'

'Well, they're certainly not rare,' I'd answered, brandishing my paintbrush. 'Well done would be good, if you can spare the time.'

He shook his head gravely. 'Nope, there's none of that in the store cupboard, I'm afraid. Parsley and sage, yes. No thyme.'

'This British humour kills me,' Dietrich commented, after we'd had a good groan.

When the penguins began laying, Dietrich challenged us all to place bets on how many chicks would be born in the colony this year. The person with the least accurate estimate had to make a cake for the one who was closest to the right number. I was lucky enough to be the winner and it was Patrick who had to make the cake for me. It was the most delicious chocolate sponge I've ever tasted, but of course we all shared it in the end.

We made a good team, the four of us.

It is evening and all is quiet at the research centre. There is a fish finger in my pocket. I sneaked it in there because the thought of eating it filled me with revulsion, but I didn't want to offend Mike, who'd cooked dinner for us both. I am actually quite proud of myself for managing the peas and potatoes. Mike is in the lab now, so I take myself to the front door and throw the offending item out across the rocks and ice. But then I realize my throw was rather pathetic and it hasn't landed far enough away. Mike may see it there in the morning, if a gull hasn't snatched it. I pull on my boots and go out. I pick it up, suppressing my disgust, and bury it further on, scrabbling at the snow and earth with my bare hands.

I'm frozen to the core when I come back in.

Soon after Mike discovers me sitting cross-legged on the floor in the lounge, elbows resting on my knees and my thumbs and middle fingertips pressed together making circles. Panpipe music drifts round the room from one of those CDs we have that never normally gets aired. It's quite nice, actually. It reminds me of owls hooting.

Mike looks dumbfounded. 'What the—?'

'I'm just practising mindfulness,' I tell him.

'Are you turning weird on me?' he demands.

'Yes, probably. Is that OK?'

'I'd rather you didn't.'

'Spoilsport.'

'Nutter.'

'Dullard.'

'Freak.'

I can't be bothered with any more banter. I'm starting to feel queasy again. 'Look, you're not helping. I'm trying to establish an atmosphere of calm serenity.'

'What's this crap, anyway?' he asks, switching off the CD player mid-hoot.

'Oi, I was listening to that.'

'Look, Terry, if you want to relax, I have a better way.'

He disappears into the kitchen and I hear a cork popping. He comes back in with a bottle and two glasses.

'No, Mike, I really couldn't,' I protest, pulling myself up off the floor.

'Of course you could. Come on, it will help you forget all about that piece of shit, Patrick.'

He fills both glasses to the brim and holds one out to me.

'I said no,' I tell him, getting irritable now.

He swipes it back so fast it spills on the mat, then curses loudly.

Suddenly I feel like crying. Mike does choose his moments.

'I'm having an early night,' I mutter, wearily making my way to the door. 'You can mop up the mess.'

He tells me to eff off then.

'When you're in England, what do you and Charlotte do at weekends?' I ask Mike as we set out together the next morning, a gust of wet sleet flying in our faces. I'm trying to get used to the concept of normal life in Britain.

'Odd question,' he replies testily.

'Is it?' I wouldn't have thought so. 'What's the answer?'

'We go to museums and galleries sometimes.'

'Oh, so she's into cultural activities, is she?'

'In her way. Not always. It depends.'

Mike is pacing silently by my side. For a moment, against my will, I picture him having sex with Charlotte. At first, he is rather uptight and scientific about it. Then she strips off to reveal her utter voluptuousness and

177

pounces on him, pinioning him to the bed, and all at once he is a changed man. I smile to myself for a moment before returning to today's hard reality. The wind is biting my cheeks, sleet is slopping down my glasses, and ahead of us is a day full of penguin-monitoring.

I tentatively put the question to Mike. 'If we have to close down, what will you do? Will you look for similar work or will you settle down in Cheltenham – with Charlotte?'

'Terry,' he answers. 'Mind your own business.'

I expect, no matter what Mike says (or doesn't say), his girlfriend does let her elegantly flicked hair down at weekends. I wonder if she's had any affairs during Mike's long absences, pinioning some other guy down with her voluptuousness. I hope not, for Mike's sake.

He heads off to his allocated area of the colony and I walk down to mine. Now I am in my comfort zone, surrounded by penguins again. The sleet has blown away, the sun is beaming through gaps in the cloud, and I can hear the soft, musical trickling of ice as it melts into water. Fuzzy penguin chicks are everywhere, so plentiful they seem to be carpeting the ground at my feet. They bumble and tumble about, playing together in the stones and puddles. Such a sweet sight.

Still, it's not much fun needing to pee so often while I'm working outside. The penguins couldn't care less, of course, and seem quite gleeful at the sight of a weary scientist pulling down her thermal trousers and knickers and squatting in the snow. I'm struck by the grossness of my own body. For some reason human muck seems so much worse than penguin muck.

I get back to work. But for the first time ever it feels like drudgery. I can't believe it. Surely I can't be getting *bored* of penguins?

I put a hand over my stomach, where my baby is growing.

A winged shadow sweeps across the snow. The giant petrel swoops down a short distance away and alights on a rock. He is eyeing up a straggling group of penguin chicks. He arches his huge dark wings and takes a leap forward, snapping at them. Aware of the danger, the chicks shrink back and form a defensive cluster. He will shortly go in and snatch one of them for his tea. I emotionally disengage myself, as I've done thousands of times before, but this time it seems more difficult than usual. I have to look away. I'm a slave to my hormones and pregnancy has turned me into a complete snowflake.

I get on with weighing chicks and recording statistics, but it's not long before I hear a ruckus behind me. I can't help looking back, expecting to see the petrel dragging a bloodied baby penguin across the rocks. But instead I see a feisty young adult Adélie shielding the little group from the petrel, both flippers outstretched in defiance. I love that protective instinct inherent in all Adélies. I slowly pull out my camera and zoom in, thinking this will be good for the blog. To my amazement I see that the brave adult penguin has an orange flipper tag. It's our very own Pip! He has become a wall between the chicks and their predator and is now trumpeting loudly to scare the petrel away. The petrel backs off awkwardly. He knows not to mess with adult Adélies, scoots off across the snow, and, with a few strong beats of his enormous wings, flies away.

'Pip!' I call out, amazed. 'I am just so, so proud of you.'

Pip reminds me that I *have* had a bit of practice raising a little one after all. And at least I've had these years here and nobody can take them away from me, no matter what the future holds. It's been a life beyond my wildest dreams and I am just so thankful for it all. I will never forget Locket Island or the penguins.

I feel much more positive now. I'm due another break so I wander up as far as Sooty's nest. Sooty isn't here but Mrs Sooty is stuffing regurgitated fish down mini-Sooty's beak. She has a greedy, demanding child, but she doesn't mind in the least, devoting her energies selflessly to his needs.

I will love my baby as she does and do everything I can. If it's a boy I think I'll call him Archie. If it's a girl . . . let's see . . . Veronica? Maybe not. Eva, perhaps. Yes, Eva. I'd be equally happy with either, but I somehow feel it will be a girl.

I don't want to go back to the UK too soon, though. It's occurred to me there's a tiny, tiny chance that the penguin project might carry on if I can be replaced and if Veronica keeps on with her generous funding.

I'm going to have to write to her again. I'm desperate for some hint of how Patrick is feeling about me – and about Locket Island . . .

Someone is shouting my name repeatedly. Of course, it can only be one person.

Mike. He is crimson with rage. 'Terry, why haven't you been answering your radio? I've been worried sick about you.'

'Oh God. I must have switched it off by mistake.' I

wear the radio hitched to my belt. I must have nudged it off when I pulled up my trousers after my unladylike squatting session.

Mike is spitting venom. 'Don't we have enough to worry about without you being so flaky?'

'Sorry. That was really stupid of me. Have you been hunting for me long?'

'Three pissing hours.'

I'm shocked at myself, too. 'Mike, I'm just so sorry.'

This is not like me. It's unforgivable. My belly is aching, my breasts are sore, I'm exhausted and I feel overwhelmed. I put my head in my hands and start to cry. I don't care that Mike sees me. I don't care that he thinks I've lost it. I can't help the flood of tears that is bursting out of me.

'For God's sake, Terry.'

But it is said gently this time. He wraps his arms around me. I sob into his chest. He has no idea about the pregnancy and assumes that this is all still because of Patrick leaving. He holds me tight. I am surprised at his murmured words of comfort, at the way he's stroking my hair from my face, stroking the tears from my cheeks.

I look up at him, my eyelashes heavy with more tears, my eyes awash with them so that he is just a blur. I must try to pull myself together. This isn't how I want to be.

He holds my face in his hands. His lips move down and touch mine.

'My God, Terry,' he whispers. 'I love you so much.'

29

Veronica

Bolder Island

Sir Robert smiles at me over the breakfast table.

'So, are you ready to talk about Magellanics today, Veronica?'

'I am ready to talk about any species of penguin at any time, Sir Robert,' I reply, as I spread a thick layer of marmalade on my toast. 'However, I believe it will be Macaronis today.'

He shakes his head. 'No, it is Magellanics. Did you not see in the schedule?'

'Forgive me, Sir Robert, but you are mistaken. I checked only twenty minutes ago. It is written in black and white. I am to report on Macaronis this morning.'

He looks me in the eye, and his handsome smile converts to an equally handsome frown. 'We are all booked on a flight at nine which will take us to the nearest Magellanic colony.'

He seems very sure, but I know that I am right.

'When you have finished your croissant we will go and check on the noticeboard,' I tell him. The poor man has been so busy it is not surprising he gets a little confused sometimes. We all have copies of the schedule but tend to leave them in our bedrooms, so the one pinned up in the common room is the quickest to access. When we are done with breakfast, we go together to consult it.

Sir Robert points to my name, clearly written next to the word 'Magellanics' under Thursday.

Can it really be Thursday already? And how could I have mistaken Magellanics for Macaronis? Somebody must have changed the schedule without informing me.

I feel rather foolish and wrong-footed, however. Luckily I manage to redeem the situation with a relevant quotation from *Hamlet*: 'I am but mad north-north-west. When the wind is southerly, I know a hawk from a handsaw.'

Sir Robert's smile has returned. He is impressed with the expanse of my literary knowledge and excellent memory. Indeed, I do believe that all the recent demands on my brain cells have only served to sharpen them further.

The day progresses exactly as scheduled, with Sir Robert, Liam, Beth, Daisy and I taking one of the miniature local planes to a small neighbouring island. Daisy is reluctant to be dragged away from her beloved Petra but, as ever, is keen to watch my filming. Her mother has nothing better to do with herself than to tag along.

Now we are gathered under a mackerel sky close to a rocky cove. We have set up with a picturesque scene behind us: the sweep of sand is pale gold and speckled with penguins, whilst the sea presents a magnificent blend of green and turquoise interwoven with ribbons of bright silver. We form a small human huddle in amongst a jumble of penguins. The Magellanics are handsomely marked, with a distinctive white ring around their faces and a horseshoe-shaped band of black feathers outlining their white chests and abdomens. When we arrived, this group were lifting their heads and braying loudly, but now that the cameras are set up things have fallen surprisingly silent.

According to Liam, cameramen spend most of their lives trying to sneak up on shy animals unobserved so as not to scare them off, but it is not so here. Shyness is not a concept known to penguins. Several lenses are focused in, watching the beaky faces of this group. The beaky faces are watching right back. We seem to have spent the last half-hour waiting for them to do something interesting. However, the penguins, equally fascinated, are apparently waiting for *us* to do something interesting.

One of them eventually takes the initiative. He steps forwards with his head held high in an attitude of swagger, eyes fixed upon us, but definitely showing off to his companions. Almost immediately he trips up and falls over in a most undignified manner. Daisy hoots with laughter. I'm not sure this was the sort of thing we wanted. If it is kept in, it will have to be put to a comic piece of music. The penguin cheerfully gets up again and returns to the exact spot where he was before, not bothered at all about losing face. The penguin-human standoff resumes.

At last an adult penguin leaps out of the sea and waddles up the beach towards us, her silhouette lurching from side to side against the backdrop of bright waves. She is heading for a large, bulbous, grey-brown chick.

'Go, Veronica!' calls Liam.

I start speaking. 'As you will observe from this charming example, my dear viewers, the parental urge is strong.' Sir Robert points to the penguins, indicating that I should relate what's actually going on as opposed to the facts I have memorized. 'This mother seems very anxious to see her child again.' I stop here, for I have learned the importance of pregnant pauses, especially when action is afoot. The cameras, my viewers and I are all watching as the mother regurgitates her softened catch into her chick's waiting beak. The chick gulps down everything that is offered and then asks for more, chasing her around.

Liam comes out from behind his tripod. 'Good, got that.'

'Are you happy to do something about their nests, now?' suggests Sir Robert.

I acquiesce. We proceed to the tufted yellow dunes and focus on another posse of penguins. I inform my viewers that parents dig burrows in the soil with their strong beaks and flippers, to protect their young from predators.

'Sea lions, elephant seals and orcas (commonly known as killer whales) are more dangerous in the sea than on land. Although they appear to be lumbering great fools, the seals are apparently quite lethal underwater. But it is the gulls and skuas that threaten these chicks and might swoop down to seize one when its parents aren't looking.'

We witnessed this happening once on Bolder Island and it was a truly bloody and tragic affair. I cannot believe the chick's mother ever quite recovered.

*

I have so far covered Gentoos and Magellanics. There are Rockhoppers, Macaronis and Kings to go. Daisy will be doing her own little narration about Rockhoppers for *I Wish*, which will focus on her delightful relationship with Petra. This afternoon, whilst I read in the common room of the lodge, she has been busy practising her words with Beth. I will say this for Beth: she is endlessly patient.

When I look up from Emily Brontë, she is hovering before me. Beth, that is, not Emily Brontë. Although I have been so caught up with *Wuthering Heights* that my wits are scrambled and for a moment I struggle to sort fact from fiction. She puts a few sheets of paper into my hand, mumbling something I cannot catch, but I believe it includes the words 'email' and 'Patrick'.

My discombobulation disperses in an instant, giving way to a tingling excitement. I thank her and seize the papers. I see there is absolutely no text whatsoever, but many photos are printed across the pages. I pull myself up from my chair as quickly as I can and retreat into the privacy of my bedroom to consume what's there.

I sit down by the window. I inhale deeply and let myself look at the first photo.

My baby gazes out at me. My Enzo. Just as I remember him, but snuggled in a blanket with a teddy bear who is an unrealistic shade of forget-me-not blue. Oh Enzo, I have not forgotten, could never forget you . . .

The blue blurs and the picture becomes a haze. So many years ago, so many decades, but at last I see him again, perhaps only a week or two after he was taken from me. I screw up my eyes. A splash of water has fallen on to the photo and is making the ink run. I dash it away and hold the paper safely out of harm's way, but I am overcome by wave after wave of emotion. I have my own memories of this same boy. Of bathing him in the sink of the nunnery. Of singing him 'It's A Long Way To Tipperary' and 'You Are My Sunshine', and Sister Amelia poking her head round the door telling me to keep quiet – and me singing all the louder because I wanted to continue looking at Enzo's smile. That beautiful baby smile!

I take deep shuddering breaths. At last I am able to focus on the other pictures, other memories that are not mine. The flow of tears does not cease, gushing freely down my cheeks and neck. My Enzo is before me, but being cuddled and adored by strangers, bounced on the knees of the young couple who took him, whose faces I scarcely remember but who robbed me of all happiness when I was hardly more than a child myself. I see with relief how they loved him, yet my anger flares because that love should have been mine.

One by one I study the changing images of my boy, year after year. Thick dark curls grow round his face, his limbs lengthen and he becomes taller. He sits on a picnic rug. He sticks his fingers in the icing of a birthday cake. He plays on a roundabout in a park. He is stomping through snow. Then he is riding a little red bicycle with stabilizers. Then he is at a zoo, looking at monkeys, pointing a stubby finger at giraffes. Then he is at school, in a smart uniform for a class photo with his friends. Then he is in a playing field kicking a football. Then he is diving from a high board into a swimming pool. The last photo just shows his face.

My heart is bursting. I can hardly bear it. He is smiling again, the most beautiful smile in the world. His dark eyes are looking straight at the camera, straight at me, his mother.

30

Patrick

Vancouver

'HELLO AGAIN!'

Denise's earrings and her smile are just as bright as last time. She pecks me on the cheek and lets me in. I dump the box on her hall floor. She is keen to go through the routine of dog-petting, tea-drinking and small talk, but I'm not having it. I've tried to ring her several times over the last few days and not got through. Now my patience has run out.

'Was his name Joshua or was it Joe?' I demand. I know I should say, 'How are you, Denise?' first, but this nasty niggle has entered my head that we might have somehow got the wrong person.

Lulu snuffles at my heels. Denise's smile drops into a frown. 'Joshua?'

'Yes, there's a photo album and loads of pictures, but the writing under them says he's Joshua,' I explain edgily.

'Let me think.' It's clearly not an activity she's used to, judging by the vacant expression in her eyes.

'Kettle, while Mommy's trying to work it out.'

I worry for a moment before I realize she's talking to Lulu. I follow her into the kitchen and she plonks two mugs and a packet of biscuits on the sideboard. I will the kettle to boil fast, which it doesn't.

Once we are back in the sitting room with our teas, I manage to force the album into Denise's hands. 'Look here. It says Joshua.'

She turns the pages. 'So it does.' She peers down at the photos, bemused. 'But I remember him as Joe. It's definitely him.'

Yes, but is it the *right* him? I want to scream.

'I wonder if Emma would remember.'

'Who's Emma?'

'My daughter, the one who's a lawyer. She's got a memory like a box of razors. She never knew Joe, of course, but she's quite up on the family history. I could ring her, after we've had our tea, if you like.'

'Do we have to wait until we've finished our tea?' I ask.

'Well, Patrick. You *are* in a hurry, aren't you?'

She's noticed!

She isn't looking so thrilled with me now, but she gets up and wanders to the phone. 'Emma, darling, it's me, Mom. Yes, I'm fine, and so's Lulu . . . Oh, that's good to know . . . Listen, honey, I've got that young man with me who was doing the research about the Fullers. He found the Fuller things in the attic and one of them was a photo album, but it seems that Joe . . . maybe *wasn't* Joe? His mother called him Joshua in the notes.'

There's a long pause. Then she beckons me over and holds her hand over the mouthpiece. 'She wants to talk to you,' she hisses.

I take the phone from her eagerly.

A brisk young voice comes at me. 'Hello, is that Patrick?'

'Yes, sorry to bother you, er, Emma, but this is important to me.'

'Understood. He's your father, after all. Listen, Mom's a bit vague about these things, I know. She's forgotten but I do remember looking into it once. He was christened Joshua by the Fullers, but he liked to call himself Joe and changed it officially later. I guess he wasn't keen on all the biblical connotations of Joshua. But it's definitely the same guy.'

I'm glad. He was cute as a kid, even if he did turn rotten later. I'd started getting attached to him, in a weird way.

'Thanks, Emma. You've no idea how good it is to have cleared that one up.'

Then she comes out with it. 'Did Mom tell you there's another box?'

'No? Another box?'

'Ah, she's forgotten that too. Tell her from me that she's hopeless, would you?'

'OK, but what about this other box?' My pulse has accelerated madly.

'It's only little: a shoebox, I think. It was sent to our family when Joe Fuller died, by one of his friends. I've never seen what's inside, but I guess it contains a few of his personal possessions. You're the one who should have

191

them now. It'll be in Mom's attic too, somewhere. She keeps all the family stuff.'

'God, Emma, you're an angel. Thank you so much.'

Just a shoebox has got to be better than nothing. Denise is still finishing her tea and biscuit but gives me permission to pay another visit to her attic. I'm out of the room before she's finished speaking.

I get a shower of fricking dust in my hair again as soon as I open the door.

The shoebox takes me some time to find but it's there, on its own, in a corner. It's gathered its own layer of dust and some mouse droppings.

I forgot to ask if I could keep the box. I don't feel I can take it away and then come back a third time to Denise's. Even Lulu is getting bored of me. But I'm reluctant to open it with Denise looking on.

I'll open it here, now.

The parcel tape is old and crackly but has gone round the box so many times it's still well sealed. I scrape it with my nail and tear it off. I lift the lid. There's not much inside. I take the items out one by one. I pull out my notepad to jot down information as I go.

A watch that stopped long ago. It's squarish, expensive looking, classic style, engraved on the back: *To Joe, from your loving parents*.

Feeling a bit resentful and jealous, I write:

– was loved by parents

Next I pull out a dog-eared leather folder edged with a zip. I unzip it. Inside are a few postcards and birthday cards from people whose names I don't know and a couple of photos. I rifle through them quickly.

It only takes me a matter of seconds to find it: a photo of a grown-up Joe Fuller. Dad. My eyes have suddenly gone watery, but I blink away the tears and stare at him. He's standing with another bloke at the top of a mountain, rucksacks leaning against their legs. Both are grinning with that 'we did it' look of pride on their faces. Dad has the kind of looks that women like – all tanned and swarthy and athletic. I can't help thinking he looks like a decent bloke, though, the kind of man who'd be a good mate. On the back it reads: *Joe, from Maurice. In the Rockies, 1967.*

I scribble it down.

– climbed in the Rockies
– had a friend called Maurice

I study the photo again and I'm suddenly filled with white-hot rage because he looks so damned unconcerned. OK, this was taken a long time before I was born, but I still can't stand that smug expression. I speak to him through clenched teeth. 'Why, Dad, why? Why leave Mum like that when you knew she was depressed? When you had a boy of your own, a week-old baby? Why run off and never, ever contact us again? Didn't you know the grief killed her? Did you ever find out she put stones in her pockets and walked into the sea?'

I am shaking the photo now, as if I could shake the shame and horror of it right into him.

'Did you ever even think about me *at all*? Did you? Did you?'

Then, as if in answer, a very small black-and-white photo drops out on to my lap.

A picture of a very new-looking baby in a blanket.

Me? It might be me.

All at once it's got very stuffy in here and I have to sit down on an old trunk. My throat feels tight and there's an odd taste in my mouth.

I don't have any photos of myself as a baby. Not a single one.

I have to remind myself to breathe.

Newborn babies all look pretty similar, but it *must* be me, mustn't it? At least that's a sign that maybe I wasn't entirely forgotten by my dad, if he kept it for all those years. I rummage through the contents of the folder, spreading out every other photo.

And at last I find the proof I'm looking for. A photo of Mum and a teeny tiny me together. She's holding me close, her hair loose about her shoulders, laughter in her eyes. Just as I remember her. And I get the voice of Joni Mitchell singing, and the smells of rose soap and cheap shampoo together with a sour tang of beer. A violent sorrow grabs me in the guts and I have to close my eyes for a moment. If only Mum had stayed. If only bloody Joe Fuller hadn't left us.

31

Patrick

Denise has let me keep the shoebox. It's sitting on my hotel floor now, by the enormous window. I'm still feeling wobbly.

I can't help being pee'd off with Granny V again. She should bloody well be here with me now. We always said we'd do this together. At a time like this a guy should have a mate or a family member nearby. Or a girlfriend.

There's nearly a week to kill before my flight to the Falklands. What am I going to do with myself? I wonder again about the possibility of getting drugs, but I don't have a clue how to set about it in Canada. I guess I should make the most of being here and go sightseeing, even though I'm hardly in the mood for it. Maybe once I've started it'll get easier.

I head for the lift then decide I can't bear to be trapped in such a small enclosed space. I start down the hundreds of shiny brown stairs instead. Speed seems necessary and I'm hurtling down so fast I trip, but grab the rail just before I do myself a major injury. Eventually at the bottom, I push through a fire door, pound along a corridor and find myself in the back of the reception area. The smell of fresh coffee mingles with the smell of new carpet. On a glass-topped table, in front of one of those architectural orchids that live on nothing but air, I find a rack full of flyers about Vancouver. I pick up a random few and skim-read.

Apparently this is a city with something for everyone, from families with toddlers to LGBT travellers (how about sad, lonely gits?). There are literally hundreds of things to see and do: looking round Granville Market, visiting Chinatown, shopping on Robson Street; exploring forest trails, sailing on the Strait of Georgia, taking a cable car up Grouse Mountain to see the views of the gridline streets and harbour . . .

Instead of all these, I home in on the leaflet for Greater Vancouver Zoo. My dad went there when he was a kid. I'd like to go there too. Also, I'll admit I'm missing Locket Island and I could really do with some penguin therapy.

It turns out that the zoo is some way out of town. I approach the girl in reception with the curly fringe. She's looking very bored in a neat, efficient sort of way, but puts on a professional smile just for me. I ask if she can recommend a local hire car company, and she gives me some pointers, the smile never leaving her lips. I bet she's thinking, *Ah, cobwebby guy will be coming back soon with more shabby boxes.*

*

Hiring a car for the day is a rigmarole that uses up my last ounce of patience but at least takes my mind off misery-guts thoughts for a while. When I finally turn off the highway in my blue Nissan, glad of the satnav, and pull into the huge car park, there aren't actually many hours left in the day for animal-watching. It will be worth it, though. Penguins have a way of making me happy, and just thinking about them helps me warm more to my dad. I *want* to like him, having seen those photos, but it's hard because I just don't get why he never got in touch with me, why he never wanted to know me.

This place is bloody enormous. It's a cold, cheerless day but I'm striding along so fast that I'm sweating anyway. I zoom around buffalo and alligators and lynxes, but can't seem to find the penguin enclosure. I was given a map at the front gate but the word 'penguins' isn't on it anywhere. Zebras, yes; llamas – I've never seen so many llamas; flamingos – I've got fricking flamingos coming out of my ears! There are hippos and jaguars and cheetahs and a good many weird animals I've never heard of, like addaxes and nilgais and onagers. But not a hint of penguin anywhere.

I spot a member of staff who's standing beside a cage of orangutans. He has an official air, a big orange badge and a giant smirk.

'Where are your penguins?' I ask.

The smirk becomes even smirkier. 'I'm sorry, sir. We don't have any penguins here.'

I can't believe my ears. I explode at him. 'What? What kind of a zoo doesn't have penguins?'

'If you want to see penguins, you'll have to go to

Vancouver Aquarium. That's where the sea life is. It would be pointless to duplicate what they're doing there.'

I swear loudly. People are staring.

'What are you looking at?' I yell, and a couple pull their children away, shocked. My temples are throbbing. I should have known. Of course there are no flipping penguins. I slope off back to the car park, drained and ashamed.

God, what kind of a person have I become?

I drive back so full of self-loathing I could weep. I drop the car off and head back to the hotel. I'm too knackered to go up all the stairs this time so grit my teeth and go up in the lift. Once back in my stupidly luxurious room, I fling myself on to the bed.

Yet again, my fingers are itching to bring up Terry's blog page on my phone. I only just manage to stop them by making them email Granny instead. I'm not good at putting thoughts into words so I keep it factual. I don't mention my abortive zoo trip.

Hi Granny,

Hope you're well – and same goes for Daisy and RS. More stuff found out today. Daughter of Denise (Emma) much better for info than Denise, so now I have a shoebox of Dad's things too, from when he was older. Also discovered he was christened Joshua but didn't like the name so changed it to Joe. He was poss thinking about this when he drew the spiral with the J in the middle?

I stop to attach the photo of the drawing I took earlier, and while I'm at it I take out the watch, leather folder and latest pictures, and take snaps of them all.

Here he is as an adult. And there's one with yours truly and my own mum. I'm hoping this means he didn't totally forget about us. I guess we'll never know why he left.

That's going to keep on bugging me for the rest of my life. But at least I have the photos. Granny will be pleased to have them too.

I gather all the bits and pieces together and put them back in the shoebox.

It occurs to me that if I search for Joshua instead of Joe the internet might give me something more. It's possible his name was kept as Joshua on some of his official documents. I boil the kettle and make a coffee with the little sachets that are laid out for me. Then I pick up my phone again and key in the words 'Joshua Fuller'. References leap up, and I scroll through, my eyelids beginning to droop as I filter through the mass of irrelevant search results. Glad of the coffee, I keep going.

Many pages in, there's a newspaper article from 1985, the year I was born, the year my dad left. At the top of the column is my father's photo, which I now recognize – the same man who was grinning at the top of the mountain, although here he seems more serious and darker, somehow. I glance at the headline.

I have to blink and look again because I can't believe I'm reading those three words. There's no mistaking them though, however much I want them to be different words; words telling of some heroic deed. And there is no doubt they're referring to the man in the picture, my dad.

KILLER FLEES COUNTRY.

32

Veronica

Bolder Island

WHEN BETH PASSES me the most recent email, I cannot keep my hand steady. My breath is suspended and I feel dizzy with anticipation. What else has Patrick unearthed about my beloved son? *Beloved* indeed, because locked away in the quiet of my bedroom, I have been looking at the photos again and again, trying to absorb every last detail. I have fallen in love with my Enzo all over again.

My voice jolts out of me: 'Thank you, Beth.' I am terse in my impatience and she shrinks from me as if I'm a crocodile.

I see at once that there are no photos this time, which is a disappointment, but there is a full page of writing. Patrick is not normally given to wordy elaborations so this can only mean he has more information to impart.

I retreat at once to my bedroom to drink it up. But the stupidest, most exasperating trifle holds me back from spending more precious minutes with my son. My reading glasses are nowhere to be found. They are not in any of my handbags. There are few items of furniture in my room, but I rummage through every drawer in the chest of drawers, scan the tops of the bedside cabinet and windowsill, and even check the high shelf inside the wardrobe.

I am proud of my memory, which never lets me down in spite of my mounting years, yet these wretched inconveniences seem to occur more and more often. If I were a less patient person, I would be incredibly angry by now.

I stomp out into the communal area and bellow to the small group who are present: 'Has anyone seen my glasses?' Conversation stops and heads turn. 'It is extremely important that I find them without delay,' I assert in an authoritarian manner. Everyone springs to action.

'Don't worry, Mrs McCreedy,' cries Keith. 'You have come to the right person. Keith will find them.'

'I sincerely hope that he will.'

The detritus of breakfast is scattered on the tables and the smell of frying lingers in the air. Sir Robert is already out reporting but Keith, Beth, Daisy and several cameramen are all now scrabbling around on the hunt for the missing glasses. Were it not for my desperation to read Patrick's email, I would enjoy such a sense of command.

It is Daisy who discovers the infuriating but vital item, tucked behind a teapot.

I thank her and dash to my bedroom, shutting the door firmly behind me, now fully equipped for any revelations that should come my way. I put the glasses on my nose, at last set to devour the letter.

But to my dismay, I now register that it is not from Patrick at all. It is from Terry.

My disappointment is palpable, yet I become increasingly riveted as I read on. What begins as a fairly chatty and innocuous newsletter turns out to be a desperate plea of a somewhat mysterious nature.

Dear Veronica,

I do hope you are staying well, not overstretching yourself (as if anyone could stop you!) and enjoying your time being amongst penguins again. Please forgive me if this email is largely about me. I can assure you that the Locket Island penguins are well and numbers of breeding couples have slightly increased since last year, which is amazing. And Pip is as much a character as ever. I see him most days, parading around, being very much part of the crowd. Whenever he sees me he comes waddling up to say hello. He was a real hero yesterday, protecting a group of chicks from a giant petrel. If you look at the blogs you'll see the video.

We are missing Patrick here and hope that, whatever is going on with him, he is happy.

She'll have no idea how much he has discovered about his father. I wonder if she still has feelings of affection for him after his crass desertion. So far, her words have been remarkably free of accusation.

Something has come up, Veronica, and I'm really, really worried. It will affect the whole future of the Locket Island project as well as my own future, and it's not at all clear to me how to go forward. Would you be able to somehow sound Patrick out and just see how he feels about me? Don't tell him I've asked you to, please, I'd die of embarrassment. I know it was our relationship problems that made him leave and not the work itself, so I wondered if you could also find out if he'd ever consider coming back if I wasn't here?

I haven't broached this option with Mike and Dietrich and I expect it's impossible but it was just a thought. I'm racking my brains for solutions.

So sorry to ask this of you, Veronica. I keep thinking about the days we tended Pip together and then about how you encouraged Patrick to join our team. I know you care for the project . . . and for us all.

Please don't let on to Patrick that anything's wrong, but just let me know where he's at. That will help me plan for the next steps.

With much love,
Terry x

This leaves me in a state of complete bewilderment. Whatever is wrong? Is she ill? Is there a problem with her family back in England? And how on earth am I to 'sound Patrick out'?

Now that I am becoming better acquainted with the mysterious ways of the internet, I am beginning to think that I should learn how to use these wretched email she-nanigans myself. It is extremely vexatious having to rely on other people to relay these missives to me all the time.

I will have to turn my hearing aid up to maximum volume and get Beth to explain it all to me. Or I could ask Daisy, with whom I'll have no need of maximum volume, her volume being naturally more than adequate. Still, I feel I have already exhausted Daisy's patience with the googling lesson. I should go to the adult in this case.

I seek Beth out and find her doing a jigsaw puzzle with her daughter in the common room. When I make my request, she says she'd be delighted to help and leads me to the office.

'I'm so grateful for everything you've done for Daisy,' she tells me on the way. 'You've helped her more than I can say. I'm not even sure she would have recovered without you; and the way you kept telling her to remember the penguins when she was in hospital – it was just wonderful. And the chance for us to be here, on Bolder Island . . .'

'It was nothing, absolutely nothing,' I answer, surprised. 'I am glad to be of use. It has done Daisy a power of good being amongst penguins. I've often thought that nature has hidden healing powers, both mentally and physically, and she has proved me right.'

Beth seems a bit weepy. I put out a hand to her.

'Sorry,' she sniffs, reminding me of Terry, apologizing for what isn't her fault.

'It happens,' I tell her.

I sit beside her in the office and wait whilst she fiddles around with the machine for a while. Then she turns to me, pointing at the screen.

'Right, I've bookmarked the page for you here, Veronica.'

'Bookmarks' are, she informs me, a way of keeping your place, as if the contraption were a real book. I am to 'click' on the said 'bookmark' and my email messages should come up in a list showing who has sent them on the left and the title of the email on the right. If you then click again on either of these, your message is suddenly revealed. She lets me practise a few times. I am pleased to say that clicking is not too arduous a task for me to handle. In fact, after the first few times I am clicking away quite merrily. She shows me how to expand the screen so that I can read the letters without my glasses. This is a most thoughtful invention, I must admit.

Beth then explains that if I want to reply to an email that has been sent to me, I have to click on the bendy arrow in the corner. Then I type my message and click on the blue box that says 'send'. Again, this is not nearly so complex as I had feared.

We see that an email from Patrick is indeed waiting for me. It contains a brief paragraph saying he has found out more and some images are attached. I glance only briefly in the presence of Beth. This time the photographs are of my Enzo's possessions and a few pictures of him as an adult. One is a portrait of a woman and baby; not me and Enzo, but the next generation. Patrick was a very sweet baby, as his father was before him. I look at the picture of Patrick's mother with interest; the woman who walked into the sea with stones in her pockets when her son was only six years old. She is wearing a scrappy scarf round her neck and her hair falls loosely round her shoulders.

Although her face is covered in smiles, I can't help thinking she has an odd, wild look in her eye.

I am anxious to study the pictures of my Enzo as an adult in the privacy of my bedroom. I have so far managed to swallow my emotions and Beth is diplomatically looking away. Now, with her help, I send a brief email back to Patrick to thank him for his efforts. I beseech him to send me anything else as soon as he finds it.

33

Veronica

FORTUNATELY, SHEETS OF grey rain are blowing across the island today and I am excused from any filming duties. Liam and Miriam are out battling the gales to try to capture some windswept and stormy seabirds, whilst Daisy, having braved the elements to see Petra first thing, is now quietly doing some colouring in her room. Sir Robert has also retired to catch up with his reading, so I am left to my own devices.

In the quiet of my room I gaze at these new photos. As a young man my Enzo looks thrillingly familiar. He resembles me a little, with his defined cheekbones and chin, but his similarity to my Giovanni is striking. I knew Giovanni of course when he was only eighteen, whereas this is a picture of our son in his twenties. His face is fleshed out a little more, but that expression . . . It brings back so completely Giovanni's boundless enthusiasm for life, unvanquished even though he was a prisoner in a foreign land far away from his family. He was quite something.

So, this is the man my baby became. He is quite something, too, standing atop his mountain as if he were king of the world. I used to wonder so often what he was doing. How I wish I could have a conversation with him now. We'd talk all about the life he might have had with me. Doubtless I would never have married; I would never have become the millionairess that, thanks to my caddish but conveniently rich ex-husband, I am today. I would never have afforded a place to live like The Ballahays, and Enzo and I would have been rejected by society for breaking its callous rules. But I would have been happy, and I hope he would too. We would have had each other. He still would have grown into this fine young man I see in the picture, imbued with the McCreedy spirit for adventure. How proud I would have been. Indeed, how proud I am – but also how bitter and jealous and stricken with the aching enormity of my loss.

It is a Madonna and child, in a painting hanging on a convent wall. Fascination draws me closer to look, but as soon as I am within touching distance of the brushstrokes I am whisked away, upwards. Now I am viewing the figures from a great height, but they have stepped out of the painting. They are a real-life mother and baby. Is it me, with my Enzo? No, it can't be. The woman has straggling blonde hair and glasses.

I sit bolt upright in bed. Of course! Electricity has been surging along my neural pathways, making connections. Whilst my conscious mind has been focused on the past, my unconscious one has made links with the present. Terry's words, imprinted on my brain, have filtered through an interpretation process and I have finally realized what is worrying her so. How slow I have been, how stupid!

I should not have needed a dream to tell me the girl is pregnant. There is nothing else that would cause her to write to me like this, to ask me to 'sound Patrick out' about his feelings for her; to implicate that she is leaving for good and enquire whether he'd come back to Locket Island if she were no longer there herself.

I cast my mind back to the day I realized I was with child, over seventy years ago. I was simply terrified. My circumstances were very different from Terry's, however. It was wartime, I was a mere schoolgirl; I had lost both parents and my lover. Being an unmarried mother in those days meant shame and rejection for the rest of my life. My first instinct was to get rid of the baby, but there was no means of doing it – at least nothing I could gain access to – and the child continued to grow inside me whether I liked it or not. I did not like it, not in the least, until the day I gave birth to my Enzo. It was then that everything changed. My heart flooded with love the very moment I first set eyes on him.

Terry is in her mid-twenties, a much more sensible age to have a child, but she will have issues of her own. She will have to sacrifice much if she is to have this baby. But there are always sacrifices involved in being a parent . . . How I wish I'd been given the chance to make those sacrifices.

I switch on my bedside light, locate my glasses, which are thankfully on the table this time, and read her email again.

Jubilant as I am at the prospect of a great-grandchild, I must refrain from premature rejoicing. I fear what she might do. If there's one thing I know about Terry it is this: she will not want to leave the penguins.

Yet if the penguins have taught me anything, it's the importance of family. Because I lost mine, I spent decades in denial of this simple truth. Now I know this: if anything can be done for the sake of your family – anything at all – then you should do it.

A plan is beginning to form in my head.

I am a McCreedy and I must act immediately, before I lose the impetus. I haul myself out of bed, pull on my slippers and wrap myself in my scarlet silk negligee. It is still the middle of the night, but I walk down the corridor to the office with firmness in my step and resolve in my heart.

Two things in this world distress me more than anything: people who should be together who are torn apart, and a baby who is lost. I must do what I can for this baby, my great-grandchild. I helped glue Patrick and Terry together once and will endeavour to do so again, by fair means or foul.

The computer is stubbornly uncooperative, and at first I can see no way of turning the wretched thing on. My own impatience does nothing to help, hindering any clarity of thought. But eventually I locate a switch and the screen springs to life. I click on the 'bookmark' that will bring up my emails and then click on the last one sent by Eileen. I click on the bent arrow at the top and start to type.

Fortune has blessed me with a ready supply of money, so I instruct Eileen to find the very quickest means of

211

getting Terry here and make travel arrangements post haste, regardless of cost. I cannot leave it too long, but as far as I know she should still be safe to fly. From Locket Island it will be much quicker for her to travel to the Falklands than to Britain, for on the world map up on the dining-room wall the distance spans a mere couple of inches. Patrick told me the ship now visits the island once a week. She could travel easily to South America and thence take a flight to Stanley airport. She could be here in less than a week. And by now Eileen must truly be the world expert in booking last-minute flights.

Having dispatched the email to Eileen by clicking on the blue box with utmost efficiency, it only remains for me to contact Terry herself. I find her email and the bent arrow and type my brief but purposeful reply. I present the purchase of her travel tickets as a fait accompli. If I consulted her in the matter, she would no doubt be a slave to her conscience. She would fret about taking advantage of my generosity and other such inconsequential matters.

I am astounded at my own perspicacity in this matter, bearing in mind how little of my life I have spent thinking about other people. I am so struck with wonder that I question whether I am still, in fact, Veronica McCreedy or have somehow transformed into somebody else.

Now that I have taken action, I am feeling less perturbed about the whole thing. Terry is sensible and will surely accept that she must come here to talk with Patrick without delay. I can only hope that they will find a way of stepping ahead into parenthood together.

I close the emails by clicking on the X in the corner.

Then it occurs to me that I should perhaps write to my

grandson as well in the form of a preliminary 'sounding out'. I click on the bookmark again. A fresh email seems to have arrived from Patrick already. I know it is a new one because the title is in bold type. It reads: 'Not good news.'

Unpleasant as this sounds, I have clicked with the mouse before I can stop myself.

Hi Gav and Beth,

Gav and Beth? Have I gone completely bananas? Then it dawns on me that I must have clicked on the wrong bookmark. This is Beth and her husband's email list, not mine.

Still, it was an honest mistake, and now that the message is sitting on the screen in front of me it would be unreasonable to expect me not to read on.

Hi Gav and Beth,

Just had to let someone know I've found this. It's been giving me hell day and night. Can't believe my own dad could have done this, but the evidence seems damning. I don't think I can show it to Granny, can I? She might never get over it.

At least I know why he left us now. Grim.

Hope you are all OK. Will be with you soon in the Falklands, Beth, and will think about whether to break the news to Granny then. Maybe better to pretend that I haven't found anything else and leave her with the happy memories. Ignorance = bliss etc.

Cheers,
Patrick

What? *What?* How dare he keep anything back from me? How dare he share something about my son with his friends when he hasn't even told me about it? And what is it that my Enzo has done? There is a line of blue gobbledygook across the screen starting with the letters 'https', then various colons, forward slashes and joined-up words. I experimentally click on it. A newspaper article pops up, filling the space. Before my eyes is a photo of my Enzo as an adult. The headline shouts at me. The words fly into my brain: KILLER FLEES COUNTRY.

I stare. The paper is dated September 1985. I skim the article, hardly able to take it in. It tells me that a man was found dead on a remote country road, having been knocked down by a car. Joshua Fuller, perpetrator of the hit-and-run crime, was discovered to have flown back to his own country, Canada, before the police could get to him. Canadian authorities had been alerted and were looking for Fuller to bring him to justice.

I read the article one, two, three times. Can this be true? No, it cannot. I refuse to believe it.

But indeed, we know Patrick's father left England very suddenly, never to return. According to the paper, forensic evidence backs up the fact it was Joshua Fuller's car that knocked the man down, the same car that he left in Heathrow's car park when he fled the country. The injured man, meanwhile, had bled to death on the roadside.

I pull myself out of the chair, but my legs don't seem to work properly and I have to sit down again. My thoughts are awhirl. There must be some mistake. I am still muddled as to the Joshua–Joe conundrum. Could Patrick have misidentified his father? I fasten again on the photo, taking in every feature of the man's face. There is the McCreedy jawline, certainly, and I perceive in him something of my own father, something of Giovanni and something of Patrick. Much as I do not wish to believe it, I know without any doubt that this is my Enzo.

As I turn off the computer, the horror begins to sink in. My son didn't call an ambulance, didn't stop to try and save the man's life. Instead he ran away. He left an innocent man to die.

I stumble back to my room, tears blinding me. My limbs will not permit me to hurl myself on to the bed, but I sink upon it in shock. I want to howl, but I mustn't let myself. Daisy is sleeping in the room next to my own. Instead I clench my fists so hard that my nails dig trenches in my flesh and I bite into the pillow, just as I did all those years ago when I was a homesick teenager who had found out my parents were dead. Just as I did when my baby was taken away from me.

My baby. Oh, my baby.

34

Veronica

FOR THE REMAINDER of the night I tussle with the sheets, floundering between disbelief and shock. I excuse myself from my early morning walk with Daisy, saying I have slept badly, which is all too true. She is cross with me because she wants to go and find Petra, but she will have to accept it. I'm sure Beth will take her out after breakfast. For my own part I take tea and a croissant back to my room, desiring nothing more than isolation.

The realization of what my son did seeps into me. It chills and curdles the blood in my veins. I cannot comprehend such an act of cruelty and cowardice coming from anyone, let alone that dear child with the radiant smile who curled his tiny fingers around my thumb.

I think back to my own parents' kindness and their moral guidance; my mother's example, checking in on our elderly neighbour, her tireless work driving ambulances to save lives during the Blitz. My father's words to me: 'There are those who make the world worse, those who make no difference and those who make the world better. Be one who makes the world better, if you can.'

Would Enzo have grown up to be a better person if Giovanni and I had been allowed to raise him? I sit in my room, my croissant untouched, and my mind leaps back over decades. I recall the first time I met Giovanni, when I noticed the way he spoke kindly to the horse that pulled the farm cart. I remember when he held my face in his hands after my parents had died. The expression in his eyes was one of sheer, burning love, sharing in my pain, seeking to comfort me however he could. He hadn't wanted to make love that evening; he thought I was too young, even though I'd lied to him about my age. It was me who insisted.

It is unthinkable that the baby he planted inside me grew into a callous criminal. It must be the adoptive parents who are to blame. If only I could have looked after him, I would have brought Enzo up to be a decent human being. I would have instilled in him the correct moral values and he would have been incapable of such an act.

When I saw the photos of my son before, I wept that I had been deprived of all knowledge of him throughout his life. But at least I was able to build up for myself a model of a kind and brave boy, a son who made my heart swell with pride. Now I have lost that too.

A knock at the door makes me jump. Sir Robert's voice comes: 'Is everything all right, Veronica? You are due to be filming in an hour and a half. If you're not well we can postpone until tomorrow, but I need to let the crew know.'

'I am quite well, Sir Robert, and will be with you shortly,'

I call back through the door, forcing my voice to sound normal.

The mirror reveals my appearance to be distinctly under par. My face is wan and my wrinkles look deeper than ever. They seem to spell out my misery.

I apply foundation in thick layers and daub my cheeks with blusher. I take the eyebrow pencil and draw for myself a pair of strident eyebrows. I add a dark line of kohl around the rims of my eyes, then select my most brilliant ruby lipstick. I am not going to be beaten by this.

I walk out of my room clad in my lilac dress with a gold cardigan and gold shoes to match. My posture is upright, my gait is unfaltering, but behind the bravado and warpaint I feel old and tired and cross; and behind the oldness and tiredness and crossness is utter desolation.

We are transported to today's filming spot in the minibus and, during a conversation about the symbolism of albatrosses, Terry reappears in my thoughts.

I see now that I was wrong in my assumption that all new life is precious. My family history is a catalogue of woes. My beloved parents, smashed to pieces in a bombing. My own miserable life, orphaned, bullied, shamed. Everything would surely have panned out better if I had never had a baby. The man who died on that roadside would still be alive, too. My son must have grown up a tormented soul indeed. As if that were not tragic enough, he left a woman who was so grief-stricken she committed suicide, leaving another child to the cruel hands of fate. And Patrick himself is mixed up and desperate. When I first met him he was on drugs. I had thought he had evened out, but he deserted Terry and the Locket Island team at the drop of a hat, didn't he?

I am furious with the boy for not being honest with me, and I fear for him as well. Unstable as he is, he may turn to drugs again, especially now. Is he responsible enough to become a father? I very much doubt it.

We have arrived. I am positioned on a flattish plain of stone beside a colony of Southern Rockhoppers but today I scarcely even notice them.

'OK, Veronica, we're off,' calls Liam.

I dredge up the words from the dusty shelves of my brain. 'The Rockhopper penguin is aptly named . . .

'The Rockhopper penguin is aptly named . . .

'The Rockhopper penguin is aptly named, for you will observe the incredible strength in . . .'

Sir Robert waves his hands at Liam to tell him to stop filming. 'Take a moment, Veronica. Breathe deeply. Go over the words in your head. You can do this.'

'Of course I can do this!' I snap back. 'I have done it many times. I was just thinking this light is quite poor. We would be better off leaving it till later.'

'The light is fine,' protests Liam. 'It's all looking good.'

'If you want to stop and leave it till later we can, though, Veronica,' Sir Robert insists.

'Not at all,' I answer tersely. 'Be so kind as to continue filming.'

Liam obeys.

'The Rockhopper is aptly named. You will observe the incredible strength in her muscles as she doggedly follows her route over these rocks despite the waves, winds and steep, hard . . .'

I clear my throat and start again.

'The Rockhopper penguin is aptly . . .'

My wretched voice keeps drying up. I try to summon the words to my brain but it is like barking orders at butterflies.

'Come on, Veronica,' Daisy whines, 'the Rockhoppers are *important*. Petra is a Rockhopper.'

I grip hard on my handbag and try again. 'The Rockhopper is aptly named. You will observe the strength in her . . . the strength . . . the incredible strength . . .'

'I think we should do this later,' Sir Robert states, scowling and shaking his head. 'You are tired.'

His patronizing attitude is more than I can bear. Anger churning in my stomach, I spew out the words. 'I do not want to do this later. I do not want to do this at all!'

There is a stunned silence. I erupt into a torrid rant, aimed at Sir Robert: 'You are just using me for your own ends, to make your precious programme more popular. The whole idea is ludicrous and was doomed to failure from the start. You expect to whistle and I'll come, expect me to humbly take it when my name is dragged through the manure by the press, expect me to lay all my own needs and emotions on the altar of your fame. You think that everyone is at your beck and call, just because you are a celebrity. Well, let me tell you something: Veronica McCreedy is made of different stuff. I am not prepared to kowtow. I refuse to be your puppet any more. I am fed up with the whole thing and I want nothing more to do with it.'

Sir Robert is motionless, except for a tuft of his white hair that is lifted slightly by the wind. His expression is unreadable. 'Do you mean to tell me you're resigning, Veronica?'

'Yes, well done. You managed to work it out. Yes, I am resigning,' I tell him, tell them all. Loudly.

Liam looks appalled and takes a step towards me. 'You can't do that.'

I strip the little microphone from my lapel, cast it to the ground and walk off stiffly, throwing the words at him over my shoulder.

'It is looking distinctly as though I just did.'

35

Terry's Pregnant Blog

Here on Locket Island there are, ridiculously and danger-ously, only two people left. One is pregnant by her ex and the other says he loves her. Meanwhile little Eva (or per-haps little Archie) is growing, cell by cell, cleverly developing tissues and organs and becoming just a teeny bit more human every day.

While Mike remains oblivious, Terry wonders how every-thing is going to pan out. Frustrated as ever with the snail-like internet on Locket Island, she has managed to research a few different birthing methods. She is questioning whether it might be feasible for her to have a water birth. This appar-ently helps the body to release oxytocin. More oxytocin from the mother helps the baby release endorphins, so Eva will presumably feel more pleasure and less pain when passing through the birth canal.

Terry is also wondering how her cervix is going to cope.

Of course, this is not the version I publish. I delete it quickly, including the title, and start again.

Terry's Penguin Blog

The Adélie chicks are growing fast. Sleek black-and-white plumage is appearing where the baby fluff used to be, and they are now left in their crèches by both parents for long intervals. The days will start getting darker soon, making it harder for the penguins to fish. As portions of the sea freeze over, the adults and their young will begin their migration north, chasing the sun and searching for feeding sites.

Once the penguins have departed en masse, our work routine normally changes. Fieldwork is focused on the penguins' environment as opposed to the penguins themselves, with studies of the krill they feed on, and the seals and other wildlife of the island. Tasks are more geared towards the lab and the office, maintaining the building and infrastructure.

That's the sort of thing Patrick was so good at.

It isn't known how fast the penguins can adapt their migratory patterns to keep up with environmental changes, especially the decreasing sea ice. We are now using geolocation sensor tags to track some of the penguins, and Pip has been fitted with one. We can only hope he will stay safe.

> Failing to survive the winter migration is the biggest cause of
> death in adult penguins and about a quarter will not return . . .

I have to stop typing. I gulp down some air and rush to the sink. I presume I'm about to throw up but instead just hang there gagging for a while. Mike is working with test tubes in the lab. It's unbelievable he still hasn't guessed I'm pregnant.

We are both pretending his declaration of love didn't happen. At the time I was so astonished I froze, and it took me longer than it should have done to break away from his kiss.

'Well, that stopped you crying anyway,' he said.

'Mike . . . I don't feel that way about you. I can't cope with this now,' I stammered.

'Shhh . . .' He laid a finger on my lips. 'This has been a shock for you. I'm sorry I was angry.'

'You were right to be angry,' I assured him. It was easier to talk about the anger than the kiss.

He shuffled about for a moment. I've never seen him look so awkward.

We spoke together: 'Mike, I—' and 'I didn't mean to—'

We both stopped. I took off my glasses and rubbed them manically.

He stepped away. 'Well, now I know you're all right I'd better be getting back to work. See you later, Terry.'

He was already walking off, becoming a silhouette against the bright snow, one hand raised in a farewell wave.

As I stumbled on through the day I tried to come to terms with this new revelation. My imagination painted out for me the extraordinary scenario of myself with Mike as a boyfriend. Or perhaps it wasn't so extraordinary? I know I can live with him . . . and if the penguin project is folding anyway . . . Mike and I might find a flat together in England. In our newly penguinless lives, we could console each other with dinnertime conversations about penguin poo. Stranger things have happened.

The idea didn't lodge though, for three very good reasons: I don't love him, I am having Patrick's baby, and I could never do that to Charlotte in Cheltenham anyway.

I did have one attempt at talking it through, over dinner, the same day.

'We need to talk, Mike,' I said into the embarrassed silence.

'No, we don't,' he snapped back.

'Don't we?'

He hurled the words out at me. 'I got carried away, OK? I said things I didn't mean. I was upset about this bloody mess we're in with the project, and then you went missing and I was relieved to find you, and you were looking so . . . so . . . My brain just malfunctioned for a moment. I was probably missing Charlotte and I flipped. So can we just drop it, please?'

I felt the blood rising in my cheeks. 'Fine. I just needed to know.'

'Well, you know now. Pudding?'

I held out my bowl and he slapped a wedge of sponge on to it, then added a shoal of tinned peaches.

'Thank you,' I said, relieved. I was severely tempted to add, 'By the way, I'm having Patrick's baby,' and watch how his expression changed, but I managed to stop myself just in time. Patrick must be the first to know.

I linger in the bathroom and do some breathing exercises, counting a slow eight while I inhale, holding it for another eight and then exhaling over sixteen beats. A few repeats and I'm able to return to my blog, feeling calmer. I've realized the vital importance of relaxation for health. Music helps enormously too. I haven't listened to the panpipe CD again because that seems to wind Mike up, but I've dug out some of Dietrich's jazz, which he doesn't seem to mind so much.

Veronica's letter via Eileen has settled my mind a little. She didn't say it in so many words, but I know from the phrasing of the email that she's guessed my secret and she will support me, even if Patrick won't. How wonderful she is! And how reassuring to know that Eva will have a doting great-grandmother, even if her father isn't around for her.

I'm looking forward to meeting Eva. I talk to her sometimes and say how sorry I am that I didn't welcome her properly, with the love she should have had right from the beginning. She is making life difficult for me, yes, but none of this is her fault. She needs me like nobody's ever needed me before. I am her mother and I feel great waves of love rolling out towards her.

I will go to the Falklands as Veronica has arranged. I will tell Patrick because I have to. That might be ugly and painful, but it's the right thing to do. After that, whatever he decides to do, Eva and I can both move on.

36

Patrick

Vancouver

I'M SOAKING IN the bath in the posh silver-plated bathroom of my en suite and I'm thinking hard about my mum.

I have squeezed myself back in time, into four-year-old Patrick's shoes. I am walking back home from nursery with Mum, my hand in hers. It's raining a bit and I've got my hood up, but I tilt up my head and I ask her, 'Where's my daddy?' I've just met a friend's daddy, a dude on a motorbike who was wearing black leathers and took off his helmet and shook out a mane of hair and had a tattoo on his wrist. I am hoping that Mum might be able to produce from somewhere a daddy for me who is just as cool. But her face becomes rigid and she looks straight ahead.

'You have no father.'

She knew, I'm sure of it. She couldn't bear to think

about him and what he did. No wonder she sounded choked up. No wonder she never wanted him mentioned. I get it now. Poor, poor Mum. No wonder she fell apart.

The picture of her holding me is propped up by the taps where I have full view of it. Her face is all made up of laughter. I remember that laughter, which didn't happen that often but when it did it came in wild scattergun bursts.

Memory is a weird thing. Can we ever really trust it? I think I can recall all sorts of things about Mum, but I was only six when she died. Maybe I just clung to tiny fragments of her that stayed in my mind, then added details of my own to fill the gaps. I may even have built up a new mother for myself who no longer resembles the way she actually was.

Yet when I look at that picture, I can conjure several scenes. Like when we pretended to be jousters in medieval England, charging at each other with long carrots. And when I brought her breakfast in bed for her birthday, a slice of blackened toast with inch-thick chocolate spread smeared over it. I wanted so much for her to be happy.

I can see her tying up her hair as well, and putting on mascara. I remember how it made sooty tracks down her cheeks when she cried. Oh God, when I think of how she stuck it out trying to be a good mother to me when she carried that terrible truth with her all the while.

I rip open a ridiculous little package of complimentary scented body wash and tip it over my toes.

This feeling of loathing for my father isn't new. For most of my life I've blamed him for Mum's death. But for some reason, last year, when I met Granny V and Terry and the guys in Antarctica, all the bitterness seemed to stop. I decided to give him the benefit of the doubt: maybe he'd just left Mum and me because he had some kind of personal problem. I thought up a whole string of possibilities; maybe his adoptive parents had got ill or he'd fallen in love with someone else or had a breakdown or something. Hell, I'd thought up nearly every excuse in the book.

I didn't think that he'd killed someone though. Funny. That just never crossed my mind.

The water is getting cold and I'm turning into a prune. I scramble out, fling the ginormous towel around me, and pad back to the bedroom. Snow is splattering against the huge windows.

I don't care that I've just cleaned myself and it's freezing outside, I'm going for a run. I rub myself dry quickly, pull on my joggers and sweatshirt, and pound out into the corridor. I take the lift. The woman on reception, a different one this time, doesn't even look up as I fling myself out into the streets of Vancouver once again.

I sprint along the harbour and into one of the huge parkland areas where there aren't too many people. Some of the trees are evergreen, but most are skeletal, their twigs outlined with snow. Running always helps my stress levels but I'm still feeling shaken when I collapse on to a park bench, panting, unable to go any further.

It would be good to have contact with someone. I emailed Gav and Beth last night because I had to share it and it didn't seem right to blurt it out to Granny. I don't want to give her a heart attack or anything.

I wish there was somebody else I could talk it over

with, somebody who was here right now. There are plenty of people around, locals who look nice enough. I wonder if I could just spill it all out to some random person. It's supposed to be easier to share with strangers, isn't it? I think of Forrest Gump at the bus stop, telling his whole life story to one person after another as they come and sit on the bench beside him. I'd like to do that. A middle-aged, rosy-cheeked woman is passing by with shopping bags. She looks as if she isn't in a hurry and might be a good listener. But she'd think it creepy, wouldn't she? Especially when I got to the bit about my father running a guy down. I can imagine her shuffling away, suddenly consulting her watch and deciding she urgently has to be somewhere else.

There's only one person I can think of in the world who'd understand.

God, how I wish she was here. I can't help it this time. I let myself pull out my phone and open up Terry's penguin blogs. I read them one after the other. There are pictures of Locket Island, looking so . . . so kind of pure, in spite of (or maybe because of) all the penguin poo there is about the place. I see Pip, every feather distinct. And there's Sooty with his little chick. What an odd-looking penguin he is. I flick through panoramic views, the colony from a distance, a black-and-white mottling amongst the rocks with a backdrop of blue mountains. There, on my phone, is the Antarctic sea; there's the lake shaped like a locket hole; there's the volcanic beach. There are the glittering icebergs and there's the snow layered thickly and scattered sparsely, flattened by the wind and driven into great white mounds and cliffs. I see penguins posed in every possible position – diving in the waves, waddling along in a penguin highway, tobogganing on their bellies, sleeping, feeding chicks, involved in courtship ceremonies, pointing beaks to the sky. That girl is obsessed with penguins, but then I've always known that. It's one of the reasons I fell for her. I've been off-the-scale angry at her these last few weeks but today I'd give anything to be able to pull her into my arms.

I read all the blogs she's written since I left. She writes about the new chicks, the crèches. She writes of Pip and his friends, of Sooty and his family, of sightings of Emperor penguins and of changing weather conditions. She mentions Mike and Dietrich a few times. She doesn't once mention me.

She's well rid of me anyway, isn't she? My daddy's a crim. Who knows what *I* might do?

I pull my hood over my head and bend forward, sickness in the pit of my stomach. I wish I'd never seen photos of my dad now. It all went so horribly wrong.

The questions keep gnawing away at me though. He kept that photo of me and Mum for all those years, so it must have meant a lot to him. Did he plan to come back one day and find us? Did he know she committed suicide? Did he ever wonder what I was doing with my life, or try to get in contact? And how did he manage to live with what he'd done?

I bring up that picture of Joe Fuller, looking so happy and triumphant up the mountain with his friend. I can't get my head round the fact this same guy left a man to die on the road. The message written on the back of the photo comes back to me, from Maurice somebody. From the

231

picture it seems like he was close to my dad. He'd be in his sixties or seventies now, most likely still alive. Joe might still have been in touch with him after my birth. He could know something about it . . .

I have a few more days in this country and I can't deal with any more sightseeing. I'll try to track down this Maurice.

I'm a bloody genius to have got Emma's phone number before I left Denise's.

I ring Emma.

Her voice sounds tired but definite. 'Sorry, Patrick. I don't know anything about his friends. I never met him, remember. You'll have to talk to Mom again.'

I ring Denise, not holding out much hope. I catch her in this time.

'Oh yeah, there was a Maurice,' she says slowly. 'It was him that sent the stuff after your father died. They were quite close, I think. They used to do climbing together.'

I press her for Maurice's surname. She ums and ers a lot. 'I'm sorry, honey. It was too long ago, and I wasn't acquainted with him personally. I'm not sure I ever knew his surname, anyway.'

Jeez, nobody fricking remembers anything.

Then she says: 'I think he might have become a writer, later.'

A writer. OK, that's something. I thank her.

I start googling Canadian writers in the seventies and eighties with the Christian name Maurice.

37

Veronica

Bolder Island

I WILL ASK Eileen to book me another flight, a flight that leaves as soon as possible. Most things, in my experience, can be changed, if you throw enough money at them. My first wish now is to be alone at my home, The Ballahays. If I cannot get a refund for the flight I am booked on two weeks hence, then so be it. Pecuniary matters are not uppermost in my mind at present.

I have no wish to shirk responsibility, but I cannot be involved in this filming palaver any more. I am incapable of it. My heart is simply not in it.

I have officially handed in my notice. Beth and Liam both came to me on separate occasions and tried to coax me into changing my mind. Liam even resorted to mild threats and said I had signed a contract with the BBC and was legally obliged to continue. I told him I cared not a whit for the BBC and their stupid contracts.

I have not been out at all since I arrived back at the lodge after my resignation. A quote is floating in the back of my mind . . . something along the lines of 'It is impossible to look at a penguin and feel angry.' At present I do not wish to look at penguins. I need to keep hold of my anger. It gives me an energy and strength that prevents me from entirely giving way to sorrow.

Sir Robert, I note, has not tried to persuade me to stay. He seems to accept my resignation with cool complaisance and continues his own work with yet more diligence than before. Indeed, I have scarcely seen him. My tirade against him may have been rather excessive in its vehemence but I am peeved, not to say rather hurt, by his lack of reaction.

Daisy is fuming at me and won't speak to me at all. She deliberately snubs me and sits at a different table during meals.

To none of these people have I confided my inner dismay. Beth must now have read Patrick's email and will know about our family's terrible secret. She does not let on . . . but then of course she thinks that I know nothing about it.

Patrick, in turn, doesn't know that the girlfriend he left in Antarctica is now carrying his baby.

The crew are out this morning, probably busy trying to make up for the time I lost them yesterday. Only Keith is at the lodge when I leave my bedroom. He is sweeping the hall floor with an oversized broom.

'Hi there, Mrs McCreedy!' he calls. 'Not out filming today?'

'No.'

He is entirely oblivious. The sooner I can remove myself from this establishment the better. I must send Eileen that email. I think I recall how to do it. I bend my steps towards the office. Everything is hushed and the computer is sitting there, waiting for me. I switch it on. With great care I click on the bookmark that is intended for me and not anyone else. My list of emails pops up before my eyes.

There is a message waiting for me, from Eileen.

Dear Mrs McCreedy,

I hope you, Sir Robert, Daisy and the penguins are well. I am still so sorry about that newspaper thing and will never forgive myself. All is well at The Ballahays and the snowdrops are just lovely.

I've received your instructions about Terry travelling to see you in the Falklands and I think I have done it! I got a bit stuck on line but the nice lady in the travel office in Kilmarnock was so helpful. I have emailed the codes and details for all the tickets straight to Terry, just as you said I should. How wonderful it will be to have her and you and Patrick all together among the penguins again! I said to Doug this morning how pleased I was for you all, and said it to Mr Perkins too when I saw him bringing in logs. Perhaps Terry can get in on the filming, seeing as she's good with penguins and so pretty to look at.

The church choir is going well and we have a new piece to learn. Very catchy. I can't stop humming it.

Very best,
Eileen

Well, it is looking as if Terry will be here soon and will at least be able to meet with Patrick. I, on the other hand, will be back in Scotland by then. I wonder for a moment whether I should wait for them both to come before I go, whether I can help in any way. It would be good to see Terry again, and it might be my last chance for a long while.

Still, my presence here is now exceptionally awkward and I am viewed as a traitor amongst the film crew. With a heavy heart I type out my reply to Eileen, asking if she can book me on the next flight back to Britain. I click on the blue box that says 'send'.

Now that the deed is done, I feel a little trickle of relief in amongst the torrent of misery. Once I am back at The Ballahays I can marinate in tea and solitude until I am able to pass as a respectable human being again.

I would like to go for a quiet walk now and breathe some fresh air. But first I feel a grim compulsion to look at my son's life again. All the emails sent to me by Patrick and printed out by Beth are in the chest of drawers in my bedroom. I pull them out and spread them over the bed, casting a glance over the photos of those possessions, those experiences, that face.

When he was my baby, Enzo was the sweetest darling . . . but people change, and I must accept that he did not turn out well. Quite the opposite. I think of the poor man left dying on the road, then think of my dear Patrick growing up as an orphan, his whole life ruined. Anger rises within me and rampages through my blood, demanding action. I fall on the photos with my bare hands and tear them apart, one by one. I rip them into as many pieces as I can – a bit of hand, a piece of brow, a section of knee and foot and eye. When this is done, I screw them up so that they are mere twisted shreds.

If there were a fire here, I would throw them on it. Instead I will go and cast them into the sea. I have no qualms about this. Paper is biodegradable and I cannot believe that the printer cartridge ink will do much harm to the environment. It is a symbolic act and I am in great need of it.

I struggle into my walking boots, stuff all the pieces into the inside pocket of my handbag, take my stick and stride out. I am alone on the path to the coast. My head is throbbing painfully and all my limbs are aching, as if my whole body has aligned with the feelings of my heart. Yet again I have lost everything: my work, my dignity, my friends. Even my most cherished memories are irreparably shattered. Why does life keep persecuting me? How have I deserved this?

I register the colony of Gentoos not far away and their cries, brought to me on the wind, seem to be keening cries of despair.

I progress towards the shore and stand for a while watching the small waves as they scurry back and forth in their white frills and green-blue ruffles. Then the larger waves that mound, curve and curl before they crash. Then the expanse of water that stretches out beyond. It is broad and deep; full of mysterious creatures that bury themselves in the ocean bed or cling to rocks or drift with the currents. Such a multitude of invisible life is out there. The earth and the seas are brimming with it . . . yet I feel so alone.

A solitary penguin waddles towards me across the sand. I am touched. This penguin, at least, doesn't shun my presence. I stoop a little and find that I am saying, 'Hello, hello, little one,' and reaching out my hand, encouraging it closer. It takes a couple of bounds and I see by the band with daisies painted on it that, as I suspected, it is Petra. She stops when she is just a foot away and looks up into my face, her head cocked curiously to one side. I am not close to this penguin as I once was to Pip but I cannot help but be charmed by her.

'Well, this may be the last time we see one another, Petra,' I tell her.

She shakes her whole body then comes a step closer. Her eyes are most expressive. She pads around me then takes a soft peck or two at my stick. I walk on. She hops alongside me.

When I am close enough to the sea I unclip my handbag. I reach for the shreds of paper, grasp a handful and hurl them at the waves. But the little bits of my son are gusted back into my face. I take more out in angry handfuls, bringing my arm back and hurling them out with all my force. The wind is stronger. The pieces swarm around me like confetti of flies, like a snowstorm of black and white; the last fragments of a bad, bad life that I unwittingly brought into this world and wish I never had.

Petra is fascinated and hops after them in a wild dance. She manages to catch one in her beak and promptly gobbles it up.

'Well done, Petra,' I call, my voice a bitter twang.

The shreds are scooped up by the wind, swirled with grains of sand and deposited again across the beach. I am too tired to gather them. They will be sucked up by the tide in due course. I have done what I can.

My eyes are watering so much in the wind that it is a while before I register the two people. The smaller one is racing towards me.

38

Veronica

'Veronica!' It is Daisy's voice. 'You found her!'

I presume she is referring to Petra. I hear my throat make a little grunty noise.

'Been looking for her everywhere. Hey, Petra!' She prances around the penguin for a minute before stopping and looking at the whirling sand. 'What are all those bits on the beach?' she asks.

'Nothing worth bothering about,' I answer, grinding one of the pieces under my foot.

Daisy tips her face upwards to look at mine. She takes me by the hand. Her own hand is tiny as it grasps mine. Her face looks small, too, with her tight woolly hat covering the thin layer of brown hair.

'Don't be sad, Veronica!' It is a command. 'I'm really sorry I was rude to you.'

'Apology accepted, Daisy. But I have reasons to be sad . . .

reasons that I can't tell you about.' I glance out and notice that the other person, who I now perceive is Daisy's mother, has dropped back. She appears to be gathering shells, but I suspect she is giving us a chance to speak together in confidence. Petra, however, is listening intently.

'You're not really going to leave, are you, Veronica?' Daisy sounds upset.

'Yes, Daisy. Yes, I'm afraid I am.'

She is hugging my whole arm now. 'Please don't, Veronica. You mustn't. You need to stay with us here. You need to carry on filming.'

I fasten my eyes on the line where the sky meets the sea. 'Is it so very important?'

'Yes,' she asserts, quite urgently. 'It is.'

'But . . .' I feel so wretched. I can feel tears coming again, spilling out over my cheeks. 'This wind is very bad for my eye condition,' I murmur, pulling my arm away from her and dabbing at my face.

'You *can* carry on and you *will*.' Her voice is hard and firm now, admitting no doubt. 'Remember the penguins!'

How often have I said this to her when she was ill and losing hope? How often have I cited it as a call for courage, fortitude and perseverance? Daisy clung on to the phrase and it helped her overcome long stretches of pain and disability – and she is only a child. I am humbled by her. I am even humbled by Petra, who is tossing her head, her fine yellow feathers like streamers in the wind, her small body surrounded by whipping sand, braced against the blasts. She almost seems to relish the challenge of it all.

'Remember the penguins!' Daisy repeats, louder, noticing that her words are having some effect on me.

What kind of example will I be setting for this child if I give up now?

It is too late, though. 'I have asked Eileen to book me on the next flight home.'

'Well, email her again and ask her *not* to! Quick!'

She starts pulling me back along the path that leads to the lodge. 'Mum!' she screams, and Beth turns round and starts towards us, the wind playing with her hair.

I look at the child once again and, as the last traces of my anger ebb away, clarity returns. My mind is made up. But we will need to hurry.

'Do you and your mother want to run on ahead? Beth knows my email details. You are faster on your feet and will get there quicker without me.'

'Yes!' Daisy punches the air with her fist then runs and fetches her mother, giving a hurried explanation. Beth looks at me quizzically and I nod my acquiescence. The two of them speed back towards the lodge.

I linger for a few more moments with Petra, before – giddy with this change-around – I follow in their wake.

I take a look inward and realize I am pleased to have been persuaded. Perhaps I needed fresh air and a sea breeze to soothe my spirits. Perhaps it was being in close proximity with a penguin that changed my mind. Or perhaps I just needed somebody to beg me to stay.

Still, I do wish that person had been Sir Robert.

39

Veronica

Dear Mrs McCreedy,

I hope you are well. I've been in a bit of a flap because I've had all sorts of emails saying you wanted to come back and then you didn't. The one saying you didn't was from young Daisy and so I thought I'd better check she wasn't having a prank. Please don't worry, though. Me and the lovely lady at Kilmarnock Travel Agents have looked into getting you an earlier flight home and there's one on Thursday if you want, but we haven't booked anything yet in case you don't. Would you be able to let me know ASAP?

   Mr Perkins has trimmed the back hedge. It does look neat.

   Yours,
   Eileen

I email Eileen and tell her that I will be returning on the original flight in two weeks' time and she is on no account to trouble the Kilmarnock travel agent any further.

I consider making a formal announcement to the camera crew at dinner to let it be known I am to resume my reporting and filming duties, but decide it is more appropriate to inform the key members of the team and let word spread organically. The first person to tell is, of course, Sir Robert himself. He does not return from his own filming until late, but I take him to one side immediately when he does.

'Sir Robert, one word with you, please.'

'What is it, Veronica?' His face is set in stone.

'I wish to inform you that I have decided to stay after all.'

He raises a beautifully bushy but disappointingly unenthusiastic eyebrow.

I hasten to reiterate my intentions in case he has not heard me or somehow misunderstood. 'I shall be working for your documentary again, from tomorrow.'

The other eyebrow slowly ascends to the same level as its partner. Both are still lacking any zeal. 'I thought you were fed up with the whole thing and wanted nothing more to do with it. I thought you did not wish to be my puppet any more?'

How exasperating that he exactly remembers those words I spat out at him.

'I was perhaps a little harsh in my terminology and hasty in my decision-making. It is the McCreedy way to be somewhat mercurial,' I explain. 'In any case, it is a woman's prerogative to change her mind.'

'I see.'

His chilly manner leaves me disheartened. I had hoped he would welcome the news with at least a modicum of jubilation. However, he seems weary and unimpressed. He states that he has to go and discuss something with the production manager and leaves the room without further comment.

Beth has informed me of some more unfortunate headlines in the British press:

MCCREEDY MESSES WITH SIR ROBERT
FICKLE MCCREEDY FREAKS OUT
GREEDY MCCREEDY MUST HAVE OWN WAY
HAS MCCREEDY FINALLY LOST HER MARBLES?

I am entirely baffled as to how these scandalmongers have obtained such information, for Eileen assures me she has imparted no news whatsoever since her original gaffe. It is all rather alarming, but one must hold one's head high and carry on.

It has been decreed that the next filming I am to do will be the piece with Daisy for the *I Wish* programme. Petra, it is hoped, will feature largely in this. Beth has been asked to say a few words about her daughter and the scourge of cancer in their lives for the film, but she has declined. I believe she is camera-shy. I, on the other hand, am not. However, I *am* concerned that my sentences will become tangled or dry up as they did before. I may have decided to honour my obligations, but I am still severely traumatized by what I have learned regarding my son.

Daisy and I have resumed our early-morning walks.

She has no idea why I am distant and dolorous and I am never going to tell her, but she helps me practise my (mercifully short) script, going over and over the words with commendable patience.

The day after my declaration that I am staying, I am appalled to find out that Sir Robert is to desert us.

'I did tell you, Veronica, at least twice,' he argues when I express my shock.

'You did not, Sir Robert.'

I will not pretend that I am pleased at this.

'I certainly did tell you, Veronica,' he urges, 'but maybe you didn't hear . . . or maybe you just forgot.'

'I never forget anything.' I am raising my voice now.

He holds up his hands. 'Look, it's only for a few days, to go to South Georgia. I need to get some more footage of Rockhoppers and of Macaroni penguins.'

'But penguins are *my* domain.' I have become quite possessive over them. I feel the colour rising to my cheeks, annoyance imbuing my voice with a cutting edge.

'It is all agreed and travel arrangements are confirmed. I fly out tomorrow. You will stay here with some of the team and do the filming with Daisy for *I Wish*. Your grandson will be arriving anyway, so you have to be here to see him, don't you?'

I do not deign to answer.

40

Patrick

Vancouver

IT HAS TAKEN forever but I think, after about five thousand authors called Maurice, I have him. At least, I've found a book written by a Maurice Timmin from about the right era and it's called *Man and Mountain*. Then there are three later books by the same author, called *Your Rose Garden*, *The Truth about Pruning* and *Roses the Painless Way*.

Now I've got his surname I key in a search for 'Maurice Timmin author' with bated breath to see if I can find pictures. Yes! He appears on my screen straight away: an older, greyer version of the man in the photo with Joe Fuller. It's definitely the same man.

'Got you!' I cry.

Having found the full name, it's easy. I locate him via

his website, where there's a contact page, no sweat, and send him a message.

Hello, sorry to bother you but I believe you knew my father, Joe Fuller, aka Joshua Fuller? I'm in Vancouver now but prepared to travel anywhere.

I'm pretty sure Granny won't mind me chucking any amount of her money at this one. I can decide later how much to tell her, depending on what Maurice says.

Would it be OK to meet up and talk as soon as possible?

And I attach the photo of the two of them up the mountain.

I go to one of the swanky coffee shops that line Coal Harbour and sit drinking cappuccinos, checking my phone every two minutes.

He replies three hours later. Yes, we can meet up. But he lives in Ontario.

It will be quickest if I fly.

I can't stand airports. And I seem to be spending half my life in them these days. I travel light, but the whole check-in and customs business is mind-numbingly tedious. Then all the sitting around waiting drives me nuts. I'm not into reading novels like Granny, and I'm not into duty-free shopping, and I'm so fed up of googling I now hate the bloody sight of my phone.

Life is way too full of arrivals and departures. I'm

knackered now and I'd actually quite like to stay in one place for a while.

I rifle through a rack of British papers at the airport newsagent's and buy a *Daily Mail*. I sit turning the pages, listlessly reading headlines and sipping a plastic coffee. It's all boring and depressing stuff and I can't really concentrate. I wish I could just fast forward time and be at Maurice Timmin's house already.

Then the word 'McCreedy' pops out at me. I do a double take. The headline reads: 'McCreedy and Saddlebow – Lovers' Tiff?' What the hell is Granny up to? *Lovers?* I laugh out loud. At their age! Those journalists are taking the hugest Mickey. I guzzle down the article anyway, dying of curiosity. It says Granny stormed off in a violent rage in the middle of filming. That's pretty bad, if it really has happened. It looks like she's not having the lovely, idyllic time she'd hoped for. I think I might conveniently forget to tell her about her son's crime. I somehow doubt she'd cope.

41

Patrick

Ontario

'Yes, I was close to him.'

Maurice Timmin is smaller than I was expecting. His face is wrinkled and every wrinkle droops as if his skin has never quite fitted him properly. His eyelids sag over pale watery eyes and his chin recedes under a thin layer of grey stubble. He doesn't stand quite upright. As he leads me into the sitting room of his bungalow, I notice his stoop is constant.

The walls are covered with pictures of birds and roses. He sees me noticing them.

'It used to be all mountain scenes,' he tells me, 'but not now. Not since Joe.'

Of course, my father died in a mountaineering accident. I've been so involved in thinking about his crime I'd almost forgotten that.

'You stopped climbing mountains yourself after . . . ?' I ask.

'Yes. I was traumatized by it. I was there, you see, when he fell.'

He waves at a chair and I sit down. It's so big and deep I'm almost engulfed in it, but my host stays standing, propping himself up by clutching the back of another chair. I see he is nervous and emotional.

'You are like him,' he comments, after a pause. He scrunches up his eyes. 'Yes, you could almost be him.'

I frown, not sure how I feel about this.

'Please sit down,' I beg, 'I want to hear everything.'

Maurice has not offered me tea and biscuits like Denise or brief efficiency like Emma, but I have a feeling I'm going to get the truth, the whole truth and nothing but the truth. He does sit down now and fixes me with those hangdog eyes.

'I wrote the book on mountains while he was still alive. We both had this thing about them; reaching a summit or striding along a ridge, breathing the pure air, seeing the world spread out below us – we only felt free when we were high up in the mountains. After his death I could neither climb them nor write about them. I had a breakdown and had to be treated for stress for several years. It's been roses ever since.'

He points out of the window at a rose garden that in summer would probably rival the one at The Ballahays but is now just a thicket of grey, thorny sticks.

I've brought my father's leather file with me. Hoping it will help him, I hold out the picture of himself and Joe up the mountain, then turn it over and show him the message written on the back.

'Ah yes, I sent him that. I thought he'd like the memory. That was taken on a wonderful, bright day up in the Banff region. I remember it well. The two of us with ropes and helmets finding footholds and inching up on to ledges; the spines of mountains all around, the glacial valleys and emerald lakes below. During the last leg of the climb we were high in every sense of the word. Your father kept singing songs at the top of his voice. He was so super-fit he hardly felt the lack of oxygen. A great, determined spirit.'

Granny would say that was the McCreedy genes. All the same, I can't feel proud.

'That was before things started going wrong for him, of course.'

There's a background buzz in the house that must be the central heating system. It seems very loud. I don't want to distress Maurice, but I'm horribly tense and in a real hurry to hear whatever he has to say. I can't quite bring myself to ask about it directly, so I just bring up the page with the newspaper article on my phone and pass it to him.

I'm expecting him to flinch and maybe utter a cry of horror or something, but he doesn't. He just says, 'Ah, yes,' again and looks at me through his sorrowful eyes. This is surreal.

'So . . . you *knew*?' I ask, goggling at him.

He nods. The buzz of the central heating seems to grow louder and louder.

I need to be sure. 'You knew that my father killed a man?'

'Oh no,' he answers, his voice steady now. 'It wasn't your father who killed a man. It was your mother.'

42

Patrick

'MY MOTHER?'

The words punch the insides of my brain.

'I'm afraid so.' Maurice is holding his hands in a tight ball on his knee.

I pull myself up from my chair and stand over him. 'No. No, you've got that wrong.'

He shrinks back and I realize I may have come across as threatening. 'Look, that's not what it says here!' I snatch my phone back from him and wave it in his face.

He blanches and shakes his head. 'That's not the way it was. It's not the truth.'

'Isn't it?'

'I'll explain.'

'I wish you would.' Again, I'm sounding a lot harder than I want to, but this is tough to take.

He swallows loudly.

'Sorry,' I tell him. 'I'm just shocked.' I make myself sit back in the big squishy chair again. 'Please tell me everything. I'm listening.'

'I know you must be close to your mother . . .' he begins. 'But Joe was a good man.'

A low hiss escapes from between my teeth.

He goes on. 'We used to talk a lot, he and I, on those long treks up hillsides and mountains. Walking encourages confidences, I always think. I never seemed to have very much to say about my own life, which was dull compared with his. But he was always having adventures. Parachuting, diving, assault courses, travel to interesting places . . .'

'And one of those interesting places was Britain, I take it?'

'Yes. That was much later than this photo though. When he met your mother he was in his early forties.' He hesitates and clears his throat.

'How . . . how is she?' he asks.

I tell him Mum isn't around any more. He gives his condolences politely but seems almost relieved. I guess it means he can speak about her more freely.

'Fay, her name was, wasn't it?'

I nod, picturing her in that photo with me in her arms. I suppress a great pang of sorrow.

'Go on, please.'

By his face I can see that Maurice has let himself back into the past again. 'He'd had lots of relationships with women by then, of course. He was a handsome and charming man and that kind of thing came easily to him.'

I get the feeling Maurice Timmin was a little envious.

'Not that I'd be in his shoes,' he continues, as if reading my thoughts. 'Not after what he told me.'

'Go on,' I say again. I'm not sure my ears want to hear this but at the same time I'm bloody desperate to know.

Maurice settles into his narration. 'Joe had a whirlwind romance with Fay during a trip to Europe. He told me he was drawn to her especially because of her gypsyish life-style and refusal to conform. He saw her as a fellow free spirit, you see. But in her case that came with a darker side.' He looks at me oddly. 'Did you know she was a drug addict?'

I didn't, but all at once it makes sense.

'Bloody hell.'

'The pregnancy was a mistake, but Joe wanted to do the right thing and stand by her, even though it was a tempestuous relationship and never easy. Together they rented a cottage in the English countryside that was little more than a shack, and he managed to find work as a farmhand to try and pay his way. He missed his life in Canada, but he was hugely proud when you were born.'

My throat suddenly feels thick and I don't trust myself to look into his face any more. I study my knees.

'I'd like to tell you Fay was a good mother . . . and maybe she *was* in some ways. You'll know better than I.'

I can't say anything.

'I'm sorry I can't recall more of the details. I remember Joe said he tried to help her, but she wouldn't help herself. He hoped that becoming a mother would be a strong enough incentive to get her off the drugs, but no. Such a terrible thing to happen to a young woman. Anyway, not long after you were born, she took their battered old car out for a drive. As often happened, Joe was left holding the baby. When she returned it was the middle of the night; she was in a heightened state and talking complete mumbo jumbo. She mentioned hitting a man, but when Joe questioned her she was very vague. He assumed she meant she had physically punched somebody, perhaps in a pub. It was only the next day when the news came out that a man's body had been found on a nearby road that the penny dropped.

'Fay, when she understood what she'd done, was utterly distraught and swore she would never touch drugs again. Joe didn't know whether to believe her or not, but wanted to. Meanwhile the police were going round door to door, making enquiries. Fay had been in trouble with the law once before because of her drug habit, and what's more, their car had been sighted speeding in the area on the night of the hit-and-run. It was only a matter of time before she'd be arrested and sent to prison. Fay was screaming at Joe to help her. What could he do?

'It occurred to him that he could take the blame. He believed he could get back to Canada if he acted quickly, then it would be assumed that he was the guilty party. And that's the course of action that he took, for better or worse.

'The police might have caught up with him before he left the country, but luck was on his side for once. There was confusion about his name. They were looking for a Joe Fuller but the name on his passport was Joshua Fuller, so he managed to slip through controls before they realized. Once he was back in his own country, he destroyed the passport and lay low, changing his name again. He didn't even feel able to visit his own parents because they might inadvertently have given him away. He did turn up at my door though, a few years later. We resumed our friendship and our mountain climbing, and his story slowly came out.'

'God,' I murmur. 'Oh God.' I'm beginning to see both my parents differently now. I'm beginning to realize Mum's suicide wasn't so much desperate loneliness as desperate guilt.

It still doesn't quite make sense though. I force my brain to cooperate and try to join the dots.

'But couldn't he have stayed and stood by us both?'

'Remember the situation. He was a foreigner in England; his real home was here. He was energetic and driven, not the sort of man who could endure being locked up for years. Would *you* – for something you hadn't done?'

He doesn't wait for me to answer. 'And he couldn't bear to see Fay – a young mother, terrified and repentant – facing a long prison sentence either. He knew nothing about the British legal system, but he suspected, too, that you would be taken away and put into care as soon as she was proved guilty. He wanted you to have a mother.'

'Well, that worked out well then, didn't it?' I say bitterly. 'If he had stayed, Mum might still be alive now.'

I tell him briefly how she died, tell him that I was brought up by foster families and only recently discovered Granny V.

'Oh my dear boy, I am so very sorry. I have kept all this to myself for all these years because I presumed Fay was alive and well, and not wanting any accusations or legal cases coming her way. I thought you were OK too.'

I bite my lip. 'Hardly.'

His face creases up for a moment. He frowns at his hands as they twist in his lap.

I try to push it down, but the emotion just keeps forcing its way up again and now I'm bawling openly, bawling my eyes out like a kid.

Maurice must think I'm wetter than an otter's pocket. Mind you, he seems to be competing with me on the wetness front. Fat tears are rolling down his cheeks and into his stubble, where they settle like quivering beads.

'Once again, I can only say how sorry I am. But I can tell you this. He only knew you for the first week of your life, but he talked about you a lot. He did love you.'

'Love me?' I growl. 'He could have found me if he'd tried hard enough. He could have made contact somehow.'

Maurice is insistent. 'He tried to ring your mother, many times, but she must have moved house. I imagine she couldn't afford to stay where she was. She didn't let him know where she'd gone, and, of course, he could never go back to England himself with no passport.'

I remember the caravan a little, and the council house that was our home for a short while afterwards. Mum would have been hard to track down, for sure.

'He might at least have written,' I argue. 'Somebody would have forwarded a letter, surely?'

Maurice shakes his head. 'But he couldn't.'

'What?'

'He couldn't write. He never learned how. He somehow slipped through the school system, paying a schoolmate to do his homework for him, flunking exams. He was what we'd describe today as severely dyslexic, which is why he struggled with it so much. These days he'd be given all sorts of assistance to help him along, but not much was known about the condition in the fifties and the teachers just thought he was slow. He only ever learned to recognize a few words. That's why he changed his name from Joshua to Joe. He couldn't avoid writing his own name from time to time and "Joe" was so much shorter and easier.'

I think of the J he drew as a schoolboy in the spiral and put up on the wall. Probably so that would help imprint on him how to write it. I understand even more now why he decided to escape back to Canada. How hard it would be for an illiterate guy from a different country to deal with all the bureaucracy of the British courts. He'd run away knowing the blame would be attached to him for ever. He did it for Mum, and for me.

43

Veronica

Bolder Island

MY POOR PATRICK. I see from the greyness around his eyes that he has been just as traumatized by the recent discoveries as I have. Perhaps even more so. I hope that over the coming days the sunshine and the presence of penguins will help him relax. It is important that he has recovered a little by the time Terry arrives.

I have, of course, disclosed nothing to him of Terry's pregnancy or the fact that she will be here in another week. It is enough for him to try to accept the news that his mother was a criminal – and not, as previously believed, his father. Of his two parents, it is his mother that he remembers, knows and loves. He is still in a state of extreme shock. We McCreedys feel things strongly and I know that poor Patrick will carry the scars for the rest of his life.

When my grandson reported the astonishing revelations of his meeting with Maurice Timmin I was utterly agog. Thankfully I was sitting down at the time and he had brewed me a good strong pot of Darjeeling. It was evening, he had returned from a brief tour of the island led by Daisy, and everyone had left us together on the veranda for a little catch-up. Yet again I had to realign the history, replace misconceptions with fresh facts. I will confess it took me some time to take it all in. But afterwards I felt quite overcome with relief.

Patrick was burrowing his fists into the corners of his eyes. 'Now I get why my dad ran away . . . but I still bloody wish he'd found a way of coming back, of being with me when I was a kid.'

'I wish he'd found a way of being with me, too,' I confessed, gazing into my tea. 'There are often reasons for running away, but sometimes there are also very strong reasons for going back and trying again.'

I let this thought penetrate for a few moments. We have both done our share of running away recently.

'It seems odd that my Enzo, with his privileged upbringing, never learned to read or write.'

'Yup, I know,' he answered. 'But Beth tells me that she worked in adult literacy for a while and you wouldn't believe how many people can't, even these days. And with dyslexia it must have been extra hard.'

I considered the J my son drew as a boy, and it filled me with inexpressible sadness. If I had been allowed to raise him, I would have taught him myself, going over every letter again and again, as many times as he needed. I am not the most patient of people, but I would have given him this gift, no matter how long it took. I would have sent him to the best school I could find, no matter how poor we were. I would have been a good mother to him, I know it.

'I wish I had kept the pictures you so kindly emailed,' I told Patrick miserably.

'Didn't you keep the print-outs? What happened to them?' he enquired.

'I tore them up and threw all the bits to the sea.'

His eyes widened in surprise. 'Just as well I've got them here, then.' He tapped his phone.

I am very grateful for this. I will ask him for fresh print-outs and frame the best ones in gilt for the mantelpiece at The Ballahays. If anyone comes to the house and sees them, Eileen can confidentially tell them: 'Oh yes, that was Mrs McCreedy's son. Such a brave soul. Such a tragic tale.'

For although he never made his way back to us, my dear son, my darling Enzo, has been resurrected again in my heart as valiant and true. Indeed, to take the blame for a heinous crime in order to protect the mother of his baby is, to my mind, nothing short of heroic. If only I could take him in my arms and hold him close and tell him how proud I am.

Patrick is less convinced of his father's heroism. After we discussed everything, he told me, 'I'm still finding it hard to accept that he ran back to Canada. But I can tell you this, Granny: never, never will I touch drugs again.' His voice was forceful and I heard the ache in it, and the resolution. 'Nothing can induce me to go anywhere near the stuff now I know what happened with my mum, how it wrecked so many lives – the guy she ran down, hers, Dad's, mine . . .

I dabbed my eyes and told him I was glad. 'We shall make a man of you yet, young Patrick.'

'Thanks. That's kind of you, Granny.'

The morass of feelings that were broiling within me has begun to settle. My equanimity has been sufficiently reclaimed. Were it not for my argument with Sir Robert and my concerns about Terry and Patrick, I would recommence my filming duties with great verve. Sir Robert is still away filming on the island of South Georgia. His manner with me at his departure was distinctly frosty.

At least I shall soon be seeing Terry again. Her presence invariably has the effect of lightening and cheering people. It is a gift she has, although she doesn't realize it. I imagine she must be very stressed at present. Nevertheless, I have high hopes that she and Patrick will resolve their issues and embark together on the marvellous adventure of parenthood. Meanwhile, I myself will be able to embark on the marvellous adventure of great-grandmotherhood.

In the evenings Patrick has been telling Daisy more and more about life on Locket Island: the snowy adventures, the blizzards, and the problems trying to keep everything working at the run-down field centre. Her eyes glisten and she never tires of hearing about the Adélie penguins, especially our dear Pip. Patrick talks about Mike and Dietrich and the team in general, but he never mentions Terry by name. I am surprised that Daisy has left off quizzing him, bearing in mind how keen she was to hear wedding bells. I am the one who is hoping for them now.

I wonder if Patrick misses Locket Island life. He must

do, surely, at least a little? It's hard to gauge how much. When I read Terry's penguin blogs I myself am frequently assailed by sharp longings for the place. For him it almost classified as home.

It strikes me that I still don't know my grandson very well at all. I find him hard to read. He has revealed the truth about his father but does not confide his feelings in me as I had hoped he would. However, he seems to get on well enough with Beth. She is the wife of his former employer and friend, Gavin, so I presume they talk about the bicycle shop and mutual acquaintances in Bolton.

What I have noticed is how excellent Patrick is with Daisy. He is a great big strong man who can take her on his shoulders and fling her around until she crows with laughter. I believe she misses her daddy and he is the next best thing.

'Did you hear the one about the small, shy pebble?' he asked her yesterday, having set her on her feet again.

'No, tell me about the small shy pebble,' she commanded.

He delivered the line with panache. 'He wished he was a little boulder.'

I was glad to note that, despite his problems, Patrick's humour remains unshakeable and as cheesy as ever. Daisy looked confused, however. 'A little bolder? Like the name of this island?'

'Yes, but it also means braver.'

'Oh,' she said. She thought about this for a minute then asked: 'So how's that a joke?'

'Well, *boulder* is a name for a great big rock.' He was beginning to look exasperated.

'So the little pebble wanted to be a brave great big rock?'

'Yeah, you got it!'

She wrinkled her nose. 'I don't see why that's funny. Because pebbles don't grow into rocks. It's the other way round. Rocks turn into pebbles by grinding against each other in the sea, Sir Robert told me. So the poor little pebble will get smaller and smaller, not bigger. He may even become a grain of sand one day. He'll never, ever get his wish. It's actually really, really sad.'

'You are hard to please,' Patrick grumbled, putting his hands in his pockets.

Nevertheless, Daisy has made a friendship bracelet for him, which, I note with interest, he does actually wear. I can perceive potential father material in him. He is approaching the age of thirty, after all, which would imply (I would hope) a degree of maturity. On the other hand, this is Patrick we are talking about.

44

Veronica

'MY DEAR VIEWERS and fellow penguin fans,' I begin. I had originally intended to use the word 'admirers' rather than 'fans' but have been instructed to dumb down and use words with fewer syllables. The reason given for this is that we are currently filming for *I Wish*, whose audience tends to be families with young children and they might not understand me otherwise. I disagree with this philosophy, bearing in mind Daisy comprehends me perfectly well; and indeed, how is the younger generation expected to improve their vocabulary when given nothing interesting to aspire to? Be that as it may, I am elated that I am to feature on this programme in addition to Sir Robert's and therefore I am willing to compromise.

'My dear viewers and fellow penguin fans, I am Veronica McCreedy and I am eighty-seven years old. Allow me to introduce you to a particular friend of mine. Her name is Daisy.'

Here the camera swivels to focus on Daisy, who waves and smiles broadly. 'Hello everyone. I am Daisy and I am nine years old. Allow *me* to introduce you to a particular friend of mine. *Her* name is Petra.'

The camera swings down and focuses on Petra, who is tucking into a piece of fish with which she has been carefully bribed.

It is my cue. 'We do not know Petra's age, but we know she is a Rockhopper penguin who lives here on the coast of Bolder Island, in the Falklands.'

Daisy is beaming with pride. She launches into an enthusiastic improvisation. 'Rockhopper penguins are my favourite penguin, now. It used to be Adélies, especially Pip. Pip is another of Veronica's friends who lives in Antarctica, and I love him too . . .'

'Cut!' shouts Liam. 'None of the Pip business, please. Too confusing for the viewers. Stick with Petra, if you don't mind, Daisy.'

We start again. By take five we manage to pass our sentences to each other seamlessly. Daisy achieves her little speech about how she found Petra and gives a few salient Rockhopper facts: that the species is pretty, strong and possesses incredible 'bounceability'. (As she puts it. Although this is a word of considerably more than one syllable, the crew seem to like it. Daisy can get away with anything.)

It is good that we have required several takes because Petra is now providing a very picturesque scene. She is admiring her reflection in a shallow pool left behind by the tide. The upside-down Petra, backed by a blue sky, touches beaks with the right-way-up Petra. Both of them are fascinated. You can clearly see every detail held on the surface of the water: her bright, inquisitive face, her yellow eyebrow tufts and, around her slightly uplifted left flipper, the pink friendship band with daisies all over it.

'Yes, look at yourself, Petra. See how beautiful you are!' Daisy enthuses.

Petra lifts her head and Liam manages to capture a little Daisy–Petra dance as they chase each other round in circles quite charmingly. Even better, their antics have attracted the attention of another penguin who waddles across from the other side of the beach to see what's going on. His outline is stout and we know by the sunflower shade of his long crest that he is a Macaroni.

First he loiters a few feet away, looking on, then he can't resist joining in the dance. He dips his head and starts running in Petra's wake, his feet slapping the sand, his flippers slightly back. Delighted, Daisy skips round them both. Suddenly Petra stops, becoming aware of the new penguin behind her. He stops too. She arches to look at him, first over her right shoulder then over her left. She slowly turns right round to view him properly. He stands there, looking a little awkward, his flippers drooping slightly. She advances. He backs off, then turns and flees. She is now chasing him. Daisy creases up with laughter. It is the funniest thing I have seen for years, and the laughter grabs me by the stomach and blasts out through my lungs. What a welcome release that laughter brings.

*

Daisy is bursting to tell her mother and Patrick about the Macaroni when they return from their walk. They listen to her enthusiasm with smiles.

Patrick, who has become quite the expert on the subject of penguins, is particularly interested. I inform him that Macaronis and Rockhoppers often share breeding sites and mingle socially. Sometimes they even interbreed.

'It's cute when different species make friends like that, isn't it, Daisy?' comments Patrick.

'Yay!' she exclaims. 'Soooo cute. What shall we call Petra's pal?'

I suggest the name Ptolemy but Daisy frowns. I suppose it is too much to expect her to be acquainted with the philosophers and astronomers of ancient Alexandria.

Patrick also proffers a suggestion. 'I think he's a Tony. Tony the Macaroni!' He says it in a droll Italian accent that immediately reminds me of my Giovanni.

Daisy, as a huge fan of both rhyming and funny accents, pounces on his idea. 'Yes,' she agrees at once. 'That is his name. Tony the Macaroni.'

Most days, whilst we are busy filming, Patrick goes out with Beth. They partake in the more energetic brand of walks that Sir Robert and I, in our relative decrepitude, have not been able to manage.

Sir Robert and I? Alas, I fear I do not even belong in the same sentence as my favourite knight. It appears I have lost his goodwill for ever. He has now returned to Bolder Island, but he is still being decidedly offish.

'How was your time on Saint Georgia, Sir Robert?' I

enquired politely when the crew welcomed him back to the lodge.

'It's South Georgia, not Saint Georgia,' he answered with an air of displeasure.

He did go on to tell me more about it, however. He informed me that the penguins there are filling just about every square inch of land in some areas. He and Miriam were lowered down on winches into the middle of the colony from a helicopter in a strong wind so as to capture the stunning vista and report from the centre of the action. Much as I resent his having taken over some of the penguin reporting, which I consider to be my speciality, I would be reluctant to be winched from a helicopter on a piece of rope during a strong wind. Indeed, under such circumstances I might have dropped my handbag on to the unsuspecting penguins beneath, which would have been upsetting in more ways than one.

Sir Robert has shaken hands with Patrick and welcomed him with cordiality, but conversation does not flow. Patrick probably didn't help matters by introducing himself as 'bum turned penguin-researcher turned bum again'.

I could see how unimpressed Sir Robert was by this. The two of them have little in common other than the passion for wildlife that we all share.

It is incumbent on me to inform Sir Robert of Terry's forthcoming arrival on Bolder Island. I take him aside after dinner and tell him in confidence, warning that he is on no account to mention it to Patrick.

'I am hopeful that their meeting will be *productive*,' I add rather mysteriously. I cannot divulge more than this.

Sir Robert's mouth turns down. 'This is not a free-for-all for your friends and family, Veronica,' he tells me sternly. 'It was agreed that you would come on tour. We then added Daisy to the trip – fair enough. And her mother had to come – also fair enough. But you insisted that your grandson should join us – and now Terry too? I respect Terry but this is not fair on the crew or on Keith. You are messing everyone around, Veronica.'

I feel defensive and upset. I have had few friends during my long life but I would certainly have classified Sir Robert as one of them. I also know from experience that friends, like the milk of human kindness, can turn sour. They can abandon you when you need them most and act more cruelly than you could have imagined.

Sir Robert's words sear deep, and not least because they make me question myself. Am I really messing everyone around? Should I cease to interfere, stand back and just let events play out as they will? Am I, as Patrick would say, a 'control freak'?

I am assailed by self-doubt and badly in need of tea. Thank goodness there is an urn of boiling water ever ready in the dining room. I make a pot of Darjeeling as my mind meanders along philosophical paths. We are not really at home in this world, this mass of human limitations, where we are forever pretending to be something that naturally we are not: where we strain towards an ideal and are always falling short.

When I thought my son was a lowlife of the worst order, my emotions temporarily paralysed me and rendered me incapable of work. I despised, as I have always despised, any sign of weakness in myself and I was

271

repulsed by the potential pity of others. Yet now I see that unfortunate episode was another instance of my 'messing everyone around' . . . And, in the process, I was making a complete fool of myself.

Few things are harder to accept than my own inadequacies.

'What's up, Granny?'

Patrick has bustled in and noticed my woebegone expression.

'I was merely contemplating what an unpleasant and troublesome human being I am.'

He lays a hand on my arm. 'It seems like you're more tolerant and forgiving of other people than you used to be, Granny. How about you start being a bit kinder to yourself? It's OK to fail sometimes. It really is. I do it all the fricking time.'

'This is true,' I answer thoughtfully.

45

Patrick

Bolder Island

GRANNY IS BEING erratic. One minute she's smiling serenely and the next she looks like she's sucking on a lemon. She's always at her best when she's with Daisy, I've noticed, so it's good that the two of them are working together. Sir Robert seems to have pretty much abandoned her and is doing his own thing. Arrogant git.

I can't help liking Bolder Island. It's soothing to feel warm sunshine again, good to see green hills and blond beaches, strange to hear bleats of sheep mingling with the trumpeting calls of penguins. The penguins are both a painful reminder and a real treat. The impulse to count, weigh and tag them is ingrained in me now and I keep catching myself observing all the little nuances in their behaviour.

I'm glad I didn't go straight back to Bolton after all. It means I can put off any decision-making too, which is just as well. When I think about my parents, I feel like I'm disintegrating piece by piece. Thank God Daisy's here to keep my mind off it all.

'I know what you should have,' I tell her as a group of us are walking back to the lodge one morning, a cheeky wind gusting us forward.

'What should I have?' she asks, all ears.

'A kite.'

'She had one,' Beth tells me. 'It crashed on the rocks and got torn.'

Daisy's keen to give me all the details. 'Yes! It was a good one. It was big and really fluttery and orange. When it crashed we found Petra, so that was fantastic and I'm not sorry. But I do miss it a lot.' She looks a bit miffed now.

'What I'm thinking is that I could make you a new one.'

She is so thrilled at this idea she stops and bangs me on the knees.

'Ow, don't do that!'

'It means I'm happy,' she cries. 'Can you really make me one?'

'Sure. What colour should it be?'

She thinks. 'Yellow. No, green. No, purple.'

'I'll see what I can do.'

I have a scout around and manage to find coat hangers, string and bamboo canes in and around the lodge and outhouses. I ask Keith if he's got a toolkit and any light, durable fabric going spare. He has. I think we can do this.

It takes me a full day and a bit of ingenuity but soon we have it. A big, diamond-shaped kite, which I hand over to

Daisy to colour as she wishes. She spends the next morning painting it all over with blobs, swirls and hearts. We tie on a long, purple tail.

'Ta-da!' she cries, showing it to Granny.

'My goodness, Daisy. What a splendid achievement!'

Out of Daisy's hearing, Granny later describes it as 'a hideously gaudy creation', but she is just as interested as I am to see if we can get it to fly. Luckily conditions are perfect here on Bolder Island, with a good wind coming off the coast. It's great to see Daisy running along the beach, with our mad, multicoloured kite flapping in the sky above her. It may be the lack of trees here, but the sky seems extra-huge. I do feel, looking up, that I could drown in it.

After jolting the kite all over the place, Daisy comes back, breathless and beaming. Even Sir Robert, who has made a rare appearance to be with us and watch, seems impressed.

He smiles down at her. 'From a distance it looked like a bird, the way you made it swoop like that.'

Liam has managed to catch Daisy on camera with a troop of curious penguins scuttling at her feet and the kite prancing along in front, its long tail looping.

'The *I Wish* people are going to love me for this,' he mutters. 'And of course, you,' he adds to me as an afterthought.

It's great to be with people again. That Keith is a good bloke and most of the crew seem OK. They're all pretty busy though. Beth is at a bit of a loose end, like me. I've known her for years through Gav, but never had much of a chance to talk to her. Because Beth and Gav share an email address, she already knows what happened with my dad and my mum, and how I found out about it.

'I can only imagine how awful this must be for you,' she commented quietly to me the evening I arrived.

Daisy is spending a lot of time helping Granny with her words and doing the filming, so Beth and I have decided to get out and see some of the Falkland sights together. These islands are curious. They're three hundred miles from Argentina and eight thousand from the UK, yet they feel oddly British. According to Keith, the cultural sights are mostly to do with the 1982 war: a Margaret Thatcher bronze bust, the Argentine military cemetery, various other memorials and a totem pole created by military personnel. There's also a shipwreck, a lighthouse, a small cathedral and a museum or two. But of course, the best thing of all is the wildlife. To get about we can use the eight-seater planes that run a pretty good service, although they're not always predictable.

As we explore, my feelings start to spill out to Beth. She's an amazingly good listener, even better than Gav. It helps to get everything out in the open.

More and more little details about my mum are trickling back. And I see how I've been unconsciously twisting and moulding my memories to fit into what I assumed was true. For my whole life I've seen my mother as somebody who was treated badly by my dad, abandoned with a tiny baby, penniless and prone to depression, whose sorrows were too much for her to bear. I saw her as the blameless victim, him as the villain. Now the memories are starting to untwist. I see guilt in her face, in her actions, in her tears.

'I know what Mum did was an accident, but to let him take the rap and never admit any responsibility . . . That's the hard thing to accept. And to leave *me* thinking all my life that he abandoned us. Why couldn't she tell me what he did for us?'

'But you said you were only six when she committed suicide,' Beth reasons. 'Far too young to be told any of it.'

'OK, point taken. But she could have written it all down and left it in some solicitor's office for me to open on my twenty-first birthday or something. *She* wasn't dyslexic. *She* could write perfectly well.'

'Don't be too harsh on her,' Beth advises. 'You can't know what it was like for her. She had a lot of demons to deal with. I'm sure she did what she thought was for the best. Most people do. They may be wrong, but they're *trying* to be right.'

'I suppose so,' I admit. Unlike Beth, I always leap to judgements. I take a swift, admiring look at her. 'How come you're so fricking positive the whole time?'

She just smiles and shakes her head as if such things are beyond my understanding.

46

Patrick

East Falkland

WE'RE ON EAST Falkland, the largest of these islands, which, with its population of over two thousand people, is a positive metropolis compared to Bolder Island. The whole crew came over today. While the others were busy, Beth and I took a tour of the marine and military monuments of Stanley, had a nosey round Christ Church Cathedral and its famous whalebone arch, then had a swift pint in one of the inns. We've finally got to Volunteer Point. I thought the filming would be finished by now, but no; Granny is still spouting her stuff, surrounded by her human entourage plus a massive array of King penguins.

'Shall we take a walk along the coastal path?' Beth suggests.

'Yes, let's.'

We walk and talk. As we top a green shoulder of land we pause to look out at the horizon. The land is rugged, with hairy clumps of grass and wildflowers and bright yellow mounds of gorse. We can still hear the distant honking of the penguin colony. The sea is washing beneath us; huge breakers have become small white combs in the streaked water. This landscape is stunning, in a completely different way from Antarctica. I think how many thousands of miles I've travelled over the last few weeks. Although I am closer to it again geographically, Locket Island seems further away than ever.

Suddenly I'm blabbering to Beth about Terry. I mention past girlfriends and how I seem to fall for a woman fast and deep. How I get obsessive and soppy. But how, with Terry, I'd felt something different. How I could look at her with my male lust and my Patrick gooiness and that was one thing, but how I could also step out of these and see all her qualities shining through, her incredible strength and goodness . . . and the awesomeness of anyone who could live out there and do what she does. Yes, Mike and Dietrich do it too, but Mike's odd and hard, let's face it, and Dietrich keeps going away to spend time with his family in Austria. But Terry . . . I can see her staying out there for ever. She loves it that much.

'More than she ever loved me,' I tell Beth, aware that I'm sounding pathetic and childish.

'You don't know that,' she answers. 'I bet she did love you, but was just finding it tricky as boss of the team, and the only woman out there. I expect she was struggling to run things well because of all the budget problems. With your clinginess, you probably weren't helping either.'

'Do you think? Mike reckoned she was only with me because of Granny's funding.'

Beth stops, surprised. 'Well, he must have been jealous and said that out of spite. She doesn't sound like that sort of a person to me. I'm sure she'd be completely horrified if she knew you thought she was so devious and grasping.'

When she says it like that, I see that she's right. Nobody could be *less* devious and grasping than Terry. It was my own paranoia and insecurity that made me believe that.

'I'm not much of a catch, am I?' I mutter gloomily.

Beth laughs. 'Oh, come off it, Patrick!' Then she sees how much I mean it. 'If you really need me to say it, I will. You *are* a good catch. You can take it from me. You've had a tough background and that's affected you, but you're good-hearted and fun to be with. Those are important things for a woman.'

'Go on.' All compliments are welcome here, any time.

'Well, you're sensitive which, believe it or not, is something we like. Macho is outdated and dull. We like men who feel deeply and aren't ashamed of it.'

I'm not sure how to answer that one. I could do with feeling a lot less, to be honest.

'*And* you're good-looking,' she adds, briefly scanning my features.

'Why, thank you! Not so bad yourself.'

She gives a little curtsey. I said it as an automatic reaction but now I notice her liquid brown eyes and I realize it's true. When I saw her in Bolton she always seemed terribly thin and waif-like, almost transparent. And her face was etched with worry lines. But now her skin is sun-kissed and she's somehow more solid – in a good way. Totally different. How happy a person is makes a hell of a difference to how they look; I've noticed that. I guess she must be relieved about Daisy.

I realize how crass I've been to go on and on about myself when this woman has been through her own nightmares, which I can't even begin to imagine.

'Daisy's getting on OK now, isn't she?' I begin.

'Oh yes, she's loving every moment of her time here, largely thanks to your grandmother. It's wonderful that she's made her very own penguin friend too. I don't know how she'll part with Petra when we go back.'

'I expect she'll order Keith to send her weekly updates. He'll probably do it, too.'

She chuckles. 'Yes, I expect so. She's good at getting her own way.'

I try to use my sensitivity that she likes so much and ask about the history of Daisy and her diagnosis. 'Oh, you don't want to know about all of that,' she replies, shaking her head sadly.

'I do.'

So she tells me the full story, which I never learned from Gav, although I'd kind of gleaned bits of it. It all began with Daisy suffering from pain three years ago, pain that went on and on. They were told various conflicting things by doctors, who finally offered a misdiagnosis along with a series of medicines which didn't make any difference at all. By this time the poor child could hardly walk. She was needing painkillers and hot water bottles the whole time. She cried through the night and was exhausted. She had to take weeks off school.

Beth tells me about the day they learned the dreadful truth, how she couldn't stop weeping and just wished she could take the disease herself, rather than see her daughter suffer any more.

'Cancer is a hideous thing in anyone's lives,' she sighs. 'When it affects a child it is a monster.'

She describes the treks to hospitals, the endless waiting in the ward after biopsies and scans and chemo. She tells me how Gav, being a very earnest Christian, assumed everything would be OK if they just kept praying, and she tells me how she got frustrated sometimes with his attitude. How she cried again when Daisy first lost her hair. She tells me about all her anxiety for Daisy's little brother Noah as well, who hasn't had anything like as much attention as he deserves.

Jeez, when I was working with Gav at the bicycle shop I was so bloody clueless. I knew the family had problems but never understood the agonies they were going through. I guess everyone has stuff going on that you don't know about, hidden strains and stresses; only some people make far more noise about it than others. I'm beginning to wonder if it's the ones who make less noise who are suffering the most.

My respect for Gav's whole family has gone through the roof. But especially for Beth, who has borne everything so quietly and bravely.

47

Veronica

East Falkland

TODAY WE ARE at Volunteer Point, which is the site of almost the entire population (1,500 breeding pairs) of the Falklands' King penguins. I am again reporting for Sir Robert's programme and he has graced us with his presence. I have not covered myself with glory, having stumbled rather badly through the first hour of filming. We are now on a break. The sun is shining, and my grandson and Beth have decided to leave us to it.

'Why do Patrick and Mum keep going off together?'

I gaze out at their two backs as they walk away from us and wonder the same thing myself.

'I expect they have a lot to talk about, Daisy. Bicycles and Bolton and whatnot.'

We are surrounded by King penguins. These good-looking birds are the most stately species of penguin I have seen. They are tall, the second largest penguin in the world after the Emperors, and they have the most exquisite markings. Whilst their backs and flippers are sleek silver-grey, their heads are an immaculate midnight-black save for the beautifully contrasting crocus-yellow strip at the base of their beaks and on their cheeks. The yellow recurs at their throats and melts paler and paler into the snowy plumage of their chests.

Their chicks, on the other hand, manifest none of their elegance. They are bulging bears with thick brown fur, small heads and big feet that stick out comically at the bottom. It is hard to believe they are real. Many of them are losing their baby down and sport little scraps of fluff around their collars or random patches on their heads and chests. They are a cross between their younger teddy-like relatives and their glamorous parents.

To enhance the scene's aesthetic appeal and to complement the colours of the Kings, I have today abandoned my favoured scarlet and ruby shades and am wearing a bright amber cardigan over a blue corduroy dress. My handbag is matching amber patterned with silver rosebuds.

'OK, we're rolling,' calls Liam.

I inform my viewers that the Kings' breeding cycle is the most complicated of all the penguin species. Parents are only able to raise two chicks in any three-year period, partly because they take a year off after all the efforts of parenting. Only one egg is laid each season. Like the Emperor penguin, the Kings do not build nests; instead parents balance the egg on their feet and incubate it in a 'brood pouch'.

From April to August (winter here) the chicks will stay on land whilst both parents are away at sea, sometimes travelling hundreds of miles in their quest for food.

Except that I don't say 'quest for food'; I say 'quest for love' by mistake.

I glance over at Sir Robert, clear my throat and start again.

I manage better this time. 'With their parents visiting the colony less frequently, the young penguins can lose up to half their body weight. It is not surprising the juveniles are looking so podgy now. They will need all their reserves in the months to come.'

Liam now homes in on the undeniably beautiful plumage of a single bird.

'These penguins are as stunning as any I have yet seen,' I tell my viewers. 'The gorgeous yellow colouring on their heads and throats is used to attract a mate.'

I am relieved to have this piece of reportage finished. I glance towards Sir Robert again. Normally he would come over and give me some form of congratulation on my work but now he is not even looking at me.

My grief for my son has, since Patrick's revelation, been greatly allayed. My grief for the loss of a living friend, Sir Robert, is as painful as ever. I must put the past back into its box and try to focus on the present. I now see how inappropriately I acted in resigning and then revoking my resignation. My attempts to make up for it have been inadequate. My integrity is in question and it is imperative that I make a formal apology. Once I have done this, I have high hopes that Sir Robert will be magnanimous and our former friendship will be restored.

Humble pie has never been amongst my favourite dishes, but I am determined to do this. Therefore, once my King penguin narration is completed, I approach him.

'Sir Robert, I should like to apologize for my former conduct. It was not as impeccable as I would have wished. In fact, it was rude and ignominious. I am thoroughly ashamed of myself.'

'You seemed very . . . upset,' he comments.

'I was not functioning well. I was deeply distracted.'

'Hmmm.' He seems distracted himself, gazing at a bird above my head.

'Will you forgive me?' If I was the young and luscious Veronica of the past, this would be so very easy. As the old, crusty, rusty me it is not. I can almost see myself from the outside: my lipstick drying up on my wrinkled lips, my expensive outfit doing its unsuccessful best to flatter my withered body, my ancient blotched hands gripped anxiously around the handles of my handbag. He must indeed find me a pathetic figure.

He flicks his eyes towards me then away again.

'Apology accepted,' he says, with a stiff bow but none of his former twinkle or warmth.

I turn my back and wander off, needing air. I am overcome with melancholy. I walk slowly around the headland, gladder than usual of the support of my stick, for each step feels heavy. I tell myself firmly to remember the penguins.

As I reach a bend in the path, Patrick and Beth come into view ahead of me, still some way off. I fix my eyes on Patrick's outline. I worry about that boy. Terry is due here soon and I have not managed to detect at all what his feelings are for her. It is not for me to tell him that his ex-girlfriend is pregnant, but I have been severely tempted. I feel I should prepare the way, but I am not sure how. My grandson is wayward and I worry that the shock of this new revelation will send him into another peculiar phase.

Patrick and Beth have stopped on the path. Their two bodies are close. Then they are closer still. Fused together as one.

I cannot believe what I am seeing. My consternation at witnessing them in such a posture of intimacy is such that I can only stand here rooted to the spot.

Wrath at last giving propulsion to my legs and seizing my throat in a tight throttle, I turn and march back the way I came.

What is this new outrage? I knew my grandson was in a state, but to make advances to his friend's wife? Never would I have believed he could stoop so low! And she, who I had thought was such a little-goodie-two-shoes, to throw herself at him within a week of his arrival! It is an anathema. A monstrosity. And poor pregnant Terry, oblivious to all of this, is due to arrive any day now.

No doubt Beth thinks she can have her wicked way with Patrick whilst she is across the other side of the globe from Daisy's father. No doubt a holiday fling is quite all right in her book. Well, it is not all right in mine.

48
Terry

Locket Island

EVERY DAY, MANY times a day, I think about little Eva growing here, inside me. I am beginning to get glimpses of our future together, different scenarios playing out in my mind. Eva is sitting in the bath surrounded by bubbles. A little blob of foam quivers on her nose. She loves the warm water and she's cackling with laughter as she waggles about and splashes me, but I don't mind. I'm laughing too. Now it's her first Christmas and she's sitting under a tree, gazing at the fairy lights. She reaches her tiny fingers up to touch the baubles, transfixed by the magic of it all. Eva's first steps will be wobbly, but she'll be holding my hand. I may weep a bit. And how thrilled will I be when she says 'Mum' for the very first time?

When she goes to school, she'll have her hair in pigtails

with ribbons, maybe a different colour for each day of the week. I wonder if she'll be blonde like me or dark like Patrick? She'll have a spirit of adventure, for sure. She'll love climbing and I might be able to afford a climbing frame for the garden. I'll help her with her homework whenever she needs me. She'll be good at science and art. Dietrich will send her his pictures of penguins and she'll draw some for me to send him too. But I'll keep most of her drawings and Blu-Tack them up on my fridge.

I lay a hand over my belly and promise Eva I'll do my very best by her. I will her to grow healthy and strong and clever and wise and interesting and, above all, kind. I'm awed at the responsibility I've been given.

At the same time, when I write my blog about Locket Island the sense of loss is hard to bear. I'll be leaving so soon, first for the Falklands and soon after for Britain, for good.

I've started to get nervous again about how I'm going to break the news to Patrick. I know he's been researching his dad, but I have no idea how he's going to feel about becoming one himself. Veronica hasn't told him I'm coming and seems to think it's a good idea to conjure me up as if by magic. I'm not sure he's going to appreciate anything so dramatic. I wonder what his face will be like when he catches sight of me . . . Will it be delight? Frankly I think it's more likely to be shock. Then another even more momentous shock when I tell him why I'm there.

Mike and I pick our way over the polished stones of the beach. When I see Dietrich coming off the ship with his rucksack and his jolly wave, I feel so many things, but above all the torture of guilt. He's told us via email that his wife is well again, and he is feeling newly optimistic about the future of our research. He'll be devastated when he finds out that I'm leaving.

As soon as he looks into my face, he knows something is amiss. He engulfs me in one of his bear hugs that lasts longer than usual. It is very welcome.

'Don't worry, Terry. You can trust us with the penguins.'

'I know I can.' I can't say anything else because Mike is here too. He and Dietrich give each other a briefer, more distant hug.

I am to leave on the same ship that has brought Dietrich back to Locket Island. It's lucky he arranged to come back right now but all the same, I wish there was time to catch up with him. Of course, I must tell Patrick my news first, but I'd have liked to have taken Dietrich to one side and confided everything. Now there's only a matter of hours to pass on penguin news and give him and Mike instructions for the week I'm away.

Mike has been snide and prickly over the last few days, but this morning he is in a better mood. He's probably relieved I'm going. I told him the reason for my trip to the Falklands is to meet Veronica and sweet-talk her into continuing our funding. No doubt he also believes I want to avoid him for a while because of his crush on me. Little does he know how that pales into insignificance compared with everything else.

At the field centre I explain how the workload is to be divided, which is easy because Dietrich will take over the area he had before and they will have half of my patch each. There will be a hiatus in the blogs, unless either of them feels inspired to write anything or post a photo. It's unlikely they will.

They both accompany me back to the Zodiac that is to take me across the shallower waters to the ship.

'Bye, Terry. Give our best to Veronica.'

'Will do. Bye, guys. Be good!'

'You too!' calls Dietrich.

The waves rock the little vessel wildly, but I ignore the nausea that rises in my throat. I am suddenly feeling hopeful again. A soft skein of mist is wreathed around the mountain peaks. The sun is dancing in and out of the clouds and I am surrounded by a dazzle of icebergs. The light makes rainbows in the spray. Just beyond the boat, a group of penguins is porpoising in and out of the water in a series of joyful arcs and leaps. The wind is tugging at my hair. It's time to face the future.

49

Patrick

Bolder Island

GRANNY IS SUFFERING from an acute case of grumpiness. This all seems to be aimed at me for some reason, and she keeps making comments about loyalty with pointed looks in my direction. I presume these are veiled references to my desertion of the Locket Island project.

I've been watching her filming over the last few days. In spite of Daisy's coaching, she still keeps forgetting the words and has to do retake after retake. She's probably thinking about her son; reliving the past, when she gave birth to him in that nunnery and the terrible day he was taken away from her. I admire her for pressing on.

I've been mucking around and putting on my jolly face, but I'm pretty screwed up inside too. What happened with Mum and Dad is gruesome, hideous and horribly hard to swallow. I can't stop thinking about it. It's just as well Beth is around – exactly the right person at exactly the right time to stop me exploding.

Granny has been prowling around all morning and snapping at anyone who speaks to her. Now she beckons me over. I spring to attention.

She pulls her coat on, along with an air of extreme importance. 'Patrick, you and I need to go out for a walk together. Yes, now. And no, Daisy, you can't come too. I have a word or two to say to my grandson in confidence.'

Her mouth is a straight line and I have a feeling I'm going to be told off. What have I done now?

She marches out of the door, wielding her handbag like a shiny red weapon. Her footsteps sound sharp on the gravel. I go out after her, a slight step behind as if she's royalty.

'What is it, Granny? What's up?'

'I have various concerns, Patrick. Various and substantial.'

She refuses to tell me anything until we are a good way from the lodge. The wind stirs in her white hair and she turns to me. Underneath her severity I can see there's an excited flicker in her eye.

'I will inform you without any mincing of words that your despicable behaviour with Beth has been noticed.'

'What?'

'I saw you two canoodling out on the coast path yesterday.'

'No!' I can't fricking believe she was watching. And of course she went and assumed that mad, bad Patrick was up to his wicked ways again. 'No, Granny. No! That wasn't what you—'

She interrupts me, her voice a low stream of venom. 'Needless to say, I am extremely disappointed in you. I know you are going through a difficult time, and I understand that, as a McCreedy, you are liable to be volatile. But this is the lowest of the low. To sneak off with that young floozy, who is not only the mother of our precious Daisy but is married to somebody you claim is your friend. I am heartily ashamed of you. I can only hope you are ashamed of yourself, too, and are not intending to take this any further.'

I hold up my hands. 'Of course I'm not, Granny. There is totally nothing between Beth and me. We were just confiding in each other and I got a bit upset about Mum, and she got a bit upset about Daisy, and we both of us needed a hug.'

'Just confiding?' she says, pricking up her ears.

'Just confiding, I swear to you on . . . on anything you like . . . On the penguins.'

For the first time in ages her lips break out into a natural smile. Then she frowns again. 'If you needed somebody to confide in, why didn't you just come to me?' she asks crossly. 'Am I not a good listener?'

'Well, in a way you are, but you can't hear what I'm saying half the time and I don't want to shout it out to the whole universe.'

'I heard *that*,' she huffs.

We walk in silence for a while. We have now reached the edge of the Gentoo colony. Thousands of short figures are waddling about on big pink feet. Conversation is getting more difficult because of the noise.

'You miss Terry, don't you?' Granny says suddenly, a very quick sentence this time that sounds almost desperate.

Well, she's offended that I haven't confided in her much before so I may as well do it now. 'To be quite honest, Granny, yes, I do. I miss her more than I can say. Every inch of me misses her. Every millimetre. Every atom.'

'Oh, Patrick,' she says with some force. 'I am so glad.' At least that's what I think she said. Her words are drowned by the wittering of chicks and trumpeting of adult penguins.

I glance over the crowd and feel a great longing for Locket Island.

Then I look back at Granny and see that she is pointing.

50
Terry

Bolder Island

IT FEELS AS if I've been sitting on this stone for ever. I may even be growing into it, slowly transforming into an odd rocky nobble. The quiet, friendly man called Liam who met me in the Land Rover and gave me a lift here said it was the exact spot where Veronica decreed I had to wait. He took my luggage with him, saying, 'Great. That's you sorted. I'll see you back at the ranch.'

I'm all alone now, which is just as well. I don't feel ready to face Patrick yet, or Veronica or anyone. I need this time to sit here, motionless, with the warm sun on my back and the calls of penguins in my ears.

Veronica has planned it down to the last detail. With her taste for drama, she has selected this spot because it's scenic and romantic. I am a little hidden from the path by the undulations in the land, but once he sees me there will be a backdrop of glittering blue sea and an elegant sweep of hill, the Gentoo colony between us providing life and vibrancy.

There's no sickness at the moment, just this ebbing feeling in my stomach and an overwhelming tiredness. I spent last night in a hotel in Ushuaia, isolated, listening to the sounds of the city outside the window. In spite of my exhaustion I fidgeted the night away, completely unable to sleep.

I watch the shadows of clouds sliding over olive-green hills. I don't know what I'm going to say when Patrick appears. I have tried out so many versions of the scene in my head but none of them ring true, and whatever happens I want it to be true. My revelation will just have to come out however it will.

I hear his voice calling before I see him. 'Terry!'

I jump, even though I've been expecting this for the last half-hour.

There is utter amazement in that voice.

'My God, Terry! You're here!' Amazement and thrill . . . and tenderness.

My heart starts thumping wildly. I long for him so much but I can't tell him that.

My body feels numb as I struggle to my feet. Patrick is galloping towards me, his arms outstretched, scattering reams of squawking penguins in all directions as he comes. Way behind him I can make out the figure of Veronica, all in reds, waving at me. She has stopped where she is, not far from the lodge, and will not approach until I've had the chance to talk with Patrick.

297

And now he is here, scooping me up in his arms and covering me with kisses. I feel those kisses showering down on me like a dried-up plant feeling the soft rain. Patrick has taken my presence here as a sign that I still love him. And I do. I do.

But I can't forget how he left us. I push him away and give him a hard slap right across the face. He reels backwards with a sharp cry. Then starts talking quickly. 'I know, I know, I don't blame you. I was crap and crazy and stupid and thoughtless and I don't deserve you.'

He keeps blabbing on and on, and his voice is just as meaningless to me as the honks of the penguins.

'Stop! Just stop, please, Patrick.'

He stops.

It's time to tell him.

The words wobble out of me.

51

Patrick

Bolder Island

I CAN'T BELIEVE she's here. It feels like a dream; a dream in which she is in my arms again. At least, it does until she hits me. Then I know I'm awake. Words of shock, apology and love burst out of me. She stills me with a single sharp gesture of her hand. She has something to tell me. Her face is strange and different and I can't make out if her news is good or bad, happy or sad.

Then I hear her say that I am to become a father.

Me, Patrick. A father.

'*What?*'

Her eyes are wet. So are mine.

'Are you glad, Patrick?' she asks anxiously. All her anger is gone; she is just waiting for me now, hanging on my answer.

'Glad doesn't even begin to cover it!'

Electrified, I scoop her up once again, kiss her, thank her, gaze at her, at her body that has done this wonderful thing without my even knowing about it. I feel as if my whole life has been leading up to this moment. That all the crazy revelations about my parents have been sent to show me how incredibly, fabulously important this is.

She smiles her beautiful smile. 'I'm glad you're glad.'

'May I?' I ask.

'Do!'

She takes my hand that is hovering by her belly and places it there, over the warm swell where our child is nesting.

'It's amazing, isn't it?' she says, beaming like a summer sunrise.

'It is! Amazing!'

After we have both carried on saying how amazing it is for some time, I notice how pale she looks. I'm worried about her, about whether she is physically OK after her long journey. I need to be sensitive, but I feel stupid and crass. I have no idea what this must be like for her. I beg her to come back to the lodge and rest.

'No,' she says. 'I've been sitting on that rock for ages. I want to walk now. My limbs need it and my mind needs it. And I'm not ready to meet the others yet.'

We stroll towards the shore, and I take her arm as if we're an old married couple. The cries of the Gentoos fade into the background and the wind swishes in the grass. Terry has not said she has forgiven me or that she loves me, but I can sense her relief. As for me, I'm so blitzed with happiness and disbelief I hardly know what to do with myself.

We start to talk of our future, all the different possibilities laid out before us. I see her eyes travel over the panorama of tawny land, rocks, sea and sand.

'It's beautiful here.'

'We could stay here, if you like?' I suggest, because everything seems possible now. 'Or go anywhere in the world you want to.'

A look of wistfulness passes over her face. 'But not Antarctica. That's no place for a baby. I can't stay on Locket Island. That life is over for me now. I have to leave the penguins.'

I see what a momentous thing that is for her, but it can't be a priority now. 'Forget the penguins. This, right here, is the important thing: our son, or daughter.'

She has to agree. We walk in silence for a while, each needing time with our own thoughts.

'It seems more real now that I've told you,' she says at last. 'I've had to keep it to myself for so long.'

'Dietrich and Mike . . . ?'

'They don't know yet.'

'Granny?'

'Only because she guessed. She made me come here.'

I'd thought as much. 'She did right.'

Again, we try to imagine what might happen in the months ahead. Terry tells me that she had thought of calling the baby Eva if it's a girl or Archie if it's a boy and asks if I like the names. I say I do . . . but also I like names beginning with a J. Perhaps Joe?

'Ah, like your father,' she recalls. 'Did you find out anything?'

'My God, Terry, so, so much. I'll tell you over time. But

yes – photos and everything, and a great big skeleton in the family cupboard. I can't quite make up my mind if my dad was a complete loser or a bit of a hero. Granny's going for the hero interpretation. But never mind about him now. That's all in the past. Now it's time to look to the future.' The sea is gently whispering sweet nothings; the sand is gleaming golden-white. 'Will you let me take care of you? Of you both?' I glance down towards her tummy again, relishing the fact that my own son or daughter is with us.

Terry smiles again and her whole face is lit up. I understand what people mean when they talk about pregnant women being radiant.

'Of course, Patrick. We'll take care of each other.'

I kiss her for a long, long time. Deep, strong kisses that burn with desire and ache with love.

Eventually we turn and start heading back for the lodge. We must talk to Granny, and Terry will have to meet the others. She's only here for a week, but in that time some plans are going to get made.

I start trying to be practical. 'We must see if there's a doctor locally who can check everything's all right with you.'

Her face clouds over a little. 'I did manage to see a doctor on the ship, but he was rubbish.'

'How come?'

Her gesture is impatient. 'He did one of those tests with a dipstick and he said that, according to my urine, I'm not producing the hCG hormone. He reckoned I'm not pregnant.'

I stop in my tracks.

'But I know I am.' She states it as a fact.

'You . . . you couldn't have lost the baby, could you?' I stammer, alarmed at the thought, not knowing how to say it kindly. 'All that overworking, and the travel here? The flight?'

She shakes her head. Not offended, just a little frustrated.

'I'd know if I'd lost her. Of course I'd know. The doctor just got it wrong. We'll get another test and you'll see.'

I waver. I don't know much about these things.

'Stop looking so worried, Patrick,' she urges. 'I've looked it up. Some women don't test as positive until later on in the pregnancy. My body has been going through all these changes, telling me every way it can. And nobody knows my body better than me.'

'True.'

She cups her belly in both hands. 'I *know* that Eva is here.'

'Or Archie,' I add. Archie, not Joe. If it's a boy it will be Archie, the name she's chosen. She deserves anything she wants, and I'll give her everything I can.

I can't believe that I've been given this second chance with her. How lucky am I? Crazy lucky. Stupid lucky.

Still, my mind will be easier once we've done that second pregnancy test.

52

Veronica

Bolder Island

WHEN TERRY AND Patrick come in they both look bright-
eyed and excited.

'My dear girl!' I cry, welcoming her into my arms.

'Veronica,' she answers, holding me tightly. She murmurs into my ear: 'Thank you for bringing me here. It's
going to be OK.'

I view Patrick over her shoulder. He is fizzing like a
sparkler and grinning like a Cheshire cat. I smile back at
him and he gives me a thumbs up.

We take Terry to the room that has been made up for
her, as now, all at once, she is overcome with fatigue. She
has been given the only room that is left. It is small and
plain, although, I remind myself, this is luxury compared
to what she is used to. Her rucksack is waiting for her on

the floor, where Liam left it. Her bed looks fresh and comfortable, and I have picked a few wildflowers and put them in a vase on her bedside table.

Patrick and I leave her to rest. I feel he must be in need of tea so I hastily prepare a pot and we bring it with us to the common room. Later we will be celebrating with something stronger and more bubbly, although Terry will doubtless only allow herself a sip or two. I can hardly express how thrilled I am that she and Patrick have been reunited. I will do my utmost to ensure their lives and that of my great-grandchild will be as blissful as possible from now on.

Patrick is now manifesting great emotion and cannot sit still.

He tells me, however, that there is a slight doubt regarding the pregnancy. He trusts Terry, who is adamant, yet we'd do well to have it scientifically confirmed at the earliest possible opportunity. I absolutely agree, but wonder how it can be done in this place of isolation. Having discussed it at some length, we decide to take Keith into our confidence. He is currently stacking cutlery in the kitchen.

When he is summoned to the common room and the situation explained he declares, as is his wont: 'No worries at all. Keith will sort it.' He is going to phone his friend in Stanley, who can purchase a testing kit at the pharmacy there and will send it over in a discreet package via one of the local flights. He will also book Terry an appointment with the doctor and will personally take her over in his boat. And yes, of course, Patrick and I can accompany her.

I must temper my excitement with a note of caution.

We decide that it might be politic to save the champagne until after Terry's appointment.

Everyone likes Terry as soon as they meet her. She has such an easy way with people, such a ready smile. I should really take a leaf out of her genial and generous book, but my habits have become rusted up over the years and it would be hard to change them now. She and Patrick spend pretty much all of the following day together, talking earnestly in her bedroom or his, the common room or the environs of the lodge. This is only to be expected under the circumstances. I have to do a short stint of filming, which requires many takes because I am rather distracted. Beth, whom I have misjudged, is meanwhile doing a marvellous job keeping Daisy occupied with games, walks, colouring pencils and whatever other entertainments she can devise.

In the evening the discreet package is duly delivered and Terry retreats to the bathroom. Patrick paces up and down by the door. I hover in the vicinity, far enough to be decorous but near enough to detect either jubilation or distress.

We wait for far longer than I would have anticipated. When she comes out there is a frustratingly quiet consultation between them. I turn up the volume of my hearing aid but just miss the purport of what they are saying. Terry quickly returns to the bathroom and there follows some loud retching. She comes out a few minutes later looking rather green. Patrick escorts her back to her bedroom. Half an hour later he emerges. He is scratching his head.

'I don't know what to think,' he confesses. 'She is still totally sure she's having a baby. I've never seen anyone so sure about anything, and she's just thrown up, which I guess is an indication. But the test has shown negative. That's the second time. What the hell is going on?'

I cannot answer this question.

'I'm sure I felt a slight bump as well,' he muses. 'Although that could be too much cake, I suppose.'

'Well, at least we have an appointment at the doctor's for her.'

The appointment, the earliest slot available, will be in two days' time. I trust that this will prove that my great-grandchild is happily and healthily progressing. Still, it is uncomfortable to have a doubt such as this niggling away in the background.

I have a swift word in Keith's ear and obtain the number of the surgery. After much persistence on my part, being passed from one person to another and waiting 'on hold' for far longer than is acceptable, I manage to speak to the doctor herself. Having listened with interest, she is unable to make a diagnosis but agrees to give Terry an ultrasound when she comes. That should certainly settle it one way or another.

53

Veronica

'BOTH THE ROCKHOPPERS and the Macaronis are migratory species, leaving these islands between April and September. They nest together on clifftops or steep cliffsides, a choice which demands immense strength and tenacity. Rockhopper males will babysit whilst waiting for their females to return. Their patience is to be applauded, as they do it willingly, eating no food themselves for weeks on end. The females out at sea must be equally determined; the lives of their chicks depend on their safe return. As the mothers head home with their craws full of food, they are hurled on to the cliffs by ferocious waves. Timing is everything. A split-second too soon and they could be smashed on these perilous rocks. Too late and they miss the chance of catching hold; they will flounder and be dragged back in. This female has been knocked back countless times. At last she has found purchase with her hooked claws on the steep, slippery cliffside and propels herself homeward in a series of vigorous hops.'

I am, in fact, narrating in a much gentler part of the landscape where a little penguin activity is visible behind me, but my voice will carry through whilst more inhospitable scenes are shown. This will comprise the footage that Sir Robert and Miriam captured on South Georgia. It is a heart-stopping piece of film: penguins flung hither and thither in the plunge and roar.

It is my last piece of work for Sir Robert's programme, to go in place of the reporting I abandoned so disgracefully. There is yet one more little piece to do for the *I Wish* programme with Daisy, however.

It is now late in the afternoon. Terry and Patrick are here, a little way off. They seem very involved in one another, but a shadow has fallen over Patrick since the results of the pregnancy testing kit. Nobody else knows the situation. Daisy is thrilled that Terry is here with us on Bolder Island. I've explained that the reason for this is Locket Island business. I instructed her specifically not to mention wedding bells to either Terry or Patrick because things are not clear for them at the moment.

'Oh, I understand,' she said. 'Sometimes Mummy and Daddy have problems, but they *have* to work together because I'm ill.'

Beth and Daisy are both here on the beach with us and Daisy has her new kite with her. Liam is here too. Petra and Tony the Macaroni have been spotted together again, so of course he wants to capture another scene with Daisy introducing them both and get a little penguin-on-penguin action.

Daisy is now keen to make a friendship flipper band for Tony like the one she made for Petra, and plagues Keith about it at every opportunity. Where will it end? I ask myself. Does she want to make bracelets for every penguin here? There are many thousands of penguins on this island, many thousands in a single colony. When you see them en masse it is difficult to believe that most of these species are endangered or threatened.

We divide into three search parties to look for the penguin pair: Beth and Liam, Terry and Patrick, and Daisy and I. Daisy's kite swoops and flails before us as we peruse the shore.

There are numerous penguins dotted about on the beach, but not the right ones. After twenty minutes we head for the dunes and are fortunate to find Petra and Tony almost immediately. They are together again, hunched side by side in the tufted grasses.

'Mum! Liam! Terry-and-Patrick! They're here!' Daisy screeches, waking the two penguins. Tony seems a little self-conscious. He neatens himself up, tucking his beak down and nibbling at his breast feathers.

Daisy holds out her hand to Petra. Petra straightens and tosses her head then stretches out her flippers and waddles up to us. I am sure she recognizes her human companion by now, bearing in mind she and Daisy have provided entertainment for each other every single day since we first discovered her. Daisy snatches her hand back just in time to avoid having her fingers pecked.

'No, naughty penguin,' Daisy scolds, delighted.

Tony is now emboldened to approach too. The two penguins waddle around with her for a while, their eyes glowing rose-coloured and their crest feathers streaming bright yellow.

As we watch, a butterfly flits past, its satin wings flashing in the sunlight. Petra and Tony are fascinated and hop after it. Neighbouring penguins notice and join in the fun, one by one, until eight penguins are chasing the butterfly around. Its motion is zigzagging and fluttery whilst theirs is a sequence of strong bounds, and although they remain in a close-knit group, their heads and bodies bob up and down at comically different rates. It is a joyous sight to behold.

'Get it, get it!' Daisy shouts to Liam, who has just arrived wielding his camera, a breathless Beth in his wake.

'Right-oh, Daisy, I'm getting it,' he shouts back, following the action with his lens.

Terry and Patrick arrive on the scene, also panting. We watch together, enthralled.

I notice Terry gazing fixedly at the bouncing birds, and then her eyes swivel and fasten on Daisy. There is a fresh bloom in her cheeks and she seems charged with an inner light. She must be imagining having her own child, examining the spectrum of wonders and possibilities that lie ahead.

I can only hope that the joys of motherhood will last longer for her than they did for me.

54

Veronica

East Falkland

I AM SEATED in the waiting room, my handbag in my lap. There is only one other person present, an aged man with a grubby-looking beard, and I am glad to say he is turning the pages of a magazine and showing no desire to communicate with me.

Patrick pokes his head around the door and beckons me.

'She wants you in with us too, now,' he hisses as I scramble to my feet. 'She's finding it hard.'

He ushers me into the consulting room. The doctor, a rather glamorous brunette in her forties, is sitting quite close to Terry, talking to her in soothing tones. Terry looks up at me but doesn't smile.

Patrick and I take the other two chairs. The room is a small, blank space. On the desk is a computer. The doctor swivels the screen round and points to a smeary image in black and white. 'Here is your evidence, if you're still not convinced,' she tells Terry. 'This is your uterus.'

We all stare at the black space, the poignantly clear lack of baby.

'I don't understand,' murmurs Terry, in complete puzzlement.

'You are definitely not pregnant. This admits no doubt.'

'Is she ill then?' asks Patrick, his eyes turning back to Terry, love and concern written all over his face.

The doctor ignores him and speaks to her. 'You seem healthy. Your blood pressure is normal, you are a good weight. I'll take some bloods and maybe you could give us a urine sample, then I can dismiss a few other possibilities. But my feeling is that there is physically very little wrong with you, despite the symptoms you've described. Do you mind my asking if you've been suffering from any stress lately?'

'Well . . .' She glances at Patrick.

'Yes,' he answers baldly. 'She has. It was my fault.'

Terry takes off her glasses. She rubs each lens very carefully with the edge of her sleeve, then puts them back on and gazes again at the screen.

The doctor then asks if she has been craving a baby. Terry shakes her head. 'No. Not at all. In fact, at the beginning I was shocked and scared. Dreading it, in a way. It meant I had to leave the job I loved.'

The doctor nods thoughtfully. She presses the tips of her fingers together and explains, choosing her words with care. She believes Terry is suffering from a rare condition called pseudocyesis. It occurs when a strong emotion causes an elevation in hormones. In turn this creates physical symptoms that mimic pregnancy. It is more likely to happen if a pregnancy is either longed for or feared. The mind has a powerful influence over the body and, once the belief in the pregnancy is established, the symptoms perpetuate. Women with the condition may stop menstruating. They suffer from sickness, fatigue, breast swelling or tenderness and a swollen abdomen. Sometimes they even feel foetal movement.

In a nutshell, Terry has been tricked by her own body.

'I'm afraid we don't operate a counselling service here,' the doctor adds, 'but if you feel you need it, I can put you in touch with a mental health professional in Argentina.'

'A mental health professional?' Terry asks, her words weighted. All the colour has faded out of her. 'Do I need help?'

'No, not necessarily,' the doctor assures her. 'But this is no small matter. The physical symptoms will probably disappear now that you have seen the proof, but you will need to be gentle with yourself.'

We leave the surgery in a daze. The sun and the wind hit us the moment we step outside but do nothing to disperse the pall that has fallen over us. Terry and Patrick are both silent.

'Oh dear me, I seem to have forgotten my handbag,' I declare, and slip back inside. I knock but do not pause before opening the door of the consulting room. The doctor is typing furiously on her computer. I pick up the handbag where I deliberately left it under the chair. In haste I ask her a few further questions. She is not very much help. She confesses that she has never actually had a patient with this condition before, although she has read about it. She believes it affects different women in different ways and can only be looked at on a case-by-case basis. Terry may recover very quickly, but she may not. At least she now appears to have accepted that she is not with child. There have been women who persist in believing in their pregnancy for two or more years, so very convincing are the symptoms.

I exit again from the building and find Terry and Patrick a little way off. They are standing apart.

'My poor girl,' I cry, striding up to embrace Terry.

'No sympathy, please,' she replies stiffly.

I am not a great giver of sympathy, having had little practice, but I do remember that nobody gave it to me when I needed it and I know how that feels. 'I believe you are due some,' I reply.

She doesn't answer.

Patrick tries to take her hand, but she won't have it. She won't even look at him.

She is physically tough, I know that, yet this unexpected news must have taken a momentous emotional toll. I owe this girl much and my heart goes out to her.

We are all still in a state of shock during the trip back in Keith's motorboat, and exchange very few words despite his efforts at small talk. He must realize something is amiss, but thankfully he has the delicacy not to probe.

When we reach the shore of Bolder Island Terry takes my arm and helps pull me to my feet.

'No, no, stop it!' I protest. 'You need to look after yourself.'

'Why?' she asks bitterly. 'There is nothing wrong with me.'

We start walking together up the track that leads to the lodge, leaving Patrick to help Keith moor and secure the boat. I glance sideways at Terry. Her pace is even but her face is rigid. She looks as if she has seen a ghost.

I glimpse a figure in the distance coming towards us. It is Beth. She smiles and greets us. Terry manages a hello and walks on by, but I hang back. Although I realize I leapt to the wrong conclusion about Patrick and Beth, it is imperative that she does not interfere. My grandson has no right to tell her about Terry, and he is himself volatile and vulnerable at present. Beth has noticed him coming up the path behind us now, shoulders hunched, and she is stepping forward as if she's about to go and talk to him.

I swiftly step forward myself and bar her way.

'Oh no you don't, young lady.'

She frowns. 'I was only going to—'

'We are only here for another week, and there are issues to be resolved. Patrick is greatly stressed and needs to sort things out between himself and Terry. If he needs to talk to anyone else, it will be to me, his grandmother, Veronica McCreedy.'

I bang my stick on the ground and draw myself up to my full height, which is just a little taller than her – and significantly taller when she is cowering.

55

Terry

Bolder Island

How could I have been so wrong? Those facts coldly spelled out by the doctor seem incredible, yet I saw with my own eyes the ultrasound image, the emptiness where little Eva should be. I somehow created all those symptoms through no choice of my own. I conjured a baby because it was something I feared and dreaded ... but then I absorbed the idea, climbed on board and started to hope and yearn and love.

I want to be strong but I'm still so confused. I reason with myself that this is good, that I can go back to Locket Island now ... yet I can't seem to stop crying. I miss Eva, the anticipation of Eva, the future of Eva.

Over the last twenty-four hours I have started to feel less swollen and sick, but I am shaken, deflated and deeply ashamed. Thank goodness I never contacted my parents to tell them about my pregnancy. Thank goodness I never told Dietrich and Mike. But I hate the fact I was so sure about it. I hate that my own body has wronged me like this, has played such a cruel joke on me. Now I feel like a criminal, a liar of the worst order. I have let down Veronica . . . and as for Patrick, I can't face him at all. I keep remembering his utter joy when he thought he was going to become a father.

'He must hate me now,' I said to Veronica when we were back in the privacy of my room at the lodge.

'What did you say, my dear?' She adjusted her hearing aid, which gave a small protesting squeak, as if it really didn't want to hear any more.

'Patrick hates me,' I said, louder. 'Because he wanted that baby so, so much and I made him believe me. I deceived him, just as I deceived myself. He must blame me for it all. And I can't help blaming me for it too.'

She looked at me sadly. 'All this blaming is not the way forward, I feel. I have spent a great deal of life blaming other people for absolutely everything, but now I see what an unhealthy habit this was. Often it is not people who are to blame, it is circumstances colliding in unfortunate ways. This was not his fault and it was certainly not yours.'

Veronica has been wonderful. I know she was thrilled at the prospect of becoming a great-grandmother and she must be devastated too, but she has shown only kindness. She is forever bringing me hot water bottles and more cups of tea than I can drink. She has gifted me expensive soaps and perfumes, which I'm sure must be her own as I don't think there's that sort of shop for miles. I don't deserve any of it.

I eat mainly by myself in my room because the noise of the canteen is too much, but Veronica sits with me a lot. Daisy and the film crew have been told that I am ill. In a way, I suppose it's true. I always thought of myself as practical and down to earth, not the sort of person who'd ever have psychological problems, yet here I am. How idiotic I was to assume that there *is* a 'sort of person' who'd suffer from these. As with a physical disease, any of us, sooner or later, might find ourselves struggling with some brutal mental health issue.

Veronica offered to look into those therapy sessions for me, but I'm booked on a flight to Ushuaia and a ship to Locket Island in just a few days and I would rather recuperate quietly here. Immersing yourself in nature is about the healthiest thing you can do, so today I've decided to go out for a short wander. I check that nobody is hanging around before I sneak down the corridor to the lodge entrance. I don't feel able to hold a conversation with anyone. I need to be by myself, to wander amongst the rocks and dunes and gaze out to sea, letting my thoughts drift as they will.

The sun seems impossibly bright as I step outside. Pulling my jacket around me I set off down the track at a swift pace towards the beach. I can already hear the caws and cries of the Gentoo colony and make out a flock of black-and-white figures. I haven't got far when I hear footsteps pounding behind me. Why can't I just be left alone? I wish I could turn myself into a penguin and blend in with them.

It's Patrick, running after me, calling my name. I wonder if he's been keeping watch. I walk faster. I know how much I've disappointed him and I don't want to see him. I can't bear it. I'm nowhere near ready.

But here he is, fussing around me. Telling me he loves me. Telling me we can still make a go of things. We can't. Of course we can't. Why is he doing this to me?

I turn on him like a tiger.

56

Veronica

Bolder Island

IN SPITE OF the fact that Daisy has made friendship bracelets for everyone, there is precious little friendship anywhere
to be seen.

Sir Robert is obstinately glacial towards me, Terry
and Patrick are not speaking to each other, and Beth is
even quieter than usual, which is saying something.
Moreover, there have been more disagreeable articles in
the gutter press which are making me dread my return
to Britain.

PENGUIN PARTY ENDS IN TEARS
MCCREEDY MOOD SWINGS ANGER SADDLEBOW
MCCREEDY CLAN WARFARE
FALLOUT ON BOLDER ISLAND

I have tried talking to Sir Robert about these, but he merely shrugs off my concerns. He evidently persists in his belief that the publicity will serve us well. He cares little that it has rendered me so forlorn. At least the evil, gossip-mongering journalists could find nothing bad to say about Daisy.

My poor Enzo still haunts my thoughts every day. I also mourn for my great-grandchild who never managed to exist at all. I worry about dear Terry, and about Patrick, who is so devastated by it all.

'It's a bloody bungee jump of emotions, Granny,' he told me when I asked about his feelings yesterday. 'And it's doing my head in. One moment my dad's a killer and a coward. Then nope, wrong; it was my mum who was the killer and coward. But hey, I'm getting back together with the girl I love and we're having a baby! Then no, we're suddenly *not* having a baby. And she won't even talk to me.'

'I'm so sorry,' I murmured.

'I know she couldn't help it and I'm gutted for her. But I'm gutted for me too, Granny. I wanted that kid. Being a father was going to be the one thing in life I *wouldn't* muck up. It would have brought out the best in me, I know it. I'd have loved my son or daughter more than life itself.'

Part of me is glad to hear this, whilst the other part weeps for him.

'My God, how I wish I'd never left Locket Island,' he moans. 'That bloody ship just made it too easy. Fricking hindsight. It's not a wonderful thing at all. It's bloody torture.'

*

Daisy and I are out together for our morning stroll. We stopped for a while on our way to the beach to admire the colony of Gentoos. But as always, Daisy pushed on eagerly in the hope of seeing her favourites, Petra and Tony.

Now we are wandering along the pathway that follows the line of windswept dunes. Gulls swoop overhead through a sky that is all made up of tufted creams and mauves. The sea, cobalt-blue in the distance, blends into lighter shades before it laps the shore in lace-trimmed tiers. The beach is a shining mirror. Daisy plucks off her shoes and socks as she does every morning when we get to this stage and takes off. I watch her small figure zipping across the wet sand, leaving a messy trail of footprints which soon fill with saltwater and swill back to smoothness.

As ever, the fresh air and the elements are a balm to my troubled spirits. I inhale deeply and focus on the scent of the sea and the sound of waves.

Daisy is running towards a dark lump on the sand. I see her stoop down, then stiffen. Her hands sail up into the air and at the same time I hear a shrill, strangulated cry.

'Daisy, what is it?' I cry, my voice small on the wind. I walk as briskly as I can to catch up with her.

As I approach, I hear hysterical sobbing. I cannot get to her fast enough, pushing my creaky legs to reach her, but I fear the worst. She is scrabbling at the dark shape. I can now see colours in it: black, white, a few streaks of yellow, some pink. She is touching it, wrestling with something that flaps in the breeze.

And as I come closer, I can make out that the lump on the sand is a dead penguin. A penguin with a primrose-yellow headdress and a bright pink band on its flipper.

'Oh no, Daisy, no, don't look!'

But of course it is too late. She has looked, has seen it all. Petra is dead.

Daisy howls. I take her into my arms, tears flowing like rivers from my own eyes. I sink down on to the beach to hold her better, ignoring the clods of damp sand that stick to my skirt. Our grief binds us together. We hug tightly then gaze on the sad sight then weep afresh.

I wonder how long Petra has been lying here, how long ago the life ebbed away from her and why. Her head is twisted a little to one side, her eyes half closed, her beak slightly open. Even now she looks sweet, although strangely transformed into this still, silent effigy. I try to analyse why she seems so very different, and conclude it is because penguins are, more than any creature I have yet seen, exceptionally full of life. Death does not suit them.

Sorrow heaps on sorrow, not just for the death of a penguin, but to see Daisy so distraught. Everything began here so well for her: recovery from her illness, the chance of a lifetime expedition and her dreams coming true. To see her in this distress makes me rage once again at life's cruelty.

Daisy's eyes are red and swollen. She is holding on to me so hard it hurts. I pull a handkerchief from my bag and wipe her wet cheeks. 'Dear child, we must go back and tell the others. They will be wondering where we are.'

'But we can't leave her here,' she moans.

I feel the same. Gulls will swoop down and tear Petra's body to red ribbons if we do. We have no spade to bury her and neither of us has strong enough muscles to carry her all the way back to the lodge with us. I cannot and will not let Daisy go back on her own, nor can I leave her here by herself.

I take off my coat and lay it over Petra's body. It is a crimson woollen coat, beautifully tailored and a great favourite of mine, but I can always buy another. I tuck it around the penguin-shaped mound. The cold air seeps through my clothes and makes my skin curdle, but no matter.

On the way back Daisy is quietly trembling. 'Poor Petra. I loved her. I loved her so much. I will love her for ever.'

Patrick comes running and Terry too. Beth, Sir Robert and a small crowd of camera crew follow. The little penguin has charmed many hearts. We form a sad, stooping circle around my coat and the small, precious body it conceals.

Beth is trying to comfort Daisy, squeezing her hand. 'Cry all you like, darling. She was very special. You made her last days happy. You were so good to her.'

'How did she die?' somebody asks. It may have been me.

Patrick crouches down and pulls back the coat to examine her. He raises his eyes. 'What do you think, Terry. Starvation?'

She comes and kneels beside him, shaking her head.

'No, she looks well fed. She was a strong young penguin.'

They puzzle it over, two penguin experts together. She gently lifts Petra's floppy head and prises open her beak. Looks down her pink gullet. 'There's something stuck in her throat,' she announces. 'That's our culprit. That'll be what caused her death.'

A bolt of guilt shoots through me. If she has choked on something, could it be one of the torn-up bits of paper I myself scattered over the beach, a fragment of my son's picture? I saw Petra gobble one up. Is it possible that she chewed one of the larger pieces and it became wedged in her throat?

'What is the thing?' Daisy demands.

If I have caused her little friend's death . . .

I'm finding it difficult to breathe.

'I need to sit down,' I murmur.

The crew washes around me as I feel my body sinking into a heap on the sand beside Petra.

57

Veronica

Everyone is fussing.

'Would you kindly desist? I am quite well, thank you. I believe I must have tripped on something.'

I pull my skirt down so it is covering my knees, from which it has twisted upwards in a most unseemly manner. My stockings have laddered and wetness creeps through my cardigan. I accept Patrick's strong arm and he pulls me into a sitting position. I shake the sand out of my hair.

'Phew!' exclaims Daisy, who has been frozen to the spot. 'I thought you were dead too.'

'I would not be so inconsiderate as to die now,' I point out severely. 'Later, maybe.'

I note Sir Robert's face looking down at me. It has momentarily lost its inscrutability. Indeed, it has become a map in which all roads lead to the state of concern. He takes off his own coat and pulls it around my shoulders. It is light but warm.

'Take your time, Veronica,' he advises. 'Don't get up too quickly.'

His words propel me to action and, not wanting to be taken for a weakling, I struggle to my feet with a little assistance from Patrick on one side and Terry on the other.

'Never mind me,' I snap. 'We must take this poor penguin back to the lodge without further ado.'

'Yes,' Daisy cries. 'We must. We need an autopsy,' she adds, astonishing me with her vocabulary. 'And then we need a funeral.'

Petra's body is borne by Patrick, still cushioned in my crimson coat, with all due pomp and ceremony. A trail of downcast humans follows behind him. Sir Robert offers me his arm and I gratefully accept it.

Back at the lodge, I hasten to exchange my sand-encrusted skirt and cardigan for a fresh outfit and reapply my lipstick. My reflection in the mirror is haunted. I am horrified at the ominous thought that my own stupidity has destroyed Petra's sweet life.

We gather round to watch the autopsy, which is conducted in the outhouse by Terry and Patrick, with the help of a pair of tweezers. I cannot bear to look but I cannot bear not to look either. After some gentle prodding, Terry draws a long misshapen object out from Petra's throat.

'What is it?' I ask breathlessly. 'Is it a piece of paper with part of a photo printed on it?'

She examines the object closely and shakes her head. 'No, Veronica. It's much more lethal than that.'

'It looks like some kind of plastic wrapping,' mutters Patrick, poking at it.

A few letters are visible in purple block capitals. We all arch our heads forward to try to see. 'Yes, it's a strip of packaging for biscuits,' he confirms.

Relieved as I am not to be personally responsible for Petra's death, it is miserable to think of her trying to eat such a thing and choking to death upon it.

'She will have died quickly and painlessly, won't she?' Beth asks Terry, raising her eyebrows and looking pointedly at Daisy.

Terry doesn't know what to say. She is a truthful girl but does not want to distress Daisy any further.

'Yes, quite painless,' replies Patrick, saving her the decision.

'I hate plastic. I HATE it,' cries Daisy with passion.

I put a hand on her shoulder. 'I do too, Daisy. I do too.'

She is overcome again with great jerky sobs. Beth leads her away for tea and comfort.

'It wouldn't really have been painless, would it?' I have to ask once she has gone.

'No, Veronica. It would have been a slow torture.' Terry is visibly angry; angry with the human race, as am I.

I bite my lip. 'I sincerely hope this wrapper was not carelessly dropped by any member of our film crew.'

'No,' she assures me. 'It looks old. It has probably been floating about in the sea for years; decades, even. It takes four hundred and fifty years for plastic to fully decompose.'

Deeply shocked, I turn to Sir Robert, who has accompanied us but remained hanging in the background, very quiet through all of this. 'As penguin ambassador I feel I should say something about this, as part of the programme.' My voice is hard and sharp.

His eyes widen in surprise, but he nods slowly. 'Yes, Veronica. If you feel up to it I absolutely agree. I think you should.'

First we head to the dining area to collect much-needed cups of tea, an Earl Grey for him and a Darjeeling for me. We take them to the office and sit together, discussing what should be said and doing a little research on the computer. Although I was aware of the issue, I had no idea how much our seas are positively heaving with litter: plastic bags, sweet wrappers, bottle caps and synthetic fibres from clothes. Soon there will be more plastic in the sea than fish. The poor birds become confused by these unnatural objects and think they are food. Ninety per cent of all seabirds have now consumed plastic (a figure that has risen astronomically from 1960 when it was just 5 per cent). By 2050 it could be a horrific 99 per cent.

This is not only disastrous for the birds themselves, but for the health of our ecosystem generally. I had believed this area of the Falklands to be one of the most unspoilt in the world, yet even here our filth is torturing and killing the penguins.

'Are you feeling angry, Veronica?' Sir Robert asks, his voice as earnest as I have ever heard it.

'Absolutely livid,' I reply.

'Well then. Let's do a spot of filming right now.'

He calls Liam, who sets up the camera outside the lodge. I speak my piece, my voice strident with rage, every word in place, as clear cut as the crystal chandeliers in the Ballahays sitting room.

Afterwards Sir Robert shakes my hand. 'Veronica, thank you. That was . . . that was just perfect.'

He looks quite awestruck.

58

Veronica

To TRY TO distract Daisy a little I have decided to disclose the contents of my locket. This takes me some strength of mind as the specimens within hold great sentimental value. Nevertheless, in the evening I lead her to my bedroom and let her lift the chain over my head, which she does with due care and reverence. She passes it back to me. I press the catch and the locket springs open.

'This is a strand of hair from my dear father's head, and this one is from my mother.' I place the brown and auburn hairs into her upturned palm. 'They died when they were still quite young.'

She gazes down at the twisted samples, silent and respectful. The next two specimens are going to be even harder to talk about. I extract the very dark tendril of hair which is still fine and lustrous, as if it had been cut from his handsome head just yesterday.

'This is from a young man called Giovanni with whom I once fell in love.'

'Oooh.' She fixes her eyes on me now, as if she cannot believe that I was ever young enough to do such a thing.

'He was Patrick's grandfather.' I will let her do the maths. I must move swiftly on. 'And this,' I say, taking the final tiny wisp of hair – of baby hair, of my Enzo's hair – 'is from Patrick's father.'

There. I have done it. I have said it without crying.

Daisy stares down at all the four specimens but is uncharacteristically quiet. I realize now that showing her the hairs from all these dead people is not the cleverest way of cheering her up. But there is yet something else tucked into the edge of the locket.

'And this is special in a different way, Daisy.' I can muster a genuine smile now. 'This is a tuft from Pip, my penguin friend in Antarctica.' And he, at least, is alive and well.

Daisy insists on a full-scale funeral. She wants hymns, prayers and a set order of service. I remember Patrick saying that her father, Gavin, is a committed Christian and I presume that Beth must be one also. They will have brought Daisy up according to their beliefs. I find myself rather taken by Daisy's conviction that Petra has now gone to a penguin heaven. I only wish I could share it.

'What do you think it's like in penguin heaven?' I enquire over breakfast the day after Petra's death.

'Well, there's lots of fish, obviously,' Daisy tells me. 'Mountains and mountains of fish.'

'It must be extremely smelly,' I remark.

'It is.' She nods enthusiastically and her eyes widen. '*Really* stinky. But penguins like that.'

'What else?'

'There's a kind of penguin playground, with a sandpit and a snowpit and a big, big bathing pool because they like swimming so much. They can do all sorts of water sports. And ice hockey and ice skating. And there are fifteen rainbows in the sky.'

'Fifteen!' I exclaim. 'How marvellous.'

'And there are bubbles everywhere, because penguins like chasing bubbles. And in heaven all penguins can fly.'

I imagine a flock of penguins soaring across an azure sky, dipping and swooping through clouds as they do through the waves. Yes, it's a good image of heaven.

'And some of the penguins play harps,' Daisy concludes.

'That must be tricky to do, with flippers instead of fingers.'

'Oh, they use their beaks and their feet as well.'

'Do you think Petra is playing the harp now?' I ask.

'Definitely!'

Patrick has dug a grave with the help of Liam and Keith. It is in a spot Daisy selected on the side of a hill, with a view over the coast that Petra frequented so often. She urged Patrick also to make a small wooden cross. I went with her to gather some wildflowers and we put together a little posy to lay on the grave. Liam has asked Daisy if he is allowed to film the funeral and she has given her consent.

'It's important that people all over the world will remember Petra.'

I am not going to be the one to inform her that *I Wish* is only broadcast on a relatively small British television channel and the funeral footage is quite likely to be excluded in any case.

Daisy slaps her brow. 'Duh. I nearly forgot the most important thing. Tony must come to the funeral. He was her best penguin friend.'

'I'm not sure we're going to be able to find him and bring him up here at a fixed time, darling,' Beth says, kissing her lightly on top of her head.

Throughout the day Daisy spends many hours wandering up and down the beach, looking for Tony the Macaroni. But he is nowhere to be seen.

We assemble around the grave as the evening is painting the sky in shades of rose and amber. We are a sizeable group, made up of TV film crew along with myself, Sir Robert, Patrick, Terry, Beth and of course Daisy. Not many penguins are given such a send-off. Beth has printed out the words of the service. It starts with the solemn recital of a poem Daisy has written herself (with only a little help from Patrick):

> *Petra, how you made me laugh*
> *Your hops and jumps were really daft*
> *Your eyes so pink, your flippers black*
> *Your snow-white tum and shiny back*
> *Your headdress flowing in the breeze*
> *I don't think you had any knees*
> *But you had big and bouncy feet*
> *And you were just so super-sweet*
> *Petra, my best penguin friend,*

Your lovely life has reached its end.
Petra, you were quite fantastic
Till you died from horrid plastic.

This is followed by the chosen hymn, 'The Day Thou
Gavest, Lord, is Ended', which is apparently one they had
at the only other funeral Daisy has attended, her grandmother's. Had Eileen been here she would have boosted
the singing considerably, but as it is we are far from being
a choir of angels. My singing voice is just a dry crackle
and Sir Robert, although his tone resonates in a fine bass,
is at minimum volume. The rest of the crew mumble
along. But Daisy and her mother both sing out, Daisy in
a high, childish soprano and her mother in an unashamed
clear and rather lovely alto.

The day Thou gavest, Lord, is ended,
The darkness falls at Thy behest;
To Thee our morning hymns ascended,
Thy praise shall hallow now our rest.

As o'er each continent and island
The dawn leads on another day,
The voice of prayer is never silent,
Nor dies the strain of praise away.

I think about my son and his life largely spent so far away,
on a different continent. I think of all the countries we
have been to between us over the past weeks, of Eileen at
The Ballahays, and of the Locket Island team. None of us

336

has been praying as such . . . but perhaps in a way, we have. We have been wishing each other well, in any case, and worshipping at nature's altar.

> *The sun that bids us rest is waking*
> *Our brethren 'neath the western sky,*
> *And—*

'Stop!' yells Daisy, holding up her hand. The singing stops abruptly and all eyes are turned on her.

'It's Tony!' she shrieks. She points to the beach and there, sure enough, is a small waddling figure with a waving yellow headdress. 'Wait!' she shouts. She pushes past the crew and takes off, hurtling down the green slope towards him, calling his name. We watch her.

'She won't be able to get him over here,' Sir Robert murmurs.

'Didn't we once have a conversation about naysayers?' I ask him, then add, 'You don't know Daisy as well as I do.'

We see Daisy bobbing her head, doing little penguin waddles herself, pretending to hold something out to Tony and leading him slowly in a little dance up to the graveside, to where we are all standing, waiting.

Tony is rather bemused by all these humans who are standing stock still and gazing at him, but he seems to trust Daisy. She coaxes him right up to the wooden cross. He pecks it gently with his beak. He has no idea his friend is buried there.

'Next verse!' Daisy announces, and we resume singing. Our voices are quieter even than before. I don't believe there is a single one of us who is not feeling choked up.

> *So be it, Lord; Thy throne shall never,*
> *Like earth's proud empires, pass away;*
> *Thy kingdom stands, and grows for ever,*
> *Till all Thy creatures own Thy sway.*

'All Thy creatures' conjures myriad wildlife in my mind, from the foxes and hares of the Scottish countryside to the seals and penguins of Locket Island. I think of Sugar and Spice, the dutiful dogs of Ginty Island. I think of Sir Robert's Abbott's boobies and all the other plethora of birds and animals he has had the privilege to witness in their natural habitat. What wonders this world holds! Yet all earth's proud empires do pass away, and none of us is as invincible as we think we are.

For a moment I remember a younger me, in my childhood before my parents were killed, when I assumed the permanence of everything ... when love and life were entirely taken for granted. Not so now. All things must pass, I reflect; but some things pass too, too early.

I glance across at the small assemblage of people and it strikes me that the death of dear Petra has brought us together and made us forget our futile human wranglings. Terry and Patrick are holding hands. Beth smiles gently across at them both. And Sir Robert is now at my side, radiating fellowship once again.

The sun is sinking below the horizon. The crew wander off slowly, respectfully. Beth leads her daughter away and Tony hops down the slope back to the beach. I wonder if he will retain any memory of the friend with whom he spent so many happy hours.

Liam remains behind the camera. It is he who has the final take of the sunset and the silhouetted wooden cross, with Daisy's friendship flipper bracelet hanging over it.

59

Veronica

Dear Mrs McCreedy,

I read in the newspaper about dear little Petra and I couldn't stop crying. Even Doug said it was rotten and hard on Daisy. After she got so fond of it too. And there was me thinking about you all so happy together on Bolder Island. I've scanned a copy of the paper in case you haven't seen it. I think there are others too.

The snowdrops are nearly over at The Ballahays but we will have daffodils soon to brighten things up. The place seems lonely without you. Mr Perkins and I are both looking forward to having you back soon. I am just so sorry for Daisy though. Do give her a hug from me.

Yours ever,
Eileen

The paper she has scanned has the headline: DEATH BY PLASTIC.

It reads:

> Amidst speculation about ruptures between presenter Sir Robert Saddlebow and Veronica McCreedy, the friendly penguin who was their muse for two television programmes has died. The penguin, affectionately named Petra by Daisy Dillon, the child who is to appear on I Wish, was found dead on the beach, choked on a biscuit wrapper. A solemn funeral for the penguin was held with all the members of the film crew present as well as several of McCreedy's friends and relations. A member of the team said: 'None of us could have predicted such a sad conclusion to our filming trip. We have all been affected by this. It highlights the fragility of our wildlife and challenges us to act more responsibly.'

I wonder who it was who said this? The funeral happened only yesterday, so they have been extremely swift, whoever they are. With Beth's help I manage to print out the article. I show it to Sir Robert, who is seated in the common room with a book, and ask if it was him.

'No,' he answers. 'It wasn't me. Somebody must be telling them in detail what's been going on here.'

'It isn't Eileen,' I assure him defensively. 'She made that mistake once and wouldn't do it again.'

'No, I'm sure she wouldn't,' he replies. He runs a hand over his brow and lays down the book. 'Ah well, poor Petra's death might do much to win the public over again.'

'Poor Petra,' I sigh. 'I would rather have her alive than the public's approval.'

He surveys me with his keen blue eyes that look so deep. 'Veronica, will you tell me what it is that's been troubling you?'

'It is a long story, Sir Robert.'

'And we have all evening,' he replies, indicating the space on the sofa next to him. I oblige him by sitting upon it. The gentler Sir Robert – the Sir Robert that I know well but have not seen for some time – is smiling encouragingly back at me.

'Please forgive me if I've been a bit distant recently,' he tells me. 'For the last week I've been suffering from a bad toothache and it's made me very grouchy. Keith gave me a clove to suck on yesterday and it has worked amazingly well.'

Although I am sorry for the toothache, it is some relief to know that I have been taking his gruffness too personally. Still, he can't have forgotten the dreadful scene of my resignation.

'Sir Robert, I know my behaviour has been inexcusable, but I have had weighty issues on my mind.'

'I gathered as much,' he answers solemnly. 'Perhaps I was unfair on you, too. Do you wish to explain now?'

He does seem very ready to listen and perhaps I am finally ready to confide. I turn my face to him, wondering where to begin. Words start to come. I tell him of my son, of the memories I have treasured for all these years, of the love that I have always felt for him. I try to describe my suspense since we have been on tour, the eagerness with which I was awaiting information about his life. Then I explain how I'd received news that turned my whole world upside-down, news that my beloved Enzo had killed a man.

'My dear Veronica!'

It is a long time since he has called me that. I go on hastily to explain that this was a mistake of monumental proportions, that my boy had not, in fact, been the killer but had taken the blame for the sake of his family. But that I was ignorant of this until Patrick's arrival.

I inform Sir Robert that I'd also had concerns about Terry and Patrick. It is not my business to impart the exact nature of these, but I mention the fraught, sleepless nights. My emotions had burst forth that fateful day of my resignation, expressed as violent anger only because I was frustrated that I was unable to do my job. A little reminder of Patrick and his water filters slips through my mind and I register what a destructive force such anger can be.

Sir Robert has been gazing at me steadily throughout this explanation and now he lays a hand on my arm.

'I hope you understand now how truly sorry I am,' I sigh, dashing away the tears that have been clogging up my voice and are now sprouting from my eyes.

'I have been very mean to you, Veronica,' he answers softly. 'All this while I had thought that you were merely being prima-donna-ish and cussed. Even when you apologized before, you didn't tell me what was behind it all. And I was very hurt by those things you said,' he confesses. 'Especially when you suggested I was exploiting you. Yes, I thought you'd make the programme better, but I wanted to give you a wonderful experience too. If only you knew how hard I worked to get you on this trip, how much it took for me to persuade the producer and director to take you on!'

I stare at him in astonishment.

'But I had no idea about the turmoil you were going through,' he continues. 'I ought to have seen there was an explanation. I wish you had confided your woes to me.'

I feel a certain chagrin at his words. I have spent a lifetime dealing with my problems on my own. I am not accustomed to this oversharing of highly personal matters that seems to be the accepted normality these days. On the other hand, he does have a point. It is far too easy to misinterpret, and I wonder how many relationships would be saved if only people told each other how they were feeling.

I have, however, detected a note of hypocrisy, which I point out without any qualms.

'My dear Sir Robert. You accuse me of not confiding in you, and yet you didn't let on that you had a toothache. Moreover, you never tell me the tiniest snippet about *you* aside from your professional trips and documentary-making adventures. I know nothing of your family, of your background, of your feelings. Your whole life is a closed book to me.' This is said with some passion. I take up his closed book and wave it in his face as a literal illustration of my point. I notice that the title reads: *No Man is an Island*.

He is taken aback.

'You are right to accuse me, Veronica. I wonder if you and I are similar in that way. We put ourselves across as bold and colourful characters, but essentially we are very private people.'

'It is the way our generation was raised,' I reflect.

He stands up and walks slowly around the room. I observe again what a fine figure he is. His perfectly upright posture belies his advancing years and he is as vigorous in his movements as a man of thirty. But then suddenly he droops a little and begins to look older. He comes and sits beside me again.

'The truth is, Veronica, that I am envious of you. You have done so much with your life. You had an affair and a son in wartime when you were just a girl. Later you married then divorced. Then you discovered your grandson. You went to Antarctica, made more bonds and saved a baby penguin. Then you took Daisy under your wing. You throw yourself into relationships. I do not.'

Here, if you were possessed of a feather, you might well be able to knock me down with it. He says such things of me, Veronica McCreedy; I, who have spent decades mouldering away friendless at The Ballahays, with only somebody as tolerant as Eileen to bear my curmudgeonly company.

'Come, come, Sir Robert. You are vastly more popular than I!'

'And yet I find it so difficult to open up to people.'

This is the moment, I realize, to take advantage of Sir Robert's rare moment of vulnerability, for his own sake. 'May I suggest you start now? I am, as they say, all ears.'

60

Terry

Bolder Island

'WHAT'S GOING ON with us?' I ask Patrick when I bump into him in the hallway.

'I wish I knew.'

Our hands reached out to each other's during Petra's funeral and are intertwining again now.

Over the last few days I've been buffeted by fierce emotions every which way. I have felt embarrassed, defeated and ashamed. I've felt abused, I've felt angry, and at times I've felt panic-stricken. But now a new clarity seems to have entered my brain. I'd like to sort things out before it disappears again.

'I don't think anyone's in the back room. Shall we take a drink in there and see if we can work things out?' I suggest.

'Good plan.'

But somebody else has already had the same idea. The door is a little ajar and there's the murmur of soft voices inside. We peep in. Veronica and Sir Robert are side by side on the sofa, talking earnestly.

We tiptoe back to the kitchen. Patrick pulls me round to face him, looks as if he's going to kiss me but then doesn't. 'Shall we go outside and talk while we walk? Talking and walking is always good.'

He's mentioned before that he and Beth have been walking the scenic paths of Bolder Island together. I was jealous at the thought of it but I'm over it now. Of course, Patrick will have wanted someone to talk to. He had a lot to deal with. Veronica told me about the family's dark secret after the funeral last night. It seems we've all been battling with demons these past few weeks. We've been so wrapped up in our own problems we've hardly had time to notice anyone else.

Patrick and I push open the door and go out into the evening. The last stains of sunset are in the sky. The wind rustles in the long grasses and we can hear the distant cries of gulls. Our footsteps make a gentle thud like the rhythm of our hearts.

'Do you remember when we first knew Veronica?' I ask. 'How she couldn't bear to have any door left open?'

Patrick shakes his head. 'No, I don't remember that. But you got to know her properly before I did, Terry. It was you and Pip that saved her, in more ways than one.'

I smile, transported back to those times. 'She made a point of being cantankerous, but I knew all along she had a lion's heart.'

I remind him that Veronica only began to tolerate open doors because of Pip; we had to let him waddle freely around the field centre so he wouldn't grow up with agoraphobia.

'Now it looks as if Granny's letting people in too,' Patrick comments. We both meditate on the scene we saw with Veronica and Sir Robert.

'A late life romance, do you think, like the papers said?' he asks.

'I don't know. I'd put nothing beyond Veronica, to be honest.'

The sound of penguins at night is different from during the day. Many of them are sleeping, but the ones who have a taste for nightlife are still chattering and calling to each other. The darkness gives a softer quality to their voices, though.

We walk on and the light fades so that we can't see the path stretching ahead of us any more. I know we are both thinking of Eva or Archie, that enchanted life that was all in my mind and never actually in my womb. I don't know what was going through Patrick's head during Petra's funeral, but for me it felt at times as if it was the funeral of our baby.

The sorrow is still there but it is quieter tonight. Yesterday it was a volcano of spouting flames and flowing lava but now it has solidified into a dark crust. I know I will never forget this strange, haunted time, but I'll eventually learn how to carry on.

The night wraps around us like black satin. The air is so much warmer and gentler than the air of Locket Island. We pause and look up. The stars here are incredible, almost as good as the ones over Antarctica. But of course, they are the same stars, aren't they? Millions and millions of worlds and galaxies and universes, teeming like tiny bright insects. My scientific mind knows they are made up of hydrogen, helium and other elements, but on nights like tonight it is easier to believe they're the shining spirits of the departed, or perhaps the souls of those yet to be born.

I reel slightly. My symptoms have abated but I'm still not quite back to my normal healthy self. Patrick puts his arm around my back to steady me. We start walking again and his arm stays there. I know already that I want it to stay there, wherever we are walking, whether it's England, Scotland, the Falklands or Locket Island. I want to be the one who walks beside Patrick.

'You told the doctor you didn't want our baby,' he murmurs, so quietly I can hardly catch the words.

'Only at the beginning,' I assure him. 'Then I did. More than even *I* realized. Sometimes you don't know what you want until you've lost it.'

'Why didn't you tell me about it the moment you suspected?' His voice is not accusatory, just seeking to understand.

I sift through my reasons. 'You didn't exactly make it easy for me, did you?'

He makes a short noise that is half chuckle and half sob. 'Oh, Terry. I only went off in such a huff because I was hurting like hell.'

I take his hand and give it a squeeze. 'I know. I do know.'

'And hell is actually way more painful than you'd think,' he adds. 'I guess that's why it's called hell.'

I chortle. That's my Patrick.

'God, it's good to hear you laugh again!' he cries.

We talk about what might have been, about how we would have brought up our baby. He speaks passionately about giving complete, unwavering love. I'm reminded that he was passed from foster family to foster family throughout his own childhood. He's done amazingly well when you think about it.

It is comforting to feel Patrick's warmth, but I remind myself with a pang that in two days' time everything will change again.

'You'll be going back to Bolton?' I ask.

'I suppose I'll have to,' he replies without enthusiasm.

'And what will you do next with your life, Patrick?'

'I haven't a clue.' He stops to kick a stone. 'You'll be off back to Locket Island, I suppose?' He throws out the words recklessly as if he doesn't care, but I know he does.

I think of Mike and Dietrich struggling on. I think of the acres of snow and rock and glacier that are my home, more than any other home I've ever had. I think of the thousands of Adélies. The Locket Island penguin project was my first baby, my true baby. Even if it won't survive for much longer, I can't abandon it now.

If we could only turn back the clock and be there together . . .

I have questioned many times over the last twenty-four hours if there's any way Dietrich and Mike would accept Patrick into the team again, but I know I'd lose all credibility if I even suggested it. He was only there in the first place because of Veronica's insistence, he isn't qualified and, most importantly, he acted like a complete idiot. The way he left us wasn't just unprofessional, it was utterly thoughtless. It put us all in jeopardy and nearly destroyed the project altogether.

Somehow I'll have to muster the strength to cope with losing Patrick all over again.

61

Patrick

Bolder Island

'CAN WE GO and see her grave?' Daisy asks. 'Will you come with me?'

Her eyes are red and puffy. I expect mine are too.

I pat her shoulder. 'Perhaps I'll just check with your mother.'

Beth is in the office writing an email to Gav. She tells me to go ahead with Daisy. It's good that she trusts me with her most precious treasure. I appreciate that.

Terry is busy packing. I'm trying hard not to think about that. We'll all be packing soon. More bloody departures.

'Let's go, then,' I call to Daisy, pinning a smile to my face.

'Can I take my kite?'

'Of course you can.'

The two of us gallop up the slope together. It's another clear day with a sharp breeze that keeps the kite flying high. Its long purple tail weaves patterns behind it as it rides the currents. Daisy chatters most of the way.

'I shan't mind dying so much now because when I do I'll get to see Petra again.'

'Daisy, stop it, please! You're not going to die until you're at least a hundred.'

'That means I have ninety-one years to go,' she tells me, proud of her maths.

We scramble up the steep side of the hill, the most direct route to the grave. The grass here is cropped short by the wandering sheep. I can hear ewes bleating and their lambs' answering cries. When we reach the site, Daisy lets out an 'Oh' of surprise. As well as her own little posy of yellow ragwort flowers, there is a single, pure white flower placed carefully on the hump of earth just under the cross.

'Who put that there?' she asks me, baffled.

I shrug my shoulders. 'Maybe it was Tony the Macaroni.'

'Hold this for a mo.' She gives me the end of the string that her kite is tied to, and crouches down to have a look. 'It's beautiful,' she cries, 'so beautiful!'

I stand and gaze out at the sea instead, the endless winding and unwinding shreds of blue. I can't bear to look at the flower. I know perfectly well where it came from. Yesterday I came up here with Terry for our last few hours alone together.

'Thank you for not thinking I'm mad, Patrick,' she'd said.

'You're the sanest – and best – person I know,' I told her.

She stared down at the grave. 'Eva was so, so real to me. Now that she's disappeared it feels like grief.'

'I know what you mean,' I told her, because I kind of miss her too. 'We could leave a flower, if you like?'

'I'd like that very much.'

We found this pretty, bell-shaped specimen growing between the rocks, and solemnly placed it here.

Later we found out that it is the national flower of the Falklands and is called Pale Maiden.

As the sun shrinks behind the clouds, I take Daisy back down the hill to the lodge. We pack the kite away then I drop her off with Beth.

I wonder if I can snatch a few more precious moments with Terry. I knock on her bedroom door. It's been left slightly ajar, so I peer in. She's nowhere to be seen but her rucksack is bulging and strapped up, all ready to go. Such a sad sight.

Terry hasn't even left yet but I am already missing her so much I feel as if my heart is cracking across the middle.

Granny and I accompany Terry on one of the mini planes to see her off at Stanley airport. The islands float on the blue below us like jagged green snippets of cloth, but I can't enjoy the vista.

Terry assures us she is physically well now, but I'm going to worry about her all the same. She says she doesn't want long emotional goodbyes. She says she's looking forward to getting back to Locket Island. There are two researchers and five thousand Adélie penguins there who need her.

Not for the first time, I want to drop on my knees and

beg her to have me back on the Locket Island team, but I know that wouldn't be fair on her. The guys would never accept me back into the fold now.

'Say a big sorry to Mike and Dietrich for me,' I tell her. 'I know I'm not in their good books . . . but I bet they miss my cooking.'

'They do, they miss it a lot. Although Mike's beginning to get used to my tinned dinners.'

I'm not allowed to kiss her, but I grip her in a tight hug. We've said we won't stay in touch. It would be too painful. I may not be able to stop myself from reading her blogs though.

She gives Granny a hug that's longer than mine and I'm jealous. 'I promise I'll give your love to Pip, Veronica. Thank you so much for . . . for everything.'

I'm proud of Granny V. She has become a TV presenter and a penguin ambassador and been on another epic voyage. She has helped me, Terry and Daisy through some horrendous issues and dealt with hard ones herself. And now she's promised to keep the Locket Island project going until the end of the year. She needs to settle back into life at The Ballahays and recover for a while, but then she'll review the situation and look at her finances, and who knows?

I'll need to do something or other too. I have vague ideas but nothing concrete yet. I do know nothing's going to be easy, but there are two things I'm sure about. One: no matter how shitty life gets, I'm never touching drugs. Two: whatever I end up doing, I'm going to give it my all. I'm not going to mess up again.

Granny and I stand together and watch as Terry hoists

her rucksack on her shoulders and passes through the gate to departures.

'Brave girl,' Granny says, pulling an embroidered hanky from her handbag and dabbing her eyes.

62

Terry

Locket Island, Antarctica
Two months later

Terry's Penguin Blog

The Antarctic winter is a challenge for us all. The wildlife, so abundant and varied in summer, starts to disappear as the temperature plummets and the days shorten. Smells fade as the world freezes over. Twilight reduces the landscape to glimmering shades of white and grey, with ice and hoarfrost coating every surface. For several weeks the sun doesn't manage to rise over the mountains at all. The silence becomes brittle, huge and all-consuming. Yet if we look upwards, we are treated to glorious displays as the invisible sun streaks the undersides of clouds with pearly light.

Pip and the other Locket Island penguins have all gone now. Dietrich, Mike and I won't see them again until the breeding season. At least this year we are able to track Pip because of his satellite device; it has revealed to us that he has already swum three thousand miles northwest. We hope he is finding plenty of krill to keep his energy up, and we have all our fingers crossed he'll come back with the others when the sunny days return.

We humans are struggling on at the research station. There is plenty of work to be done, analysing the data we have collected, studying the penguins' environment, and working our way through a long list of jobs to keep the centre running. It is the hardest time of year for us and I know we are all missing absent friends, both flippered and human.

I sigh and press 'publish'. How strange that our Locket Island team has shrunk back to the original trio, as if the whole of last year didn't happen.

But it did happen, and it has left me full of memories, questions and a strange, unidentifiable sense of longing.

I wasn't ever going to tell Dietrich and Mike about my phantom pregnancy but, to their immense surprise, it all came out one evening when we'd been drinking rather too much prosecco a few days after the penguins had left. It was an evening of tipsy confessions, in fact; the same evening we found out that Charlotte in Cheltenham didn't actually exist.

'But the photo by your bed?' I asked Mike, not believing my ears.

'Her name is Emily Brocklebank and she's a hairdresser.

We went out on four dates. I thought it was a nice picture, so I kept it . . . and she just kind of transformed into Charlotte.'

'Mein Gott!' Dietrich cannot believe him capable of such a lie.

But I think I understand. He was wanting to demonstrate that he was more than a boffin, keen to prove he was very much up to a long-term relationship with a beautiful and intelligent woman. (And I'm sure he is. He will find his real-life Charlotte one day, and she will pinion him down with her voluptuousness, and he will be a changed man . . .)

After that evening Dietrich and I pretended we'd forgotten the whole conversation, but we hadn't, of course.

Charlotte from Cheltenham has not been mentioned since. Mike is always keen, though, to drag Patrick's name through the mud at any opportunity. I try to change the subject when this happens. It doesn't make for a happy atmosphere.

'I have been in touch with the Anglo-Antarctic Research Council to see if they might consider giving us more funding next year,' I tell Dietrich and Mike, as I hang my laundry over the clothes horse next to the propane heater. It had to be hand-washed because our washing machine packed up two weeks ago.

'And?' Mike asks.

'They don't think it's worthwhile to keep our research centre going. We're too small an operation and they want to put money into their state-of-the-art new station on mainland Antarctica.' I keep my tone light but, as ever, worries about our future are grinding away under the surface.

Dietrich's features settle into resigned acceptance. 'So we just hope Veronica might carry on helping us.'

'Same old, same old,' Mike groans. 'It would be nice if she'd commit herself once and for all. But I suppose she isn't going to do that until her precious Patrick has made up his unbelievably slow mind.'

I am not going to be led down the let's-insult-Patrick path. I sniff one of my socks to make sure the smelliness has been removed by its long soak in a bucket of detergent.

'How is it?' asks Dietrich, noticing.

'Much better,' I assure him. I spread the sock and its partner side by side on the rack.

'There's a very slight possibility the AARC might recon-sider,' I go on as I pull a fleece out of the washing basket. 'We could apply for a grant if we were to expand the pro-ject to encompass Chinstrap penguins and Emperor penguins as well as the Adélies. We'd have to join forces with the state-of-the-art place and become a kind of sister centre.'

'You *what*?' cries Mike.

'That sounds like *a lot* of extra work,' Dietrich com-ments, also looking alarmed. 'And a lot of compromise.'

'Yes, it does. I just thought I'd mention it, though.'

I take myself off to the computer room. Before I start typing I sit staring into space, letting my mind wander. It keeps doing that these days.

It was so hard, so very hard, saying goodbye to Pip. Often I go and stand at the top of the slope and gaze down at the site that just two months ago was so full of the hustle and bustle of penguin life. It's deserted now, like a ruined castle or amphitheatre; just a shell of scattered grey stones and pebbles lying silent in the dusk.

The penguins will repopulate the valley come October . . . but will any of us be here to see them? I wonder.

63

Veronica

The Ballahays
Late July

THE RHODODENDRONS HAVE been superb this year, thanks to Mr Perkins and his green fingers. The Ballahays roses are magnificent too.

Next to a fine floral arrangement on the mantelpiece sits the reprint of an old photo in a gilded frame. It shows a handsome young man standing on a mountain-top with his friend. When Mrs Perkins dropped in with some of her homemade jam the other day, I happened to be lingering in the hall and I heard Eileen showing it to her.

'Ah yes, that was Mrs McCreedy's long-lost son,' she said. 'A brave soul. It is such a tragic tale.'

I will always hold Enzo dear and regret that I couldn't

362

have played a greater role in his life. These reminders – photos, stories, hairs in a locket – seem to become more important as the years grind on and the mass of life that is behind becomes ever greater than the mass of life that is in front. Each memory is precious, and I will never stop missing my darling son. I am one of the many people who walk this world with a dark clod of sadness inside.

At least several decades' worth of questions have now been answered. I shall move on more peaceably with whatever remains of my time on this earth.

Very little has happened since my return from the filming voyage, although I was summoned to a studio in Edinburgh and a few extra voice-overs were successfully recorded. I have been plagued many times by pestiferous journalists, but sent them packing without too much ado. I also attended a concert featuring Eileen and her choir, who warbled a selection of fa-la-la type madrigals and some monotonous church anthems, all of which sounded flat to me, but one has to show willing.

Daisy has been officially proclaimed by doctors to be 'in remission' which is the hugest relief although not altogether a surprise. I do feel that her renewed strength and vitality is largely due to her expedition to the Falklands. *I Wish* was broadcast last month and featured Daisy's penguin adventures for a full eleven minutes. It showed some of the most endearing scenes of Daisy with Petra on the beach of Bolder Island. It also included an excerpt from the funeral. I have no doubt that all but the most hard-hearted of viewers shed tears as they watched. It segued on to show Daisy in the television studio in London accepting her 'I Wished . . . And My

Wish Came True' medallion. We were all immensely proud of her.

Subsequently Daisy set up a project at her school, making and selling penguin-shaped cookies to raise money for conservation and cancer charities. She has coaxed many school friends and several members of staff on board and has already been featured in a local newspaper. Her parents want to protect her, of course, but she is thrilled with her modest allotment of fame and crows often about it. I feel this is excusable in one so young who has been through so much.

Daisy hasn't been the only one to act for change since our renowned filming venture. There has been a large-scale shift in the mentality of the general public and several movements towards making this planet a cleaner and safer place. A woman in Norfolk has started up a new anti-plastic campaign on social media posting horrendous but efficacious photos of animals and birds gruesomely dying from plastic strangulation. I am told she has 53,000 followers and counting. A leading supermarket has announced they are phasing out non-recyclable plastic packaging and others have followed. There have been petitions to persuade the government to legislate against any such packaging and put a tax upon it. This sudden surge of public virtue has been partly due to *I Wish*, but largely because of all the newspaper stories.

It was eventually discovered that Liam – quiet, pleasant, boring Liam – was the one who leaked all that information to the press whilst we were away. In the end it promoted penguin awareness and became superb publicity for both programmes, so we must not judge him too harshly – although he will not be working for Sir Robert again. Sir Robert values loyalty, as do I.

Ah, Sir Robert! I have realized that sometimes one has to go through difficult times with a person before one really knows them. One must witness their reactions to the more brutal sides of life, how they respond when they experience desperate, raw emotion. One also has to recognize that they may deal with these afflictions in their own way.

Whenever I am assailed by the slings and arrows of outrageous fortune, I become a firebrand and woe betide anyone who comes near me. Sir Robert's ways are different. He feels deeply but takes himself off into the wilderness to watch the sea eagles. I know now that he has his own private losses. He has told me about the young lady he knew many moons ago, a dynamic beauty who was a news reporter he met through his work, who was tragically killed in a bombing. Sir Robert has never fallen absolutely in love with anyone before or since. He has formed embryonic attachments but always taken care to nip them in the bud. He is all too aware that overnight the spring blossom of love can transform into the rotting canker of grief.

I respect him for that. As I stood beside him at Petra's funeral all those months ago, I thought I heard the faintest sob issuing forth from his heart; and I know now that it was for this deeply missed woman. It is strange how the death of one little penguin affected us all. It reunited us, and it simultaneously eased our mourning for other lost loves.

Sir Robert and I have shared much and know that, for the remainder of our lives, we will be the very firmest of friends. At any age that is an achievement not to be sniffed at.

I have asked Eileen to go and collect Patrick from the station. He has been in Bolton ever since we returned, which was many months ago now, but he has yet to find a job. This is most unsatisfactory. I have offered to fund his training as an electrician or engineer or mechanic, as he is naturally adept at practical work and I believe he would be quite capable of this kind of thing. But my suggestions were rebuffed with a less than enthusiastic response. I've even said I'll pay for him to train as a chef, bearing in mind his abilities in that department, but he brushed that away too. 'No. No, Granny. You carry on funding those penguins. Don't worry about me. I'll manage.'

When Daisy comes to stay, as she has done twice since our return, she tells me she hasn't seen much of him either. He has rented a flat in Bolton but only helps her father Gavin occasionally at the bicycle shop. Patrick's correspondence is, as ever, scant and non-specific. When I ask him what exactly he is doing, he answers, 'This and that,' which is infuriatingly evasive. However, I will endeavour to extract some information from him during his forthcoming stay.

Terry is currently in the United Kingdom, visiting her parents in Hertfordshire for a few weeks whilst it is midwinter in Antarctica. I am hoping I will be able to coax her to The Ballahays at some point before she returns. I am half wondering if I can mastermind a meeting between her and my grandson, but I fear they both might find it too upsetting.

*

I have just completed the penultimate clue of the *Telegraph* crossword when I hear the front door opening and Eileen's voice call: 'Coo-eee! We're here!' She has made good time from Kilmarnock.

I rise to my feet and put the kettle on.

'Hi, Granny!'

I turn and am pleased to see that my grandson is looking very well. Indeed he is quite flushed and full of something. He gives me a tight squeeze. I rearrange my pearls and offer him tea.

'Yes, please. And a little snack if that's OK? It's been a long journey.'

Eileen locates the ginger thins whilst I select my second-best tea set and lay out three cups and saucers.

'Make that four, would you?'

Who said that? It wasn't Patrick and it wasn't Eileen. An eager face pops round the door, with round glasses and untidy fair hair.

'Oh my goodness!' I shriek. 'Terry!'

She leaps into my arms. 'Hey, Veronica, we thought we'd surprise you.'

'You have done. I am wholly astounded. I am utterly speechless.'

She is looking a hundred times better than when I last saw her. It must be that Antarctic air. Or is it something else as well? My gaze travels from her to Patrick and back again. Their presence here together seems miraculous.

'Well, don't just stand there grinning like a pair of drunken apes. Tell me everything.'

Over the Darjeeling and ginger thins I learn several

facts. Firstly, I find out that Patrick has not, as I had feared, been squandering his time since we arrived back in Britain. On the contrary, he has been doing voluntary work with various conservation organizations in Yorkshire, Suffolk and Wales. He has also done a first aid course and has been pursuing excellence by means of online classes, gaining not one but two qualifications in environmental science. On top of this, he has been putting himself through an extreme fitness regime.

'I didn't want to accept any more hand-outs from you, Granny, but I did have an aim in mind. I missed Locket Island so fricking much I wanted to do something somewhere with penguins.'

Meanwhile, the Locket Island team had been making their own plans for the future. A grant had been unexpectedly forthcoming from a funding organization. It was, however, provisional on their joining forces with another research centre further south. The extra work involved meant they had decided to advertise for another worker to help them.

'I mentioned it in one of the blogs,' Terry tells me, 'and said I'd be doing interviews in London this summer. I said we were looking for someone to fill Patrick's place.' She pushes back her hair and beams. 'There was one outstanding candidate.'

Patrick clears his throat. 'You weren't in the least bit biased, were you, Terry?' he checks.

She pats him on the arm. 'Well, you were the only one who'd already had experience with Adélies. And the only one who had a reference from Sir Robert Saddlebow himself. Also, I happen to know you're extremely good at

368

cooking, which might just have tipped the balance in your favour.'

'So they're both going back to Locket Island!' Eileen proclaims blithely, as if I am too stupid to have worked this out for myself.

'Are Dietrich and Mike in agreement?' I ask, thinking they will surely be less forgiving than Terry, particularly Mike.

'Yes, I've emailed them,' she answers. 'They took some persuading, but the better-the-devil-you-know argument worked in the end. And Patrick has shown his commitment. They want to give him another chance. We all do.'

She gives Patrick a swift kiss on the cheek. I can detect the heady, sweet scent of love wafting through the air of the Ballahays kitchen.

I am immensely proud of my grandson and could not be happier for them both, although I will miss them sorely. Whilst they are here, I will have to make the most of their joyously combined company.

There is now a fine collection of house guests at The Ballahays, but Patrick and Terry keep stealing off on their own.

Eileen confided in me that she spotted them in the rose arbour earlier ('Oh, Mrs McCreedy, it did look so romantic, with the petals blowing all around them') and now they seem to have disappeared again.

As I pass by the photograph of Pip that is up in the hall, I glance at him, as I always do. His raised flipper seems to be waving at me. I am in no doubt that this is the wild construct of my vivid imagination, but it puts a smile on my face nonetheless.

I catch the sound of soft voices in the snug. Ha! I turn up the volume of my hearing aid, just to check that all is well.

'Do you think we'd have got back together if Veronica hadn't summoned me to the Falklands?' I hear Terry ask.

Patrick is silent for a bit. 'I doubt it, to be honest. Would you have asked me back?'

'Hardly. Not after you left like that,' she answers.

He sighs. 'We could so easily never have met again.'

'Well, thank goodness Veronica forced my hand. But she did it because of our baby. It was our poor, non-existent baby who brought us back together. His or her ghost life inside me hasn't been in vain.'

There is a kiss-sized pause here. 'You'll make a fantastic mother one day.'

'And you'll make a wonderful dad. Not yet though.'

'Nope. When we go back to Locket Island I'm going to take a whole suitcase full of—'

At this point my hearing aid, which I have been steadily turning up, squeals loudly.

There's a peal of laughter and Patrick flings the door open.

'Granny, were you spying on us?'

'No, not at all. It is Eileen who snoops, not I. Anyway, I have an important announcement to make. I just came to tell you: it's time.'

64

Veronica

THE EVENING SUNSHINE streams through the bay windows of The Ballahays, highlighting a fine network of tiny spiders' webs in the corners. I will have to ask Eileen to whisk them away with her duster. If my guests have noticed this oversight in household hygiene, they are too polite to say so. There is an atmosphere of celebration in the assembled company.

Sir Robert and I each have a sherry, which shines a lovely burnished colour in the Dartington crystal glasses. Patrick and Terry are sharing a bottle of beer. Eileen, who has of late become touchingly teetotal, is pouring out a lemonade for herself, for Daisy and for her brother, Noah. Their parents, Gavin and Beth, are both sipping from very modest glasses of white wine. Ripe strawberries are laid out on the table along with the best Scottish shortbread from Kilmarnock Stores, which, I should like to point out, was bought loose with not a shred of plastic packaging.

Daisy has become quite a princess and now has a thick mop of shiny brown hair. She is all in pink. According to her parents, she used to be more interested in dinosaurs than fairies, but now she is suddenly addicted to wings and frilly dresses, a phase that most of her contemporaries went through when they were several years younger. Daisy likes to be different.

'Look at my hair!' She holds out a strand of it for Terry and Patrick to examine. 'It's long enough for me to be a bridesmaid now, so you two can get married.'

They shake their heads, laughing.

'Don't you want to live happily ever after?' she asks, annoyed with them both.

'It's quite possible to live happily ever after without getting married,' replies Patrick. 'And that's what we're going to do. We'll try our best anyway.'

I look at them standing together and I know that Terry will support him in everything he does or says . . . until he goes wrong, and then she will gently set him right again.

Eileen is wearing the nosy expression I know so well. 'Tell me, Daisy, what do you think you're going to be when you grow up?' she asks as she presents the lemonade.

'A penguin ambassador,' Daisy answers immediately. 'Like Veronica.'

'Some are born great, some achieve greatness, and some have greatness thrust upon them,' I mutter.

'I am *every* kind of great,' Daisy asserts, stroking her 'I Wished . . . And My Wish Came True' medallion. She wears it with pride and has exchanged the scarlet ribbon for a pink one. Noah rolls his eyes.

I look at her severely. 'Do not become a precocious brat,' I warn.

'Why not?'

I am not sure what is the most politic answer to this question and so I pretend not to hear.

'Before the programme commences, Daisy and Noah, I have a little gift for you both.'

'Ooooh,' they cry, simultaneously bouncing up and down on the sofa so that I fear once again for its springs. I hand Noah his gift first, which is a chess set with finely carved wooden pieces. I was in rather a quandary about my choice and did wonder whether something like a bat or a ball might be more suitable, but Daisy has told me many times that he is a boffin so I hope he will like it. He seems pleased enough anyway.

Next, I give Daisy her small parcel. She strips off the expensive wrapping paper in two seconds flat. 'It's a locket!' she declares, her eyes wide.

'It is indeed, Daisy, a locket, just like mine.' Mine is actually an antique that was passed down from my grandmother Violet and it has a V etched amongst twirling vines. Daisy's, on the other hand, is brand new, from an exclusive jeweller's in Edinburgh, and has a D etched upon it and a light daisy-chain pattern engraved in the silver.

'What do you say, Daisy?' Beth reminds her.

Daisy puts her arms round me. 'I say: thank you, Veronica.' She gives me a kiss that makes a small popping noise on my cheek. 'Can I have one of your hairs, to put in it?' she adds, letting me go suddenly.

'Oh no, you don't want a silly white hair of mine,' I protest.

'I do,' she insists, 'I do.'

'Well, I will ask Eileen to cut off a specimen for you when there are scissors handy, if you really are certain. But there is something else. I have no wish to be mawkish, but I thought you might like this.'

I open my handbag and extract something from the inside pocket, where it has remained safe for all these months, light, pale yellow and very soft. A tiny tuft from Petra's crest. Daisy knows at once what it is and her eyes fill with tears. Her lips mouth the words 'Thank you' again. She places it in her new locket and closes it with reverence.

We ceremoniously take our places in front of the television and Eileen switches it on. Sir Robert's programme *Who Cares About Seabirds?* will go out shortly. I catch him looking at me now, a smile playing at the corners of his mouth.

The titles are accompanied by some tasteful classical music and scenes of a gull sailing in the sky above a rolling sea. For all his faults, I have to admit Liam is a highly accomplished cameraman.

At the beginning of the programme we see puffins and gannets and then Abbott's boobies with their extraordinarily blue feet, all the while with Sir Robert extolling the marvels of marine birdlife. Soon after he introduces me as penguin ambassador, mentioning my credentials as rescuer of Pip on Locket Island and litter-picking queen on the Ayrshire coast. I see myself addressing my viewers with a certain aplomb and authoritative air, my outfits always colourful and elegant, my handbag ever present. I see myself with the Maremma dogs of Ginty Island and the Little penguins waddling around at their breeding site. Sir Robert reappears, telling us of shearwaters and albatrosses and cormorants. Then we witness the tribes of Little penguins flung ashore and processing home, washed in the light of a most romantic sunset.

I watch my first narration on Bolder Island, in the midst of the Gentoo colony, the reporting of the Magellanics and the Macaronis and the Kings. Sir Robert expands on the lives of oystercatchers, teals, grebes, skuas and southern giant petrels. In between the main scenes are cameo appearances of shining seals on the windswept shores, sea lions basking on the rocks, and Merino sheep grazing in the wild acres of grassland. We see Petra, and the camera homes right in on her eager, beaky face. She is admiring her reflection in a strip of silver water. Tony the Macaroni penguin joins her and a little flock of penguins bounces along after a sunlit butterfly.

At this point I take a quick look at Daisy. She is glued to the screen but caressing her new locket gently in her hand.

My narration about Rockhopper penguins is accompanied by a surge of penguins hurled about in the waves and then the camera follows them as they hop up a steep, jagged cliff face. Finally we are presented with Petra's death by plastic. Her funeral is not shown here – it was considered far too sentimental for a nature programme. But my anger is shown.

This was the footage that was taken after Petra's death. The camera has drawn close. I speak out of the screen, my face like thunder, my words spilling out in fury: 'I urge you, my dear general public, to think. Devastation is so often wreaked not through malice but through ignorance. Ignorance kills. Thoughtlessness kills. Negligence kills. Taking the cheapest, easiest option kills. Plastic kills. Poor Petra is just one, one of thousands upon thousands of creatures who have died because of human idiocy.

'I am sickened by the filth that is now filling the sea, the land and the air. I shall not be around for many more years to see how life on this planet fares in the future, but I fear for it. I care about it, for its own sake and for the sake of our children and their children and their children. Don't *you*?'

I stop momentarily to take a gasp of breath then continue. 'Don't you? I beseech you, dear viewers, to remember Petra and her flippered friends. I beg of you to ask yourself when you are at the supermarket: do you really need all that plastic that's in your shopping bag? Tomatoes do not need a polythene tent around them. Plastic spoons should be a thing of the past. As for tea, I offer you my personal guarantee that loose leaves are far, far superior to packaged teabags.

'You might think that the actions of a single person make no difference, but let me remind you it was a single person who caused Petra's death. If that one person had disposed of their biscuit wrapper responsibly, Petra would still be alive, joyously hopping amongst the rocks and surf of Bolder Island. If millions of people changed their habits it could clear the seas again. Dear viewers, when you buy salad wrapped in a cellophane bag, remember the penguins. When you pick a disposable water bottle from the shelf, remember the penguins. When you throw away the polystyrene box of your Chinese takeaway, remember the penguins. Remember Petra, remember seabirds, and remember all the lives upon this planet which are interconnected, of which you are one. Life does not need to be strangled and choked and slowly poisoned. Life needs to ... to *live*. Please let it. That is all.'

The second part of my rant has been accompanied by the most exquisite shots of penguins in all their beauty, strength of character and comic glory. Then there is the briefest shot of Petra lying dead to the sound of a mournful chord on some musical instrument I cannot identify. Then my face again, etched with sorrow.

'I thought you were going to say "Amen",' remarks Patrick, breaking up the heavy mood that has beset us as we watch.

'Was it excruciating?' I ask with some anxiety. I have been watching with clenched fists, feeling my wrath all over again, but it is quite possible the others were simply embarrassed by this passionately proselytizing old bat.

'My dear Veronica, you are an utter inspiration,' Sir Robert assures me. 'I couldn't have done it better myself. In fact, I'm rather fearing for my job now.'

'My dear Sir Robert,' I return. 'None of it would have been possible without you.'

377

65

Veronica

THERE IS SOMETHING wistful about the arrangement of rosemary and heather that sits on the table between us. Still, real flowers are a mark of quality, I always think. Sir Robert and I are at Thurlstone House, our favourite restaurant in Edinburgh. The decor is pleasing, and the food is not only sourced locally but is a delight to the taste buds. We have ordered Scottish salmon confit with fennel.

'I will confess I am amazed, my dear Sir Robert, that our trip taught me as much about humans as about penguins,' I remark, as I spread my napkin on my knees. 'At the age of eighty-seven you would have thought I'd learned all I was going to learn.'

'Not at all, my dear Veronica,' he replies. 'And you won't have done by the time you're ninety-seven either.'

There are various assumptions embedded in this statement, and I only hope he is right. The next ten years are looking distinctly flat in comparison with the last two, however.

A sigh escapes me. 'If I am to continue learning, I shall somehow need to garner some new experiences,' I point out.

'I'm sure that could be arranged,' Sir Robert answers enigmatically. Then he adds, 'I still have a great deal to learn myself.'

In his eye there is a very distinct twinkle of the mischievous variety. I envy him that twinkle. I fear my own twinkling days are long gone.

We discuss Daisy and her laudable charity schemes, then, as often happens, our conversation turns towards the topic of penguins. We talk of the Locket Island project and what tremendous work the team of four are achieving. Between them, they have already paid several visits to their sister centre on the Antarctic peninsula and new scientific opportunities are opening up before them. Terry is particularly excited about this. She may employ more staff as time progresses, although I gather Patrick is working harder than ever and is keen to take on new responsibilities. Recent events have evidently knocked some sense into him.

The team are monitoring Pip through his tracking device. It seems only yesterday that he was a bedraggled little pompom wobbling around in the snow, about to take his last gasp. Yet now he has made a journey of many thousands of miles through icy waves, and Terry assures me he is still swimming strongly. He is an example to us all. In my mind's eye I see him gliding and leaping through the crystalline waters of the Antarctic Ocean, ever enthusiastic in his quest for fish.

When our own fish dinner is ended, I excuse myself and retreat to the facilities to reapply my lipstick. Thurlstone House boasts a particularly good ladies' powder room with luxury handwash, scented towels and a patina of natural light filtering through the delicate lace curtains. I pat my hair into place. Then I reach inside my handbag and remember that I have come out completely lipstickless. I am currently engaged in an experiment: I have purchased a strange creation called a lip *pencil*. It is true, I have many, many lipsticks in differing shades of red and pink that must be used up, but as they are inevitably encased in plastic I will not be buying any more.

As I locate the lip pencil, I mull over the evening, which has been most satisfactory. I am already looking forward to meeting and conversing with Sir Robert again. How splendid it is to talk with a person with whom one has so much in common; moreover, a person who knows all one's faults and yet likes one all the same. I do wonder what Sir Robert was referring to when he mentioned new experiences, and when he said he still had much to learn himself . . .

I draw a line of ruby red along the outer perimeter of my lips and colour it in with care. One must always strive to do one's best with whatever one has been given.

I pause. Something in the mirror has arrested me. I look again. And I am surprised and delighted to observe it there, in my eye: a small but irrefutable twinkle.

Acknowledgements

Readers, I wrote this book for you . . . because I was getting the impression that, for some reason, you liked Veronica McCreedy! I am so grateful to you for making *Away with the Penguins* a success and I do hope you've enjoyed this, Veronica's second penguin adventure. I travelled across five different continents in my head as I wrote *Call of the Penguins*, but it was Lockdown and I couldn't physically visit any of the places I describe. Some of them (Locket Island, Ginty Island and Bolder Island) are entirely made up. Others (Ayrshire, Bolton and Vancouver) are not. I have done my best to research these and have filled in the gaps with my imagination. I hope you'll forgive me if any of the geographical details are wrong – this is a work of fiction, after all!

There are many people I'd like to thank, who have helped more than I can say. I am truly indebted to all of these:

My amazing editors, Francesca, Sarah and Imogen, who have put their brilliant heads together and brought out the best in this novel. Also Alison and Ruth (my super-lovely publicist and marketeer), Irene Martinez for the gorgeous cover design, and all the other fabulous folk at Transworld.

My agent, Darley Anderson, and Mary, Georgia, Kristina, Rosanna, Rebeka and the rest of the team. They have worked miracles yet again, both in the UK and abroad. It's incredible to see my penguins waddling across the world!

Everyone who has given endorsements and supported me on social media. I am particularly grateful to Lorraine Kelly for her wonderful enthusiasm, and to my fellow authors Trisha Ashley, Phaedra Patrick, Clare Mackintosh, Celia Anderson, Tracy Rees, Jo Thomas and Samantha Tonge. Wow, I now know how very busy you are and how unbelievably generous to give this extra time and head space.

Richard and Judy, for choosing *Away with the Penguins* for their book club and bringing it to many more readers who would otherwise not have discovered it, especially during that horribly difficult year of 2020.

Likewise, Radio 2's Book Club and the board of librarians who selected *Away with the Penguins* for one of their top reads. Huge thanks, as well, to all the other book clubs up and down the country who have helped spread the penguin love.

Ursula Franklin, dear friend and 'crazy penguin lady', who has provided me with masses of glorious penguin inspiration, not to mention endless encouragement.

Sue Flood, who has so kindly answered all my questions about wildlife filming on location.

Paul Gibbs, for helping with my research into family histories, and the other lovely people at Periwinkle Tea Rooms and Clematis Cottage in Selworthy.

Lionel and Jo from Brendon Books in Taunton for beautifully hosting my book launches, even if they do have to be postponed multiple times because of lockdowns!

All my friends, for sticking by me through the good times and the bad.

My sister-in-law, Rosemary, who bought so many of my books for Christmas presents that she may well be the reason *Away with the Penguins* became a bestseller.

My small but oh-so-important immediate family, Jonathan and Purrsy, for being there for me when I need them, which, let's face it, is ALL THE TIME!

Finally, I'm going to thank penguins – for being one of the loveliest, funniest and most courageous life forms on this planet. With the ice-melt in Antarctica, overfishing and the pollution of our seas, they will need all their powers of fortitude and resilience to get through the years to come. I only hope they will still be here for future generations. Long live the penguins!

HAZEL PRIOR lives on Exmoor with her husband and a huge ginger cat. As well as writing, she works as a freelance harpist. Hazel is the author of *Ellie and the Harp-Maker* and *Away with the Penguins*, which was a number one bestseller in ebook and audiobook. *Call of the Penguins* is her third novel.

Veronica McCreedy lives in a mansion by the sea. She loves a nice cup of Darjeeling tea whilst watching a good wildlife documentary. And she's never seen without her ruby-red lipstick.

Although these days Veronica is rarely seen by anyone because, at eighty-five, her days are spent mostly at home, alone.

She can be found either collecting litter, trying to locate her glasses or shouting instructions to her assistant, Eileen.

Veronica doesn't have family or friends nearby. Not that she knows about, anyway . . . And she has no idea where she's going to leave her considerable wealth when she dies.

But today . . . today Veronica is going to make a decision that will change everything.

'Unflinching, stubborn, funny and moving, Veronica is an unlikely heroine who will sneak in and capture your heart.'
TRISHA ASHLEY

'A glorious, life-affirming story. I read it in a day.'
CLARE MACKINTOSH

Meet Ellie. She's perfectly happy living her quiet life with her husband, Clive. Happy to wander the Exmoor countryside and write the occasional poem that nobody will read; happy to dream of all the things she hasn't yet managed to do.
Or is she?

Meet Dan. He thinks all he needs is the time and space to make harps in his isolated barn on Exmoor. He enjoys being on his own, far away from other people and – crucially – far away from any risk of surprises.

What Ellie and Dan don't know yet, is that a chance encounter is about to change all of this.

This book also contains a pheasant named Phineas . . .

'Uplifting and full of heart. Perfect for fans of *Eleanor Oliphant is Completely Fine*'
JO THOMAS

'A beautiful love song of a story, wonderfully told with a warm heart and much hope'
PHAEDRA PATRICK, author of
The Library of Lost and Found